WAR OF TORMENT

Books by Ronie Kendig

WAR OF TORMENT

THE DROSERAN SAGA
BOOK 4

RONIE KENDIG

Arilamet Ocean

Napai

DEEP SHADOW

SASADA

Va'Una Issi Desert

Desert Gorges

Shadowsedge

Sea of Tribute

Wastelands

GREYEDG

Vysien

Rebel's Bay

HIRAKYS

HAVENMEAD

Forge River

LIGHTHO

East River

Rhinnock Bay

Capital River

Waterflame

Saigo

Shadar

ROHILEK

KURU

Anticipation tremored in his veins—it had come. The Progenitor's War had finally arrived.

"Admiral on the bridge!"

"What's going on? What was that swarm of ships?" Amid grating claxons and pulsing orange lights running around the bulkheads of the Command deck, Fleet Admiral Domitas Deken strode past the offices and conference rooms to the central Command hub of the newly christened *Cronus*, the flagship of the Symmachian armada. He glared up at the array hovering in the air between him and his handpicked officers, who had been transferred from other ships in the fleet.

"A fleet, sir." Grim-faced, Captain Lasson Pount stood with the executive officer.

"What fleet?" Domitas demanded. "We have the only fleet in the Quadrants!"

"Unknown, sir." Commander Wellsey Dimar, onetime XO of the *Macedon*, recorded the images and waved them to Command. "None we have record of, and the ships are . . ." He frowned at what he saw. "They're entirely foreign. Fast. Advanced—incredibly so."

Domitas compared radar to the moments before the arrival of the new ships. "Where'd they come from?"

"As far as we can tell," Pount said with a shake of his head, "the jumpgate at the *Chryzanthe*."

"Can't be. Baric reported it damaged by that spherical ship." Never would Domitas forget watching that alien ship explode from the jumpgate and come around, firing. The relay vids of the incident had taken nearly a day to reach the *Cronus* on its route to Drosero.

"Maybe they slipped through in time?" The captain quirked a blond eyebrow.

"Baric said it was damaged beyond repair," Dimar noted. "Perhaps the ship came through one of the other Sentinels."

"They're not operational yet. With Baric's flair for the dramatic, it's possible the *Chryzanthe* isn't as damaged as he reported." Probably wanted a way to keep anyone from nosing into whatever he and that alien were doing. Domitas indicated to the array, then flicked the screen, rolling back the time. "Those ships are moving fast."

"Like we were standing still," Dimar noted.

"Any idea where they're headed?"

"I'll calculate," Pount said, tapping on a console, then nodding at the results that splashed through the air between them. "Course and speed suggest a trajectory for Drosero. In fact"—his fingers flew over the console—"the exact same course the first craft took."

"We *think*," Dimar added with a look to Domitas. "The engine signature of the first craft is so slight that, while we can confirm that fleet followed its course, we cannot say if they ended up at the same place."

Not comforting. "Do we have a lock on the sphere's final destination?"

"Speculation only, sir."

Domitas waited for said speculation, and when neither officer expounded, he lifted his brows. "Is there a problem?"

Pount and Dimar exchanged glances before the XO sighed. "Long-range scans suggest it entered Droseran orbit, but since we have yet to hear from the *Damocles*, we don't know if those projections are accurate."

Drosero. This war sure was waking up the 'verse, wasn't it?

Damocles had been running recon and made it farther into Herakles, so he'd tasked Vice Admiral Acrisius, a man he trusted and respected, to park over Drosero and wear them down with limited, focused engagements. The fighters and Eidolon had put out a solid effort in prep for the arrival of the *Cronus* with the rest of the fleet.

Still, Domitas needed more intel. "Lieutenant Loren, any comms chatter from those ships?"

"No, Admiral," the petite brunette said from her station. "We've been poring over radars and pinging, but nothing. And I mean . . . *nothing*. It's strange, sir."

"Agreed." Domitas reviewed radar and intelligence reports on this incursion by an unknown. "You don't blow into the Quadrants with an entire fleet and not communicate your intent to the local armada."

"Maybe they tried," Pount suggested.

"Maybe." Dimar jutted his jaw to the array. "Clearly, they're advanced. I mean, with their speed and the long-range scans of weapons we don't recognize. And with little to no engine signatures to track . . ."

"You're not making me feel better." Domitas tossed down a flex screen and glanced at Loren again. "What about subspace?"

"Same, sir. Dead silent."

Voids. He again flicked his hand in the air, running through the minuscule intelligence they'd gathered. However much he hoped that ship was what he thought, carried who he thought, he had to refrain from betraying his hand. Decades toeing the line couldn't be thrown away with a misplaced smile. "Keep looking, people. We have an entire ship-city depending on us to make reasoned decisions. XO, how long till we're parked over that accursed planet?"

"Three days, sir."

"Sir," Loren spoke up. "Admiral Krissos is hailing you."

Domitas straightened, eyeing the static screens hovering in the air. "Keep on it. Hundreds of ships can't hide. I want to know where they went, and extra shore leave to whoever finds out where they came from. Engineering, boost our engines. I want to hit Droseran orbit tomorrow."

The unrealistic command received the obligatory concession even as he stalked to his office. It was an impossibility, but maybe they'd find a way to speed it up. Anticipating why Krissos was waving him, he entered his codes to secure the room before opening the channel. A blue halo circled the bulkheads as he twitched a hand toward the wallvid, bringing to life not just Krissos, but in split screens across the feed other members of the Xenocouncil.

Ambush, huh? Rolling his shoulders, he tucked aside his irritation. "A surprise, friends." He used that term loosely. Very loosely. "I must have missed the wave scheduling this meeting." Which should've come since he was the admiral of the fleet. Who'd called this one? Were they trying to eliminate his voice?

Another square opened and a new face appeared. It took everything in Domitas not to snarl. "Baric." He folded his hands behind his back. He hadn't understood why Tascan Command had rolled over for Baric and that alien in their single-minded vendetta against Drosero, a backward planet bereft of tech, industry, or even desirable resources. Hadn't understood until Baric's revelation that Xisya, in her magnanimous genius, had discovered a power source on Drosero hitherto unknown in the Quadrants. Elefthanite, a mineral ore that, when refined, could power all seven new gates for a century or more. A convenient excuse that hid deeper motives. Darker ones.

It took a minute for the message to come through. "Admiral," Baric drolled, "why are you surprised we would call a meeting? Clearly you're aware of the ships that came through the gate less than an hour past. You wouldn't be admiral of the fleet if you were slacking in your duties, Domitas." Blond hair trimmed short, he bore a smug expression beneath his bulging eyes. "Now, what can you tell us?"

"Besides the fact you lied to us, Zoltan?" The lag times were digging into his thread-thin resolve not to cut the wave. "Are you not in charge of the *Chryzanthe*?" Domitas tilted his head. "You vowed there were measures in place to ensure the gates were only used by the TSC. Tascan Command spent more than three hundred billion soleris to build these things. Now we find out—what? They're not secure? Whatever happens is on you, Baric. You swore no foreign species could use the gate."

For the moment, Domitas was glad for the lag to get all his thoughts in before someone cut him off. "And yet, hundreds of ships just screamed past the *Cronus* like we were standing still! Now my fleet will face Pyres-know-what. You put all of us, our planets, these ships, our people at risk!" He leaned back, his heart running a little hot after that tirade.

"Come now, Admiral," Baric replied in his patronizing tone. "Let's not overreact. The ships did nothing to you or your precious armada." The slimy captain was entirely too relaxed about the arrival of an alien force.

"What of the other gates?" Domitas challenged. "What if more come through?"

"You borrow trouble—"

"Borrow?" Domitas wasn't waiting for the rest of that message. "Your apathy endangers us all, *Captain*. As it is, the *Cronus* is woefully behind that fleet that *you* let into the Quadrants. We'll continue course to Drosero, while sweeping wide with our sensors to track that alien force down."

"The admiral is right—it's a potential threat we can't ignore," Admiral Waring said, finally inserting herself into the argument. As silence rattled through the feed, she straightened her uniform jacket. "But since Admiral Deken is already probing for the alien fleet while en route to Drosero, let's return to the concerns on the agenda."

"What concerns?" Domitas demanded. "Why was I not provided the agenda or notice? Maybe you've forgotten that as admiral of the slagging fleet, I am to be kept abreast of all council meetings and memorandums. And since I'm taking the *Cronus* and a dozen support ships to rendezvous with the *Damocles* over Drosero to lead the effort there, you would be remiss not to keep me informed of all changes in our plan."

"How far out are you?" Krissos asked. "I've got the *Argus* a week out."

"Seventy-six hours."

"Can you get there faster?" A new voice spoke, one that did not match those queued in to the feed.

That's when Domitas realized the square vidscreen on the right was not empty but simply blackened. It suddenly produced a white-robed iereas. "Theon." A feral anger rose through him, one he had to rapidly suppress as he stared at the priest, who appeared to be aboard the *Macedon*. Behind him stood the thick-chested Droseran, Rufio. "Brought your lapdog, I see."

"Cheap barbs show your weakness, Admiral," Theon hissed, his feed coming through faster since they were both in Herakles. "I would hope you are as committed to our cause as Rufio. He has lost much."

"No sympathy—he threw away his loved ones for soleris. Betrayed his people. Who is to say he's not betraying us, too?"

"And yet, Rufio delivered a significant blow, reducing Kalonica's second-most powerful clan to rubble, buying the loyalty of another clan leader, handing us the prince of the realm, and—"

"Leaving the throne wide open for a more powerful player to plant his backside there," Domitas growled.

"We got rid of him," Krissos said, "and have the majority of the remaining Kynigos in reminding chambers, making slag of their brains, turning them into willing servants."

"Any more grievances you'd like to lodge?" Rufio sneered.

"If you truly got rid of him, you're only begging for trouble by targeting the Kynigos—"

"Marco is returned," Baric announced unceremoniously.

Domitas's heart punched his ribs even amid the crackling silence as the members stared blankly from the screen. Xisya had intended to get the Progenitor far away, stop him from fulfilling his role, but Domitas knew the blood running through that man's veins. His return must have infuriated the creature.

"How?" Krissos asked. "How can you possibly know that?"

"When the ship came through," Baric said, "Xisya could smell him.

I confirmed via comms his presence on the sphere ship that attacked the *Chryzanthe*."

The captain was in communication with Marco? And hadn't notified anyone? While curses and epithets peppered the call, Domitas sat back, stunned to learn that alien had so great a reach. He should not be, but the news drove home how powerful she was. "Marco's return changes nothing. The war is already in play. We will be over Drosero in less than two days and level their capitals, then we can start excavating for the elefthanite to power the new gates."

"Benefitting us both," Waring noted. "The people will be ripe for the offering. We'll send down supplies to meet local needs, then set up registration camps to bring the population under our control. If they want food and a means to buy anything"—she shrugged—"they register."

Krissos chuckled. "I have to say, it has been much easier than I expected after all they put us through with that treaty. Never thought I'd see the day."

"They may not have weapons like yours, but Droserans will fight," Rufio said. "At first."

"Like children throwing a tantrum," Waring said. "Make life a little uncomfortable, and most people will beg for their comfort back." Shifting in her chair, she leaned forward. "Jair, what about your teams already on Drosero?"

"Good. Successful engagements." Admiral Krissos commanded the Eidolon, elite Marines assigned to various ships across the fleet, and active units currently on the *Damocles* were running clandestine ops on Drosero. "Thanks to the drug Xisya compounded, we've subdued a savage population and turned them against the ruling governments. We've armed some locals and are training them."

Domitas had been trying to sort out what exactly was in that concoction, to no avail.

"Deken, what about the *Damocles*?"

"Last word from Acrisius was that a successful strafing damaged key locations and capitals, yet left enough populace to keep the planet active and ripe for integration."

Krissos lifted his chin. "And Cenon?"

Domitas ran a hand down his beard. "With the technology already in place there, the promise of more trading routes and more profit brought them quickly into the fold—happily. Their gate is well underway." He tried not to think about it—opening another portal into the Quadrants for more of Xisya's kind.

"It's incredible!" Emesyn Waring leaned forward, hands clasped on the shiny surface before her. "Tascan expansion into Herakles was unfathomable two years ago. Yet, here we are, sliding in without much effort. Once Deken arrives and obliterates the opposition, we will have control and access to all the energy we need. This planet has been a thorn for far too long. It is time they submit—for their own good. Once Droserans see profits rise and have interplanetary and intergalactic travel available, they will thank us."

Domitas grunted, amazed at their ability to justify wiping out thousands, possibly millions, of lives.

"You disagree, Admiral Deken?" Theon sneered, always looking to start a fight.

"I don't care if they thank us. That ore will fuel the gates—that I care about." And not in the way they understood his words.

"Speaking of," Krissos said, "the cargo freighters left Thyrolia with the drilling equipment. They arrive in a month, so that's how long you have to quell the opposition."

"Forgive me, Rear Admiral Krissos," Domitas said, "I did not realize our orbs had been swapped."

Hard eyes stared back. "Just stating facts so we are all on the same page."

"A page I wrote." Domitas really was starting to hate this game. "I have work to do. Deken out." He ended the wave and scrubbed his fingers through his hair with a growl. He had a lot to do before the *Cronus* entered Drosero's outer orbit.

The next thirty hours were spent reviewing schematics for a certain effort on Drosero—not the one the Xenocouncil plotted but the brainchild of another faction, one that held his loyalty and his heart. Certain towers that were likely to be the end of his career. Decades of orb-kissing and strategic positioning come to fruition in this one act of defiance. He scanned the topographical to pinpoint the strongest points for each base, real estate away from Symmachian camps so the construction of the towers wouldn't be interrupted.

Eyes dry from the hours of reviewing details and updated intel, he read the daily reports and grabbed some lunch. When the bridge waved him, he washed down his food and hit his thumper. "Deken."

"Admiral, I think you'll want to see this."

Domitas tossed the remains of his meal into reclamation and strode out to the bridge.

"Admiral on the bridge," Dimar announced and walked with him to the array. "We started getting sensor readings about an hour ago. It was limited intel, so we sent out some pings and launched an intermediary relay satellite."

Domitas bounced his gaze to the digital images hovering over the main Command hub. "You found them?"

"Waiting on confirmation. We're still too far light distant. But . . ." Dimar's blue eyes brightened as he nodded to Lieutenant Loren. "Show him."

She smiled. "I picked up a very unusual particle emission and used it to trace the ships"—her fingers danced in the air, bringing up a representation of the trail, the array giving the emission a distinct green haze through Herakles—"to Drosero."

"Why didn't the *Damocles* notify us?"

"I wondered the same and pinged them. No response yet. They may have taken fire from some of those civilian ships—"

"Mercenaries," Domitas growled.

"—and lost their communications array."

Leaning in, he could not make sense of what Loren pulled up. The ships weren't in any familiar attack or flight formation. "What am I seeing?"

"Well, that . . ." Loren faltered. "We don't know, sir."

The screen showed the new fleet spread out around Drosero in a web of tiny dots. Over the whole planet. "Looks like they're mirroring the atmospheric barrier."

"Could be, sir. The alignment of the ships is exact," Dimar noted. "I mean, so precise it's uncanny. A computer could render a simulation, but actually pulling it off? Human error would forbid such precise alignment."

"I'm not tracking." But he was. He just needed to hear someone voice the unfathomable ideas forming in his head. Ideas that made him wonder *what* had come through that Sentinel.

"It's—"

"Sir! Satellite images are returning now," Loren announced. "Downloaded. Rendered, and—" With a gasp, she sat back, frowning at her display.

"Lieutenant!"

She flinched. "Sorry, sir. Sending to the array now."

Domitas stood with Dimar as the images bled to life in the air. Like the XO said, the delta-shaped ships held an uncannily symmetrical formation. "Barrier," he muttered.

What were the chances that some armada would appear out of the blue and set up formation to protect the very planet the TSC intended to raze? Less than thirty hours after that sphere—which Baric claimed held Marco Dusan. Kynigos. Medora. Royal pain in Command's backside. Progenitor.

Looks like Drosero has a powerful ally. His smile almost made it to his lips. Could it be . . .?

One way to find out if they were protecting that planet. He motioned to the far station where two officers stood monitoring readouts. "Tactical. Are we in range to fire a pulse cannon?"

They both tapped into their systems. One looked up. "Within range, sir."

Domitas nodded. "Target that desert"—he tapped in a location and sent it to their screens—"and light it up. One pulse."

"Yes, sir. Sending one pulse."

"Admiral," Dimar said, angling toward him with an expression of concern and fear, "we aren't ready to attack—"

"No attack," Domitas countered, shifting to watch the array. "If I'm right, we'll have to go back to the drawing board on our attack plan."

"Sir?"

"One pulse sent," Tactical confirmed.

The bridge went deathly silent, tension anchoring them in suspense. It felt like zero g on his chest watching the system mark the pulse's trajectory as it sped across space toward the delta-shaped ships.

Loren sucked in a breath as it reached the formation, probably expecting them to be destroyed. However, instead of destroying anything, the pulse struck and splintered. Scattered over the formation like lightning traveling down the branches of a tree, dispersing into nothingness.

"Scuz me," the XO muttered. "The ships are forming a defen—"

Claxons screamed through the ship.

"Sir!" Loren shouted, her face blanching. "We have one, two—a-a dozen or more weapons launched. It's the net! They're firing back."

The array showed a half dozen delta ships firing, and those blasts merging into one. "Slag." This was going to hu—

The *Cronus* thundered beneath the searing rebuke of the deltas.

A bulkhead popped open. Crackling and groaning scampered through the decks.

Domitas lifted his eyebrows, stunned at how fast that response had reached the *Cronus*. "Guess they didn't like that."

The slack-jawed XO slid his gaze over a schematic. "Neither did *Cronus*. Shield buffers are down forty percent. They took out one of our starboard engines and number four weapon array."

Problem with their shields was that they absorbed *most* energy, but not all.

"Should we return fire?" Tactical asked, readiness in their tone.

"Negative. Stand down." Amazed, yet bewildered by the new fleet, Domitas paced and studied what the array was telling him. "We return fire and there's no telling what they'll shove down our throat."

"Damage reports are coming in," the XO said. "We have fire on decks twenty through twenty-four." Those closest to the engines. "Long-range satellite sustained damage, but shields prevented structural damage."

Long range . . . Interesting. Had they done that to prevent *Cronus* from seeing and targeting them? Clearly, they had superior weapons that were faster and more accurate. Why did they stop?

"They attacked us, sir. What's our response?" Tactical itched for combat.

"That wasn't an attack," Domitas murmured. "It was defensive. A viper striking when the foot gets too close. They didn't like us firing."

"Our shot was ineffective," Loren assessed from her station.

"Mm," Domitas grunted. "But it was still a shot, and they want us to know they can wipe us off the grid. They sent a warning." He cocked his head. "XO, slow our approach. Notify Command about this first encounter."

"Aye, Admiral."

"Sir," Loren said. "Just before we lost the long-range satellite feed, I caught something on Drosero."

Domitas eyed his comms officer.

"The sphere-craft that engaged the *Macedon* near the *Chryzanthe*? It's down there, sir."

Huh. Baric said a certain young hunter had returned. They'd given him up for dead, but now it seemed wherever he'd been, he'd found his way home in the dark. How did he do that?

More importantly, where did he get that sexy ship?

Death breathes heavily this night.

As a canopy of fiery stars, ships hovered above Kardia . . . Kalonica . . . mayhap even all of Drosero. Belltower peals clanged through the city, mirroring the erratic rhythm of his own heart. Tired, adunatos bruised and battered, Marco Dusan tried to shut out the evil hanging over them like a death knell. However, the panic of thousands saturated his receptors, making his head ache beneath the strain.

He'd barely bathed, enjoyed a meal, and laid down to rest with his beloved before being alerted of the ships' arrival. Of the fact he had unwittingly brought the enemy to their doorstep.

We are doomed. Because of me. Because of his desperation to find Isaura.

Threading fingers with hers, Marco drew Isaura closer. If they were to die, at least it would be together.

"What are they?"

"Where did they come from?"

"Should we send our fighters?"

Was there hope? The fetor of fuel seeped through his receptors, telling him that in the months of his absence, Drosero had managed the unfathomable. But how many?

Amid the onslaught of questions and fear around him, Marco sought Ixion. "What fighters have we?"

His First's dark visage, cut through with that scar, swung in his direction. "Your kyria commissioned hundreds of machitis to join and train with Vorn's armada."

Marco snapped his gaze to Isa, who smiled. "Well done," he whispered, but then recalled the Jherakan king's pronouncement of but fifty ships. "Armada?"

"If you can call it that." At his left, Master Hunter Roman deBurco scanned the sky. "This planet's flight capabilities are a pitiful fraction of the Tascan fleet." Yet there was no hint of worry in his words or features. But then, confidence—not concern—had always been a hallmark of the master hunter.

Uncle. Before his death, Darius had named Roman their uncle. Was it true? Did it matter?

It did not. Could not. Not at a time like this.

"If they are here to attack," Ixion said in that gruff way of his, "we are without hope." His expression shifted. "I beg your mercy, but even with you returned to us, sire."

What have I done? Had he not returned, the Draegis wouldn't have found their way here. How . . .? How had they gotten through the gate? He'd destroyed it.

Obviously not.

Could Drosero survive against so many fast-attack crafts? Easily hundreds.

"What do you fear, Marco?" The master shouldered in.

"Must you ask?" Marco gravely nodded to the heavens. "I thought I'd return to prevent . . . *this.*" He shook his head. "Ixion is right—what hope is there?"

"Uchuvchi," came the near-chortling tongue of Daq'Ti from behind.

Marco ignored the Draegis's mention of the pilots and focused on their options. How had so many Draegis made the jump so fast? They must have been right on his tail—that or jumped months earlier, which wasn't possible because he hadn't yet brought the coordinates. Their presence here defied logic.

"They shouldn't be here . . ." The *Qirolicha* should've bought at least a month-long advantage. He'd hoped for more time, a chance to see his daughter born. "What are our armaments?"

"Armaments?" Ixion scoffed. "Forget you we are Droserans? There are but few contingencies outside Vorn's armada. We can review that when you are recovered—"

"Do not pander—"

"Never would I, my medora." Ixion tucked his chin, gray eyes casting around the bailey. "These questions would be best put to Rico, who is even now at the underground base. Or Vorn, as he leads the armada. What knowledge we have here is outdated and ill-informed due to distance, lack of intel, and experience."

"The only knowledge that matters right now is that they"—Bazyli stabbed a finger heavenward—"have scores more ships. What can defend us—"

"Uchuvchi—"

"Not now, Daq'Ti," Marco huffed.

At least a head taller, his skin now a gray-mottled dark brown, the Draegis warrior stood before the fair-haired general who was not much older than Marco's own twenty-eight cycles. No, twenty-nine—he had passed a birthday while in Kuru, he realized.

Nerves rattled through Isaura's efflux. "Your . . . friend repeats that word. What does he mean?" She eased nearer.

"It's their word for pilot."

Daq'Ti lifted his chin and trilled, as if the translation alone gave him satisfaction or comfort.

It did neither for Marco. He yet again considered the ships spread out from horizon to horizon like a giant net. It made no sense. He'd returned, believed it ordained that they could defeat the enemy, but now they stood on the verge of annihilation.

"To what end does he speak such?" she pressed.

"I don't know." It surprised how very much Marco did not want to be associated with Daq'Ti. "He has called me that since we were held aboard the Draegis dreadnought and does not use my name."

The onetime Lavabeast and his unyielding servitude to Eija had always unnerved him, though not as it had Reef with his jealous rages. Had the girl not whisked away, Daq'Ti would likely yet be with her, serving her. Protecting her. But he was here. Stranded in a Quadrant he did not know, with people he did not know, and who did not know or understand him. In truth, the effluxes around them spoke of their outright fear of the strange man. It did not surprise, as they had no experience with aliens, nor had they watched the transformation he'd undergone.

"Pilots." Ixion angled his broad shoulder in. "Does he refer to the pilots of those ships overhead?"

A question Marco had not considered. "Mayhap." Obviously they had to be piloted, but it did not necessarily follow that—

"Uchuvchi *guide*." Daq'Ti's thick, leathery hand motioned to the skies. "The *Qirolicha* guide them."

Considering the Draegis, Marco recalled what Eija had said—about the hive, the pilots. But they'd jumped away while the pilots were yet in regeneration pods. What did the *Qirolicha* have to do with the ships in orbit?

"Uchuv—"

"I know," Marco bit out, wishing the Draegis would stop talking about the pilots left behind. Men who were likely Kynigos.

"Gi'Zac pilot drones and—"

"Daq'Ti, I get it." He shifted to face him. "But remember? We destroyed the Sentinel on the way out. There wasn't time for the Uchuvchi to make the trip to the neighboring gate and jump. Not this fast." Confusion and curiosity wafted around them. The reek nearly drove Marco to his knees. Or mayhap that was yet his exhaustion.

Ixion folded his arms. "Even had we twice Vorn's armada, there would not be a prayer."

With a quiet growl, Daq'Ti grabbed Marco's shirt by the collar and drew him around. "Listen to me!"

Shouts and swords sang out.

"No!" Marco's command was lost amid the chaos of men training weapons on the alien.

Regia flooded in, shielding and separating him from the Draegis, as Bazyli urged him from the line of sight.

"Stand down," Marco ordered. Frustration and anger swelled. Feeling heat in his brand and chest, knowing this would end very badly, he bellowed, "Yield!" He shoved forward, hands out to calm the men, and Daq'Ti, whose weapon-arm warbled with heat. "Though I know it may be hard to believe, this man is an ally—no threat to you or me. Injure him and you injure me."

It seemed a little extreme, and he doubted they would understand why he protected this alien who could weaponize his arm, but Marco must make clear the protection Daq'Ti had here.

Uneasy murmurs whispered through the night beneath the thrum of ships parked in a low orbit.

Marco did not need to look skyward to verify their presence because he felt the vibration of the fetors against his receptors. "We are the ant facing the rhinnock," he said. "If they have not yet attacked—"

"No! They are Uchuvchi!" Daq'Ti's thick hand nudged Marco. "You are Uchuvchi. Gi'Zac is there." He pointed up.

Understanding struck. Marco's pulse beat a little faster as a face flashed into his mind—that pilot in the facility who'd refused to come. Hope leapt as he touched Daq'Ti's chest and indicated skyward. "Gi'Zac? He's there?"

Daq'Ti's thrumming seemed a yes. "Come." He started toward the northwest lawn, to the *Qirolicha*.

What strange mahjuk existed between Marco and this alien that left a curious void-rimmed odor in his nostrils?

Roman remained close as the tall alien led them through the remains of Kardia. They trudged to the burned knoll where Marco had landed the odd ship with its arcing arms that somehow held the large center orb in place.

The alien swung a large, ash-gray arm toward the sky with a chortle. "See Uchuvchi."

Confusion saturated the crowd gathered on the lawn, yet from Marco arose an efflux ripe with . . . awe. Admiration. And a darker note that Roman would later need to unpack. "Marco?"

"Can't be." Black hair shorn, scars marring his yet-young face, Marco moved closer, his gaze shifting from the orb to the skies filled with the glittering dots. He laughed, touching the ship's hull. Now came surprise and relief. But something even deeper waded into the mix. It was unique . . . loyalty.

Not understanding the change in Marco and concerned where that loyalty might lie, Roman focused on his nephew. "What is this . . .?" Worry over what may have happened to him among the Fallen threatened his peace. "Speak to what you reveal."

Marco grinned. "I am not sure I can. They're here because of me." A small laugh. "I don't know how—they were in regeneration pods when we stole onto the *Qirolicha* and absconded with it."

"You make little sense." Roman had caught the unusual note to Marco's Signature when he'd stepped off that ship two days ago, a note that reeked of singed machi wood. Should he be worried about the strident undertone? Or was it all part and parcel of being the Progenitor?

"So . . ." General Sebastiano began, his downworlder mind likely struggling to comprehend such advanced technology. "Those ships . . ."

"Marco! They've summoned Symmachia. It's an attack!" Duncan shouted, running toward Marco with a flex screen. "Look-look-look!"

They huddled around the flex screen.

"Where are we getting this footage?" Marco's brow furrowed as he studied the device.

"Jubbah's civilian ship," Duncan explained. "It's orbiting the big moon, staying out of Symmachia's sight."

Roman focused on the screen, feeling the others crowding around him.

In low orbit, just beyond the netlike formation of fast-attack vessels loomed a Symmachian battle cruiser, tagged *Damocles* in tiny letters. Nervous scents peppered the air, and even Roman found himself holding his breath as the massive ship bore down on the much-smaller crafts.

Unsettled, Roman glanced up, though the cruiser couldn't be seen. Standing on this planet, knowing the enormity of such a ship, he felt small, weak . . . powerless. "That's a lot of firepower," he noted quietly.

Morning light glinted off Isaura's blonde hair as she looked to Marco. "Will they attack the small ships?"

On the screen, a bright light erupted from the dreadnought. It seemed to take hours for that pulse cannon blast to reach the ships. Roman tensed, anxious that the power yield of that weapon could destroy an entire city. The pulse streaked toward the ships . . . closer . . . closer . . .

"We should get you and the kyria inside," Ixion insisted, trying to herd them.

"Crushed beneath steel or stone, it will make no difference if they are our enemy," Bazyli said.

"No need to make it easy on them."

A flash.

The pulse struck a net ship, and Roman tensed, waiting for the detonation. Yet, instead of exploding, the ship all but shook off the shot, which splintered out like electricity from one drone to another, dispersing the light the farther it rippled from the epicenter of the blast.

"The smaller ships are our allies—the Uchuvchi." Marco's voice firmed. "It's a protective perimeter. Barrier."

A stream of violet fire poured from the smaller ships. Strange and small, the counterattack—whatever it was made of—seemed like a child wielding a stick at a rhinnock.

"Fools," Ixion growled. "They only anger and incite Symmachia to respond."

"Then they'll flee, leaving us exposed again," Galen muttered.

"Nay," Marco said with confidence. "They will stand. And not only stand, but fight."

"How can you know this?" Bazyli demanded, his hair beads clacking as he shifted.

"Because I met the Uchuvchi in Kuru." Marco turned to the general. "Do we have a quick way to reach Vorn?"

"Aye, via your vambrace tech."

Marco considered the blond-bearded general. "I am glad you have embraced the technology revolution."

Bazyli looked chagrined. "Embraced is . . . overreach, my medora."

"No," Marco said, thrusting a hand toward the sky. "*That* is overreach." He rounded on Daq'Ti. "The pilots—I need to talk to them."

With a low trill, the big guy inclined his head and resumed his path across the rear gardens.

Roman followed, watching his nephew, who two hours ago seemed as death warmed over. Now . . . invigorated as he strode with his Draegis envoy and Isaura. The guard assigned to Marco, which consisted of two regia and two Kynigos, trailed him, Bazyli, and Ixion. Good men.

Roman just prayed they were strong enough to be the support Marco would need in the days ahead.

As Daq'Ti banked toward the rear ramp and started up into the *Q*, Marco faltered. Strange, the trust that had grown between him and Daq'Ti, who had not too long ago looked like volcanic rock. But there were limits. Why was he taking him into the ship? Was there a means inside to communicate with the other Uchuvchi?

"What is the matter?" Isaura asked, instantly detecting his concern.

Ten strides beyond them, Daq'Ti must've sensed the hesitation as well because he slowed, turned. Though his eyes were now oval, they pulsed as if they were still slits. "You asked to talk to them." He motioned up into the ship.

Though Marco did not fully understand what Daq'Ti meant, he chose to trust him. He patted Isaura's arm. "All is well."

"No," Ixion said. "We cannot know—"

Marco frowned. "You yet question my judgment?"

"I question an alien creature your own lips not long ago named a combatant."

"Aye, and once I was a hunter unwelcome in the lands I now rule." Anak'ing Isa's tremoring nerves at his back, he forced a grin he did not feel. Did nobody trust him now?

Marco reached behind him and caught Isaura's hand. Her tension almost instantly lessened. Frustration abated. Very aware of the surprise roiling through the effluxes around him, he grew weary. After months of smelling little save fuel, Eija, Reef, and the elements—the plethora of scents proved exhausting.

He eyed the Draegis climbing the ramp up into the ship and started after him. Felt Isaura tug back.

"I . . ." Wide green eyes traced the darkened interior of the bay. She swallowed and found his gaze again. "Is it safe?"

"It brought me home, did it not?" He huffed away his frustration, then erased the gap that had distanced them. Though but one step, it felt a league. "No weapon or ship is itself harmful until wielded by a person. This ship? *I* wield it."

Isaura drew back, her delicate brow rippling in confusion and concern.

"Come. I will show you." He led her up the ramp and moved to a side access panel. Still unsettled that he could do this, he lifted his arm, tension tightening his muscles over what he was about to do, how they would react. He wasn't exactly proud of this. Still, he rotated his wrist and released his hold.

Pale blue, his brand glowed through his shirt. Though not visible, his mind's eye recalled the way the piece of tech had leapt from the Draegis ship back in Kuru—a strange, octagonal disc—and embedded itself at the center of the brand. Tiny talons dug into his flesh . . . and from there it had grown. As if developing a shell to protect the disc, to protect his skin from burning off beneath the half-dome mound through which the blasts erupted. Gray and scaly similar to the hide of a rhinnock, it was really an incredible bit of technology. Once he got past the horror of having some alien device growing like fungus across his arm.

As his palm met the ship's cool alloy metal, the brand seemed more a host to an alien creature than a mark connected to the prophecy of the Ancient. He felt he should regret it, but somehow, he did not.

From the panel a black tube snaked out, its tip dipped in the same pale blue. It clicked into the scaly armor.

Immediately a thrum ran through the ship, the tubes detached from the hull and coiled around his arm.

A pull on his mental and physical energies made his gut tighten. Remembering how much easier this went when he didn't fight it, he relaxed into it. Shoved back the memories of being trapped in the *Prevenire*, the startling moment when the *Qirolicha* seized him . . . Though nothing plugged into his temples or back here, those ports burned.

Isaura's quick intake of breath tugged his attention. Fingers over her lips, she watched, the ambient glow washing across her features.

"All is well." Admittedly, he didn't like it. Didn't like her reaction. Didn't like the way it reflected on her skin. Didn't like—

Another tendril sprang from the ship and spiraled toward her.

Isaura yelped and stumbled back. Uncertainty flashed through her, but not outright fear, proof she trusted him if not this ship. It was too strange, too advanced, too—

The black tube snapped toward her belly.

With a strangled cry, Isaura curled her arms around their unborn child, her expression wild with panic and shock.

"Isa!" Not even thinking, Marco reached with his thoughts to snap back the tube.

A blade sang, and Ixion sliced the tube, deftly planting himself between Isaura and the threat.

Marco staggered. Felt the searing heat of that blade, though it touched him not. Felt the stinging condemnation of his First. Confusion rang through the ship, through the regia and . . . even Roman. All stared at him, aghast.

"It . . . it will not happen again . . ." Stunned, he palmed the command console, processing what he'd sensed in the split second that the ship reached for— "The babe. The ship—"

"I care not," Ixion hissed, his face unusually bright. "This place is not safe for our kyria."

Shaken, angry at the way they gaped at him—was he the monster they would now fear?—he gave a curt nod. Struggled against the drain of the ship on his faculties and body. Finally surrendered the connection. "She does not belong in the war anyway. Take the kyria back—"

"No!" Isaura's rejection reverberated off the hull. Hand on her pregnant belly as if protecting it, she moved toward him again. She kept her chin up, courage wrapped about her like a glowing aura. "As long as you are in this ship, I will be at your side." Fear saturated her efflux.

Remembering all too well the isolation and subsequent desperation at being apart from her, he agreed. "Never again will you and I be separated."

Relief rushed through her Signature as she gave him a tentative smile.

Sword yet in hand, Ixion stepped forward. "Isaura—"

"You address your kyria!" Marco barked, something hot and feral spiking through his chest and radiating into his arm. "Remember yourself, Mavridis!"

Cheek muscle twitching again, his First shifted his gaze to him. "Aye, my medora. As long as the same holds true for . . . all of us."

"Do you yet again challenge me? Is this—"

"Blood and boil," hissed Bazyli, pulling their gazes. He stood, mouth agape as he looked at something behind them.

Marco glanced over his shoulder. Shock rippled through him.

A panel in what he had thought was the hull of the crescent part of the ship had opened. Energy pulsed out, light dancing and ribboning toward the orb. The field warbled around a bridge that slid up to a hatch in the now-open center. Through it emerged Daq'Ti, leading dozens, mayhap hundreds, of men.

Aghast, Marco stared. "Impossible."

"On your medora!" Bazyli growled, his sword singing free of its sheath.

"Nay!" Marco commanded, motioning them back from the small army.

"Who are they?" Isaura angled closer, her hand in his growing clammy.

"Progenitor." A man behind Daq'Ti pronounced the name, which reverberated down the phalanx of men still emerging from the energy tunnel between the two sections of the ship.

Inclining his head, Daq'Ti shifted aside and let the leader step to the front.

Marco startled at the face. "Gi'Zac."

"Progenitor," the man said again with a sharp nod as he stalked forward. "We have not much time. The pods cannot be unmanned for long, but we were told you summoned us."

"Of what does he speak?" Bazyli's efflux fluctuated between wariness and fear.

"The greater question," Roman inserted, his scowl deep, "is how you know these men."

"They're . . ." Marco breathed, his mind racing. "Uchuvchi." He thought of all the times Daq'Ti had said that. All the times he'd answered Marco's queries with that singular name. "Pilots." He shuddered a laugh. It explained so much, yet confounded. "They're the pilots of those drone ships protecting us in orbit."

"You rejected my invitation to come, said it was not your fight."

In the lower ballroom gathered the Uchuvchi leaders—five of the hundreds who had come on the *Qirolicha*. All, like Marco, had the plug ports, but the lifetime spent in those pods on Kuru had taken their toll. Legs and arms were longer, thinner. Torsos seemed stretched. Thin, gaunt faces were made all the more haunting by ashen skin so like Daq'Ti's.

"Your homeworlds, families . . ." Marco could not fathom leaving Isaura again. And now that their daughter was coming . . .

Gi'Zac swayed.

"They struggle," Daq'Ti thrummed. "The air here is . . . different."

"Sit, please." Having set his vambrace to speaker mode to translate the alien language for everyone, Marco drew out a chair and pointed the others to seats as well.

Beyond the chamber, he anak'd nervous effluxes as word spread through Kardia of the aliens who had returned with him, the aliens who could help balance the fight against Symmachia. Down the passage where she now rested, he touched Isaura's Signature, relief yet again acute at being with her.

"The fight in Kuru," Gi'Zac said, leaning on the table, "is lost. Most of the six planets have been turned by the Khatriza. They bleed Draegis and violence. Those who have not been killed or turned are plugged into ships. After you left, after your concern and what you said, we investigated. You were right—our women are long dead, despite what we were told. My wife and daughters as well. Whether we stayed or left, our people are enslaved. It will not change." His stick-like fingers motioned to Marco's entourage. "Here, we can fight. Here, we can bring hope." Near-black eyes held his. "Even if we fail, at least here we die in honor, not isolation and slavery."

"We will not fail." Marco made sure the man knew he meant it.

With another roll of his fingers, Gi'Zac touched his temple port. "*Siznin nuringiz bilan.*"

Though the phrase didn't translate, Marco somehow knew its meaning. *By your light.* More than that, he understood it was a sacred oath spoken only to their most revered. To their leader.

Gi'Zac wavered again, and the reality struck Marco then—the exhaustion, the bone-deep exhaustion from powering a ship using a gift long ago corrupted . . . he knew it very well.

Marco stood and looked to the general. "Arrange quarters for the Uchuvchi to rest and eat." He returned his attention to the alien, who billowed to his feet. "You are my guests. I know the toll piloting takes, so I suggest rest. Since you said the ships cannot be unmanned, mayhap do so in rotations."

Again, Gi'Zac rolled his hand and fingers, touching his temple port.

Instinctively, Marco mimicked the gesture—a sign of gratitude and respect—and watched them leave.

Would their presence and fast-attack craft be enough?

Aye, they were skilled pilots of advanced spacecraft. However, they faced an armada they did not know. If more Uchuvchi somehow came through, mayhap led by Eija, there might be a prayer. But in the Quadrants, they were—like the rest of Drosero—sorely outnumbered. If they could barely walk here, how were they to stay alive long enough to fight and annihilate this threat?

The door opened, and the revelry beyond shoved its way into the quiet chamber. In the commons, aerios and regia were laughing, talking, cheering the Uchuvchi. Already celebrating a victory in a war not yet fought.

"Your efflux betrays you."

He did not turn to the master hunter behind him. "So much for the Codes that forbid anak'ing Brethren." Irritation clawed his spine, but he channeled it and faced his men. "Foolish the hope they put in an alien race simply because there is more technology and things of which they have not heard."

"Think you we are lost then?" Bazyli angled his head, blond beard twitching.

Marco reached for a tankard of cordi. "If they were our savior, there would be no need for what yet burns in me."

And burn did it ever. The heat of the brand had begun to pale to the more demanding fire from the weapon. While it invigorated, it also depleted his patience and seemed to inflame . . . thoughts.

Case in point: "Tell me, Uncle, do you anak them?"

Roman did not hesitate, falling right into the pattern of master to hunter.

"There is a void around them."

"Liodence."

At that, the master recoiled.

"Huh," Marco grunted. "I am not surprised you know of it."

"How can they—"

"Because!" He rolled his gaze to the hearth fire and sipped the warmed cordi. "The Uchuvchi are part of the Draegis race and have been captives all their lives, serving as pilots for ships." He traced the rim of the tankard, struggling against the fury of the memories. "On the *Prevenire,* I was trapped in the lectulo for six weeks. For them"—he nodded after Gi'Zac—"it is the entirety of their existence. All they have known."

"How did you come to learn of liodence?"

"An old man." Marco stretched his neck at the memory. "Qadimiy found me on Rohilek, the Draegis homeworld." He gave a mirthless laugh and set down his tankard. "He was not what he appeared to be."

Hesitating to tell the tale, he wondered how this would be taken. Few times had he felt more awkward. But the master must know. They all must. "Right in front of me, he . . . transformed. And I do not mean that figuratively." He roughed his hands together. Stared the master hunter in the eyes so there could be no doubt of what he would speak. "He was . . . Vaqar."

Shock and rage rushed through Roman's visage. "Vaqar!" Snatching Marco up by his tunic, he pulled him face-to-face, drawing the regia, who faltered, unsure of what to do. "What say you?"

Knowing it blasphemy to speak such, Marco shoved out of the grip. "Do not reprimand me, I—"

"No." Roman's breaths heaved and worry touched his brow. "Vaqar . . . you know his name is sacred to all the Brethren. But . . . more than that . . ." He gave a strangled cry. "Marco, it was *written.*" He rested a hand on Marco's shoulder, his efflux one of awe. "The White Temple scrolls predict '*the Progenitor with war in his hands will walk with he who hunted and felt the first touch of the Ancient in his nostrils.*'" His brows dug down in earnestness. "Speak true. You saw him—Vaqar?"

Why did it anger Marco that this, too, was in the scrolls? That he would be questioned and doubted in this as well? "As true as I see you."

Roman sniffed. "All this time . . ." Another shake of his head. "We thought it merely . . . symbolic."

Marco could not account for writings he had not read, but never would he forget looking the First Hunter in the eyes. "I assure you, it was not symbolic. And neither was he. Nor was he gentle with me."

"Did you expect him to be?" Roman asked around a laugh.

"I *expected* him to care! Care about what I'd been through. The harm done to me and Isaura. Those creatures digging in my head, a feeling not unlike a pulse blast—"

"*You* are not the focus." Roman edged closer. "Not of that trip, not of this war. That is why he did not coddle you, and I am ashamed you expected it. The people face—"

"I'm aware of what the people face!" Marco growled. "*I* saw the cruelty done to the Draegis. Through centuries of dosing them with liodence, the Corrupt have altered this race into beasts they use as mindless drones. At those same hands, *I* suffered, my body punished, my receptors *brutalized* as they sought to harness this so-called gift of ours. Probes shoved into my nose and down my throat—"

Burning, the memories choked him. He swallowed, suddenly aware of the silence that had fallen in the room. That he had spoken what he'd vowed not to. That they stared. Grief and revulsion blanketed the air.

Marco snagged the tankard again. Downed the cordi—now cold. He grimaced, wiped his mouth, took a few measured breaths. Did his best not to anak their reactions. And like everything else he'd tried, failed.

Without a word, he strode from the hall.

He was not the same man she had bound herself to, but he was still Dusan. Still powerful both in presence and influence. Especially over her heart.

Isaura had followed him to the ship, up into it—though the thing terrorized her—and then gaped in . . . shock? Horror? She could not put a name to what she felt as the ship . . . came alive. Like some monstrous creature from tales told to children to make them behave. It had attached to him in a way that was neither natural nor . . .

What, normal? Is that what you would speak?

Horrific, how that thing had gone after their child. What was *that*? Even now, cold dread crept over her shoulder. She feared the ship would reach through the stone walls of Kardia and come for her, for Aeliana.

Ridiculous! Truly, she did not know what to feel. The very ship on which Dusan returned had also disgorged itself of those strange-looking men. Granted, through that experience, she understood on a much deeper level that he had endured a lifetime of events and traumas in the six months they were apart—and, somehow, it had been even less time for him. No wonder he was much affected, altered. How she ached for him.

Sitting at the mirror as Kita combed and plaited her hair, Isaura glanced down at her belly and ran her hand over it. Felt a soft, assuring thump from the baby.

Oh, my precious girl . . . thank you for bringing him home to us.

Her thoughts moved to the master hunter. Quite ill-humored throughout the morning as they talked and visited the ship. Very stern. Disapproving. More so than usual. As if he, too, feared how Dusan had changed. Feared his future.

"You are well?" Kita reached around her and set the brush on the vanity.

Isaura looked up at her friend's reflection. Then saw her own. Circles under her eyes. Downturned mouth. He had yet been back two rises and still she feared falling asleep. Feared he would be taken from her.

Or that I will be taken from him.

She swallowed, again gazing at her belly. *My time with them both is short . . .* The truth of that spiraled through her, twisting her heart and thickening her throat. She bit her lower lip to keep it from trembling.

"My lady?" Kita squatted beside her. "What grieves you?"

Clasping the lifeline of her friend's hand, Isaura met her honeyed gaze. Felt tears welling up. "What this war will bring." She choked back a sob. "He has only just returned to me, and I fear our time together is short."

"Oh, tsk." Using a handkerchief, Kita wiped away a tear. "You will be with him long—"

"No," Isaura groaned. "I will not. Ignorance is not how I went into this life, and I would not leave it in that manner. Before our binding, Dusan told me of a foretelling he had—of himself and Kersei . . . with sons." She felt her vision blurring. "I was not in it. But I so ardently do not want to lose him when he has just returned!" Tears burst free, and she was grateful for the reassurance of Kita's warm arms encircling her. Comforting her.

A door thudded open in the main room. "Isa?" His voice was urgent as he sought her.

Frantic he would see her blotchiness, she straightened. Silly, since it seemed he had already detected her struggling emotions. "Coming." Skirts in hand, she left the dressing chamber.

"You are well?" he called as he turned in her direction. His brow furrowed and he stopped short.

Her heart alighted when his silvery gaze connected with hers. It felt as the heat of a hearth. Relief that he was yet here, that the ship did not take him, swam thick and heady through her. "Dusan."

Four strides carried him across the room. "What grieves you, my aetos? I anak'd it and could not focus."

"No grief, just . . . concern. Over this war." She should not lie to him, but she would not have him stressed regarding her.

Wary, he considered, then brushed his knuckles over her cheek. "Isa, I know concern from grief. They hit my receptors differently."

She rested her head on his shoulder. "I beg your mercy. I just . . . I fear this war, Dusan. I fear losing you all over again."

He wrapped her into his arms. "My aetos . . . I will not let it happen."

Strange how an unkeepable promise could so vehemently latch onto her heart. She hugged him, treasuring every moment they had together.

"Isa, earlier . . . the . . . ship." He shifted back and cupped her face. "I vow to you, the ship—"

"It is well." She pressed her fingers to his lips. "We are well."

"It would not harm you, I assure you."

Though she wanted to believe his words, she faltered. "How can you know this?"

"I . . . it is hard to explain, but I . . . I control it." He peeked at her like a recalcitrant child. "Somehow, with tech I cannot explain nor understand, it responds to me. I wouldn't have let it harm you." But something in his silvery eyes betrayed hesitation. "Too, I wonder . . . mayhap what is in me is in our daughter. Mayhap the ship sensed it . . . her."

"That does not allay my alarm," she confessed. "However, I trust your word." She would not question it or him, but neither would she again go near that ship. "You are returned to me, and I am glad for it and your protection."

Again, he drew her into his hold. "My refuge." He kissed her neck, then the hollow of her throat. With a groan, he trailed kisses up to the tender, ticklish spot behind her ear.

Trills ran down her spine at the intimate gestures. Surprised at his sudden flare of passion, she wrapped her arms around him, missing him, loving him.

"Every moment I was away, I ached for this." He burrowed in and stayed there. As if . . . hiding. "For you. To be here, in your arms."

"I as well," she said, sensing something amiss. "But what brought this on? Are you well, Dusan?"

He dropped back onto the bed behind him, slumping. Roughed a hand over his face and beard. All so contradictory to who he was, the confident hunter who commanded respect. "I do not know, Isa. I don't know if I'm well. Or . . . what." The way that last word lashed out made her hurt for him. "I want to sleep in your arms for a hundred years, yet there is barely time for one night's rest. And even then, I cannot find it. When I sleep, I dream. And it is not . . . pleasant." He looked up at her and something shifted in his expression as he huffed. His hands slid up her thighs . . . hips . . . and framed her belly. Eyes sliding shut, he leaned in and kissed her womb. "Little One . . . thank you."

A solid thump startled her.

Dusan twitched back. His silvery eyes shot to hers. "She heard me."

Isaura laughed, hand resting on his shoulder, her legs and lower back aching. "There is no doubt she did or—considering those kicks—that she is your daughter."

He grinned, and her heart melted as the Dusan she had fallen in love with sat before her once more. Confident. Focused. Not lighthearted, but never had he been such. In this brief moment, he was not burdened by the survival of the Quadrants.

She traced his face, the beard he had grown . . . the stubble of his shaved head . . . "I have missed you, Dusan."

Please, Ancient, give us more time . . .

An ominous warning snapped Marco from the heavy shackles of sleep and thrust him into the cold, black void of night. Drenched in sweat, he struggled against a weight pressing on his side. He glanced there and found a sea of wheat. Hair. Strands so golden, even in the inky hour, her skin nearly white beneath the amber glow of touchstones lining the walls of their apartments.

His heart settled and the nightmares scampered into the shadows, as he watched her sleep. Amazed that he was truly here with her. That it was no tormenting dream.

Even so, he reached out and touched her hair. Felt its silkiness.

Oras later as he yet drifted somewhere between waking and sleeping, watching the moonlight stretch across the bedchamber to her lithe frame and the glorious swell of her belly. Incredible—his child grew within her. What would she be like? Dark-haired and brooding like him, or fair and light, full of gentle courage like Isa? His gaze strayed again to his bound's smooth cheek, unfurrowed brow.

The nightmare returned to him. Words of warning, so clear in his head, as if—

Squeezing his eyes shut, Marco growled and lurched to his feet. "No." When his voice reverberated across the stone floor, he yanked his attention back to the bed, hoping he had not awakened Isaura. But the bed was shrouded in darkness. No moonlight, no gleam of hair.

What . . .? His heart lurched, realizing what this was. "Where is she? Do not torment me!" He stepped nearer the bed, his thoughts torn. "I would have *peace*," he hissed.

Light glimmered and danced across the foot of the bed, a sea of black.

He drew closer . . .

The black thickened . . . reddened . . .

Dread coiled as a scent rose like a wispy, taunting tendril. A sweet, metallic scent snaked across the room.

Blood!

Spinning around, he felt his feet tangle. He pitched against the edge of the bloody mattress. Hands splatting in the viscous substance. It stuck to his palms. Spilled down his arms.

Then he saw her.

Isa in a pool of blood. Asleep—aye. An *eternal* sleep.

"No!" As panic ripped through him, Marco was diverted by a powerful fragrance permeating his receptors. To the right.

Blackness surrendered to a shape.

He stalked toward the figure sheathed in light and mist. Felt a tremor of anger at the toying with his mind, with his heart. The words she'd spoken on Iereania. The future he'd been forced into—endless heartaches, cruel battles, long days . . . *"Change this! Do not let her die because of me!"*

"Remain strong."

A barbed tendril bit into his chest. *"Have I not returned? Have I not faced enough?"* he demanded. *"I nearly died in that accursed system! Do you tell me I escaped only to see her die?"*

"Stand between Life and Death."

"Answer me!"

But she was gone.

"Augh!" Marco awoke with a jolt. Cold sweat plastered his shirt to his chest and back. He found himself abed, Isaura beside him.

It'd been a dream . . . within a dream . . . He groaned. Hooked his hands over his shorn scalp with a shaky moan.

"Dusan?" Isa rose and caught his arm.

Hunched over, he gripped his head and fought the torment.

Warm, gentle hands touched his back. "Are you well?"

Far from it. He grunted, cast a wary glance over his shoulder. Saw her. Fair, beautiful Isa. Not dead. Not bleeding. Instead, radiant, hair free and beautiful.

With a shuddering breath, he dropped against the feather mattress, and she was there. Her cheek came to rest on his chest. He coiled his arms around her, feeling her heart beat steadily against his own.

My burden and measure. Burden and measure.

What did it mean? She was no burden—she was an anchor. A lifeline! The aetos that guided him home—by carrying their daughter.

"The ship again?" she whispered into the darkness.

Never would he speak of that dream—of her death. "Aye."

The first night back, he'd dreamed of being trapped in the *Prevenire*. Tubes of iron holding him hostage. Sucking the life from him. But tonight . . . Horrific.

Readily would he endure the lectulos a thousand times over as long as what he dreamed this night never came to pass.

Please, Ancient. I beg you. Keep her and the babe safe.

He pulled her closer and bathed his receptors in her Signature. Breathed her in. Breathed again. And again. He felt the roundness of his heir pushing her mother's belly out. Hand over the swollen womb, he reached with the anaktesios to the babe who had drawn him home with a Signature so powerful that even the Ladies could not hide her from him.

Isaura's cool, gentle fingers traced his shorn head. "Still cannot believe you shaved your hair."

"Do you hate it?"

"It is not possible for me to hate anything about you except your absence."

Marco propped himself up on his elbow. Brushed her hair from her face. Reveled in the twin lights in her eyes—hers and the babe's.

Her fingers moved to his beard.

"And that?" he asked with a smirk.

Her serene smile had been a haven since they met in the wastelands. "You would test me?"

"I want to know if your feelings are . . . altered."

She cocked her head, brows knitting together. "Do you suggest that my affection and loyalty are so fickle as to be altered because your appearance is much changed?"

No . . . Yes. "So you do find me much changed then?" Why did his heart race at that?

"Your appearance, aye. But then"—she moved his hand to her swollen womb—"are not we all 'much changed'?"

"You, my aetos, are only *more*—more beautiful, more shrewd, more wise, more . . . mine." He kissed her, remembering the innocence with which she had become his. It seemed a lifetime ago. And that innocence . . . Aye, much changed.

Mentally, his attention fell to his arm. To the bandage over the brand now covered by the weapon. The one calling to him, urging him to war. To vengeance. Soft flesh was stiffening, hardening into a crater-like pattern that was too reminiscent of rhinnock hide. He kept it hidden and would continue to, especially after the incident on the *Qirolicha* with Isaura.

"Step from the shadow of honor . . ."

The words of Vaqar again demanded his focus. But . . . step into *what*? The question ate at him. Vaqar said to focus on *who* he was. Did that mean Marco the hunter? Dusan the bound? Marco the medora? Marco the Progenitor? Which one was he to focus on? The First Hunter seemed to suggest he set aside his training, what he was . . .

Uchuvchi.

His heart rattled against his ribs, remembering the men he'd unwittingly flown to the Quadrants—Gi'Zac and the others. How very much Daq'Ti now resembled that man as *Ovqatlanish*—Tamed—though there were indications he would never be fully restored. Reminders of what he'd done, what he'd been . . .

Like my sigil. Or like the brand that allowed him to pilot the ship. Attracted a weapon. One that responded to his will. Powerful. Instantaneous. Recalling how Daq'Ti had kept his weapon arm, Marco couldn't help but wonder if it would aid them in the war against Symmachia. They were so outgunned as it was—wouldn't it benefit them to have a powerful weapon such as this? What could it hurt?

He dreaded the day Isaura noticed the change. Dreaded the way she might look at him.

"Will you tell me?"

Marco twitched. "Hm?"

She lazily traced his beard as she rested in his arms. "Your thoughts—where were you just now?"

A dark place. "Here. With you." He kissed the top of her head.

Hurt flickered through her Signature but was quickly tucked away, replaced with a deliberate, saturated happiness. She snugged into his shoulder, her breath whispering across his throat. "We are glad you are returned to us." Arm over his midsection, she relaxed and sighed. "The Lady told me the name we are giving our daughter."

"Did she?" he scoffed. "A miracle since even I have no knowledge of it."

"A surprise to me as well. Yet, even as I heard it, I knew it was her name."

"Enlighten me, so I am in on the secret."

She laughed. "Aeliana."

Marco grunted.

"Do you like it?"

"Have I a choice if the Lady spoke it?"

She sat up and stared down at him, her curtain of blonde hair draping her shoulder. "Always. We always have a choice, Dusan."

"Not true!" His words came out stronger than he'd meant them to, that burning in his gut once more demanding voice. He extricated himself from the sheets and climbed from the bed.

"How can you speak so?" She rose and donned a dressing robe, following him.

Where had his choice been on the *Prevenire*? Or, long before that, with the brand, when his life was ripped from his control? When he anak'd her worry and the surprise written across her fair face, he chose redirection. Chastised himself for nearly spoiling their time together. "Not when I met you."

She faltered, uncertainty pinching her delicate features.

He met her, teasing a kiss over her lips and jaw for distraction. "There was no choice once I saw your green eyes." Though she leaned into his affections, hesitation guarding her response, he felt the thickness of it and hated it.

She framed his face. "When you are ready to speak of what happened, I will be here. And my love for you will be unchanged."

He would not speak of it. Because it was not what he had done. It was who they had made him. Neither was it what happened to him—the past. It was very much what he would do. The venom in his veins, writhing through the brand, somehow translating into the weapon. He felt those mechanical barbs digging harder and deeper into sinew and bone. The anger churned with a heat so cruel and relentless. Thirsting, demanding blood.

Too long had she spent in selfish bitterness, absorbed in willful determination to have life as she saw fit, to disregard the good and blessed fortunes that had come her way. Too late had she discovered the well of happiness that had been before her very eyes all along.

In the family crypt below Kardia, Tyrannous Kersei stared at the machi wood coffin that bore Darius's body, his life surrendered when he saved Medora Marco from the crazed Irukandji raider who sought his blood.

Of all the things . . . you brave, stupid man.

Tears slipped down her cheeks as she sat holding their son, grateful for the solitude before the others arrived for the interment service. With the upper halls of Kardia destroyed in an attack and the new ships in space over their world, the residents of the royal house were forced to remain belowground. Therefore, the prince regent could not be placed beside his forebears in the mausoleum overlooking the Kalonican Sea.

I vow our son will know you, Darius.

Through most of their marriage, she had made a mess of things but managed to find solid footing just before he sacrificed. In that one moment, he proved himself and his mettle.

Unlike me. What had she done but be selfish? And lose everyone who loved her. 'Twas one thing to take her life by the reins, quite another to force a path and leave destruction in her wake.

Ma'ma had wanted to teach her the subtle art of wielding power—not with a sword, but with the heart. And Kersei had eschewed it, cast it off as frivolous. With no male heir, Father had never rebuked her for training with the machitis, but neither had he encouraged her. Regardless, she had seized that fallow gap and sown her own will, pushing boundaries, caring not a whit for how it might reflect upon the man she so admired and sought to make proud.

Darius had loved her from the beginning, a love so ardent and true that he believed it left him no choice but to claim her as his own. Yet, that fateful night on the Plains of Adunatos, all she had seen was how he interrupted the plans she had for her future, which included sparring, not binding, and especially not with a petulant prince. The same one who had negotiated with Uncle Rufio—*cowardly, traitorous beast*—to train her. Father had agreed, believing her first sparring injury would send her running home to Ma'ma, begging for embroidery and frippery. In that, she had let them all down. With no regrets.

"You're a bad liar, Kersei."

At Darius's all-too-accurate remonstration, she tucked her head. Fought tears. She *was* injured. Far greater now than the day he had spoken them, when she had bruised her ribs sparring Aerios Myles. There had been such concern and affection in his eyes when he came to her aid. Oh, she ached to hear him again. Longed to tell him, assure him, of her love. He had not heard that from her enough.

How I wronged you, Darius. "I beg your mercy," she whispered, her words scampering through the darkness. Emptiness. Like the chasm left in her heart from losing him. She closed her eyes and did her best to memorize what little of life they had shared together.

With a squeak, Xylander squirmed in her arms, and Kersei peered down at their infant son, who had inherited Darius's thick mop of sandy blond hair and her brown eyes. "I am so glad that he saw you born, but I wish you could grow up with him," she said, her throat raw with grief. "Despite his bullheadedness. Of which I, too, am guilty—so, in that, you may have a double portion. Ancient save us." She laughed around a sniffle. "Your father was a good man. A brave one." She thought of his cockiness, his assuredness. "Arrogant, though I suppose we cannot fault him that, since he was a Tyrannous." She bounced the babe, rocking him back to sleep. "He loved you deeply."

So much that he had sacrificed his life for Xylander, for her . . . for Marco. Now, she was alone. Truly alone. No family. No Darius. No one. A sob snatched from her lungs, and she buried her face in the swaddling.

"Princessa." The title was but a grunt from Myles, his boots scritching where he stood guard at a nearby column. His intrusion into her grief was a warning that others approached for the memorial service.

As if his alerting her had given them permission, voices and the staccato cadence of shoes slipped through the passage to the crypt.

General Bazyli was the first to reach the crypt torchlight, followed by onetime elder, Ixion Mavridis, who led a dozen or more aerios and regia. The master hunter, head high—so like Marco—entered with several Kynigos.

Dressed in his crisp military white-and-green uniform, Bazyli inclined his head. "Cousin," he gruffed, stepping in to set a kiss at her temple. "A grave loss." His large hand slid over Xylander's downy hair. "Ladies and Ancient, protect this babe." His touch on her shoulder bled through her thick black bliaut. "And his mother that they may serve You."

The old blessing touched a nerve. Had not the Ladies been the ones who led Darius to his death? And since—as her mother insisted—she was of Faa'Cris descent, did not that guilt also condemn her?

Galen Sebastiano stepped from behind his older, broader brother. "Duchess, I am sorry for your loss."

Kersei gave a nod. The title still smarted. She and Darius had lost their right to succession when he confessed to treason before finding his true path.

"Our condolences." Sir Mavridis approached and touched her arm. "Your loss is ours."

She thought to respond but ached too much, so she inclined her head. They could not possibly understand the grief—but more, the guilt.

In his traditional brown garb, recused iereas Ypiretis walked down the aisle, offering a solemn nod before he gained the front dais to officiate, per her request. Considering Theon's complicity in the betrayal of Stratios, she had refused any other iereas.

The kyria's lady's maid, Kita Lasdos, appeared and curtseyed. "Begging your pardon, Duchess, but I would be honored to assist you with the babe during the service."

"I would be glad for your help." Kersei passed Xylander to the woman and shuddered a breath, only then realizing how tired her arms had grown, how much his warmth had chased off the chill consuming the small chapel.

A regia snapped to attention at the front. "All rise for—"

"No," a feral growl crawled the stone walls and floors, preceding its owner.

Although Marco rejected the deference, those seated still rose at the arrival of their medora. On her feet, too, Kersei felt her heart thump at the thought of facing him again. She had not seen him since the night of his return, when he had shouted and demanded to know where Isaura was. When he had nearly crushed the throat of his First to free answers lodged there, thickened by shock at his medora's sudden return. When he had fallen at the feet of his beloved kyria and wept.

"This ora is not for me," Marco said, his voice low and fierce, unyielding.

"Today, we honor my brother."

That he named Darius "brother" after all that had transpired stirred Kersei's heart with gratitude.

At his side, his radiant kyria wore a dark green gown, hair tied back in a respectful knot atop which sat a circlet. Isaura. Her thickly embroidered gown draped a womb swollen with Marco's progeny.

Elegant, beautiful Isaura who had besotted the entire kingdom with her wisdom, loyalty, and steadfastness in the absence of their medora. Despite being a year older than Kersei, she had the youthfulness of someone much younger. Even pregnant.

"Duchess." Tall and still broad-shouldered, Marco paused before her, and Kersei found grief forbade her from meeting his gaze. Feared seeing those blue eyes so like Darius's. "I am sorry for your loss. Truly."

She lowered herself into a curtsy. "I thank you, Medora Marco."

Isaura glided forward and wrapped her in a hug. "Our deepest condolences. If there is anything we might do to assist, you have but to ask."

"You are very kind. You have my gratitude for allowing Darius to be buried here, for—"

"It is his right." Fierceness crackled through Marco's words and his eyes . . .

Not like Darius's at all. She marveled that the Tyrannous blue was gone, replaced by an eerie, haunting silver. *What is this change?*

"As Isa spoke—it is wholly meant. And the least I can do, considering he saved my life." Marco shifted away and placed a hand at the small of Isaura's back, guiding her to the opposite row where they sat for the memorial.

Twisting her hands together, Kersei returned to the seat, ready for the formalities to be over. Yet her gaze again found the machi wood coffin, gilt and adorned with a finely woven tapestry of the Tyrannous sigil that marked Darius as a prince of the realm. His honor restored to him. All at Marco's insistence and in spite of the Council's argument that deeds could not be undone.

"Beloved and blessed," Ypiretis said, opening the memorial, "allow us to yield our hearts and thoughts to the Ancient as we return his steward to the earth."

Even as the aged man led them through the service, Marco draped an arm around Isaura. Unusual for a royal to publicly display such affection. But the way his hand cradled her shoulder, the knuckles nearly white . . . He grieved.

As do I.

Tears slipped free and Kersei did nothing to stop them.

KARDIA, KALONICA, DROSERO

"He is much changed."

"No." Roman set down the pitcher of warmed cordi. "He is who he has always been."

Ixion glowered. "How can you speak so? You raised him, mentored him. Saw the man who was taken from his bound that night." He pointed toward the door of the lower reaches of the palace. "The man who stumbled off that ship and called those aliens 'brother' *is* changed. He is . . ."

"He is Progenitor." Roman tossed back a cup of the warmed juice. Wished it were fermented.

"Blood and boil, if I hear that name one more time . . ." Ixion shook his head, his long white hair shifting uneasily.

"You will hear it. See it—*him*! See what he was chosen to do and be very glad for it, though the price will be painfully high. At least we will exist if we persist."

"Will we?" Earnest and steadfast, General Bazyli Sebastiano stared across the table as they waited for Marco to join them to discuss war plans. "You see what remains of this capital. Those ships are said to be on our side, yet none of us can fly them or know the loyalty of the alien pilots. How long will they hold off the specter of death that hangs in orbit above us? Symmachia will not just go away."

Rico grunted. "What about the man—if you can call him that—who returned with Marco? The one who will not leave his side and has that reeking thing for an arm! And a strange, foul scent!"

Bazyli stretched his jaw. "Should we be worried?"

"No." Marco's voice ricocheted off the low stone ceilings as he stalked into the chamber alongside the creature in question.

Roman appreciated the change in his nephew—the short hair, the leaner but meaner build, the shadow rimming his silvery-white eyes. Guilt harangued him, not that he'd had any control over Marco being chosen as Progenitor, but he had been the one to retrieve his nephew for Reclaiming.

Had been tasked with watching over the boy . . . training the lad . . . honing the ardent, intense young man into one of the finest hunters to come from the Citadel.

"Oh Roman, must you?" Athina's cries that night in these very walls had not been about the boy's removal for training, but what she had known even then was coming for her son. Her grief had nearly decimated his willingness to take Marco to the Citadel, knowing each day brought him closer to this point when he was known not as Achilus or Marco or Kynigos, but as Progenitor.

The path had been chosen long before any of them had taken a breath.

"There is nothing to fear from Daq'Ti." Marco squared off in front of the gathered. "In fact, treat him with the same respect you give me because he, too, has been Touched by a Lady, and we will honor that."

Ixion shifted, his expression grim as he considered the alien. "In what manner was he touched?"

"Touched," Marco said, "just as Kersei and I were with the brand."

That would necessitate a Lady . . . beyond the Quadrants. Which was impossible. "In Kuru system—there was a Lady?" Roman heard his own words pitch and wished he'd asked more firmly.

"Aye," Marco said a little too easily.

"But that's—"

"Impossible?" Marco challenged, eyes bright. "Tell me, Uncle, how is it you know so much about the Ladies?"

Surprised to have Marco's irritation aimed at him, Roman stilled. "Knowledge of the Ladies is easily attained, if one—"

"No! No more secrets!"

"Marco—"

"Clear the room!" he demanded, glowering at Roman.

Hesitation tightened the tension in the confined space, regia unwilling to leave their newly returned medora and the Kynigos unwilling to abandon a confrontation between two hunters. Then there was Ixion, who did not seem to know what to do with the young man who had wed his daughter, fathered her unborn child, become medora, vanished, and returned stronger, more powerful—and angry.

"Leave!" Veins strained at Marco's temples. Even as his roar died, the door closed them in together. Hands pressed to the table, he leaned against it and took several long breaths. Closed his eyes.

Along his inner right forearm came the warm glow of the brand. And . . .

something more Roman could not discern. Something not visible but very much playing against his receptors and adunatos. The concern that had been taunting him regarding the dark corners of Marco's foul mood resurfaced.

"Why did you never tell me?" Marco sounded miserable.

"That we share the same blood?"

"That you knew all along what I would become one day."

Roman faltered. "The brand—"

"No." Marco peered up from furrowed brows. "You know far too much about the brand and the Ladies to be an innocent—"

"I exert no will or power over either, but it is true I kept our kinship in the dark. I felt it would muddy your training, your direction."

"Direction."

Roman could admit to being a little disappointed.

"Why did you not prepare me?"

"Didn't I?"

Marco skated him a glower.

"Am I Vaqar or the Ancient that I can alter the path your feet were set on? It is no mistake that I am your uncle, that you are a hunter gifted with the anaktesios, that I claimed you for the Citadel and trained you. What was I to add to your training that would have better prepared you?"

"Warning," Marco ground out. "Warning of the price."

His nephew had aged years in the months he was gone. Before him now stood not a confident, brooding hunter-turned-medora, but a warrior, a father, a king . . .

A very broken one.

"Warning of the emptiness." Marco pushed away and stalked the room. "The silence. Weeks-long isolation trapped in the hull of a ship, drained of life and hope."

"No man could have known those things." Roman swept in and caught Marco's arm—thrumming with heat and power, its virulence nearly setting him back a step—and pressed their shoulders together. "I knew you were Progenitor but also that Isaura was your beacon. Your daughter—"

"Enough." Marco jerked his arm free. "You watched over them, and for that, I will forgive you."

"Forgive me?"

"I see it," Marco hissed, his eyes like liquid silver beneath unshed tears. "I see her death—Isaura's." He snarled. "It torments my sleep." Misery clawed at his beard and shaved head. "The price"—his body shook with rage that vibrated through his muscles—"*she* will pay. For loving me."

"It was her choice. She knew—"

"No! *Do not*!" Marco barked, his lips taut yet trembling. "*I* am the reason she will die. Me!" Tears freed themselves and dropped onto his beard. "And this . . . *this* is what I have returned to bring about. To endure—guilt that *I* will kill her."

Stunned, Roman could not speak. Grieved, he could not move.

"The war?" Marco's lip curled. "Give it to me. I will face it. Her death?" His beard twitched as he struggled to restrain the flood of his grief. "Bleed me now because I cannot face failing or losing her."

Roman gripped his nephew's upper arm tight. Squeezed it. "You have been granted a love that cannot be removed or destroyed, not in life." He tucked his chin to be sure Marco listened. "Nor in death. She *gave* you her love—a gift. One that can *never* be taken from you."

Nostrils flaring, Marco exerted tremendous effort to control what was raging within, an efflux rank and searing. "She *will* be taken from me. And when that day comes . . ."

Heat wavered, spreading along Roman's fingers. "Focus not on—" With a grunt, he fought the heat that washed over his hand, up his wrist, hotter and hotter. Until he couldn't. He released Marco and glanced to where they had touched, startled, though he should not have been, to see the brand glowing . . .

Red. No. That was . . . off. Wrong. That color—

"Marco . . ." He hooked the back of his nephew's neck as answers flooded his synapses and receptors, shock writhing on the wake of a realization. "What have you done?"

Defiance flared through eyes nearly white. "What was necessary," he said around bared teeth. "What kept me alive. Brought me back to Isa, to my child!"

"But this—"

Marco shoved away and fell into a fighting stance.

The same stance Roman stepped into on instinct, then shifted, alarmed at the rage radiating off his nephew. A concern he had never before considered choked him. "Marco, please release it. What you reek of rots your adunatos. You must—"

"Never tell me I *must* do anything. Ever again." Marco stretched his neck.

"I do not answer to you."

"My medora?" Hand on his hilt, Ixion was at the door, glancing between them, ready. Worried. Behind him stood uncertain Ramirus and Ulixes.

Marco dragged a hand across his eyes even as the Draegis thudded to his side, the odd cadence of his words too low for Roman to understand. "I am well." His nephew patted the alien's shoulder, then glanced around the room. "We council!" Once the leaders were seated, he motioned to Daq'Ti. "Show them."

Skin leathery and tinged gray, Daq'Ti hummed as he drew up his tunic. There, slightly off-center, a gently pulsing blue handprint. "The mark of Xonim," he trilled and bowed his head.

Roman jarred, recalling that mark from the sacred texts, the Retellings. Did "Xonim" mean Lady? He glanced at Marco. "Who was she?"

"So well-versed with the Ladies that you think you'd know her?" Anaktesios was not needed to detect Marco's accusation.

Unnerved but not cowed, Roman inclined his head. "I am acquainted with some, yes." He was not at liberty to speak more.

"Her name is Eija."

He stilled. Craned his neck forward, eyebrows lifted. "You are sure?"

A bitter note ripened Marco's efflux. "No question. Eija is the one who found and saved me in the *Prevenire*." He gave Roman a speculative glance. "You know this Tascan pilot?"

"I . . . do not. But her name is familiar."

Marco waited.

"She is well-known on many worlds."

"Not surprising since she's Vaqar's daughter."

"And Eleftheria's—their youngest. Fiercest." Roman had no idea what to do with this revelation, that Marco had encountered the renowned warrior. "She's . . . terrifying."

"There is a legend," Bazyli said, his voice clear and stern, "rampant in the western territories about the Bloodbreaker, a Lady who takes children—"

"Meijatsia," Ixion rasped, his tanned face unnaturally white. "She is known in the wastelands for sacrificing children to break the bloodlines of the wicked."

"Those tales are inflamed," Roman said. "Meijatsia did not *sacrifice* children, but she was tasked by the Ancient to wipe out entire cities who had grown corrupt and perverted in their practices."

"Lieutenant Eija Zacdari was a sweet, endearing, insecure young woman." Looking drawn, Marco considered him for a long moment, his efflux rank with resignation. "But admittedly that was before she learned her true identity, which had been mindblocked so she could safely leave the Quadrants. Vaqar challenged her, helped her recall who she was. When I returned, she was supposed to be on the ship with me, but Eija remained in Kuru . . . her work not yet done."

"But Marco, you don't understand—"

"I don't care who Eija is or isn't. She's not my concern. This war is. And no matter how much I resent it or would avoid it, war is upon us." He pointed up. "Not only do Symmachians outnumber us, but if the Uchuvchi can come through, the Draegis can, too. And trust me, that's a nightmare you don't want. Pray Eija is successful, because they outnumber us with weapons we cannot begin to fathom. What I saw, what confronted me in Kuru . . . If"— his nostrils flared beneath a restrained breath—"*when* they come, we will not have a prayer." That weariness tugged at his features again, and he sagged. "But we are not yet dead. What good fighting will do, Vaqar knows. But if we are to die, then I'm of the mind to take as many of them with me as possible."

And so, the hunter has become the master.

VYSIEN, HIRAKYS, DROSERO

"It itches."

"Stop tugging at it or you'll draw attention."

Tigo Deken glowered at the woman gliding through the streets of Vysien as if she owned them. "You could dial it back a little. Practice that whole *not-drawing-attention-so-we-don't-end-up-dead thing*."

"I am Faa'Cris. If I choose to be invisible, then I am."

He stretched his arms and scratched his back. "Meanwhile, you stuff me into the worst material known to mankind."

Rejeztia rolled her eyes. "Stop complaining."

"This isn't complaining. This is stating facts." He tugged at his collar, which was rubbing his neck raw. "But hey. If you want complaining, let's start with the fact that, since you're Faa'Cris, you could've transported us straight into the palace to avoid—"

"*Hiyaaah!*" came a feral shout from the side.

Snapping his right leg back and rolling his pulse weapon to the front, Tigo deflected a singing blade that swept at him. He shoved in, forcing the man back, but then the air riffled. Glinted from a dagger.

Tigo pulled up sharp, using a knifehand to drive the man's short blade away. He shifted and hooked the man's legs out from under him. Dropped him. Nailed the guy's chest with his weapon and fired.

Huffing out his breaths, Tigo drove his gaze to Jez, not surprised to find her standing over two more attackers, moon discs tucking away as she seemed ready to yawn. He wiped sweat from his brow. "You could've warned me."

Stepping away from the unconscious men at her feet, she straightened. "Hard to get a word in with you stating all those facts."

A blur blindsided Tigo. Knocked his weapon aside. They rolled. Tigo flipped the man onto his back, yanking the dagger from his boot. "Do you yield?" Tigo asked blandly, the blade to his throat. "Or shall I sate my blade with your blood?"

Dark-skinned and gaunt, the man bared his teeth. "I'll—"

Tigo tweaked his dagger so that it pricked the man's flesh. "Blood it is—"

"Wait!"

"See?" Tigo slid his gaze to Jez. "A little conversation goes a long way."

"So do swords." She arched her eyebrow even as he heard the song of steel.

"Hirakyn, I would stay that blade lest you be delivered to Shadowsedge at my hand. Or worse—hers."

Air gusted, drawing the man's gaze—and Tigo's—to Jez. He couldn't help but grin as her armor manifested around her, wings fanning the air with that distinctive minty smell that made him feel like he was in zero g.

Can we say sexy?

He glanced at the attacker. "Not sure about you, downworlder, but I'd yield."

"Y-yes. Of course." Once Tigo released him, the man scrabbled on the dusty earth like a fish out of water and flopped onto his belly, nose pressed to the sand in subservience. "Lady, I am your servant."

Tigo sheathed his dagger as he met Jez's glower. "It's cheating, you know."

Rolling her shoulder and tucking her true form back into . . . wherever it went, she narrowed her violet-fading-to-caramel eyes on the man. "We would speak with Crey of Greyedge. Take us to him."

"I can't—"

"Hey." Tigo scratched his jaw. "I know this world is dominated by patriarchal rule, so hearing a woman command you is not something you're used to, but I wouldn't push her." He put a hand over his heart. "I made that mistake once. And—unlike her—it wasn't pretty. In fact, it was humiliating. So, do yourself a favor and take us to Crey."

"No-no. I mean—really, I can't." His expression was earnest and bordered on panic.

Anger palpable, Jez rolled her shoulder, and with that move, her eyes once more grew violet. Her armor—

"She doesn't take rejection well," Tigo warned.

The man raised his hands, whimpering. "Wait, wait, wait!" Stumbling backward, he looked like he might wet himself. "Ican'tbecausehe'snothere." He seemed to sweat with the effort of shoving those words out fast. "He took an army west to locate and destroy the Symmachian stronghold in Irukandji territory."

"Void's Embrace." Tigo pivoted to Jez as he ran a hand over his military reg haircut. "They'll be slaughtered." He paced. "We have to do—"

Hot and tight, Jez's grip on his wrist yanked him around as her mintiness pumped through the hot afternoon and blurred where they stood.

Oh no. "Wai—"

An infusion of heat and light shot through his chest and field of vision. Drowned him in a brightness that both seared and chilled. His limbs felt like rubber, his nostrils as if someone had miswired his PICC-line and fed it through his nose, searingly cold. Yet hot. Agonizing.

With a thunderous crack, the illumination snapped off.

"Augh!" Darkness drenched him, left him aching as if a dreadnought had collided with his body. He gripped his knees, waiting for the rest of his self—his brain, his organs, his breath—to catch up with the fold she'd just effected.

Through his brows, he glowered up at Jez. "I—augh!" The world canted. He pressed the heel of his hand to his forehead. "I *hate* when you do that. And why can't you give me a warning?"

"What? And miss more of your facts?"

He huffed. Staggered, glancing around, trying to get his vision to adjust. Pinching the bridge of his nose, he grunted. "I think you do that just to make me hurt."

She whisked aside and crouched.

Not able to trust his own body and instincts after that light-flare experience, he followed her lead. "Isn't prayer more effective *before*—"

"Quiet." She nodded past him.

He finally noted the field stretched before them. An array of tents laid out on a grid. People walking about as if they were in a city on a normal day. But it wasn't normal people or a normal day. These were Irukandji raiders, and this was their base camp.

"And now we die."

An impossible war without hope.

Crouched on the ledge of the roof, Marco scanned the destruction that was Kardia. The sight rent his heart. Forearm resting on his right leg, he swiveled and took in his ancestral home and surrounding property. While he was gone, Symmachia had bombed the castle in an effort to eliminate his home, his bound, his heir, his people. Destroy any will to fight. In orbit, Symmachia and the drones had been in a standoff for weeks. A silent one. Most in the city now went about their business, forgetting the threat that loomed overhead.

Marco would not forget. Ever. And if he could bring the war, he would. He just didn't know how . . . Infuriating!

His brand burned as if responding to what stirred in his gut, curling his fingers into a fist. A helpless people would eventually be pitted against a vicious, vastly more advanced enemy. And what hope were they given but, years past, marks seared into the flesh of innocent children.

Yet his brand had allowed him to power a weapon and pilot a ship. If there were more prototypes like the *Qirolicha* . . .

His gaze skidded into the oddly shaped ship still resting on the ruin of the north lawn. It had returned him to Drosero, to Isa. His daughter. And transported the Uchuvchi within its orb, thereby also summoning the unmanned fast-attack crafts that even now littered the heavenlies.

Fast-attack crafts. Pilots. Uchuvchi. The pods in that facility . . . Him. Trapped in a similar one on the *Prevenire*. Locked in that hull. Veins burning. Mind careening into the very void that had swallowed them.

Cold. It'd been so cold. Lonely. Terrifying in its isolation. Running his trembling hands over his shorn hair, Marco slumped back against the wall, remembering the scents. Smelling . . . sensing the crew but unable to talk to them, reach out to them. They were there, and that knowledge alone had been a strange comfort that helped him hold on, despite everything else hitting his receptors that said otherwise.

Afraid. The rancid, insidious fear said he'd never get home. That he would die in cruel isolation, unable to call for help. The joy that had warmed his heart and adunatos would never again be felt. Never feel Isa's love, never love again, never . . . respond.

But he *would* respond now. In some powerful, violent way to those who had torn his heart and courage apart. He'd let Xisya and her kind know that humanity had a will. *He* had a will and would no longer be their pawn nor the means of transport via his receptors. He'd sear them out before he allowed that again. Symmachia was a puppet master no more. The Corrupt must pay for the subjugation of mankind, the destruction of civilization after civilization.

"You reek."

Marco startled—not at the words but that he had not sensed the master's approach. "What's new?"

"Your attitude."

With a grunt, Marco alighted from the ledge onto what was left of the balcony, landing with a soft thump. His bones jarred, still struggling after six weeks of forced solitary confinement in that metal contraption and little activity since. His body atrophied, no longer strengthened by the vigorous workouts that had once been as normal to him as breathing. But he would beat his body into submission as he had today, hopping from ledge to ledge. Doing his best—and failing—to avoid broken walls or precipices. Scrapes, cuts, and burns were but reminders to do better next time.

He wanted no lecture or talk, so he turned to head down to the lower reaches, to Isaura, her scent yet a lure to his weary, hungry soul.

"What of honor, Marco?"

"What of it?" he snapped.

"You seem little concerned with it."

He adjusted the vambrace, considering the weapon that had embedded itself in his forearm. No one here would understand—not his men and certainly not his master. They already looked at him as a monster. "Do you know what Vaqar said when he appeared to me in Kuru?"

Keeping pace, Roman eyed him, his Signature rife with an odd concoction of wariness, eagerness, and admiration.

"He said to step from the shadow of honor." Marco winged an eyebrow at him. "Seems it's overrated or something. Apparently, I had come to put too much stock in honor and not enough in"—he shrugged—"whatever it was he wanted me to grasp."

"Give care. You mock the First Hunter."

"I mock this game!" His barked words echoed across the eerie quiet that was Kardia. "The game of life, this war that has turned those I love into javrod dummies, bludgeoning their hope and heart. Aye, I mock it." His chest rose and fell unevenly. "Is this what we've become, Roman? Sacks of straw to be run through and—"

Marco flew backward. Slammed against the wall in a move so fast and violent, he did not know it had happened until his breath knocked from his chest.

The master's forearm jammed into his throat, his large hand pinning his shoulder. "Give. Care," Roman warned. "I hear your grief, nephew, though the reek of it is enough to draw a herd of rhinnocks. Whine if you must, but ready yourself. Being Progenitor—dare you suggest Vaqar and the Ancient chose poorly?"

Marco stared at familiar blue eyes, then cupped Roman's elbow and wrist. Twisted them and freed himself. Squared his shoulders as he held his ground. "I resent who they chose."

"I am beginning to feel the same."

Always had he felt weighed and found wanting in his master's eyes. How was this different?

"Do you think you're the only one with pain and loss in this war? You sit and whinge about what you have suffered when in your hand is the power to prevent anyone else from experiencing that. At least be grateful the end is nigh."

Were his words in reference to the weapon? The mess it was making of his arm? He must distract . . . "Should I, *Uncle*?"

Roman sagged a little. "I should have told you sooner."

Swatting a defeated hand in the air, Marco started for the door to the crumbling passage that led to the lower reaches.

"Your mother is alive."

His boot slipped and nearly planted him on his backside. Catching his balance, Marco jerked around, staring in disbelief at his uncle. Hearing the words yet not believing them. "What say you?"

Roman already seemed to regret his words. "I was not supposed to speak it." Always, he had been about the law, the upholding of it, the executing of it. "But I would not have any more secrets between us."

His mother . . . "Where . . .? How—"

"She is a Lady. A Resplendent."

Marco squinted, trying to make sense of the word. Of the possibility that she was yet alive but had not spoken or come to him. That she was a Lady explained . . . everything. And hardened his heart toward them a little more.

"That's their highest rank. Their elders of a sort. Among the Resplendent, she is the eldest"—he lifted a shoulder in a shrug—"next to Eleftheria, of course. They call her Revered Mother." Studying the ground for a tick, Roman huffed. "When I removed you to the Citadel, it shattered her. But you will not hear her whine about not being a part of your life. Alanathina—" He seemed beleaguered when he dragged his gaze back to Marco. "I cannot say that she will come to you or even that she wills it, but . . . she *does* believe in you. As do I. Which is why I cannot stand to see you moping around the ruins of this place or hurling that anger about."

"Moping." Marco sniffed and shook his head. Turned away. Then came round again. "I have been back not even a fortnight—my strength fails, my mind fails, and in the dead of night finds itself trapped in that ship. Then there's the other dream where my hands are coated with Isaura's blood, my honor—" He heard his voice crack and steeled himself. Or tried to. There was no steel left. "Failure is all I know!"

Heat coursed through the weapon.

Except that. With the weapon he had not failed. It was a . . . strength. One he hadn't had before. One none would understand, yet it gave him an edge, did it not? Even Daq'Ti had chosen to keep his when Eija healed him. Like the brand, it burned. Drove.

He did not want to face the master, looking into those disapproving eyes, so he glanced down the dank, dark passage. So symbolic of his life right now.

A scent wafting from the passage pushed the dour from his mood. Lavender and white oak called to him. He drank it in and sighed. "Later, Uncle. I . . . must rest."

Marco strode the forty paces through the darkness and found her, touchstone light caressing her fair features as she smiled at his approach. He slipped his arms around her waist and hugged her. "You are my strength," he murmured into the crook of her neck.

Pleasure permeated her Signature, which flared with the minty tinge of their daughter. So beautiful. So perfect. "And you mine."

A solid thump hit his abdomen. He drew back and laughed, looking at her, then her belly. "Was that—"

"Your daughter again," she confirmed.

"She kicked me!"

"Only fair, since these many months I have been her punching bag."

Marco laughed, then crouched and framed her belly with his hands. Kissed the brocade fabric of the gown. "Aeliana," he whispered, "I can't wait to meet you."

Again kissing the womb, he felt the tiniest of thumps. He barked a laugh. "Clever girl." He peered up at Isa. A swell of joy pulled him to his full height. "Who would have thought in the tent outside Moidia when you ripped the sheet down to see me unclothed that you would one day be my bound."

Isaura's laugh echoed in the passage. "I did not do that on purpose! It was an accident."

"So you keep saying." Mesmerized by her green eyes, her beauty, and the way she carried herself, he grinned. "I'll never forget your expression as you stood atop that chair. You were mortified, but then . . . you appreciated what you saw."

"It was your fault for being so . . . sculpted."

"Sculpted? Am I now a statue?"

Isa traced his beard. "Quite." She kissed him and he responded, returning the kiss. Grateful to stay in her arms. Needing to stay here. For as long as he could.

A throat cleared. "Begging your pardon, Majesty . . ."

Marco clenched his jaw at Ixion's intrusion. "Yes?" he said in tandem with Isaura, who blushed.

"King Vorn has sent word that he will be here in two rises."

Jealousy wove a tight cord at seeing Marco so intimately set with the wastelander beauty as they descended from the upper levels. The two had paused, talking intently, then he touched Isaura's cheek, caressing her pregnant belly . . . kissing her . . .

Long ago had Kersei given up the notion that it should have been her in his arms. Now, the ache that struck hardest was that, with Darius gone, she no longer had love. She was alone.

Heart riven, she slumped back against the wall, hugging the parchments to her chest. She closed her eyes and refused her tears the freedom to roam her cheeks.

"Duchess, you are well?" The sweet voice of the kyria embraced her, ticks before a touch on her elbow.

Lifting her chin and courage, Kersei pushed off the wall to find Isaura before her, Marco a few paces behind and silent. "Aye. Thank you, Your Highness." She nodded, fastening her gaze to the kyria's. "I . . ." Swallowing gave her a moment to compose herself. "I had hoped to gain your attention"—she held out the parchments—"to address these matters."

Inclining her head, Isaura angled to see them better, no hesitation in her manner or concern. "What is this?"

"A list from the kitchens. It seems the bombings affected our market and food stores. Also, there is need in the city for food and clothing."

"Of course," Isaura said with a smile. "Whatever we can do. It is so nice to think we will have peace for a while—at least from the skies, thanks to the Uchuvchi. And I am most grateful to you for attending to this, especially so soon after being delivered of a son."

Was the comment a chastisement that Kersei had so soon left Xylander to tend the people, or was it legitimate praise? Unsure, she tucked back an unruly black lock. "'Tis naught. Clearly needs are great during wartime, and the people are our responsibility."

Kersei could not help but feel Marco's presence and, though he spoke nothing, his disapproval that shouted through his silence as he held back, observing. Curiosity getting the better of her, she finally braved a glance.

Arms at his side, he stood in a pose that might appear casual to one not acquainted with the man who had long been a hunter. But to those who knew him, it spoke of readiness as he stared down the passage in the opposite direction. Frowning. Tense. He seemed half ready to vault away.

Was something amiss?

In light of the recent attacks, the incursion of raiders, and Symmachians on Droseran soil—even here at Kardia—Kersei felt her nerves fray.

Isaura hesitated, looking from her to Marco. Concern now touched the kyria's delicate brows. She shifted to the side and caught the medora's hand in a gesture so familiar and intimate. "Dusan?"

With a twitch, he snapped back to her. "My aetos." His gaze flicked to Kersei for a tick. The powerful intrusion of those eyes into her adunatos sent a charge of heat so keen through her chest that she nearly jerked back. Then his silvery gaze landed firmly on his bound's. "I must go."

"As you will," Isaura said, watching him depart, then gave Kersei a radiant smile. "Please, do as you would regarding the stores. Tell the people their medora sends the needed aid, that he thanks them for their courage in this dark hour."

"Thank you." Kersei hugged the parchments. "I will tend to this and ensure the people are cared for."

"My great thanks." Isaura smiled and followed the medora.

Hurt flayed open old wounds—Marco had not even spoken to Kersei. No hello. No smile. No warmth. *I am but a stranger to him now.* Grief rose anew on her crestfallen hopes of a friendship between them.

"My lady," came a deep voice.

Kersei tore her gaze from the darkened passage and faced her loyal bodyguard. Saw in his tanned and ruddy complexion sympathy—he had witnessed the entire exchange. She would not be mocked or pitied. "We have much work to do, Myles."

He angled into her path. "I am sure he does not mean to wound."

"I would have neither your pity nor your advice." The words were fast and sharp, and she immediately regretted them. "And now, *I* wound." Yet he should know his place was not to counsel her. "Come. Let us work."

MAHURAT, KURU SYSTEM

"I am really wishing I'd let you drop me to my death."

Crouched behind a transformer, Eija ducked. "It would have made many things easier."

A fiery volley barraged them, pushing them lower, their faces nearly to the cold, hard floor.

"You know," Reef muttered, his voice pitching oddly, "now that you're god's daughter, you've got a lot of attitude."

Ducking, Eija rolled her eyes. "I'm not—" She growled. "Never mind. Just shut up and—"

"*Down!*" Reef dove into her, sending them careening backward.

Her head cracked against a wall and her teeth clacked. Anger plowed through her veins and she punched outward, her span acting as jet engines adding thrust to her shove.

Reef vaulted aside, into the open.

Cursing her temper and carelessness, Eija sprang to protect him. Saw a Draegis contracting his arm to fire. She spiraled out and cast a shield about her as she reached an unmoving Reef. Regret digging in, she snatched him from the ground and shot upward.

Heat streaked along her span. At the fiery pain and acrid smell of singed feathers, she tightened her jaw. Aimed for the catwalks of this enormous facility. Angling to alight on a steel grate that spanned the open area and provided support to one of the many pod towers, she hoped Reef wasn't too badly injured. Or that the Draegis firepower wouldn't reach them.

Eija touched down and bent her knees, lowering him—

"Always did want to be in your arms."

Half startled, half annoyed, she dropped him. "You are a galaxy system too late in realizing that."

Though Reef huffed a laugh, he rubbed his chest—the spot where she'd inadvertently pushed him into the open.

Concern lashed her. "Are you okay?"

Gray eyes hit hers as he paused, but he gave a curt nod. "Alive at least."

"I didn't mean—"

"Bigger space aliens to fry right now." His brow furrowed. "Hey. Eij . . ." Warning thickened the way he said her name. "They, um, wouldn't bring in a ship to destroy this place, would they? I mean—this is their breeding ground. They'd want to protect it. Right?"

"I suppose."

His gaze hit hers again. "Unless?"

How did he know she was thinking that? "*Unless* they believed the greater risk to their survival was not losing all these spawn, but . . . something else." *Like me.*

"Then we might have a problem." He nodded past her.

Eija glanced over her shoulder. Scanned the shadowy darkness of the catwalks, the beams—"I don't"—the shadowy glass that served as the dome roof to this hexagonal structure, past that to—"Oh no."

"Maybe you should kiss me."

Eija jerked. "*What?*"

"Well, in the novids, when the heroine and hero believe they're about to die and kiss, they always survive." He shrugged. "Can't hurt to try, right?"

She sniffed a laugh. "How did you ever become an Eidolon, watching all those novids?"

"Where do you think I learned tactics?"

She balked.

"Kidding! Kidding." He shook his head.

Draegis below. Draegis above. Where were they supposed to go? They were cornered. She couldn't just abandon this location or her mission. There were too many spawn here to leave unaddressed. Yet, with the sea of Lavabeasts down there and more moving across the lawn to join the fight, they were impossibly outnumbered.

"Djell," she whispered, the word discordant now that she understood where her subconscious had picked it up.

"*Come down, Little Eleftheria,*" shrilled a Khatriza.

The sound scraped through Eija, hollowing out her compassion. Forcing the warrior in her into action. "How does she know who I am?" Not quite ready to face that side of herself, she restrained the impulse.

"Who?" Reef frowned, his gaze darting between her and the incoming craft.

"The Khatriza."

"What?" His eyes widened. "Here?"

"Didn't you just hear her tell me to come down?"

He cocked his head, brow rippling. "No . . ."

"How could you not—" Eija sucked in a hard breath. "Lifespeech. They still know how to use it." That was really not good. She had expected that to have been bred out after this long of a separation from Deversoria and so many genetic mutations.

"*I know what you are,*" the Khatriza hissed in her head. "*Bloodbreaker.*"

Nausea and dizziness swept through Eija, and she swayed.

"Whoa!" Reef caught her shoulders. "Easy, easy. You okay? Take a hit I didn't see?"

She shook off the Khatriza's words, the truth of them. Her . . . past. The terrible task assigned her as the sword of the Ancient. Daughter of Eleftheria and Vaqar.

"Eija."

She looked at Reef, mind still drenched in the past. That this creature knew who she was. "It's been centuries," she muttered, grasping how truth prevailed after all this time. "*How* does she know . . .?"

Again, Reef cocked his head, his gray eyes leaden with concern. "How does who know what?"

"Never mind." In a crouch, Eija rotated, glancing around, searching for her adversary. Amid the sea of black bodies pulsing with red veins and the pods teeming with new life, the creature was here. Somewhere. "Show me. Let me be your blade." Uttering that prayer would mean she had one option: be the part of herself she'd been more than happy to repress.

"Show you what?" Reef's tone was nervous. "Ei, we don't have a chance down there. We need reinforcements. Backup. More weapons."

In one corner, she saw a halo of light—no, not light; it was simply a *lightening*, an enhancement of her vision—that revealed what was hidden.

There you are. Giddy pleasure soaked her span as she riffled out. Her helm shuttered around her face, glittering as it formed to protect her.

"Scuz me," Reef breathed. "Eija, what're you—"

"*Xiomara,*" she imbued in Lifespeech, "*this is not a battle you can win.*"

"*Child, you are the one outnumbered and naively arrogant. I will not patronize you with the suggestion to surrender.*"

Eija tucked her chin and drew closer to the Corrupt. "*Neither will I, because Eternal Embrace is the only solution for violators.*"

"*I am not the one in the wrong system.*"

"*Xisya was the successful pawn in the Corrupt's plan to reinvade the Quadrants. Guilt is thereby assessed to all Corrupt.*" Heat thrummed in Eija's hand as she readied her blade and prepared for battle.

"*Have you counted, Child?*"

Counted? Counted what?

"*Or has arrogance yet again defined your doom?*" Xiomara laughed.

Only as Eija brought her weapon to bear did understanding strike. Count . . . count the scents. The presence of the Corrupt. She drew in a breath, anak'ing . . . Her gaze again rose to the pods, to the spawn. These were hybrids, yet . . .

She shifted her gaze to the center column. Noticed the slight color variation in the cocooning djell. Tentatively reached out and felt the acrid zap of corruption. Eija recoiled, her head throbbing from the punishing touch.

Xiomara laughed. "Ah, now you see."

"How . . .?" Dread coiling around Eija's breastbone. "It's not—"

With a feral scream to the Draegis, Xiomara sprang at her.

Instincts dulled by the revelation and shock, Eija had unwittingly gotten too close. A razor-sharp talon sliced her face as Reef howled a shout from the rafters. Spinning, cheek afire, she vaulted up. Arched backward and locked onto Reef. Behind him, beyond the windows, aircraft spewed a fiery bombardment.

In the frozen terror of that moment, she faltered at the pulses streaking toward them. Which gave Xiomara the chance to catch her left dorsal wing and yank.

Too aware of her mistakes, her folly, her—as Xiomara had accused—arrogance, Eija used her elliptic wings for a tight, controlled burst to free herself and reach Reef. Saw the split-second shock that froze him. Heard the breath he sucked in. Felt that same breath gust out as they collided.

She folded herself—and him—through time and space. Extended her thoughts to the nearest safe haven.

Shad.

The distortion of time surrendered.

Darkness gaped. Air popped. Crackled.

They were still in motion when the surroundings came into focus. *Too fast.* Instinct wrapped her wings around them as they barreled at an earthen wall. But not before they crashed through a table. Upended pottery. Something wet drenched them as they struck the hardpacked dirt wall.

Pain exploded amid a sickening crunch. Blinding, white-hot agony snatched the scream lodged in her throat. Breath slipped out . . . and did not return. Neither did her lungs expand. The ache proved crushing. *I failed.* "Did not . . . see . . ."

Consciousness fled.

"The sight of you does much good for my heart."

With a smile, Marco inclined his head as he met the powerfully built Jherakan king in a back-pounding hug. "Likewise." He stepped back, not surprised when the slightly taller Vorn scrubbed a hand over Marco's shorn hair. "You should try it. Saves time in the bath."

"Why would I want that? It's the one time the sergii leave me alone." Vorn's deep, resonant laughter echoed through the chamber. He clapped Marco's shoulder. "I see hair is not the only thing altered about you."

Marco had the strange urge to shift in his boots. "And you, have you gone soft since the birth of your son?"

Vorn barked a laugh. "Aliria would vow I am a lamb when it comes to the boy."

"That would be a sight." Marco nodded. "How is your queen?"

"As beautiful and beguiling as ever. In spite of the trials of new motherhood, she is relentless in her efforts to prepare our city for whatever those accursed skycrawlers bring upon us next." The king's gregarious style was refreshing. With him there was no pandering, awkward conversation, or hemming. He touched the scars at Marco's temple. "I must thank our enemy."

Marco frowned.

"They made me more beautiful by scarring your face."

Though he did not want to, though he anak'd the shocked and wary scents around them, Marco chuckled. "Anything to strengthen our alliance."

Vorn rubbed his large hands together. "Now, we must plot their destruction."

"With pleasure. As you have noted, Lampros City and Kardia sustained damage, but we yet stand. What of Forgelight? I heard the castle lies in ruins."

"Not wholly, but there is significant rebuilding to be done. I thought that holding the Conclave in a hidden part of the castle would be enough." He gave a grim shake of his head. "Foolish."

Marco chose not to voice his irritation with that faulty thinking, though Ixion had already relayed how Isaura had been injured in that attack. "Have you considered that mayhap you were betrayed, that someone leaked the location to the enemy?"

Sharp, shrewd eyes stabbed at that accusation. Vorn's cheek muscle twitched. "I would argue no, but only a fool would not consider every possibility in this war. Regardless, we will not allow those skycrawlers to dictate our lives. And there, I would offer an apology for the injury done your queen when they attacked during the Conclave."

"Had you been able to prevent it, I know you would have. Isaura is well, so let us spend our energy on strategizing how to best utilize the Interceptors against Symmachia."

"Agreed." Eyes pinched with that frequent smile, Vorn nodded, though he hesitated.

"What weighs your thoughts, friend?" Marco instinctively anak'd the Jherakan ruler.

Sucking a breath through his teeth, Vorn swiped a hand over his beard.

Processing the scents, Marco knew to speak up. "Let me save you the strain—you fear my allegiances. Wonder if, during my captivity, Symmachia divided my loyalty. If I am a spy." Despite the restraint he exercised, he could not keep the edge from those last words.

"Put yourself in my boots." Vorn slid his hands into his pockets. That position made most men seem soft, but it only added to the breadth of Vorn's shoulders and persona. "The one sovereign on this accursed planet able to effect change and with whom I share goals and values is taken. Gone for more than half the cycle, then returns with a tale as outlandish as his tattooed nose and glowing arm."

The thudding of his heart sounded as war drums. "And yet they are as real as my loyalty to Kalonica, our treaty Kyria Isaura signed, and to Drosero!"

"Yeh." Vorn shifted forward, his countenance taut yet . . . kind. "As believed, but I had to come myself. Had to look you in the eye, so the words told me by advisors and Rico, your advocate, would be borne out in that pale gaze of yours. We cannot afford to lose you as our ally and champion, but we can less afford to be deceived."

"Understood. And appreciated." Marco huffed. "If anything, this ordeal has only hardened my resolve. That fear you speak of? It pounds in my own chest, torment that we are up against an impossible adversary. However, after what I saw in Kuru, after what happened to me—"

"Will you speak of it, what was done to you?" Vorn's brown eyes darted over Marco's face for several heartbeats.

Irritation coiled around Marco like a vise.

The burly king with his dark hair and dark eyes stepped closer, his nose almost touching Marco's. "I see it, friend. I see the change and would understand its source. Men like us—leaders, rulers—guard zealously the wounds perpetrated against us. But those same wounds are the ones that dig deepest into our adunatos, threaten to rot us from within." He gripped Marco's upper arm. "I would not see that happen to the second-most handsome man on this planet."

The humor fell flat because the proximity and the challenge to speak openly of the terrors he had suffered were as suffocating as the hull of the *Prevenire.* "Your concern honors me—"

"It does more than that."

Marco tensed.

"If we cannot have honesty between us, what do we have?"

Anger bubbling, he narrowed an eye at the king who was yet a breath away. "You imply I lie." He pushed the man back.

Lightning fast, Vorn seized his shoulders. "We are *kings,*" he hissed, his voice low, angry. "We cannot afford to coddle injuries done us by the enemy. What example is that to a scared, feckless people who have had to fight for little more than the food at their table. We are kings," he said again, this time with more emphasis, less volatility, "of people running to the mountains to hide because what have their leaders done besides the same? If they do not see us acting with shrewdness and precision and aggression, *they* will hand us over to the enemy to buy back that complacent sense of peace they have gorged themselves on these many years."

With a grunt, he ruffled the back of Marco's shaved head and stepped back. Drew up his chin. "I would know, Tyrannous Marco, what sort of king you are. The one who hides after the enemy has dealt a blow? Or the one who will bombard that enemy with everything in his arsenal and more."

"Think you I choose weakness?"

"Aye, I do." His eyes blazed. "Where is the king who was willing to align himself with the Errant to have ships and technology that every other sovereign on this planet had forbidden? Where is that man?"

"Where is he?" Marco stabbed a finger at the port plug scar on his temple.

"Here." He thrust up his sleeve to show the brand with its ever-glowing arcs and whorls . . . and also the weapon hardening his flesh. "Here." He tugged open his shirt where more scars pocked his torso. "Here. Pieces of me are littered across this system, across another. Where is that man you knew? Dead. Gone. Left somewhere in the Void." He slapped a hand over his chest. "This is Marco now. This man who wants to see the Khatriza obliterated, Symmachia put down like the feral dogs they are!"

Awareness flared through him of the effluxes invading the chamber. Shock, fear, sadness, anger . . . He pivoted to those with them—Ixion, Bazyli, his regia and the Furymark detail. "I know your fears—have tasted them, lived them, breathed them! I have seen you walking on eggshells around me, wondering if I can do this, if I am the leader you once knew." He tightened his lips. "I am not!"

Ixion clasped his hands before him, staring hard.

The general shifted and tucked his chin, listening. Hearing.

"Do not ask me as Vorn has done about the things done to me." He scanned the men who were his vanguard. "They are not my focus. They are my fuel. The fire in my veins to see this planet and its people protected. To see our enemy vanquished—annihilated!"

"Vanko Marco!" Bazyli shouted, and it became a chant, resonating through the room.

When his gaze met Vorn's this time, Marco started at what he saw—a smirk. And cursed the man's shrewdness. "You did that on purpose."

Vorn gave a cockeyed nod. "I do little without intent."

"Why? Do you doubt me?"

"Your men doubted you. Too many unanswered questions, the changes in you unnerving."

"You have been among us but a few hours—"

"Too long did I live in the shadow of that doubt, too. I only needed to set foot on Kalonican soil to see it here. Our road is not a pretty one, Marco, and they will hate us before it is over . . . But when it is done, and we yet stand, they will thank us." He lifted a shoulder. "And likely still hate us, blame us for the costs, the damages to homes and cities. All the more reason you and I must be of one accord."

"I feel like I should have been the one to say that."

Vorn grinned. "So, not only am I now prettier but also smarter."

"It's hard, is it not?" Wizened Ypiretis smiled at her as they passed through the makeshift chapel and aimed toward the royal chambers.

This was not her favorite route, what with the dimmer lighting and the lack of rugs and tapestries to ward off the chill of the stone from which the passage was hewn, but it was shorter. And for that, Isaura was glad, anxious for a chance to put up her feet.

"What is hard?" she asked, tugging a wrap around her shoulders.

"Having him back."

His words surprised. "Hard?" She paused shy of the first step up into her quarters. "Nay, not at all." Determined to gain some privacy and yield to the ache in her lower back, she lifted her skirts and climbed the four steps. "It is wonderful to have him returned to us, an answer to many petitions I laid before the Ancient's feet—along with an abundance of tears. Not until he walked into that passage and took me into his arms did I realize how much energy went into existing without him." Holding the amulet that tied her life to his, she remembered that moment. "I saw those beautiful eyes and felt the relief of his presence. Then sudden exhaustion swept over me."

"But?" the old iereas prodded.

"I . . . I grant it is strange." Oh, how her back ached. *Blessed child, must you sit so perfectly on my spine?* "Not the having him back, though mayhap"— she bobbed her head—"that is part of it. Undoubtedly because without his return, I would not have these feelings. And I am glad he is back—would have it no other way . . ."

"As you said a moment ago."

Greedily, she eyed the open heavy carved machi wood doors at the end of the hall.

Curious. Why were they open? Dusan was yet abovestairs, and none should be here without herself or Dusan. Why had others intruded upon their sacred space?

"Then what is strange about his return?"

Pulled back to the conversation, she rubbed her lower back. "I . . . I have spent these six months . . . working. Being the representative of our realm. Exhausting, overwhelming tasks and duties that have rightly returned to his very capable hands, but . . ."

"You enjoyed it?"

She fiercely settled her gaze on his. "Aye." Her heart thudded with the realization. "For the first time in my life, people listened to me. Carefully considered what I said. Sought my thoughts." She shook her head. "Never has it been so, and now . . ."

"Now, he is returned, and you no longer feel needed or wanted."

"Aye," she whispered. "It feels wrong to confess such."

"It is not wrong—it is well earned. I know Marco is grateful for all you have done to secure the realm in his absence. Clearly, the Ancient knew what he was doing."

"Of course. And if no one else sought me or my advice again, I would be glad for Dusan's need of me." She smiled at him. "Am glad for him."

"He may be the medora and bear the responsibility of the realm on his shoulders, but I know that while your counsel may not be as heavily sought, you are a glowing example and inspiration. Kalonica is better for her kyria."

Jez started forward.

Correction: Jez *shot* forward. As if fired from a pulse cannon. There had been no lead-up. No bending of the knees and leaping into the air. No shout. Nothing. One tick she knelt at his side, the next she was spiraling through the air. Each revolution warbled as her ethereal armor blurred into focus. Her longblade screamed into existence, light flicking off its razor edge. A beacon for those it came to defend. A terrible omen to those it came to confront.

Voids, what a sight!

"Tigo!"

Her commanding voice in his head rattled him. With a twitch, he realized he was standing. In plain view. Drawing attention . . . of their pulse rifles. He leapt into motion. *"Thought you could use a distraction."*

"Perhaps not a dead one."

Good point. They'd been on the ridge scouting the encampment when Jez leapt from their hidden position. Superheated air seared past him. Like a tap on the shoulder that said, *"Duck, idiot!"*

Crouch-running, Tigo raced down the rise in the direction Jez had flown. Using bush scrub to conceal his movements, he advanced on the raiders, who were yet firing on his original position. Weapon up, he grunted.

He'd thought her crazy, looking for Crey and getting deathly close to the Irukandji camp, where there were hundreds, if not thousands, of raiders dotting the terrain. But try telling a centuries-old warrior woman that you know better than her. Yeah, she didn't listen. He'd tried to tell her they didn't have a prayer against so many. Again, didn't listen.

Not for the first time did he wonder how he had come to this—defending a forsaken downworlder planet with no tech and the fury of Symmachia breathing down its neck.

Wings snapping out and striking one raider, Jez brandished her longblade and struck fast and true on a second.

Focused on the ambush, Tigo saw a third fleeing to the south. Back to camp. To warn the Irukandji and Symmachians.

Can't let that happen.

He sprinted after the blue-marked raider. Wished he had his mech-suit that made him faster, his pulse rifle aim perfect, and protected him from ordinary blows. Hot wind buffeted him as he gained on the frantic man. Also wished for comms.

Then again, that Lifespeech did the trick. If you didn't mind a hundred Ladies able to speak directly into your thoughts. Which he did.

"Tigo!"

Gritting his teeth, he glanced through the scrub. He'd nearly closed the gap with the raider, the two of them on a parallel course. He cut at a diagonal to head him off. Leapt onto a rock and pitched himself into the air. Saw more than felt the searing blast that scuffed his shoulder. Fire ignited across his skin. Ignoring it and Jez's repeated shout of his name in his head, he rocketed into the raider. Took him to ground. They rolled, and he managed to land atop the writhing mass of flesh.

Tigo threw a hard right cross. Heard it connect. Felt an explosion of pain in his hand.

"No, Tigo!" Jez alighted next to him so fast she skidded in the rocks and dirt. Caught his arm. "Stop!"

He scowled at her, confused.

"This is him." She pointed to the man beneath him, arms up to block the blows. "*This* is Crey."

Shifting his stance and lowering his fists, he stared at the now-bloodied face. His mind wouldn't work the truth into manageable thought. "But . . . he's *marked*. And in a raider camp."

Beneath punishing lines and arcs radiated shock and anger. Knuckling away a stream of blood from a busted lip, the man scooted back. Sat up and spat to the side. "Not in the camp. Scouting it. Trying to find out how they're changing the crazed raiders."

"Which is why I was sent to him."

The ricochet effect of her words hit Crey first, then Tigo, then a fourth man who came up behind the supposed rex.

Tigo frowned at Crey. "Why'd you run from her?"

"I wasn't! Gratefully"—he inclined his head to Jez—"she killed the raider who had me pinned down since first light. I was running back for the weapon I'd lost." He held up his hands, made a quick jaunt to a ridge, and retrieved a pulse weapon. With a smug grin, he returned. "My thanks to yeh, Lady."

"Hold up." Irritation skimmed off Tigo's aforementioned astonishment as he looked at her. "*Sent?* I thought—"

"Not now." Span tucking elegantly into her clypeus, she trained her attention on the Hirakyn rex. "Crey of Greyedge."

Uncertain what to do or say to this man, what *Triarii Rejeztia* would do to this man or why she sought him, Tigo bit his tongue. Had learned the hard way about offending a Faa'Cris.

Brown eyes dusted their boots. Stretching his jaw, Crey came to his feet but never brought his gaze from the ground. "Mercy, Lady." His tone went beyond greeting. It reeked of conciliation, subjugation. He again wiped at his bloodied lip. "I would not have yeh look upon me in such a state." More than once, he seemed to try and hide the marks indelibly etched into his skin. His sins, wrongs.

"You cower here among the enemy—"

"Nay!" Crey's gaze snapped up—then bounced right back down. "I do not cower, my Lady. As said, I am spying, trying to find out how they are making them right in the head."

Rejeztia studied him for a long second, taking him in. What was she looking for? Did she find the Hirakyn rex handsome?

She glowered at Tigo and rolled her eyes.

Okay, so not attraction. *And stay out of my head.*

A hint of a smile tweaked her fierce visage, but she erased it with little effort and refocused on the man who ruled these dark lands. Even in their Eidolon days, Jez had always been formidable, so much that he hadn't dared attempt to worm his way into her heart.

She commanded respect and loyalty as easily as people breathed, but this . . . this was impressive to watch. Beauty unparalleled—that too had always been there—she radiated an authority that could likely bring down the heavens if she desired.

Was it her Faa'Cris blood that brought him to his proverbial knees? Or did he just love Jez Sidra, the incredible Eidolon lieutenant he'd trusted like few others?

Either way, he found himself praying she wasn't seeking out this ruler for an alliance. For *that* kind of alliance. It was a real possibility, since that's how the Ladies perpetuated their race—sought a powerful ruler to align with, promised him an heir, then a Daughter for her.

"Whatever yer purpose here, Lady, I am yer servant."

Jez extended her hand to the Hirakyn and rippled her fingers around to form a fist.

The rex gasped, clutching his left chest. He stumbled to a knee, and the other Hirakyn darted in to steady him.

Concerned as well, Tigo felt himself inching forward to assist.

"No." Straining, Crey stayed his buddy and Tigo with a shake of his head. He scanned his arms and laughed. Peered up through thick brows at Jez. "Thank yeh, my Lady," he wheezed out. Nodded. "A small relief but noticeable and appreciated all the same." He wavered onto his feet. "Even though yeh didn't take the marks, the loss of the pain—I am indebted to yeh."

"You are indebted to your people, Crey of Greyedge." Her voice was like steel on steel. "No more are you to cower as a criminal in the gorges. You have come here to learn the truth of the change in the raiders, and I can answer to an extent: via the water source here, they are being given a drug that dulls them to the pain of the marks. To any pain, in truth. You and your army must push the raiders from their camps, force a migration north so they can no longer consume the water here."

Something akin to annoyance tweaked his cheek above the brown beard. "Easier said than done, my Lady."

"*Easy.*" She sniffed. "You endure those marks and fight to take back your throne. You have an army at your command."

"Yeh," Crey gruffed back, unabashed. "The marks—" He bit down on the words and turned away. "I may have taken back my throne, but it is harder to take back my people. To them, I am the same as these dogs. The marks brand me a traitor, a savage."

"Your methods have indeed been savage." If it was sympathy or leniency sought here, Jez would not give it to him. "The cravings of the flesh have driven you, been your guiding source, and left indelible marks on your adunatos. You had warnings and did not heed them, Crey. After me comes another who will not speak sweet words."

She thought these sweet?

"Rather than allowing the Ancient to be your inspiration, you have chosen pain to inspire your actions. Do not so quickly look for a path that is easy."

"Yeh twist my words," he balked.

"Choose instead the one that is right, that will bring healing to the land." Her violet eyes blazed. She reached out and rotated her wrist, again rolling her fingers in that fluttering move that ended in a fist. "And to you."

"Augh!" Crey slapped a hand over his face and bent in half, staggering back. Slowly, he straightened. Tentative fingers touched his cheek.

Tigo started. Two seconds ago, a blue arc had bisected the man's bearded jaw. Now, the interruption of his beard was of flesh made new.

Crey looked to his buddy, who also gaped. "Is it . . .?"

"Gone." The man shrugged and shook his head, all in a move that looked like a giant shudder. "I ain't never seen anything like this."

"You, Crey of Greyedge, are the Spear of Hirakys and must drive the Symmachian dogs north."

"North is Kalonican lands," Crey said, hesitating. "I would not make an enemy of Marco."

"Neither will you." She started to turn, then paused. "Look not for comfort in the arms of the woman you once thought to call your own. She is wholly corrupted." Jez lifted her chin. "Do you yield your will to the Ancient, Crey of Greyedge? To see this through?"

A defiant jaw jutted. "Aye, I do."

Jez smiled. "Good. I have been instructed to inform you that as your inheritance for choosing to serve the Ancient and your people, there is a Daughter who would join you and your legacy." Her gaze drifted, almost making its way to Tigo. "If you so choose."

Crey blinked. Grinned. Barked a laugh. "Do yeh jest with me, Lady?"

Rejeztia slowly slid her gaze back to him. "I do not. But first, before your binding to her can be made manifest, there is yet a war to survive."

"I think yeh mean win."

She smirked, then gave Tigo a sly smile. "It appears you are not the only Licitus on this planet with a brain and courage."

Her taunt no longer had the barbs it once did, but as Tigo moved to follow her, there *was* a barb that had lodged itself in his chest. Right where it mattered. Something that bothered him the more he considered it . . .

Someone hooked his arm, drew him around. He found himself staring into the brown eyes of the new rex.

"Yer Symmachian. I've smelled enough of them in the wastelands to know the reek of them."

"What? Are you a Kynigos now?"

Crey barked a laugh. "Ah, so yeh know Marco, too?"

"Helped him escape my ship and its captain."

Another laugh, this one loud and raucous. "Are not all our ways woven into the same cord that ties us together?"

Tigo nodded. "It seems so." He sighed and repeated it, softer. "It seems so."

Same cord . . . Yeah. Mind churning the facts, he took his time catching up with Jez as she stalked across the land, her armor sliding out of sight and her humanity re-emerging. Or at least the appearance of it. Granted, he preferred her like this.

"Because it is a form you can control?"

He heaved a sigh. "You've *got* to stay out of my head."

"Truth hurt?"

"I like your human form because it is the first side of you that I met. The first side I did ops with." *The first side I loved.*

Her gaze flicked to his, wide and . . . vulnerable.

"Jez," he growled.

"There is nothing in there I do not already know."

"And yet there is, because I saw your surprise and vulnerability right then. When you heard me say I loved you."

"You love all women."

He groaned.

"Your words, Tigo. Don't get angry with me when I speak them back to you."

"This isn't anger, but if you want to see anger, then"—he pivoted and pointed back to where they'd left Crey—"what was that?"

She paused beside him, her eyes almost level with his, which was scuzzed because when she was Rejeztia, she seemed meters taller, stronger. But here she was, Jez with honey eyes and caramel skin and—

She wasn't arguing. Her chin tipped up. Challenge. Superiority again.

"Never mind." Trudging on, he hung his head. Buried his thoughts and feelings deep so that she couldn't pry them out. It wouldn't matter anyway.

"We should go to AO."

Tigo stopped short, a spasm in his chest over seeing anyone from the 215. "Seriously?"

"Yeh, why not? I think—"

"Wait." He held up a hand. "You going to make him a king, too?"

Her left eye narrowed for a fraction of a second. "Crey was already rex by blood. I just chastened him—"

"I noticed you left out the name of the Faa'Cris he'd get—"

"He doesn't *get* us. We make a mutual—"

"—all so he'll comply with what you want him to do."

"What he *needs* to do. We have a part to play in this war, too, and must ensure measures are in place, so when the time comes, the war is won— by us."

"Whatever. Let's go see AO." Tigo stalked across the rugged terrain, acutely aware she had deflected his not-so-subtle implication.

"What in the Voids is going on over there, Deken?" demanded Admiral Waring. "I thought you said bringing this planet to heel wouldn't take long."

Domitas palmed his control console, unwilling to let her goad him into feeling as if he'd done something wrong.

"The fleet has been over Drosero six weeks and you haven't—"

"Forgive me, Vice Admiral," Domitas growled, cutting off the tirade, "but I believe those are full orbs on your shoulders, not galaxies." He paused for his words to relay and for that full meaning to take effect. "Now, get back to your own ship and crew. I have a combat engagement to oversee."

The fewer questions he was forced to address, the less likely he was to misstep, betray his hand. Lie. Ancient knew he'd spilled enough of those across the Quadrants in the thirty-plus years he'd given to Symmachia and Tascan Command. A short time in the scope of humanity, but more than enough considering humanity's fragile existence. Regardless, he couldn't afford to screw this up with a careless word or slip of the tongue.

After verifying the crew on the other side of his door were busy at their watch stations, Domitas pulled up the surface schematic of Drosero and tapped into the comms feed. "Chief, how's it going?"

"Did you know they have slagging rhinnocks here? I thought those things died out centuries ago," Slice said.

Domitas smirked. "Drosero is the last of its kind in the Quadrants in many respects."

"You could say that again."

He pinged their location and grunted. "You're not as far north as planned."

"That would be because of the rhinnocks, sir. Wember broke his leg escaping one, but we set it and used the nanite cast. It's healing but needs time. We are en route now."

"Heads-up, Two-one-one: there's a lot of activity around the capital."

"Copy that, sir. It's visible from this plain. Fire on the mountain, too."

Slice huffed a few times. "Air's a bit tight, so we're rationing O_2 to avoid getting caught with our tanks down."

Domitas nodded. He'd warned them about that. Each planet was a little different, the ratios different. Thankfully, Drosero was pretty similar to Symmachia.

"We've seen some wildlings with marks on their bodies. Crazy and unpredictable, they surprised us by having the Trace-IX pulse blasters. Kind of wondering how that happened. Had more than one encounter with them, but they weren't a match for us."

"Of course not."

"Still, if we come upon more than a handful at a time, we might be scuzzed."

"Then don't."

"Copy that," the chief said with a laugh.

"You need to get up into those mountains and recon the terrain and movement."

"Yessir."

"I want this finished and done right. I trust you to do that, Slice."

"Hoyzah!"

"Keep me post—"

A tweedle momentarily preceded the hiss of his office door. "Admiral! We're in!"

With a flick of his hand, Domitas cleared his screens and arrays, effectively ending the call and preventing Dimar from seeing the comm channel. "In wh—" He punched to his feet, realizing the answer before he asked the question. "The net—"

"A hole, sir!" The XO backed out as Domitas stormed onto the deck. "Admiral on the—"

"As you were." Domitas strode to the Command arrays, where officers were monitoring incoming relays and reports. "What've we got, Captain Pount?"

"A slagging breakthrough, Admiral. Finally."

The XO paced Domitas to the arrays where chatter and chaos reigned, tactical and flight control spitting information back and forth, logging intel and formulating plans with their personnel and pilots.

Pointing to the radar, Dimar grinned. "Here. Baru Five-three-two spotted an anomaly. They tested the net-ship—not by firing on it, but by diving between it and the nearby linked ship." He beamed. "They got through!"

Heart pumping harder than it should at his age, Domitas scanned the readouts. "Is that the only one?"

"Yes, sir. But Five-eight-nine and Four-one-five got through as well." Dimar rested his hands on his belt. "This is it, sir. We have a navigable hole."

It was here—the hour in which he could no longer control the narrative, convince Command or the *Cronus* crew that they were powerless. They would have to commit.

"Sure seems that way, but let's not get ahead of ourselves and end up holding our jewels for all the galaxies to see." He strode to another station, sliding into his temporal skin as Admiral Deken and shedding his disloyal skin. At least for now. "Zarense."

Tactical officer Lavikia Zarense, a lithe woman older than Dimar but younger than the captain, straightened and faced him. "Admiral."

"Instruct your fighters to ready for engagement, but await my order."

She fairly radiated with excitement, and he wondered not for the first time if she had Faa'Cris blood. "Yes, Admiral."

He moved along the planetary array, scanning the outer ring on the digital readout. "Loren"—he waited until her head swiveled in his direction—"work on that array. I want the ship with the faltering readings a different color. Check the others for similar failures."

"That . . . The readings will fluctuate as the planet rotates. There will be times we won't have an accurate reading, sir."

"I care about right now, Lieutenant."

"Yes, sir."

"Zarense, tell your fighters beneath the array not to—"

"This is Baru Five-three-two taking fire!"

At the pilot's sudden comm'd intrusion, Domitas bit back a curse, motioning to the array for someone to wave it up there. As it went live, a stream of orange laserlike bursts turned into a river.

Oaths echoed around the deck.

"Baru Five-three-two, what is your—"

"Engines are dead," the pilot barked. "Lost control. About to hit the atmospheric barrier."

Even from hundreds of miles up, the impact that turned into a fireball was clearly visible. "What the scuz just happened?" Domitas demanded, mind racing. "Is the net viewing them as enemies now that they're below it?"

"Seems so," Pount muttered, while Zarense communicated to her pilots to remain above the net.

"Negative," Dimar countered. "It's not going after the others."

"Sir," Loren said quietly. "Baru Five-three-two fired on the net."

"He what?" Domitas barked. "I ordered them—"

"Sir." Zarense bore a stony expression. "I—" She faltered, her dark hair glinting beneath the bulkhead lighting. "I suggested the pilots who got through should test the net from below, see if—"

"If *what?*" Domitas demanded, wanting to inflict some pain for her disobedience. "See if their weapons are as powerful underneath?" He muttered an oath and shoved a hand through his hair, then sent a scowl around both levels of the Command deck. "Tell the other two to cut engines to minimal and power down weapons. They are to do everything they can to convince that net that they're not threats. Nobody does anything until we know what kind of slag we're dealing with now. Clear?" As a chorus of "sirs" filtered around the bridge, he refocused on the array. On the intel Loren and Dimar were feeding him.

This . . . helps. He could drag it out. But for how long? He felt the answer in the marrow of his old bones—not long enough.

"Sir," Loren said, her voice small and submissive. "I've adjusted the digital readout of the net per your orders. Onscreen now."

Domitas took in the ship network as the image rotated. "Where did Five-three-two get through?" Even as the schematic swung around, he saw the hole.

"Here, sir. Orange is the less-operational ship."

Less operational. Good way to put it. They clearly had the ability to access their weapons, even if somehow they weren't able to extend shielding.

Eyes on the array, Domitas mentally shuffled through options, his heart sinking with every one examined and discarded. In whatever manner this played out, people would die in Lampros City.

"Admiral," Captain Pount spoke from his left. "We should send more ships through these openings. Have them draw attention and fire while Five-eight-nine and Four-one-five target the Kalonican capital."

Domitas's gut tightened. "No."

"But, sir—"

"You assume, Captain, that only the ships we fire upon will fire back." He nodded, peering up through his thick brows at the array. "There are over three hundred ships there. All with firing capability. You saw what they did to our shields that first day. Are you willing to risk your theory with the lives of hundreds of pilots and thousands more in the fleet? What happens if they decide to turn those weapons on us?"

"We're ready, sir."

Domitas barked a laugh. "Are we? If we're so ready—"

"Admiral, wave from the *Argus*."

"—how are we still shut out of that planet and—"

"But we're not," Pount said, his face bright with frustration. "We have a clear entry point."

"What's clear is that we have *one* entry point. Tell me, Captain Pount, do you know those ships? Can you swear that the signature change is failure and not some other alteration? They've already proven themselves far more advanced than we are. What if that fading signature is an all-quiet before readying more powerful weapons? Or a trap to lure us under the net?"

"I think if that were the case, they would've already struck."

"Again, you assume too much, as if you know their intentions."

"They've destroyed several of our ships. Intentions are clear, Admiral—they're here to destroy us."

"Wrong. They've never attacked. Only acted in self-preservation. Nothing else." He set a hand on Loren's shoulder. "Any response to our subspace communications with the ships?"

"No, sir."

"Sir. A word."

Domitas glanced over his shoulder to where a group of five Eidolon stood. Were he the type to worry, he'd feel dread right now. "Halling. What're you doing on my ship?"

"A message from Captain Baric, sir." The freckle-faced Marine nodded toward his office. "In private. Please."

"Halling, who is the admiral of this fleet?"

The guy faltered. "You, sir."

Rankled at the audacity of the commander, Domitas turned back to the array. "Tactical, tell those two Rapiers to do maneuvers—sans weapons—around the planet. See what those ships do. Flight chief, tell the other ships to start forming up to slip through that gap once I give the order."

"Sir," Halling snipped.

"Quiet, Commander, or I'll have you removed from the Command deck."

Domitas stalked to Dimar and shouldered in.

"Want me to ready security?" the XO asked, then smirked. "Or medical?"

"Just make sure nobody fires any—"

"Admiral, the *Argus* again. Also the *Apelles* has waved a few times for an explanation on what's happening." Loren stared over her shoulder at him from her station.

"Send a fleet-wide communiqué that we've found a gap in the net but have not met with success getting to the planet. Nobody is to attempt to send any craft or troops until we know more. We're anxious to get in there and get to work, but let's be sure it's a victory, not our slaughter."

"Won't know until we try." Halling's voice was a lot closer than he'd been two mikes ago.

Before Domitas could turn, he heard a scuffle and did not doubt that security was making sure Halling did not again enter the bridge until granted access. With an apathetic look, he peered back where the Eidolon were held at bay by his guards.

Halling glowered at the guards, then his irritated gaze found Domitas. "Admiral, I will be glad to remove myself if you would first allow me to deliver this message from Captain Baric."

Convinced it would not go well if he kept delaying the man, Domitas started to his office. "With me, Halling. Security, escort his team off the Command deck—and him, if he's here longer than five minutes."

"Aye, sir!"

In his office, Domitas waved up the security protocols and watched the glass and doors go opaque as Halling punched them open. Though he thought to make some surly remark about how the only person willing to put up with his antics was a half-crazed captain nobody wanted to deal with, Domitas held his peace. Stared down his nose at the Eidolon, who took up position on the other side of the desk and clapped a hand to his chest. "Admiral, thank you—"

"Get on with it. Clock's ticking." Proverbially.

Irritation twitched in the commander's cheek. "Captain Baric asked me to relay his . . . understanding that you have been following his efforts to expand the jumpgate program."

Domitas stared, silent as the grave. Neither confirm nor deny was his motto.

"And he would point out, sir, that he has evidence you shielded and protected your son, one Tigo Deken, former Eidolon commander of the Two-one-five, when rightful and lawful charges were set against him."

Apathy and ambivalence went a long way against the arrogant.

"And that you, sir, helped him escape custody and the TSC *Macedon*. A criminal offense."

Ah, there it was—a threat.

"Along with critical, confidential intel related to many Tier One projects, including Tascan Command's efforts against Drosero."

Domitas checked the clock. "Minute thirteen left, Commander." Nothing had been said that concerned Domitas.

"Aren't you worried, sir?"

"Not in the least."

"But sir, what of the fact you are a traitor?"

Domitas barked a laugh, mostly to hide the way his heart thundered. "Is that right?"

"What will happen when Command learns you are not working in the interest of Symmachia or their allied planets, but for the Faa'Cris and for the one known as the Progenitor? What will happen when they learn *that* is why you have delayed an incursion onto Drosero?"

How had he learned so much? The dark side of his supernatural self waded to the surface, thrumming through his veins. Domitas reined in his anger, his vengeance, and made himself speak in a slow, controlled tone. "If what you speak were true, Commander, I would be afraid to stand in your boots right now."

"I fight for a more powerful Symmachia. If I am to die—"

In a split second that human minds could not perceive, could not recall, could not comprehend, Domitas kept his visage impassive as he cracked his wings like a whip at the impudent pup.

A red line split the commander's lip. It would take a moment for the pain to register.

Halling twitched. His hand went to his lip even as surprise lit through him.

Now Domitas put expression into his face. "Commander, are you okay? A bloody nose?"

Cupping a hand over his mouth, Halling frowned, his confusion complete as he stalked from the office.

"A little childish, Domitas?"

"Perhaps," he replied to Renette, dropping into his chair for a moment and

glad she was here, though shielded—thankfully, since he had not deflected the in-room surveillance. *"But it felt really good. Tell me you didn't enjoy seeing one of Baric's pups get some kickback."*

"It would be wrong of me to say so."

"But you did." He grunted, knowing she would not agree. *"We have a problem."*

"Only one?"

He made his way out to the bridge, feeling the future of the Quadrants resting on his shoulders. *"I can't hold it off any longer, Renette. Bombardments will start soon, if not today."*

"We know and are grateful for the time you have bought the Progenitor and his seed."

"Prepare them."

"We have been preparing all our lives. Remember?"

"Parabellum." Domitas gripped the console, aching for what was to come. He looked to where Zarense waited. "How are our ships doing down there?"

"Below the belt, all is quiet and clear."

Heart heavy, he nodded. "Send in Echo squadron. Loose formations, no weapons, for now."

"Aye, sir."

Straightening, he swiped a hand over his beard. "Okay, people. If these maneuvers go smoothly, we'll begin phase two to bring Drosero into submission. You have your duties. Let's get it done." He indicated to Dimar. "Ready our fighters."

The needle pierced his eye and slid into his brain, sending shockwaves of electricity throughout his body. Each jolt rattled his bones, his teeth. Marco tried to scream, but the tube in his mouth forbade him. He reached to pull it out, only to find his arms tied. Glancing down the length of his body, he saw . . .

No . . . No no no.

The lectulo. How? How had they gotten him back? He'd been with Isa.

Kersei stood there, smiling at him. Sneering. Her brown eyes turned violet, then that pale, pale blue of their brands. Hissing, she lifted a hand to strike with another bolt of electricity. Only it wasn't a hand. It was . . . an appendage. Her curly hair became leggy tendrils supporting her too-long body.

"Augh!" Marco jolted upright, breathing hard. Sensing trouble.

Boom! Boom-boom—BOOM!

He vaulted out of the bed as the walls shook beneath another bombardment.

"They yet again attack," Isaura whispered, her fear strident as she scooted from the mattress.

"But how, with the Uchuvchi in place?" He shook his head. "After weeks of peace, this is alarming." Without thinking, he turned to the door just as thuds reverberated through the thick wood. He paused and glanced at Isaura, concerned for her.

She slipped into a lacy duster and nodded. "Go. I will be well."

Marco returned and kissed her, then rushed out into the passage, where Ixion waited. "What happened?"

"From what Daq'Ti tells us, three Symmachian fighters got past the net," Ixion said as they made their way to the war room. "An Uchuvchi ship lost power and failed, allowing a few fighters to get through."

When they entered the war room, Marco saw Roman and Galen Sebastiano standing over a screen that showed the Uchuvchi array.

"Sire," Galen said. "The fighters that slipped through strafed the city, but nothing since."

Odd. Marco swung his gaze to Daq'Ti. "What do you know?"

"Due to the long efforts to protect the planet, the ships are beginning to fail, lose power. Weapons drain the core. Gi'Zac believes the Symmachians inadvertently discovered the dead ship. More attempted to come through, but the Uchuvchi forced them back."

"How many are dead in the water?"

"Only the one. The Uchuvchi altered their array to bridge the gap caused by the failed ship. For now, the shield holds, but not forever."

Marco ran a hand over his shorn hair and saw movement on the radar. "What's that?"

With a grim nod, Galen sighed. "Those are two of the three Symmachian fighters that got through while the gap was open. One attempted firing on the net, but our friends destroyed it. The remaining fighters released a bombardment against Kardia and Lampros City, then pulled off. Nothing since. Doesn't make sense."

"Mayhap they fear being fired upon by the Uchuvchi," Ixion suggested.

"They have been effective," Daq'Ti agreed in his trilling way. "But I think the Symmachian ships cannot get out. The array works both ways. If they attack again, they know we will be ready."

Marco wasn't as convinced. "So they're biding their time and could be mapping our efforts here and relaying it to the ships in orbit." He looked to the Draegis. "Is there anything we can do to help the drones, keep them running?"

"Not that we know at this time." Daq'Ti nodded to the computers. "So little knowledge there. Too many things unknown or only in books."

"Reek," Marco muttered. "So." He huffed, scratching his bearded jaw. "We start losing the ships, we lose our protection. We lose that protection . . . Time's up." *We are dead*, he thought to himself. "Contact Vorn and Rico, update them on what we know." He eyed Sebastiano, feeling an old resentment toward the Xanthan. "What solutions do we have if that array goes down?"

Fresh-faced Galen started. "Sire?"

Marco pointed up. "If—*when* that array goes down, what are our options? How do we keep from being annihilated?"

"Unless we have a way to power up that ship you came in on . . ." Galen shrugged. "Nothing, sire. We spent the six months you were gone searching for solutions, options. Besides the few ships we have, there is nothing."

"Except me."

"You take too much on yourself," came Roman's deep, authoritative voice.

"Do I? Seems I was named Progenitor."

"Aye, which means *originator*, not Ender of All Things."

The sarcasm was not appreciated. "Then what are we to do?"

Roman's gaze shifted.

"Exactly." Marco turned to the others. "There has to be a solution. Let's put our heads together and see what we can come up with."

Over the next several oras, they reviewed previously considered—and ruled out—options. But they were severely handicapped as a nonindustrial planet. A fact that infuriated him most times, and especially with relation to this war.

"If we could just find a way to neutralize their advantage of flight," Roman commented.

"Meaning?"

"If Symmachia did not have technology and the war were on the ground, it would give Drosero a fighting chance."

"If Symmachia did not have technology," Marco growled, "this war would not be upon us at all."

The master considered. "Faulty thinking."

"Not entir—" A panicked efflux from Isaura vaulted Marco out of the seat and into the passage. "On me!" he shouted, following that scent. Not to their chambers as he'd expected, but up to the main level of the damaged house and out into the bailey.

There, he spotted a cluster of horses, sergii, and aerios.

"Please, no!" Isaura rushed toward a sergius, her efflux now frustrated, angry.

"Isa." Marco gained her side, ready to do violence on her behalf.

She drew up, her Signature rife with confusion and surprise at his appearance. "Dusan." She considered those who came behind him, frowning. "What do you here?"

"I anak'd your panic." He yet searched for what had alarmed her.

Confusion knotted her delicate brow, but then she deflated. "I beg your mercy—aye, we saw a ship overhead and thought they had come to bomb us. But we realized it was our own."

Annoyed, but relieved, Marco indicated to the sergii. "You were angry with them?"

Isa tucked her chin. "Aye, but I should not have been. Your child within me saps my strength and makes me a bit irritable. They brought the wrong blankets, though I had instructed which were to come with us."

Marco took in the bailey, crowded with wagons, pack mules. "With who? Where are you going?" He spied two Brethren. "What's going on?"

"Dusan," Isaura said, touching his arm. "Please . . . it is imperative. You see the smoke, hear the crying coming from beyond the wall. The people—your subjects need to see us. Need our help."

Was she mad? "No! It's not safe."

"Aye," she said, her eyes sparking with meaning. "Nowhere is safe. Do you not see the damage done to Kardia—the upper levels destroyed? While I was yet in them!" She tilted her head to the side. "Though unharmed, I learned danger will always exist and refuse to let it paralyze me. Rather would I die working to help our people than hidden beneath walls and useless."

"Speak it not," Marco begged, shoving away the images from his nightmare.

Isa faced him. "Kersei and I have visited the city after each attack without issue." She shrugged. "Save Mavridis's strong objections."

The Stalker scowled. "I have cautioned them, but they will not listen," he said. "Venturing out is dangerous and reassurances fall flat. All know we can do little against Symmachia."

"Precisely!" An angry flush rose into her cheeks. "Yet our visits encourage Kalonicans all the same. Were I to sit in these walls while they are pulling their children or loved ones from rubble, House Tyrannous would be seen as coldhearted and uncaring. I have done what little I am able to reassure them that we do care. That we are here for them."

A nervous efflux from the right drew Marco's attention to Isaura's lady's maid, the diminutive Kita, who stood hugging herself. Watching . . . Her scent startled him. This was not simply a woman waiting on her kyria. No, Kita's efflux tended in the same direction as her gaze—Ixion.

His man shifted, his gaze stony and hard. Yet his scent told he was aware of Marco's curiosity and the woman's anxious . . . *attraction.*

What was this? The fifty-something onetime elder of Prokopios, founder of the Stalkers, father of Kalonica's kyria, and First of the medora . . . Had he yet again found love in the winsome Kita? Long had there been an affinity between the two, but Marco always guessed it had to do with the role of elder to one under his charge.

How she stares after the Stalker.

"It is too dangerous," Ixion groused to his daughter. "You, the duchess, and Lady Kita should remain within the walls."

Interesting that he added Kita.

To the side, Kersei stood holding what looked like a heavy bag, not speaking. Waiting, nervous . . . Was that over her fear that they would be prohibited?

"We are packed and ready," Isaura said firmly. "We have regia, aerios, and Kynigos. It is necessary, and"—she lifted her head—"I will not defer in this."

"It is not safe!"

Marco put a hand to Isa's back as he looked to Kersei. "What say you, Duchess?"

She twitched almost violently, squinting up at him. "Sire?"

He caught her efflux and tried to push it away before his brain interpreted the signals . . . surprise . . . nerves . . . "This venture—what importance does it hold?"

Hesitating for but a tick, she seemed to grow an inch. "Every importance, my lord. The kyria speaks true. Kalonicans must see our concern and compassion. Men appreciate help to gather belongings and supplies from damaged structures, and we have ample aerios to assist in such tasks."

It made sense. "Agreed. If we cannot battle, we will work." Marco offered Isa his hand. "I will go with you."

She started, delight in her scent . . . then adoration, one favored so much he might search out a million other means to it.

As the entourage saddled up, he did not miss the way Ixion moved rigidly past Kita, who had also gone unusually still. As if both were afraid they might betray what Marco could clearly anak.

With a laugh, he looked to his First. "Ix—"

"Shh." Isaura tugged his lapel, straightening it. "Thank you for supporting me in this. You know I would not unnecessarily risk ourselves. As for what you have detected between your First and a certain woman, I noticed it shortly after you were taken from us." Her green eyes sparked with mischief. "This quiet aside of ours does afford a certain gruff Stalker time to sink deeper into his affection for my lady's maid." On tiptoes, she kissed Marco. "Find a way to encourage him, please?"

"You would have me—"

"Aye, I would." She grinned. "Men of the same caliber as you and my father are quick to act . . . except in matters of love, where you seem to be caught in some bubble that holds your wits captive."

"Brutal accusation." He spotted his First now at the ladies' carriage.

"But true all the same." She had not yet moved. "Are they done?"

After hoisting young Mnason into the carriage, Ixion held the door and extended a hand to Kita. Blushing prettily, she accepted his hand, her eyes briefly—coyly—meeting his. He said something to her and the woman faltered, looked over her shoulder at the white-haired First of the medora. She smiled, ducking within, giving him a reply of some sort. Whispered something in return.

"Whew!" Marco chuckled. "That is a strident efflux coming off your father. If he can ignore that surge of attraction, I will be most impressed."

"Do not be impressed," Isaura said with a giggle. "Be assertive. Annoy him. Push him. My father does little for himself, and this joy he finds in Kita—I would see it fulfilled."

"You would be without a lady's maid."

"Not necessarily," she said around a mischievous grin. "He would want her safe, and there is no better place for her than here at Kardia."

"Ah, but I doubt the elder of Stratios would want his new duchess *working*."

Defiant to the last, Isa raised her nose. "You will dim neither my pleasure nor my plans, Dusan."

"I would never dim any pleasure of yours, my aetos."

Radiant in her conniving, she smiled. "They will be together, and we will be a big, happy family. Imagine the Delta Presentation dinners!" That giggle of hers was contagious.

He could not help his own grin. "I look forward—"

"Your Majesty!"

Marco shifted toward the regia Kaveh.

"There is no need to wait for the duchess. She has gone ahead into the city."

Hand on her belly, Isaura gasped. "Kersei! She is alone?"

Instinctively, Marco opened his receptors and pushed outward, rifling scents in the city. He found hers, wavering between nerves and outright fear. "We ride!"

Hurrying along back alleys with Myles, Kersei kept her chin tucked and clung to the thin thread of hope that Ephaza's storehouse had not been damaged. That the sustenance for the people was not jeopardized. Of course, the greater concern for the aerios pacing her was that her wellbeing not be endangered. Aye, it had been a foolhardy, impulsive act to set out on her own. Yet, no longer could she look upon them with their giggling and kissing.

She eyed Myles as he hulked along, hand on his longblade, eyes ever roving. This man with whom she had sparred, a regia she feared and respected. "My father spoke often of you."

Myles faltered, giving her a sidelong glance. "I would have gone to the ends of the earth for Elder Xylander."

She trailed him to the right. "You knew of Darius's duplicity from the start, did you not?"

"I would not speak ill of the dead, my lady."

"You do not. We discuss truth." Lengthening her strides to keep up with him, she realized how much being pregnant and giving birth had dulled her athleticism. She must remedy that.

He pulled aside. "Wait." The word was but a breath.

Raucous laughter rattled the quiet street as two men swept past their hiding spot.

Surprise told her she had not been alert enough. Were ne'er-do-wells to happen upon the Duchess of Stratios in the city with but one guard . . . Or worse, if there were truly enemy raiders or Symmachians in the city as had been rumored, and they found her . . . She felt keenly the folly of her rash decision. Still so brash.

Myles lifted an eyebrow as if to confirm her self-admonishment.

She gave him a nod. Had she learned nothing in the last cycle? She must do better, be better—for Xylander. Since Marco had returned with Darius's body, she had spent much time with her thoughts, sorting out her future, what life would look like as a widow. What she must make of it so her son did not want.

"Safe." Myles stepped back and motioned up the alley.

With another nod, she started the climb, this road on a perpetual incline as it passed through the northernmost side of Lampros City where it met the foot of the Medoran Mountains. Her calves were already aching, and the breath struggled up her throat.

Myles smirked at her. "Mayhap it is time for a rematch."

More surprise leapt through her. "With me on Bastien, you do not have a prayer."

"Is that an official challenge?"

Kersei laughed. "Mayhap."

"If you break a rib this time, it is Medora Marco I will answer to, and I do not know a man willing to accept that fight."

"Marco?" Kersei huffed, batting aside a rogue curl. "If it is not blonde and green-eyed, he does not concern himself."

Myles gave her an appraising look but said nothing.

Her legs were leaden, and there were more delicate matters that would soon demand her attention—like hastening back to Kardia for Xylander's next feeding.

He swung his hand in front of her yet again and stepped aside, nudging her back.

This time, three women with baskets that radiated the aroma of yeast and herbs into the dusty, smoky streets scurried past. One had a baby swaddled to her back and a large basket propped on her hip. Worry trailed them, though they walked swiftly and confidently.

The little smudged face of the infant peeking from the carrier served as a poignant reminder to Kersei of what was at stake. This was their city, and the familiarity with which they moved through it spoke to her. The attacks would not stop them from delivering food—for that was likely the errand that had them venturing out so soon after an attack. Once, she had been as assured and comfortable, walking the cobbled streets of Stratios. Belonging . . . that is what they had.

"I want to rebuild Stratios," Kersei murmured.

"It *is* being rebuilt," Myles said as they resumed their course.

"I mean the city. Since the attack that took down the hall, our people have lost faith."

"They lost more than faith," Myles countered, his expression grim beneath those red-brown eyebrows. "Stratios Hall was not all that was damaged. Many lost their loved ones—a pain you know too well—their homes and livelihoods."

The words struck true. Kersei slowed, her mind wandering the truth he spoke. Hand on a wall, she came to a stop. "Why . . . why have I not considered that? Them?"

Myles stepped back to her, then glanced around and met her eyes. "You have had much grief to battle. Much change."

"Aye," she said heavily, grievously, recalling Ma'ma's words as Kersei labored in the sanitatem waters.

"You never were able to see anyone else's pain past your own."

Bewildered, suffering, Kersei had gaped at her mother. *"And you never allowed me the pain I felt."*

"You are wrong—I allowed, but you wallowed . . . How long will you wallow, Kersei?"

"She was right." The ache was raw, the truth painful. She slumped against the wall, sagging internally as much as physically. Shoving back the hood, she struggled for a breath that did not hurt.

"My lady, we should hurry." Myles's hand hovered by her elbow, concern raw and powerful, warning he would do whatever she needed. Protect however she needed.

Hands on her hips, she squinted back in the direction the women had gone. Considered the ever-rising road. Back to the women. "What am I doing?" she whispered through the dust and fog of the early morning. The acrid odor of smoke tickled her throat. She coughed.

"Making sure the city is well stocked," he said, confused.

Her eyes snapped to him. Aye, there was that. But her question tended in a more . . . philosophical direction. One of the heart. She thought to splay her heart out before him, but . . . no. He was her regia, not her confidant. "Of course." She pushed a smile she did not feel into her face. "Come." The word came around a cough, the air thickening with smoke. They were not far.

She shoved onward. Burrowing beneath her cape, she skipped a step to hurry herself along.

They rounded a corner and there—

"No." Hand flying to her mouth, Kersei gaped at the rubble that had once been the tavern and gathering hall. The small storage building in the rear reduced to debris and ash. Smoke and patches of flame still rose from it. Embers hissed as men tossed buckets of water on the smoldering pile. They worked hard, taking turns in the choking haze. One bedraggled man glanced straight at Kersei. He locked onto her as he used his forearm to wipe sweat, smearing ash in a black swath across his face. Another man elbowed him and leaned in, whispering something. The sneer that found the man's ruddy face . . .

It pushed Kersei back. Forced her to look away, to will his attention to move on.

A low-flying aircraft sent them all scrambling and shouting.

Myles yanked her back. As they cowered beneath the overhang of a shop, she watched the ship scream overhead. "We were safe . . ." No more. Their brief respite was broken. "Please, Ancient."

As the ship came around and descended again, her breath backed into her throat. "Why must they torture us? We have done nothing to them!"

"We exist," Myles growled. "It is enough."

Sunlight shoved past the smoke and glinted off the ship as it glided overhead—and instead of ordnance, the ship spat out a thick mist.

Kersei drew in a breath. "Water!"

The fire hissed its objection to being snuffed out.

Cheers went up through the street.

She smiled at Myles. "A brilliant solution!"

His cheek twitched. "Effective—"

"What's this?" a gravelly voice erupted behind her. "Found the traitor's bound out in the open, did we?"

Kersei pivoted, her feet tangling as she sighted the smudge-faced man from the bucket brigade. When had he gotten so close?

"Be off," Myles ordered, tucking her behind himself. "You will not—"

Expression full of hatred, the man lifted something and aimed it at Myles. A Symmachian weapon!

"No!" Kersei darted around him even as the man's finger twitched over the trigger. "Stop!" Her hand struck his chest, and light exploded. She froze, fearing another attack. But then she saw the man's face contort. Heard his strangled shout as he gripped his chest.

Heat seared around them.

The man had fired—*shot* Myles. "No!" She whipped to her regia but found him standing there, shocked. "Myles." Touching his shoulders and chest, she searched for a wound but found none. "Are you well? Did he—"

"Fine—" His bearded mouth taut, his gaze trained on something over her shoulder, he gruffed, "My medora."

Kersei jolted. Spun back around, stunned to find Marco there atop a destrier, his expression one of . . . abhorrence. And he wasn't looking at Myles. He was aiming that terrible expression at her.

Disgust tightened Marco's chest. He stared at the scene before him. Not at the buildings in ruin or the fire smoldering and smoking—nearly quenched, thanks to Daq'Ti's quick thinking—nor at the men pulling bodies from the rubble.

But at Kersei.

At the man who all but knelt before her, just as Daq'Ti had once knelt before Eija.

Repulsed, Marco slowly drew his Great Black around. Met Ixion's gaze. "Get the duchess back to Kardia. Clearly it's not safe." For the people.

His heart twisted and roiled. Is this how the Ladies would solve their problem? *Tame* normal men? Make them puppets via the *Ovqatlanish*?

He couldn't believe it.

What other explanation was there? He had seen it with his own eyes— Kersei Taming a man in the middle of the street. How long had she possessed this gift? Or was it a curse? He did not know, but he would address it. "Bring her to the council hall for questioning."

The steely eyes of his First held fast. "As you will, sire."

From the carriage, Isaura peered out, her pretty face knotted. "Dusan, what—"

"We return to Kardia," he barked the order to the regia. "At once!"

"Wait," Isaura said, breathless and frantic, reaching from the carriage. "Please."

Though he did not want to, Marco held up a hand to stay the order. He urged his mount closer so they could speak privately. "You would argue with me?"

"No," she said quickly, then wrinkled her nose. "Mayhap a little?"

He caught the carriage's open window. "How little?" It amazed how those green eyes and pink lips so easily untangled the anger from his thoughts.

"Very little," she said with a smile. "But I beg you—think how it will appear to your people if we depart. They have seen you." She set her hand over his. "Even now they watch, hope you would speak with them."

His heart marched to the cadence of her voice. "Few are able to stay my hand. Command me, my kyria."

Her smile grew. "I beg your mercy for doing it publicly," she said softly, "but I felt it must be done. We should stay."

"You saw what just transpired."

At this, her smile faltered. Though he'd made his point, it did not make him happy. In fact, it angered him more to see the sun in her pretty eyes overshadowed by a cloud of concern.

"I cannot pretend to know what . . . happened," Isa said, "but I know our people must see *you*. Here, in the city. They heard of your return, yet also heard you were mortally wounded by Symmachia. Rumors abound. It is imperative they see their medora, alive and well."

She was right. She always was.

He sighed, glancing around, anak'ing scents and Signatures. Raking the crowd for trouble. And it was there, no question. But trouble could come in the form of pickpockets and rascals. He detected no real harm. "And your command?"

"Walk with me among them. Speak to them. Show them you care."

"About you?" He winged up an eyebrow. "Easy enough." After one more sweep of the area, he met Theilig's gaze, telegraphing his intent, and dismounted. He smoothed his duster and approached the carriage.

Regia Cetus swiftly opened the door, setting down the step.

Marco held out his hand as Isaura ducked out. Delicate fingers clasped his as she alighted from the wheeled box. She curled toward him and touched his chest. Pressed a kiss to his cheek. "Thank you."

Cheers went up along the street.

Arm around her waist, he savored the tangibility of her and the grand approval of the gathered Kalonicans. Even after weeks together, he found it hard to believe that she was real. *Really* with him. "You weaken my knees, my kyria."

Gliding toward the swiftly growing crowds, she asked, "Should I send for a pharmakeia in case you faint?"

Marco sniffed. "If I faint in front of these warriors and my people, do not call a doctor—run me through."

She laughed, focusing on the people. On a young girl clinging to her mother's leg. "Ah, Asanteri, how are you?" She cupped the girl's face.

"The big noise scared me."

"It was large and frightening, was it not?"

"Medora Marco, who flew that ship?"

He looked for the man who'd spoken, but there were so many faces watching, so many eager effluxes. Nervous swells. "A friend, the same one who helped me fight my way back home. You will meet him in the coming days."

"Is he one of *them*?" came another shout.

"If you mean a Symmachian, no." Marco moved on, not yet willing to answer questions about the Draegis.

"How are you feeling, Kyria Isaura? Is the babe well?"

Isaura waved. "All is well." She glanced at him, her beauty a halo around her head. "Especially now that our medora is returned to us."

"What about the food stores?" a stout woman asked, arms folded tightly over an ample bosom as she nodded to the rubble. "They were destroyed. It's all fine you sitting in the castle with your sergii and silver spoons dipped in thick stew, while we—"

"I am so glad you asked, Berai," Isaura said, touching the woman's arm. "That is why we have come. At the insistence of Medora Marco, I have already inquired of the mayor so that we might set up a temporary food store and shelter in the lower keep."

"Thank you, Medora Marco!"

"Aye, thank you!"

"The Ancient be praised for sending you back."

Marco shifted under praise he had not earned. "Your kyria—"

"Vanko Kalonica! Vanko Marco!" The shouts went up and prompted many more to thunder through the street.

"The ships—are they friend or foe?"

"Friend!" Marco called over the echoing shouts. "They buy us time to prepare."

"Prepare? How do we prepare against the skycrawlers?"

"With our own skycrawling craft," Marco replied. "Already we are training select machitis to fly ships, defend our skies."

"How can we sign up?" asked an eager man.

"A militia," another man asserted, stepping toward the royal contingent.

Marco faltered, realizing it was the same man who had been Touched by Kersei.

"With your approval, sire, I would readily start one." He squared his shoulders. "I served in the Hardick Wars in the time of your father."

Had Marco not been gifted with the anaktesios, he would have disregarded the man's offer and suggestion as that of a fool. But the scent rising off this man was clear and ardent. His Signature one of focus and determination. And a militia . . . They would need every fighter they could get when Symmachia sent down Eidolon to finish off what the ships had started.

"Come to Kardia with a list and plan," Marco said. "We'll consider your idea."

"What the scuz happened?"

At the chief's demand, Reef cradled his head in his hands, hunched as he sat on the earth-hewn steps of the in-ground hovel. Heat from the cook pit, which doubled as the hearth, did little to ward off the chill of this Voids-forsaken planet. He lifted only his gaze to the table, now a makeshift gurney, where Shad tended an unconscious Eija.

"I told you," Reef said, weary of the questions, the accusing glances from both the chief and the onetime medical officer of the *Prevenire*. "I *don't* know. We were doing fine—albeit in a heavy engagement with the Draegis—but she had it. Never seen anything like it. Then, in a blink, everything went south. A Khatriza showed up and gave Eija what-for. It got bad fast—"

"Yeah, and Zacdari's dying."

"Dying?" Reef was on his feet, heart rapid-firing. "How? She—"

"Step off, Jadon." Chief glowered. "You don't want to test me. Not now."

"This isn't about you—"

"And it ain't about you either, slagger. Except that you had one task—to protect her, and now Shad is stressed, trying to clean up your failure."

"Stop being melodramatic, Sev," Shad said as she set aside an instrument. "She's just unconscious."

"Yeah," the chief grunted, gray eyes watching Reef, "but when he thinks she's dying, he acts more like he cares instead of sitting there feeling sor—"

"You—" Baru help him, Reef wanted to throw a punch. Instead, he charged past the burly chief to the table. Stood over Eija, taking in the cuts and bruises on her face and shoulder. The inflatable splint on her arm. But her face. The brown hair with red glints. A dusting of freckles that always made him crazy. She was adorable and beautiful and . . . amazing. Intelligent. Smartest Shepherd he'd encountered. "She would've made Eidolon had we stayed."

Shad's cheek twitched in a near smile as she worked. "She just wanted to fly."

With a snort, he slid his fingers under her limp hand. "Not going to be a problem now that she has wings."

"I meant piloting."

Nodding, Reef searched her face again, hoping to see those brown eyes. See the green flecks in them. Even if they were blazing with irritation over something stupid he'd said or done.

"I take it the facility is still there." Another reproof from the chief.

"We were trying to destroy the main shaft that had a couple hundred pods when she realized something terrible," Reef said with a shrug. "Didn't make a lot of sense to me, but she redirected her efforts. That's when the Draegis fired on us from above and that messed-up creature-queen thing skittered in. Screeched something at Eija, and the two went at it. I nearly fell to my death, but Ei scooped me up. Then we're spinning as if we'd lost attitude control." He scruffed a hand over his face. "Next thing I know, we're crashing through your hovel."

"*Home.*" Shad's correction was laced with hurt as she stowed an electronic device in a large box—something she'd clearly brought from the *Prevenire*. "I see no brain swelling or fractures to her spine, so when her body is ready, she'll wake." The diminutive woman shook her head as she stared down at her patient. "It's . . . amazing. Even with the wings—and I saw them—when I do a scan, her anatomy is as normal as mine. You'd never know . . ."

"Good thing, because I'm betting if Xisya had figured out what Eija was, she would've vented her first chance she got."

Voices carried outside, growing nearer.

Shad jerked to the chief. "They'll take her if they realize she's returned."

"You mean they'll kill her," the chief said with a scowl. "Take them to the dugout."

Shad nodded sharply and pointed to Eija. "Pick her up. Hurry."

Though Reef moved quickly to comply, he wasn't sure where exactly they were supposed to go in this two-room hovel. Hoisting Eija up, he met the chief's gaze. And was struck by the concern he saw. "She's no threat to them."

"There's no convincing them of that. The Khatriza are all they've ever known." He jutted his jaw. "Hurry. I hear Belcmeg, and he's not known for patience or leniency."

Reef pivoted, curling Eija against his chest, surprised at how light she was. After seeing her with the wings and larger than life, he'd expected more heft.

Shad held open a heavy door to a storage area that wasn't even as big as his bunkroom on the *Prev*.

"You kidding me?" Adjusting sideways, he frowned. "No way this hides—"

"Get in." Two-handing the knob, Shad tugged the door closed. Pulled it tight, a move that required the petite girl to rise on her tiptoes.

Darkness closed in, and Reef shifted in the cramped space. "I hate to tell you, but—"

Crank. Pop! Thuds from the front of the hov—*home*—carried into the hidey-hole.

Reef froze. "They're here."

"Hurry," Shad said.

"Hurry where?" he balked, then saw a release of darkness to his left where Shad faded out of sight. "Wait." What? He blinked.

"C'mon!" Shad urged from somewhere he couldn't see. "The panel only releases when the door is closed. If you aren't through and they open the storage door, you can't get through."

Through what? Tentatively, he took a step, expecting any second to get coldcocked by the wall. Instead, the gaping maw of black only swallowed them deeper. Grew colder. A draft whispered against his neck.

When Eija moaned softly, he stupidly looked down. He couldn't see anything, only felt her muscles contracting. "It's okay," he whispered, hoisting her into a better hold, eyes straining in the darkness. "Shad . . .?"

Nothing. No answer. His gut tightened.

"Shad!" he hissed.

Steps approached and he heard her grunt. "You *have* to keep moving."

"I would if I could see!"

A touch on his arm made him flinch, then a tug, and she led him through the blackness. A half dozen steps farther and darkness surrendered to a hazy gray.

"Here." Shad was a ghostly shadow as she pointed to a cot. An electronics panel—how much had she jury-rigged from her escape pod?—illuminated the space, throwing its faint glow along earthen walls with roots and branches twining across the top. Flat stones served as a floor. "Stay here until I come for you. There's water and bread."

"Wat— *Wait*. How long—"

"Just stay." She vanished back into the dark passage. A not-so-subtle thump dropped a barrier over the entrance, sealing them in.

After depositing Eija on the cot, he straightened and turned, taking in their hiding place. Not much to see in the dimness. The cot, a basket with blankets, and maybe clothes. A small stool served as a table, on which was the aforementioned water, and wrapped in a cloth, he guessed, was the bread.

Air . . . How were they getting air? He scanned the ceiling of roots and twigs and dirt. No obvious air holes. So . . . would they run out of air if Shad never came back?

"No, I'd claw my way out first." He folded his arms and paced, partially to keep warm but also to keep himself busy. Going over what happened in the facility. Her freaking out about the pods. Asking if he'd heard someone—how she'd expected him to hear anything over the claxons clanging through the steel-and-glass facility was beyond him.

But *she* had heard something. That Khatriza? From there, things went bad. What had she seen? Why had she been strong and assertive one tick and panicked the next?

He paced another round, glancing at the barrier that had closed them in. It pretty much soundproofed the hideout. Would he hear if the locals ransacked the home? Could they see the light of the panel? He considered the medical machine. That thing put off a pretty stiff glow. Should he power it down?

He wasn't thrilled about sitting in darkness. But he also didn't want the locals to take Eija or him. They'd vowed to either kill her or put her outside the wall. Of course, if she were conscious, she could protect herself. And him. She'd do that, right?

They hadn't exactly been nice to each other right before he'd spotted the fast-attack craft cutting across the sky. After all, this was a lot for a guy to take in. Finding out the girl you're hot for is a freaking Heavenly—so elevated she was the daughter of god or something. He'd never really been into the lore of the Ladies.

Guess it wasn't really lore, but . . . historical facts?

After deciding against killing the power on the device, he grunted. Slid down the wall and sat on the floor. Knees up, he rested his wrists there. Studied Eija. Would she ever come out of this? He wasn't sure why she was unconscious. Even Shad said she was fine. But had to admit—he'd take a long nap, too, given the chance.

This whole mission had been scuzzed.

Had Marco gotten home?

His chest tightened at the thought. Wondered . . . Wait, weren't they nearing the Al Sans Baru Festival? Symmachia's biggest holiday of the year was one celebration he'd never missed. Never failed to head to the falls for some R & R.

Slag. Had that much time really passed? His channelers weren't working, so he had no way to verify the passage of time, but it seemed right. Either way, it had been a long time. He'd known even back then that the possibility of never returning was high.

Did anyone miss him? His sister? Parents?

Why did he care? He was here. With someone who made him want to be better. His family was filled with a long line of Tascan officers, so being an Eidolon had come too easy to him. For her, it'd been a battle day after day in the Academy. But for the first time in Reef's life, he'd met someone who both challenged him and made him feel . . . like himself. But this whole fighting to save the galaxy thing? That was more than he'd signed up for.

His most ludicrous moment? Believing he could stop Eija from teleporting or whatever it was she did. He hadn't known where she intended, but all that talk about sending Marco back, about what he and Marco had to do . . . He'd seen it a fraction too late: she wasn't going back. And stupid PICC-neck that he was, amped on his own arrogance and unwillingness to consider alternate paths, he'd tried to pin her down.

Failed. Fell right into her teleportation tunnel or whatever it was. And that? That's when failure had a cascading effect.

Next he'd tried to protect her in this very village.

Failed.

After that, protecting her in the facility.

Major fail.

Now, they were here . . . cold and alone in a hole in the ground. Hiding. From local downworlders who wanted to flay her open because she had wings.

Another snort.

Wings.

That was never going to get old.

An ache wove through his chest with a strange burn that had started . . . in the facility. When she'd shoved him and told him no. Clenching his jaw, Reef tugged his collar out and peered down at his chest.

"Slag," he breathed, seeing the thrumming imprint over his heart, bright in the darkness of his thick shirt. "Scuz me!" He could feel the odd warmth pulsing into that drumming organ. Dual warmth—his blood and whatever heated the imprint—coiling around each other.

Feeling sick, he released his shirt, thankful the fabric completely covered the glow. Since he hadn't devolved like Daq'Ti, what would the Touch do to him? He was changing. He could feel something strange in his veins. Just didn't know what it would mean, what it would alter. And honestly, he didn't want change.

The whole connection-to-Eija thing was cool. In a sick, twisted way. But . . . he didn't ask for this. And resented—

"Reef? You okay?"

He started at the croaky words, shrugging as he glanced across the small space. "Yeah." Did she know what she'd done to him? He saw her face beneath the device's ominous blue hue. "Just making sure teleporting didn't turn my guts inside out."

"What happened? Where are we?"

"The Khatriza in the facility—"

"Right," Eija murmured. "She grabbed my dorsal wing right after—" She sucked in a hard breath and bolted upright. "The pods!"

"Quiet," he said. "You zapped us back to Shad and the chief. The villagers came looking for us, so we're hiding. Loud words and bright explosions of light from you might not work in anyone's favor."

"It's not like I do it on purpose."

He frowned. "Really? Because you are Faa'Cris. You—"

"Just stop."

He gritted his teeth and bit his tongue. Wait. Was this her commanding him and he was yielding . . . because of the mark? Like Daq'Ti?

He would not be controlled. "No."

She flicked him a glower.

"I'm not a dog to sit and heel on command."

"So you *can* heel?"

Indignation rushed through him.

"I was kidding!"

"Were you?"

"Djell," she breathed, touching her head, "what is wrong with you?"

"I don't know—the whole annihilation of mankind and beasts reducing my friends to ash, Marco jumping back to the Quadrants without us, me stuck here with—" He snapped his mouth shut, realizing how loud he was. How angry. What he'd been about to say.

He lowered his head and pinched the bridge of his nose.

"Well, don't stop now."

Reef flicked his hands in the air. "What do you want, Eija? Tell me, because I've tried everything your way, and look where we are. Say what you want, what we're supposed to do, O God's Daughter."

Anger flashed through her eyes, which were suddenly violet.

"Great," he scoffed. Closed his eyes and leaned his head back against the dirt wall.

"I'm sorry."

Surprised, Reef considered her. Couldn't remember the last time she'd apologized—ever. And the way she was looking at him with those vibrant violets . . . Did she know? Had she realized what she'd done to him? That he was Touched? Tamed?

She held his gaze . . . and kept holding it.

He didn't dare pose the question. If he asked about the imprint, and she didn't know, he'd give it away. Somehow, that felt worse than her already knowing. And why did he feel ashamed? Angry? It wasn't his fault!

"I didn't mean to—"

Thud! Bang! Thud-thud!

Reef hopped to his feet and moved in front of the door. "Sure wish I had a mech-suit." He shifted his right leg back and readied for whatever was trying to come through the door. "Or my pulse rifle."

"Close quarters," Eija noted quietly. "Too dangerous."

"Hmph."

A touch on his shoulder drew his gaze around. He felt the heat of her touch—not the romantic heat that made his gut tight or knees weak, but the heat of her Lady side, the one that snaked down into his chest and coiled around that handprint. Might've just been him, but it seemed something illuminated between them. Her gaze was startlingly violet now. Pulsing her light, her purity into him.

Definitely knows.

And was that pity she was throwing at him now?

Scowling, Reef shrugged away from her.

The panel gave way. Light flooded the room.

Chief shouldered in and scanned them. "Half expected to find you two galoching."

"Like you and Shad?" Reef pushed past him, leaving the room. Leaving the questions, leaving Eija. But he had a feeling that no matter how far he ran, no matter how many planets he put between them, he'd never be able to escape this.

What the scuz was going to happen to him?

Never had she expected a look like that shooting from Marco's beautiful eyes, condemning her. Mayhap he did not realize their connection was still there. He clearly suppressed it. She, however, yet felt it keenly. His rejection. The revulsion. Over something she could neither explain nor control. Whatever happened in the city had been unintentional, and how it ailed her to think she had somehow hurt the brigand.

She was not even sure *what* she had done, save that she stopped the man from shooting Myles, prevented a crime from being committed. Yet *she* had been detained—*detained*!

Hands fisted at her side, she paced the hall, sensing the disapproval of Thorolf and Belak as they guarded her.

"I am sure he will come soon," Myles said quietly.

"You spoke those words forty minutes ago." Kersei stretched her neck. "This is absurd." She shoved her fisted hands under her arms, feeling the tingling in her chest that signaled Xylander would soon need to be fed. "What wrong have I done that he would seek to punish me? It is ludicrous and unfair!"

"Uh"—Myles ducked—"my lady, I—"

"Duchess."

Kersei leapt to her feet. Had he heard her disrespect and petulance? The twitch of his cheek, the way he would not meet her eyes, told her he had.

Stony-faced, Marco stood at the door to his receiving chamber, a hand indicating that she should precede him into the room.

Moving past him to enter swept her nerves with fiery shivers and forced her to realize how she feared him. Feared his anger. Feared she had somehow trespassed upon an unwritten rule or command. Feared he would send her away. Inside, she stopped and clasped her hands tight, noting his guards positioned silently in the corners.

With a thud that made her flinch, the door swung closed.

Marco strode around her to the side table, where he poured a steaming mug of what she assumed to be cordi. "You fear me." His words rumbled and coiled around her heart.

She thought to argue. Lie. But never had she been one to placate, nor would she now. Besides, the truth of her feelings was easily picked up by his discerning senses. Might as well save herself the humiliation. "After what I saw in your gaze in the city, aye."

His icy eyes struck her as he sipped the cordi. That sigil still intimidating. He lowered the mug and set it aside, then motioned to the chair. "Please."

Swallowing, Kersei seated herself. "I am uncertain to what end you have summoned me, but I would have you know my son needs me soon."

"In other words, get on with it?" Twisting the Tyrannous ring on his left little finger, he wandered along the bookshelves but said nothing. Would he not yield to his own admonishment?

A side door opened and Isaura swirled in with the tall, dark-skinned alien who had arrived on the ship with Marco.

Radical was the change that swept over Marco as he set eyes on the kyria. His scowl vanished, his near smile that rivaled a smirk all but glowed, and his shoulders relaxed. He held out his hand and Isaura glided to him, placing hers there. So casual a move, so familiar. So . . . adoring. They stood close, so intimately set that Kersei felt she intruded.

Pushing her eyes elsewhere, she visually bumped into the alien—man. His skin was neither black nor brown but mottled like ash. It was not smooth, but more . . . pocked. His shoulders mostly melded into his neck, and though his eyes were oval like most humans, there was an up-and-down lengthening to them that was . . . odd.

"Have you met Daq'Ti?" Marco's voice stabbed her conscience and felt accusing, as if calling her out for staring at the newcomer.

Kersei shifted, crossing her legs at the ankles. "I have not." Her heart thumped that she had not answered him properly. "Your Majesty."

"But you are aware that he returned with me from Kuru."

"I am." Already this had begun to feel like an interrogation. "To what end—"

"And have you heard Daq'Ti's story, of his . . . transformation?"

Kersei frowned. "Ah," she said, lifting her hands, "there you have lost me."

"So." Tapping on the device attached to his vambrace, Marco gave her a sidelong glance. Then, he detached a flat, square screen and handed it to her.

"Since I was not here, tell me—has this image been shown to any here on Drosero?"

She tentatively took the device. "I can speak but for myself." When she saw what the screen captured, she recoiled. "What is this? The diabolus?"

Now towering over her, he fixed his hauntingly pale gaze on her. "Of some Draegis that name could likely be used. When I first met Daq'Ti, I may have even called him that myself."

She frowned, glanced at the alien. "I do not understand."

Resting a hand on Marco's arm, Isaura inserted herself. "You are frightening her."

"Good," he pronounced. "There is much to be frightened of."

"Why? What wrong have I committed?" Kersei's heart raced with her thoughts.

"The image on that screen"—he pointed to the device—"was Daq'Ti three months ago."

Glancing at it again, Kersei gave a laugh she did not feel, waiting for him to share the joke. When he did not move or laugh or explain, she faltered. "Surely you . . . jest." She studied the enormous creature on the screen, his body as embers in the flame, blackened, charred. Massive. Hideous. "Figuratively, you mean."

"Literally."

She scoffed. "Impossible." Waited again for him to tell her it was all a great diversion. When he did not, she considered Daq'Ti. Then Marco. The alien again. "People do not change so much as what you suggest."

Marco stared at her, hard. "What did you do to the man in the street?"

Her heart skipped a beat. Then another. Remembered the flash of light. The odd current that shot over her arm and riffled her hair. The man's gaping mouth. Wide muddy eyes. Foul breath that punched from his throat. "I . . ."

"You did something, Duchess. *What* was it?"

Feeling cornered, condemned, she swallowed. "He . . . he threatened me. Produced a skycrawler weapon and aimed it at Regia Myles. In my defense, I but used the training learned among my father's machitis to stay him." It was mostly true. Everything until her palm touched his chest. "That is all."

"No, Kersei, that is not *all*." His gaze locked onto hers, forbidding her from moving, breathing. "Much, *much* more transpired." He looked past her and nodded to Kaveh, who stood in shadow near the door, which he opened.

Led by two regia, the man from the square entered the room with his head held high. When he set eyes on her, he broke free of the two regia and threw himself at her feet. "My lady! Lady, please!"

With a yelp, she leapt from the chair and scrambled back. "Remove yourself, you brigand!"

"Restrain Mr. Haltersten," Marco complained and turned his disapproving gaze on her.

The guards wrested the man into a firm hold, keeping him on his knees.

"To what end is he here?" Kersei balked. "Did you not hear me say he accosted me? Attacked Myles?" Did Marco not care? "Darius would—" She clamped her mouth shut, fighting tears. Wishing Darius were here to defend her. But she was alone. Had no defender. No answers.

"Dusan?" Isaura said, her soft words somehow breaking through Marco's raw intensity.

His focus adjusted. "There was a girl on the ship I was trapped in," Marco said, his voice suddenly . . . distant. Hard. "Her name was Eija—"

"*Meni xominga qaytaring.*" Daq'Ti's voice was peculiar and melodic, despite its deep resonance.

Marco slid his gaze to the side but did not look at the alien. He nodded, almost as if to himself. "She was a pilot, the one who found me trapped between the bulkheads. When the Draegis boarded our ship to kill us and steal the coordinates to the Quadrants, Daq'Ti was part of the raiding party. He killed one of the crew, ripped open the escape pod that Eija—"

"*Meni xominga qaytaring.*"

"—had been trapped in. He grabbed her by the throat and yanked her out, trying to kill her as she kicked and writhed."

Kersei gulped adrenaline, not finding it hard to believe this alien-man could easily kill. But also grasping shocking glimpses of what Marco had endured during his absence.

"Somehow Eija—"

"*Meni xominga qaytaring.*"

"Why does he keep saying that?" Kersei asked, the words nearly choking her.

"It means 'return me to the Lady,' and more than his own life or breath, he wants to be with her again." Marco huffed. "It is not a romantic overture. He is by blood and transformation her guardian. He lives to serve her alone and will accept perilous injury, even let himself die, to protect her."

Unable to fathom such a resolute commitment, Kersei studied Daq'Ti.

Saw in his gaze grief. Somber helplessness. Truly, he only wanted to return to this Eija. "I . . . That is incredible." Mind swimming, she blinked. "I—"

"Daq'Ti." Marco looked to the alien. "Show her the mark."

Mark?

With a warbling sound, the alien-man shifted, unfastened the first four buttons of his tunic, and drew aside the material. A blue handprint pulsed over his heart.

Embarrassed at seeing his chest and what lay there, Kersei drew back. "What is it?"

"In a moment." Marco jutted his jaw to Kaveh, who moved in front of Haltersten and tugged at his shirt.

"My lady!" Haltersten cried out and started thrashing. "Do not let them harm your servant. Please—I must protect you. My lady!"

Protect me? She needed protection *from* him.

As the regia again wrestled to control the wiry man, Marco spoke. "I learned after she changed Daq'Ti—"

"Changed him?"

"—that she was not merely Eija. She was in fact the daughter of Eleftheria and Vaqar, her identity hidden from even her for this mission. She was—"

"A Lady." Even as she said the words, Kersei saw the Kalonican's chest. More accurately, saw a barely visible impression of— "A handprint."

"Correctly, *your* handprint. It's the *Ovqatlanish. Tamed* is the translated word for this process. The mark is yet faint, but as he changes—"

"*Changes?*" Mortified, Kersei jerked to him. "Of what do you speak? He is human! What is there to change?"

Marco's lips quirked in a smirk. "The heart, the very adunatos of a man." The smirk became a sneer. "It seems your kind have been adept through the years of plying a man's heart and will against himself."

"How dare you suggest that I—"

"Forget you to whom you speak?" Theilig demanded, striding across the chamber.

Kersei yanked her gaze down. "Nay, I do not forget, but when accusations are—"

"Do I accuse you?" Marco hissed, closing in on her. "Aye, I do." He pointed to Haltersten. "There is your evidence. You are born of a Lady, and that mark gives witness to the blood in your veins. That you can imprint him and change his will to something you find more palatable—"

"Pala—" Kersei drew up sharp. "He would have accosted me! Killed Myles!"

"Do you tell me Myles is too weak to subdue *this* man? If you say true, then I will have Myles, a regia, flogged for so thoroughly failing House Tyrannous and one of its own."

Kersei gaped. "What is this?" she balked. "Why do you rail at me, treat me as if I have done wrong to this man when this . . . this Eija—"

"*Meni xominga qaytaring.*"

She growled. "When she commands respect from you?"

"Because she is Taming a race of heinous monsters that reduce humans to ash. Because *she* is yet there, *fighting* the creature who strapped me to a metal bed and stuffed me into the hull of a ship with tubes plugged into my body, my mind stuck in an endless dream that I could neither end nor change."

Appalled by his ordeal, Kersei drew back, heart seized. "Marco . . ."

He faltered. Glanced aside. To Isaura, who hurried to him, speaking softly. Then his narrowed gaze found Kersei again. "The *Ovqatlanish* in Kuru is vital to the survival of a civilization. Here, used on men when there is a system of justice to correct abhorrent behavior, it is a *gross* violation. Against your own people! Your own kind! I will not allow it!"

She could agree, yet— "It is . . . I do not know how I did it. Where it came from—"

"Wrong! You know well its source. Or will you now lie to me again and say you are not a Lady?"

How? How did he know? She had not spoken with anyone of her time in Deversoria.

"As thought." He turned away. Went to the carafe and poured more cordi. "Go back to them and learn to control that power. Wrongly used it is a blight, not a blessing." He dumped back a mug of warmed cordi. Swallowed. Palmed the table. "Do not again use it against any man, or I will have you banished."

Her shock assaulted his receptors and his conscience.

The stunned silence of the others proved gaping and remonstrative, stinging his nostrils. Yet, Marco would not alter the vow. He stared at the table, still working through his anger over the *Ovqatlanish* manifesting here in the Quadrants, being used against normal men. And by Kersei, of all people.

The thought repulsed him. The wielding of one's will over another . . .

"Dusan," Isa whispered, her hand warm on his back.

"Go," he ordered in the direction of Kersei. "All of you." To be sure Isa did not mistake him, he threaded their fingers. Grateful when her glorious efflux said she understood, though she clearly hurt for Kersei. Curious that. With her nearby, he paced the length of bookcases lining the north wall as the room cleared and the doors were shut.

"Dusan," she said quietly, seating herself on the cushion, rubbing her belly, "are you quite certain that was the ri—"

"The right thing?" He scruffed his head, noting he needed another haircut. "Aye. Not only right but necessary."

"But if you are correct, she is a Lady. They are not beholden to human authority."

"Wrong." Marco did not speak that tersely or angrily. Just . . . plainly. "The Ladies, the Blades of Vaqar, were charged with *protecting* mankind. But rather than do that, they drew in on themselves and wielded their gifts to the detriment of men. If they choose to remain in Deversoria, fine. But they will not surface to turn the men of this planet, or the Quadrants, into pawns or puppets, holding the will of men captive to their own whims. I have already been that once—albeit to a Corrupt—and will not allow it here."

"But you must grant that this man, Haltersten, was wrong—"

"Egregiously so, and had she not ripped his will from his chest, I would have addressed the matter violently." He recalled sitting on the destrier, seeing the malcontent pull the weapon, and hiking a leg over to deal with it when that light blinded him. "No one will touch a member of this House without repercussion."

She scooted out of the chair and stood, with some difficulty. "Dusan." Her gentleness, her soft words, her Signature radiated her peacemaker's heart.

"Give no reproof, Isa. I—"

She cupped his face. "No reproof, my love." Staring into his eyes, a gesture that seemed to reach right into his adunatos and pull out the more tender of his inclinations, she slowly smiled. "Ah, there you are."

He frowned. "Who?"

When Isaura tiptoed up to kiss him, her belly pressed between them. "The man I love." She smoothed her hand over the scruff of a beard. "I know how this pained you. I felt your concern."

"Kuru—" Even thinking of that Ancient-forsaken place made him gulp adrenaline. "So much was wrong there. Men subservient, spineless puppets. Women all but gone and the few who remained were Khatriza—so cruel and lost to their depravity . . ." He shook his head. "I cannot allow us to become that. Will not."

"Then do not, but neither become what you forbid."

He scowled. "What?"

"You threatened to banish Kersei."

"Aye, and if she yet persists in turning men into her puppets, it will be done."

After drawing in a long breath, she slowly released it. "I was there, Dusan. It did not seem her intent was to do anything but stop an assault. If she truly sought a puppet to do her will, why there, in the street with hundreds of witnesses?"

He drew back. "You side with her."

"I side with justice, and you do as well." Head tilted, she considered him. "It does my heart ill to see more members of this family turning against each other. Mayhap had there been a discussion with Kersei—"

"Discussion." Why did his heart drum so? *Why* did she question him?

"You and I both saw that Kersei knew not what happened on that street. If you simply encourage her to find a mentor to teach restraint of the gifts the Ancient has seen fit to bestow upon her . . ."

His irritation bottomed out. The gift . . . the Ancient . . . just as Marco had gifts. That was her point, was it not? He saw the wisdom of her words. "You are right. The point is valid."

"Then you will rescind—"

"I will not."

Isaura drew back, her brow rippling in confusion. "I do not understand."

She didn't, did she? "The *Ovqatlanish* has no place on Drosero—it was designed to Tame a person, right a grave injustice to a race who had no choice in how they became the monsters they were." He loved this woman, but her naïveté regarding this situation curdled in his gut. "Daq'Ti—"

A hum trilled the air as the Draegis thudded closer.

"—tell me true," Marco spoke to the former Lavabeast as he held Isaura's gaze, "were you given a choice to become the Draegis beast who destroyed with impunity?"

He trilled softly. "No, we were grown in pods."

Still staring at Isaura, Marco did his best not to be swayed by the hurt and sorrow swarming her efflux. "What Kersei did, even in ignorance, has forever altered the life of a man who made his own choices to become what he is today."

Isaura straightened and swallowed. "I—"

"Regardless of Haltersten's intention to harm her and Myles, his choice has been removed from him. His will. His ability to direct the course of his life." He silently begged her to understand. "That is never acceptable."

"If that were true," she said, her voice wavering with the slightest of tremors, "then would not your calling as a hunter be in question?"

Challenged, angry, he stepped into her personal space. "Each person I webbed was delivered for justice, not stripped of his will. Not altered into a mindless drone whose only wiring was to *obey* a Lady." He scowled, angling his head toward hers. "Tell me you understand that. Tell me you do not condone—"

"Dusan." Her touch was gentle yet firm, like the way she said his name. "Please, you are frightening me."

"It frightens me how easily you're convinced she did no wrong."

"Never did I speak such words." She was still pressing her palm over his heart. "You are angry. And for arousing that, I beg your mercy, but the line seems very slight. How are you certain what you speak is truth? Your time there, while a lifetime to me, was short. Your experiences—as spoken by your own voice—limited to the ship and captivity."

"You question me?" He gaped, stricken.

"I would have you consider that Kersei was innocent in the charge of willfully injuring another."

"And yet, Haltersten is a puppet to her—you saw his pleading of her. The mark she has imprinted on him without his consent. How can you defend that?"

"Intent, Dusan. I speak to intent. Kersei did not *intend* to do this thing, but this man did intend to harm her. Would have killed her regia with that weapon. Had that happened, would it not have removed *Myles's* ability to direct his own life?"

"Indeed, and my response would have been just as strong. But never should this man have been stripped of his ability to think for himself. If that is ever acceptable to you—"

Her eyes widened and she stepped away, shocked.

How keenly—terribly—he felt the emptiness of her withdrawal. Realized the harshness of his words. The mistake. He let the emotions fall to the floor between them.

"Now who would remove another's will?"

He frowned.

"Am I not allowed to disagree with you, Dusan? Is that a crime, one that would elicit a punishment of me being banished from your life?"

"Isa." Hearing his thoughts on her tongue startled him, scared him. "No, that is not . . ." But it *was* what he meant. What he'd been about to speak—without thinking. The realization sickened him. "I . . ."

What was wrong with him, that he would so easily strike such a severe chord?

"You are right." He held her close and exhaled shakily. "Even now you are my beacon." He hated the tension in her body, tension he had put there. "I let my anger speak." He cupped her face, peering into those green eyes he so dearly loved. "I would never remove your will or you from my life. Not when there is breath in my lungs."

"Even when we disagree?"

"Even then—now. Forgive me?"

She sighed and nodded. "Of course. Will you tell me? Help me understand."

"What?"

"What it was like in Kuru with the Draegis. Your reaction was overharsh, in my opinion, and never have I known you to be so cold toward anyone who was not an enemy. Especially not one who once held great claim on your affection." It startled that she would speak of it, but Isaura smiled all the same. "Thus, I would understand what has created in you this abhorrence of this inadvertent thing the duchess did."

His veins twitched with irritation, fighting to lash out at the challenge. "Were you not my aetos, I would believe you intended those words more as remonstration than search for understanding."

Hurt played havoc with her Signature. "Truly, I would understand, but I . . . I will trust you. Yet I would ask that you hear my concern and give it consideration."

"Always. Now, I must speak with Daq'Ti and make plans. I will see you for the evening meal." Even as he watched her go, Marco noticed the thrum in his arm. The heat it gave off, so much worse than the brand. As the door closed, he expelled a thick breath.

"How may I serve?" Daq'Ti asked.

Marco shifted gears, not an easy task after such an encounter. "I would have you start training the Uchuvchi. Ask Ixion to charge a Stalker with teaching all of you hand-to-hand combat. The ships will not last forever, and we could use their hands."

"Their hands?"

With a sniff, Marco smirked, holding his forearm. "A figure of speech. They would be helpful in fighting the Symmachians."

Daq'Ti trilled his understanding. Started to leave.

"One more thing." After a brief hesitation, Marco rolled up his sleeve and extended his forearm to the Draegis. "Do you know what—"

"*Chirish!*" Daq'Ti all but growled, his expression fierce and dark. "*Chirish* is not good." His gaze raked over Marco. "Let it go, Uchuvchi."

"You say this when you asked Eija to let you keep yours?"

"I regret it," he muttered. "Too late to go back." His oval eyes met Marco's. "Release it, Uchuvchi. It is too dark."

"I . . . I have no choice. It attached to me."

"No. Let go."

"You aren't listening—it embedded into my brand. I can't get it out." Not sure he really wanted to either.

Daq'Ti trilled, grabbed his arm.

"Hey!" Marco shouted—and it earned a response from Theilig and Kaveh, who hurried in. "No. It's okay." He seized the chance to step back. "We were done." He hurried from the room, unsettled, shoving down his sleeve and buttoning the cuff. Unsure what worried the Draegis, Marco knew one thing: he wasn't letting this thing go. He had an effective weapon. He needed it. Drosero needed it.

"I'm a little confused."

"Only a little?"

Tigo glowered at Jez as they hiked. "We're going to see AO, right?"

She nodded, moving easily across the untamed lands of Drosero.

The trek had gone from grassy plains to forbidding, cracked desert. He recalled hearing of the wastelands and wondered if that's where they were now. "So, what're we still doing on Drosero?"

Head tipped down, she tried to hide her smile—unsuccessfully.

"Your apples are glowing."

"Excuse me?"

"Apples of your cheeks. I see them—means you're smiling. Which is nice."

"You're trying to annoy me again."

"You mean, I *am* annoying you, since I hear it in your voice."

She huffed.

But why was she smiling? He hadn't said anything funny. "Want to let me in on the joke?"

"Took you long enough."

What? Tigo stopped, letting her continue on. "Were you in my head again?"

Now she paused, too. Slowly came around. "No," she said with more than a little shrill in her tone. "Since you are a man of logic—at least, I thought you were—and logic would dictate that if we're looking for AO, we should be on Symmachia or a Kedalion planet, not the downworlder planet that has obsessed Xisya."

"Xisya?"

She lowered her head. "Please, we should—"

"It's really cold."

Now she scowled. "We're in the desert."

"Are we? Because to me, it's freezing cold in the empty vacuum called

All The Things You're Not Telling Me. It's a scuzzing island you've left me on without answers or direction."

A knot grew between her eyes, tugging her brows. "You trusted me once," she said, more than a little hurt in her words.

"Right back atcha."

Again, she dipped her head for a second, then shifted closer to him. Her fingers laced his, and everything in Tigo turned to goo as her glittering caramel eyes met his. With her pervasive presence, she somehow rose into his personal space with a sultry look that drifted down to his mouth.

"Not fair," he murmured before her lips teased his.

Voids! Kissing her was perfect. *She* was perfect. Tigo slipped a hand to the back of her neck, deepening the kiss she'd started. Appreciating the way her hands came to rest on his chest, then around his neck. He hooked her waist and snugged her into his arms. Felt dizzy. His head went . . . weird. Not surprising—she'd always messed his head up and made him—

"Augh!" When he tried to move, he wobbled. "I *cannot* believe you did that. Kissed me to shut me up!"

"Tigo."

Voids if all he could think about was kissing her again. "Not fair!"

"You're missing the important part."

"Yeah, kind of hard to think after that kiss. Glad to know you're having trouble, too."

"Tigo."

"*What?*" Why was he so ticked? And why were his eyes and throat burning? "What am I missing, Jez? Because I'm tired of you—"

Her eyebrow arched. And somehow she had yet again reduced him to a complaining, simpering—

Hold up. Behind her. The scenery behind her tugged at his attention. Drew his gaze. Breath backing into his throat, he stilled.

Her ebony eyebrow arched. "Ah, there you go."

"Holy . . ." He turned a slow circle, taking in the mountains that looked . . . shaved. Barren. Not like desert mountains, but majestic ones that had been stripped bare of their beauty and life. The sky was a strange gray, cloudless yet hazy. "What the scuz . . .?" Then he really got it. "You kissed me to distract me from folding."

"You're used to space travel, but not moving across time and distance."

"So, time travel."

She cocked her head. "Of a sort. You can fly a ship and wear a mech-suit, but crossing galaxies in a blink is hard on a body not used to it. You nearly passed out just folding from Deversoria."

"But Deversoria isn't really a place. Or belowground. It's a different plane or something." Tigo gave her an opening to set him straight. "Right?"

Jez stared down the rocky slope. "We need to get going before the sun is gone."

He glanced at the hazy sky and frowned. "What sun?"

She was moving farther away, her attention on the ground, which was shifting and slipping beneath her feet.

Obviously she wasn't going to answer. She always felt superior. And right now, he felt . . . well, *not* like an Eidolon. He hadn't felt like Commander Tigo Deken since she'd forced him down into Deversoria.

"I didn't force you."

He growled. "What do you call it then?"

"I saved your life!"

Okay. Valid. "I should've had a choice."

With a sigh, she rounded a bend in the twisting of the land . . . planet . . .

He touched his temple, trying to steady his warbling vision. But it wasn't his vision that was warbling—the actual location was. It was . . . scuzzed. "Where are we?"

"Now you want to know?"

Would it always be like this with them? Kissing one second, snarking the next?

"No."

Hold up. Why would he complain about that? It'd mean more kissing. And . . . okay, so if she wanted to be in his head . . . *She must really like kissing me.*

"AO."

Tigo nearly barreled straight into the overgrown man who'd once been a member of the 215. "Eggleston."

"Commander." Salt-and-pepper hair framed a weathered, heavily tanned face. "Thought that was you on the ridge." Eyes crinkled from a still-hidden smile. "Getting closer with each visit." He winked at Jez.

Hold the O_2. What was that?

She shifted and tilted her head. "How is it going?"

Not for the first time, Tigo noticed his eyes were itching, burning. The planet . . . Jez had mentioned interplanetary travel in a blink. So . . . what planet were they on? It wasn't Symmachia.

Eggleston indicated to a path. "Terraforming on the southern rise seems to be holding."

Arms crossed, Jez moved to get a better vantage. "Nice. Any luck finding the deposit bed?"

"Not yet. The underground systems are vast"—his gray eyes raked the land—"with desertlike conditions. But the people are glad for the terraforming attempts." He inclined his head toward her. "I've told them who is responsible."

"I wish you had not."

"When this is done, they should know who to thank."

And who to blame.

"This is their home," Jez said as she climbed the last of the incline and stood with the big guy. "It must be *their* efforts that save their planet, or they will eventually come to resent us all the more."

"Even if they know the truth?"

"Which truth?" She looked out over the valley below as Tigo slid into position next to her. "The one that we hold to, or the one *they* hold to?"

"You make truth sound conditional."

Tigo eyed the gouges in the valley floor, the multi-storied troughs and structures. The mines. Hazy atmosphere. Squalor of livelihood and existence . . . His heart skipped a beat. "Tryssinia." It had a whole different meaning to him, shoving his thoughts right into the arms of Teeli Knowles.

Voids.

"To them," Jez went on, as if she hadn't heard his thoughts skip to the attractive medical officer from the *Macedon*, "their truth is absolute. To them, our truth is a convenience they feel we can afford, since we are removed from this . . . place."

"Just like the land, attitudes are changing." AO folded his thick arms over his chest. "It's healing, and I think they're ready to let go of the poisoned past to allow their hearts to heal as well."

The hatred here is too strong toward us.

Well, no scuz. Who would let go of that anger when they were constantly watching their loved ones die? When they were trapped on this forsaken planet? When they had gained a reputation for being contaminated, both the land and the people?

Hold up. Tigo flinched—because that thought about hatred being too strong . . . It hadn't been his thought. Nor the earlier one about blame. The voice paired with them was Jez's.

Like that made sense. He wasn't Faa'Cris. Couldn't pull thoughts out of her head the way she always did his.

Jez lifted a shoulder and shifted.

"Reading my thoughts again?"

Her gaze dipped to the ground, then to the side.

"Does he know you like kissing me?"

"He will blame you because, like me, AO knows you have always loved the ladies."

"But none like you."

Her cheeks went pink, which was so beautiful in her caramel complexion. *"There are none like me. I am unique."*

"Definitely true."

"Do you two need a room?" AO's voice still had that old-man resonance that always made Tigo feel like he was talking to his father.

"Watch yourself, Licitus." Reprimands came too easily to her. "And—"

"Wait." Tigo's brain finally caught up with her words. *"Licitus?"* He stared between them and frowned at the big guy. "You know that term?"

"Know it? I *lived* it."

Tigo's thoughts spun into a frenzy. *"What?"* He angled away from Jez. "You said no man leaves once he's entered those dark halls."

"Jaigh hasn't *left*," she said coolly, and though her armor didn't manifest, there was an aura of it around her face. "Not officially. He has undertaken a mission on behalf of the Faa'Cris."

"And . . ." AO prompted.

Jez lifted her chin. "And AO is not a mere . . . Licitus."

AO grunted a laugh. "Calling me Licitus is as accurate as calling a Marine *nephesh*."

Though Tigo tried to decipher that, he struggled. *Nephesh* was a derogatory term that meant ghosts and was a reference to Eidolon. So was he saying that he was an elite Licitus? How did that even make sense? Or did he mean—

Forget it. Tigo scratched the back of his head. "Okay, give it to me. Read me in on . . . whatever this is."

"Later." Jez flicked a hand in the air. "Right now—"

"No."

Violet eyes sparked at him.

"That just makes you more beautiful." He knew that would annoy her, but it stopped her argument. "I want to know. No more leaving me out." He didn't care if that ticked her off, which it had, if the wake rippling off her was any indication. "Does he know you've walked away from the Daughters?"

At this, AO jolted. Arms came uncrossed. "For *this* Licitus?" As he waved at Tigo, he scowled. A storm moved through those gray eyes. "You abandoned—"

"I abandon nothing or no one, and Tigo is as much a Licitus as you are."

"I call foul," Tigo snapped. "And have no idea what you mean."

Words sharp, glower sharper, Jez seared AO with a fierce look. "If you must know, Tigo has formally challenged and chastised the Faa'Cris. To my astonishment"—the way she worked that satiny jaw said whatever was coming next must be painful—"I agreed with him."

Tigo almost laughed. "Not easily." Kind of proud he'd managed to do something that brought her to his side. "It took a lot of heated discussions . . . and kissing."

AO didn't smile. Nor seem entertained. "What you have done—"

"Is none of your concern." Jez's nostrils flared. "Nor his."

"Excuse me?" Tigo winged an eyebrow. "You left *with me.* Remember the whole hand-holding thing as we walked out?"

"You would leave for him, but—"

"Enough!" Rejeztia gloried before them, her wings flicking dust into Tigo's eyes. "We must focus."

"Oh, I *am* focused," AO said, his voice . . . deepening. A hint of a metallic echo exasperated his words. "We had a deal, *Triarii.*"

Things had swung far south of where Tigo had expected them to go. And he didn't like it. Didn't like that the big guy knew her Faa'Cris rank. Had a bad feeling about this, but the bigger issue was that they still hadn't told him how AO came by all this knowledge. "How can you be Licitus and have been an Eidolon? We were told you—"

"You were told what you needed to be told," AO said. "I am no Licitus, not in the way of the sniveling dogs whimpering down the cobbled streets of Deversoria and licking the heels of the Ladies."

To know those phrases and the cobbled streets . . . to feel that revulsion . . . This wasn't just head knowledge. It was *experiential.* Especially with that much venom laced through his words.

"AO, please. Don't—"

"Don't *what*? Tell your most recent love toy the truth?"

Bad feeling turned to horrible feeling. "I'm sorry—what? Toy?"

Jez focused on the big guy, the one who'd taken to Kersei Dragoumis like a father. "Things are too complicated—"

"No, they're *real* simple." AO's words sent a surprising echo banging around Tigo's head.

"I beg you," Jez pleaded.

He lasered in on Tigo. "Have you heard of the diabolus?"

"Is that . . . rhetorical?" Tigo sniggered, then shrugged. Everyone had heard about the diabolus. "Devils. Evil beings whose reputation long ago escaped Drosero."

"It was not just their reputation that escaped," AO snarled. "They are not devils, though the Faa'Cris would have people believe that to keep them fearful, hostage, and distant. The name simply means *slanderers*." His chest rose and fell raggedly. "That is what we were named when they cast us out of Deversoria centuries ago because we would no longer subjugate ourselves, be under the feet of the Ladies. We once stood at their side."

Those words . . . "Scuz me," he hissed, considering the man who had spoken what had come out of Tigo's mouth in those sacred halls. He smirked at Jez. "Wow, Jez. Sound familiar?" Yet . . . "Hold up." His mind would not cooperate with what was trying to cram itself into his believability ranks. "*We?*"

AO's face now seemed alive and sinewy. Grief tugged at the weathered lines around his eyes. "I am among the last of my kind. When Vaqar was blessed with immortality for his sacrifice in defense of the Fierian, two races were raised up and endowed with powerful gifts. In each other we found comfort, love, and built families together. Centuries later, the Ladies went into hiding, and we went with them—for a time. Our purpose was not to hide, but to war, to lead. Existing in that way became untenable, so we departed Deversoria."

"Wait." Tigo's head spun. "You mean . . . *you*"—that's what the big guy meant, right?—"you're one of these . . . basically . . . male Faa'Cris." And since the Ladies only allied with powerful rulers . . . "You were a king?"

AO barked a laugh, but then his gaze grew serious. "I am not Faa'Cris." He was still the Eidolon who had served with him on the *Macedon*, but was now much, much more. "I am"—his gaze slid over Jez in a familiar, somehow intimate gesture—"Do'St."

"That was a long time ago." Jez's voice echoed now, too.

Watching these two was like standing between two rhinnocks engaged in a very long, very tense standoff . . . that spanned centuries. Tigo felt like he was about to get smashed in an epic collision of will and power.

"We are off-topic." Jez indicated to the sleepy mining town. "They are the point."

Not sure I buy that.

"Leave it, Tigo."

"Stay *out* of my head," he growled.

With a somber gaze, AO put a hand on his shoulder. "I can teach you how to shield your thoughts."

Tigo started. "That's a thing?"

"A necessary one," AO asserted.

"You have distracted him long enough." Air riffled and wings again dusted the air.

"Ah, Rejeztia," AO said, his voice once more rumbling like rocks. "So nice to see you again." He grinned at her. "Have I hit too close to the mark, informing your newest toy of the dark secrets of the Faa'Cris? Does he understand how far you Ladies have fallen?"

Her armor sparked, as if rubbing shoulders with the atmosphere created its own friction. "You now see, Tigo, why his kind have died out."

AO's deep bass chuckle even seemed born of the elements. "I yet live, so we are *not* dead. No matter how much you will it."

"Yeah, okay . . ." Tigo squinted, still struggling to keep up. "So, you're . . . immortal?"

"That belongs to the Triada alone."

Triada?

"The Ancient, Vaqar, and Eleftheria," Jez spoke into his mind.

Nodding to himself, Tigo felt like he was sucking at empty O_2 lines. "Ancient One . . . AO . . . because you've been here a very long time . . . Were ruler—" His gaze hit the land, recalled their convo. "Scuz me! Here—Tryssinia. This was your kingdom."

AO inclined his head solemnly. "Over the area that now grows green under the terraforming efforts and long before the Faa'Cris banished their deranged Sisters to this planet."

"The Corrupt came here of their own volition. We did not send them."

"You are responsible for what you threw upon an unsuspecting and unprepared universe."

Anger sprouted in Tigo's chest, watching these two. Realizing the utter backbirther he must be to them. "You were on my team, part of the Two-one-five . . ." The dig hurt. "And . . . what?" He squinted at them. "You thought it'd be great to play me for a fool?"

"It was thought you needed the protection of us both."

Tigo stared at them blankly. "Why?" He sniffed at Jez. "Was it that important for me to come and challenge all your beliefs and convince you to walk away from them?" As soon as he saw her armor shimmer, he held up his hand. "Hey. Just asking because this is making zed sense!" Then an idea struck. "Was this about Teeli?"

Something twisted through AO's face. "A great loss."

"Teeli was special, but not an imperative in your journey." Was that jealousy he heard in her voice even still? "Tigo, there is much we do not have time to explain. So many pieces in play that can never be expressed. AO joined my mission to be at the ready by your side for reasons that include and affect Kersei—"

"The Droseran? Affect her how?"

"And your father," AO inserted.

"What?" That spinning in his head was happening again. Like he'd lost attitude thrusters.

"Jaigh," Jez hissed a remonstration.

"He should know."

"This was not—"

"My father . . ." Tigo thought of his barrel-chested dad walking the Droseran prince out of Deversoria. "What about him?"

AO huffed and shook his head. "Why have you never wondered how you got to this place? Tell me, *please*, that you've wondered how you ended up in this role, among the Ladies, speaking truth and challenging—"

"What role?" Fed up with the half-bits of intel, Tigo felt his anger rising and tumbling over these two he'd once commanded and considered friends. "If I had not rebelled against Faa'Cris customs, *I* would be that dog licking their heels."

"But you *didn't* lick those heels," AO growled, mischief glinting in his eyes. "Did you?"

The question felt like a mine waiting for Tigo to trigger.

"Enough!" Jez shouted. "We are here for the Tryssinians. Your people, Jaigh."

"No, *I'm* here for the Tryssinians." AO bared his teeth, a move that Tigo half expected to force Jez to draw blade. "You've come to stare down that perfect nose and deliver edicts."

"There is no edict." Her voice was sharp but also resigned. "I no longer rank among the Ladies."

AO snorted. "Like scuz you don't." He remained undeterred. "I may not be Faa'Cris, but your kind exist beneath the same rules as the Do'St. If you are able to reach into your adunatos and yield your will so the armor can emerge . . . if you can fold across a galaxy"—he cocked his head—"you are yet Faa'Cris." The emphasis on those last words hit like a hammer on a mech-suit. "Corrupt and Forsaken *cannot* wield the light."

Tigo faltered. Was that true? He eyed Jez, whose face twisted. She was furious, not that a lie had been spoken. But because truth had been.

And it amplified the irritation in his gut. Made it roil. Pitched him back to that moment with Crey on Drosero when he'd had a suspicion, a speck of doubt he had shouldered aside. A betraying thought he refused to believe. Not wanting to accept that . . .

"He's right." Voids that hurt to admit, and even that angered him. "Isn't he? You're still Faa'Cris—actively working. A mission." Why had he believed her? "Nothing has changed."

Her armor slid away and before him stood the lieutenant he loved.

Correction: thought he loved.

Because looking at her now, seeing how she had treated him so cruelly, looked down on him . . . "You lied to me. Manipulated me." It was all so suddenly clear.

"Tigo—"

"All this time, I thought . . ." He huffed. "I actually believed you were listening. Thought you were taking what I had to say seriously."

"I was. You know me—"

"I *thought* I knew you!"

"Don't be unreasonable."

"Unreasonable?" He scoffed. "That's your department with your snapping wings and flashing swords."

"We have no time for this." She caught his arm.

Tigo twitched free. Stumbled back.

Her eyes were pleading. "The Second Sundering is coming, and Tigo—"

"Leave him be," AO rumbled. "Too long have men lived beneath those armored boots and wings." He jutted his jaw. "Go. Leave. I will train him as you know I should—we train our own kind."

Her eyes widened. "No." She shifted to Tigo. "Listen, I know—"

Own kind? Disbelief tightened his irritation. He gawked at her, then the big guy. "What're you saying? That I'm . . ."

"Spit it out." AO almost seemed to mock him. "It's not going to hurt you."

"You can feel it already. The heavy weight of that identity," she asserted. "The Do'St left not only Deversoria and the Faa'Cris, but the way of the Ancient."

"You don't know what you're talking about," AO growled.

Jez's mockery and cynicism fled. "*This* is why I didn't tell you, Tigo. I do not want you to become him—them."

"It wasn't your choice, Rejeztia," AO said.

Heavy weight, yeah. Definitely. But— "You knew?" His mind was going to explode. Blow gray matter all over this dead planet. "You knew I was . . ." He eyeballed the big guy. "Dosed?"

"Do'St," AO corrected and touched his neck. "Say it from the back of the throat."

"I don't scuzzing care how you say it," Tigo balked, looking at the big guy. "You want me to turn against her because she lied to me. But whether by manipulation or omission, you are guilty of the same. Right?"

Gray eyes burned.

"Thought so."

"Our legacy is not one we easily or lightly announce. To many, it is a curse. Reprehensible. We cowered beneath it for many a century, but finally broke free of the condemnation. Accepted what we are. Used it, strengthened it. To us, it means one more chance to become what we were designed to be."

"And what is that?" Jez railed. "A race absorbed with power?"

AO growled—audibly. Like a diabolus.

Drawing a breath, Jez shook her head. "Right now there are far greater things to address. Marco is returned. The Draegis are coming. Xisya is deepening her tendrils in Symmachia. We are about to face the biggest battle in our existence—an extinction-level event. The only question is who will win. Are we going to kill each other over petty differences and let *them* be the last ones standing?"

"You do well for nearly eight months, Your Majesty."

"What is happening within me has little to do with my efforts." Isaura threaded her arms through her overcloak, shivering away the chill that had shrouded her during the pharmakeia's examination.

"I think you are mistaken, my lady. You see, it is well-known the babe responds to the emotional state of the mother, so your joy—or sadness—will directly affect the child." The wizened man gave her a smile, then started for the door. "I shall return in a fortnight, and thereafter, each sabbaton."

"So often?"

"The closer to the heir's arrival, the more attentive we must be, in case this one is impatient."

Wondering if Aeliana would be, Isaura hugged her belly. A portion of her wished it so. She would see the babe. Look into her little face and see which features were borrowed from Dusan, which from her.

"I had thought the medora was to be in attendance today," the pharmakeia said somberly as he caught the knob.

Isaura had become a master at deflecting barbs over his absence during his captivity. "It was his intention, but well you can imagine the stressors on our sovereign in this time, what with the skycrawlers prowling for yet another opportunity to attack."

Gray-haired yet straight-backed, the pharmakeia clucked his tongue. "Indeed, these are strange times. Never had I thought to see such things in our skies. Hard have I tried to explain to my grandson what is happening." Another cluck. "No easy task that."

"I would imagine not, so you can fathom the task set before Medora Marco." She smoothed a hand over her gown and belly, still feeling a bit undressed before the pharmakeia. "He will be with us next time."

He bowed his head. "Of course, Majesty." With that, he left.

As the door shut behind him, she slumped against the mattress. Did her best to bury the hurt. Dusan had promised to come, to be with her for this visit, but he had been overly distracted since the Symmachians were managing to slip fighters into the gaps that were increasing with time. She knew his heart—knew he wanted to protect them. Likely would take to the skies in a ship. He did so love to fly. Yet he remained here. With her.

Mayhap not *with* her. But within these walls. Afraid to leave her. *Oh Ladies, he is . . . tormented. I know not what to do or say. Please, help me.*

"You are well, my lady? The pharmak—"

"Well." Brushing away the tears, Isaura smiled at Kita as an idea came to her. "We are both well. Thank you." Would it work? Aye, it would. "I beg your pardon, but I must speak with Dusan."

Kita inclined her head. "Of course."

Isaura left the bedchamber and crossed the adjoining room, feeling Kaveh and Theilig fall in step with her. "Same place?"

"Aye."

"Has he broken his fast?"

"Not to our knowledge, Majesty."

Oh, Dusan . . . She lifted her skirts and climbed the stairs to the upper level. "Kaveh, have the sergii deliver a tray to the gathering room. He will need to eat."

"At once." Kaveh pivoted and hustled back down the stairs.

"Theilig, find Elder Mavridis. Have the medora's ship readied."

Theilig's gaze snapped to hers as they trod the hewn stone steps. "Majesty?"

"What few ailments I have had, stuttering was not among them." She slid her gaze to the intelligent, middle-aged regia.

"No. Of course not." His gaze drifted down, then slowly rose again. "But the medora—"

She stopped and faced him. "Well I understand that our medora has returned and it is *his* voice that holds final say. However, I am still kyria and have made plain my wishes." What was this, so odd coming from this man? "Never have you so consistently questioned me as you do now. Is it because I am but a woman—"

"Nay!" He blanched and yanked his gaze down, contrite. "I beg your mercy. It is merely . . . We lost him once, and I would not have it happen again. This time, with permanence."

"Aye," Isaura agreed wearily. "Neither would I. It is why I go to him now. Why I insist that his ship be readied."

"I . . . I do not understand, Majesty."

She gave a longsuffering sigh. "Few men do." She shook her head, then laughed at the mortification that twisted his dark blond beard. "Oh, Sir Theilig. You are an easy mark." Her laughter grew fuller. "You would do well to bind and steady that irascible spirit within you."

He tripped over the last step. Cracked his shin.

It really was too much fun, distracting him so easily. Laughing, she hopped up the last step to the royal residence that lay largely in ruin.

The small hall was attended by Ramirus and Ulixes, who held casual but alert stances along the marble floor that now ended rather abruptly in a gaping maw that had once been the solar. Ceiling gone, the chambers she had shared with Dusan lay open to the elements. At the far edge, where the balcony would have been, stood a medora just as broken as the walls piled in heaps around him.

Hands at her side, she admired the view. Though he had lost weight, Dusan was still athletically built and strong. The scar at the base of his neck was visible. He said it would not heal like the others had because it was some type of port that was of a more permanent nature. That many skycrawling soldiers had them to assist in flying and using mechanized suits.

Whatever that meant. It was not just the scars that had changed Dusan. It was something deeper, something he seemed to be nursing. Hands in front of him, he held his right forearm, and it then struck her that he had rarely removed his vambrace since returning and wore long sleeves when he did.

"It is good to hear your laugh."

My laugh? Ah, yes—with Theilig. Isaura glided toward him. "It is good to laugh. There was little while you were away." She reached him and enjoyed the way his hand slid easily and possessively around her waist, tucking her close. "The pharmakeia asked after you."

Dusan flinched. Groaned. "I missed the appointment."

Head against his shoulder, she sighed. "Aye, but little happened save listening to the heartbeat."

"A sound I would have been glad to hear. Forgive me." He squinted out at the waters and the lands to the north, then back to the south, a view afforded thanks to the heavy damage wrought by the bombardments. "Mavridis said Symmachia targeted this part of the castle to kill me."

"Aye?"

"I disagree."

Isaura frowned. "How so?"

"I was not here and Symmachia knew that—and also that you were here, alone." He firmed his touch on her back. "Which means they intended to kill you. All while I was lightyears away and could do nothing to protect you."

Her heart drummed a little faster. "Me? Why?"

His icy gaze struck hers. "Because of our daughter."

Now, she scowled and placed a hand on her belly. "What of her? What has Aeliana done to deserve—"

"Symmachia is merely the puppet. The string puller is that creature, Xisya. She wanted—wants Aeliana dead."

"Why?"

"It is but a guess, but I believe Aeliana to be powerful. In what way, I cannot know. What I do know is that she sent her Signature to guide me home, and that may have been reason enough for Xisya."

"I agree she is powerful—if her kicks are any indication," Isaura said with a laugh. She looked around the ruins of their chambers, then to the ocean pitching itself violently against the cliffs of Kardia far below. "What draws you here?"

It took a moment for him to answer. "That anger you feel?" He nodded and shifted his gaze back to the ship-dotted sky. "That is what brings me here, the reek that fouls the air, because it is not just you. It is the people of Kardia, of Lampros City—Kalonica. All of Drosero. They are angry. And powerless." He paced from her, and she could see the mirror of the sea's rage in his movements. His hand again went to where the brand lay beneath his jerkin. "It forces me to consider things I would never before have entertained."

That scared her most.

Isaura swung in front of him and framed his face, knowing her time to divert his attention and anger was short. "I know well how it torments you. And it is my belief that you are bored—"

"I am where I belong."

Sweet words kindly meant. "Above all, I think you would be with the pilots . . ." Oh, it was so hard to speak, but she managed a smile. "Yet you will not go."

His expression sharpened. "I will never again leave you."

More sweet words. "When you come up here and I am in the lower reaches, have you *left* me?"

"You mistake my meaning," he said around a scowl. "If I am yet here in Kardia, at least I can—"

"Do nothing," she said resolutely. "Dusan, if they bombard the house again and the stones fall just right . . ." She shook her head. "No man can do a thing to stop them from falling where they will."

Anger tightened his lips.

"I mean no offense and imply no ill regarding your incredible abilities as a Kynigos or determination as my bound, but sitting here, staring out at the sea . . ."

"What?"

She ached for him to understand, to hear her counsel, but the anger seemed to have a firm root in his thoughts. "It is not good for you, Dusan."

Hesitation skipped across his olive complexion, twitched the beard around his mouth, then flashed out of sight. "Absurd."

"Aye," she said with an arched eyebrow. "You are definitely that."

"Do not mock me, Isa." He turned away, and that hurt more than anything.

She saw this happening a lot of late. "Never would I mock you when you are the best man I have ever known. But no matter the crown on your head or the ring on your finger, you are a hunter at heart and must be hunting."

His gaze rocked to her. "I am no longer a Kynigos."

"You will always be a Kynigos," she argued. "And I think it is time for you to stop climbing the walls—and I mean that literally, like yestereve when you scaled the bailey gatehouse."

Chagrined, he gave her a sidelong look. "You saw that?"

"And the time you hopped up the turret that was in shambles from the last attack."

"The loose stones provided a greater challenge." He was like a boy in his first year of training.

"So, I would ask"—mercies it hurt to do so, scared her—"before you make a target of yourself, before you end up beneath a pile of stones, take to the skies. Search for the enemy. Protect our people and our home—our child—the way you were designed to. Not here, petulant and moping in the shadows."

He straightened. Considered her. "What are you saying?"

"Go fly your ship, Uchuvchi."

Brow rippling, Marco took a step in her direction. "You are sure?" Another step, then faltered. "No." Again he faced the seas. "Too risky. I must stay—"

"Risk is everywhere, Dusan. You were not made to be contained within walls and ceilings. You are made for air and hunting."

He tilted his head to the side and craned his neck. Shoulders rolled forward.

Isaura laughed. He need not be so dramatic in anak'ing her. "Tell me, Kynigos, do I speak true?"

With a softer expression now, he cupped her face. "No truer lady has ever spoken."

"Go," she whispered. "Fly. Let me see that giddy hunter once more."

Dusan kissed her. "Giddy?"

"In Jherako when you saw those ships—most definitely giddy. Make no attempt to deny it."

He grinned. "I might have been a little happy."

"Then I would love to see what elation looks like."

Dusan angled his head and caught her mouth with his, deepening the kiss even as it started. He lifted his head and peered at her with hooded eyes. "You already have. In Jherako."

"The ships—"

"*Not* the ships." Meaning danced in his pale eyes. "Another, much more intimate moment."

Heat seared her cheeks. She gave him a playful push.

"Kyria Isaura."

At the intrusion of the new voice, she jerked out of Dusan's playfulness. "Aye, Sir Theilig?"

"They have readied the ship."

Dusan started. Looked from the onetime army commander back to her. "Wha—"

"Go, fly your scout, Kynigos. Protect your people."

MOUNTAIN FLIGHT BASE, KALONICA, DROSERO

Conflict thrummed through Marco as he signaled flight control his readiness. Excitement kneaded every tense muscle, begging for release. But it brought back the *Prevenire*, being trapped in the hull. At least on the *Qirolicha*, he'd been in a large open space. Here, he was nearly as plugged in as he had been on the *Prev.*

"Aetos Actual, you are cleared for takeoff."

Marco flipped a few more switches and dialed in the target—he wanted to get closer to the Draegis net watching over them. With all the skill and familiarity he'd gained flying a scout as a Kynigos, he tapped the pad on his left and felt the Interceptor shift from its landing supports—with just the slightest of wobbles—and hover off the ground as said supports retracted. Grinning, he slid the thruster control with a gentle touch.

The Interceptor surged forward, thwapping Marco back against the headrest. He barked a laugh, thrilled with the responsiveness of the newer craft. His scout always had a bit of lag to her, but this beauty . . . "Incredible."

"Aetos Actual," the tower comm'd, "good liftoff. The sky is yours."

Marco whipped the craft up, feeling the pull of gravity as he shot toward the atmosphere. He'd have an escort—the two most adept pilots.

"Aetos Actual," another voice intruded in his headset. "Might go easy on that trajectory. Interceptors are known for maneuverability and speed, but they need to be finessed."

Chagrined at the warning, Marco eased off the thrusters, savoring the high vantage and its view. "Good copy, base," he said, his fun dimmed only a little. "Appreciate the tip."

"Thought your bird falling from the sky wouldn't be a good omen."

Marco laughed. "Agreed." He leveled off and headed back toward Lampros City from the mountains, where some of the ships had been relocated. When he'd visited Vorn eight months ago, there had been only fifty ships on the planet. Now, Kalonica alone had fifty. A decision Isaura authorized with the Council's approval after Jherako was attacked. It dispersed Drosero's fledgling fleet across the planet, forcing Symmachia to deal with multiple targets rather than one.

Feeling more hopeful than he had in months, he angled toward the castle, determined to do a flyover, let Isaura see his ship, know he was grateful.

I do not deserve her.

She had seen through his gruff manners and terse words, understood that being grounded, being unable to assist in the effort to defend Kalonica and the planet was eating at him. At his adunatos.

"Aetos Actual, this is Aetos Two on your right wing."

Marco glanced to starboard to where another bird came even, the sun glinting off the slick surface of his Interceptor.

"Command wants me to help you get familiar with the weapons. First, we'll bring up the targeting array. Believe they showed that to you on the ground."

"Copy that," Marco said, remembering the instructions and activating the array. A blue haze warbled into place over his vision, making him tense. Reminding him of—

"Good," Aetos Two comm'd. "It's as simple as point and shoot."

Marco grunted. Knew anything said to be *that* simple wasn't. "Copy."

"The ship's system will guide you through target acquisition and neutralization. Really is that simple."

"You aren't from Kalonica," Marco said, watching as a red blip appeared on the shimmering grid.

"*Target identified*," came the automated voice from his ship. "*Firing Solution Ready.*"

"No, sir, I'm not. Can you see the target?"

"Yes."

"*Fire in three . . .*"

"You'll have to do it manually, sir. Safety precaution."

"Safety?" Marco balked.

". . . *two . . . one. Fire. Fire. Fire.*"

Marco depressed the button. Once. Twice. It seemed like overkill. He hit it a third time. Watched as something in the distant sky blew up. "What did I just destroy?"

"Practice target, sir. Nothing to worry about."

"Except debris falling from the sky."

"No debris. Disintegrates upon impact."

Marco squinted through the targeting screen even as it vanished.

"*Threat neutralized*," the system intoned.

"Great job, sir."

Marco snickered, somehow disappointed with how automated this was. "I think my unborn daughter could've done that."

A chuckle carried through the comms. "I'm sure the princess could, sir."

Princess. He hadn't really thought of her like that. "You kiss up this much regularly, Aetos Two?"

"No, sir," came the reply. "Toned it down just for you."

Marco couldn't help but laugh.

"Didn't want to come across too strong on our first date."

More laughter. "Where are you from, Two?"

"Thyrolia, sir."

With a grunt, Marco glanced to port again. Saw the other Interceptor peel off and dart away. Thyrolia. Baytu Smirlet and her husband, Jubbah, were

Thyrolians. He'd webbed Jubbah, whom he'd later discovered was the trader supplying Vorn with ships. "What are you doing defending Drosero, Two?"

"If they succeed here, they'll be unrepentant and unrelenting across the Quadrants. Can't let that happen, sir. Not if I can help it."

"Copy that."

TSC *MACEDON*

Hands planted on his belt, Captain Zoltan Baric stared at the static maps hanging between him and the Command deck.

"He is near," Xisya hissed into the air as she bounce-glided toward him. "I sense the Progenitor."

"Because he's on the scuzzing planet," Baric bit out. He'd followed this creature, listened to her, allowed her to alter his genetic makeup in ways that were painful and cruel. Little benefit could be seen so far. At least not for him. For her . . . well, the pull of her will against his made for a constant struggle. "Which does us no good since we can't get past these ships."

"They will fall," she shrilled. "They all fall."

"But they haven't, and we're running out of time."

"No," Xisya crooned. "Time is ours. Find him. He is there, closer than before."

Baric clenched his jaw. Looked to the lieutenant sitting at radar. "Anything new?" It was a waste of a question.

Brown eyes scanned the arrays. "No, sir. They're running maneuvers again. Just—" She snapped her mouth shut. Sat up straighter. "Wait . . ." She leaned in, her gaze darting over the dots and readouts.

"What?"

"I . . . sir—there's three."

"So?"

"They fly in pairs, sir. All the time." She indicated to the panel. "There are three here, two hanging back from the other." Her gaze came to his. "An escort."

Adrenaline charged through Baric's veins. "For a king." He snapped his fingers and grabbed the comms mic. "WEPS, firing solution now. Straight through that hole in the net. Grid One One Seven Mark Five Two Four."

"Copy, Captain. One One Seven Mark Five Two Four."

Baric held his breath. Was it possible? After the weeks of standoff since Marco had come through the Sentinel, destroyed the Sentinel, then bolted back to his Quadrant and taken shelter beneath this out-of-nowhere alien armada . . . had they finally found a way to destroy Marco and his impudent little planet?

"Target locked."

"Send it."

SOMEWHERE OVER KALONICA, DROSERO

"Aetos Actual, return to base."

Before returning, Marco veered up and to port, eyeing the Uchuvchi array, the pilots struggling to keep the net working. A hole was dripping Symmachians into their atmosphere, but it was too small and the pilots too effective for many ships to tempt their firepower. A few had made it through, leaving the dirty work to the Droseran armada. Skimming the underbelly of the Uchuvchi net, which sat on the other side of the atmospheric barrier, Marco eyed the ships. Marveled at the unique ability of the Uchuvchi to drone pilot those ships from the *Qirolicha*.

"Aetos Actual, RTB. Now!"

"Copy that." Marco brought the Interceptor around.

"*Unrecognized ordnance inbound*," the ship announced.

Marco sniffed. Keyed his mic. "We ended the instruction demo already. I'm—"

"*Incoming fire.*"

What?

"*Target solution not found. Impact in ten . . .*"

Was the ship malfunctioning? "Two, what—"

"Get out of there, sir! Now!"

Reek! Marco peeled away from the net and dove back toward the planet.

The shrieking of the Interceptor's alarms hammered his head.

"Aetos Actual, we have inbound enemy—"

Pulse pounding, Marco focused on the threat. No—*escaping* said threat.

"REATTEMPTING TARGETING SOLUTION," the ship droned. "UNSUCCESSFUL."

Though Marco maneuvered and tried to avoid the blast, the screaming alarms warned him he was failing. He pushed the throttle full forward and dove. Felt in his head the drop, then dialed it back, the ship shuddering but pulling it off even as gravity fought them.

"IMPACT IN FIVE . . . FOUR . . ."

The claxon was getting faster. The *beep beep beep beep* so close together, it almost sounded as one.

Out of the blue, he remembered his training. To relax into the hunt. To let training and instinct take over. He glided his hands to the control. Took a deep breath.

"THREE . . ."

Beepbeepbeepbeepbeep.

Banked hard right. Throttled down. Hard left.

Beep beep beep . . .

"RECALCULATING."

Bought a few seconds. Not much, but maybe enough to get out over the ocean. Avoid fiery debris hitting a city or village.

Beepbeepbeepbeep

Reek! Where had it come from? How had it reacquired so fast?

"IMPACT IMMINENT."

"Dusan," came Isa's soft, gentle—but worried—voice in his head.

"I love you," he replied, the only thing he wanted her to know as death came for him once more. "Forgive—"

Gray blurred in front of him. His ship auto-adjusted to avoid the collision. Two! "No!"

Light exploded. Two's Interceptor erupted into a ball of fire. The concussion slammed into Marco's ship as he howled another shout. Wanted to scream more, but he focused on keeping the craft from crashing. From wasting the sacrifice Two had made.

In a spin, system panels flickering, Marco struggled to bring the bird out of it. The force of the out-of-control Interceptor whipped his brain to mush. Somewhere in the din, fighting against the ship to regain flight control, he heard someone announcing Aetos Two down.

Vaqar, please . . .

Should have stayed on the ground. With Isaura. Maybe he deserved to die for leaving her.

The ship came out of it. He pulled up and got his bearings. Set the autopilot control, the Interceptor redirecting them back toward base. "Altas base," he huffed, head woozy. "Aetos Actual . . . RTB."

Eyes stinging, all too aware of how Two had sacrificed himself for him, Marco felt the rage of righteousness. "Augh!" He struck the canopy with the ball of his fist. He was sick of the Symmachians ripping away lives.

"Dusan."

The sweetness of Isa's dreamspace voice felt as a gong. She would want him to promise to never fly again. Want him to stay there with her. And how could he refuse when she had endured so much, carried such a burden for him, carried his child . . .

He flicked up his helmet visor as the ship descended into the heavily treed mountain. Pinched the bridge of his nose.

"Dusan, please."

"They must pay, Isa. And I must make them do it."

Bittersweet air swept his receptors. *"Aye."* It was definitive.

Did she understand what that meant? What the future held? For him? For her? It gutted him, thinking about it.

"I just . . . needed to hear your voice."

"And I yours." Ancient will he should never lose it.

The white halo around the bulkheads went blue.

Domitas lifted his gaze from the tactical array even as a curvy, brilliant form blurred into focus and she activated the secure privacy shield. His heart thudded a little faster, as it always did at her arrival. "I could get used to this."

Renette's smile said she had come not for him but with intent. "Have you recruited the Hirakyn yet?"

He could not keep the irritation from his voice. "You could have asked via Lifespeech."

"Xisya got too close to killing Marco, so the timeline is advanced."

"Aye, Baric was unrepentant about defying my orders not to fire," Domitas growled, "and your kind will not leave the stone walls of Deversoria." He gave her a grim nod. "Do not think to instruct me on what I have done for centuries."

"And what is that?"

"Protect *my* kind. Going to the planet will tip my hand. Put the others at risk." He had not revealed himself to any being in over a century, and he did not relish the thought of yet again being named a diabolus. "Unlike the Faa'Cris, Do'St do not enjoy controlling men with our appearance."

She rolled her eyes. "Crey is integral, but the situation around him is tenuous, and he is being defiant. Rejeztia charged him with sending the raiders north, yet now he has returned to his palace and squanders time."

"I am well aware, Renette."

She eyed him speculatively but stopped short of arguing. "Go to him, Dom. He's too important to lose."

He sighed. "I was just about to wave him."

"Symmachia will intercept any such communiqué, and it will expose you both. With Krissos here, you can be sure he has spies as well as hidden cameras. Shield yourself and go."

Blast all to the Voids! He knew she was right but hated that she was here, ordering him about.

She glided forward. "No order, Dom. An *urge*. Please."

Tapping the array, he sent a pulse to the device in the palace, letting Crey know a message had come through. There wasn't a message, but there would be . . . the 1.89-meter messenger. "If I didn't love you so much . . ."

Renette came to his side as he leaned over the console and laced her arms around his neck. Kissed his cheek. "This is not just for me, Dom."

He grunted. Slid a hand around her waist as he straightened. "No, it was for me," he said and stole a kiss. "Now, to blow this Hirakyn's mind."

Once the feed showed Crey closing himself into the secure room, Domitas gave Renette one last kiss and folded himself across time and space. Before he allowed himself to be seen downworld, he lifted a device from his pocket and set off a small electrical disruptor to prevent anyone with tech from seeing his presence in the Hirakyn palace. Domitas stepped from the fold.

With a shout, the rex leapt backward, eyes bulging as he took in Domitas's span. "Blood and boil!" His normally tanned face went white as plaster. "Diabolus!"

Growling at the term, Domitas held a hand to the doors of the saferoom, which rattled beneath shouts to know if the rex was okay. "Answer them."

"A-Admiral?" Crey faltered. "Ye-yeh. Of course." He looked to the doors, but his gaze returned to Domitas as he barked at his guards. "Leave off. I need time to think." The wide-eyed rex gaped at him. "What . . . are yeh?"

Not answering would create a problem between them. A needling annoyance. "I am Do'St, the counterpart to the Faa'Cris."

"B-but yer . . . a man."

"Quite."

"And Symmachian."

"A suit I wear to pass through time." He lifted a hand. "Our time is short. I have come because I would have you as an ally, Crey of Greyedge. Marco needs your efforts here."

"Marco and I are already allies."

"Are you?" Dom challenged. "What of the charge laid at your feet to push the raiders north?"

"I . . . I returned just last eve." Crey smoothed a hand over his face.

"Your people fall to the Irukandji and—"

"Because of weapons and Ladies-know-what-else yeh Symmachians gave the raiders."

"And now the power lies in your hand to change that. Will you hide here or act?"

Crey angled his head and narrowed his eyes. "If yeh are this thing"—he motioned up and down at Domitas—"then why in the world did yeh let it come to this? Why do yeh not do more?"

Because we were resistant? Tired of dealing with humans and Faa'Cris? Because we wanted to just . . . exist. Because we grew comfortable and complacent, too focused on self, *rather than our purpose in this existence. Because, as much as the Do'St resented the Faa'Cris, the Ladies had it right—this was not their war.*

Of one guilt, he could be absolved. "Although I've spent the last three decades working my way up the military ranks, there are things that slipped past my awareness. By the time I realized what was happening within our research departments," Domitas conceded, thinking of Baric and the Corrupt, "I was too late. The enemy I sought to thwart already had a foothold." He had too long ignored the cries of Renette. But then, she had always been one to over-worry, so he had not thought much of it.

"No, you had not thought. Period," came her melodic but stern correction.

"I concede my laxity. Condemn me not." He already condemned himself.

"Theule granted a stronghold here in Hirakys to Symmachia. You have taken the throne, but you must use your army to push them from your lands so that you can stand with Marco when the time comes."

"What time?"

Domitas inclined his head. "You will know."

"Listen, after that display of yer wings and all, I fear to say no to yeh," Crey said, "but we are in dire straits here." He stabbed a finger to the west. "Long have the Irukandji been banished to the hills, and yeh spoke of the raiders and troops, but have yeh seen what is happening there?" He shook his head. "It is a *city*—an entire new empire. They have organized and set up government. Driving them north is not as easy as mounting our horses and herding them off our land."

"Government." That was news to Domitas. Who had implemented that plan? What was happening that he hadn't been informed? How had he again been caught unaware, when he had worked so hard to have an eye across all of the TSC? Granted, he was tasked with the fleet. Krissos . . . Hmm. He'd need to dig around. "You are sure?"

"No doubt." Crey nodded. "How yer people are managing to reason with raiders whose minds are lost is beyond me—your Rejeztia said something about the water—but it is reshaping the entire infrastructure of this continent."

"They use a drug. Symmachian forces on the ground have been dosing them with a counteragent in the water. She told you this. That is why you were instructed to drive them north. Remove their access to the contaminated water, and you remove their reason. What is left behind will not harm those not crippled by the Lady's mark."

"When yeh brought the prince here"—Crey's eyes clouded—"yeh said Symmachia had no interest in overtaking our world."

A lie, he must admit, though only lately, with the revelation about this elefthanite energy source, had he learned just how big a lie it was. "I said what was necessary to convince you to take the prince and to buy your loyalty."

Crey studied him. Shrugged. "That is it? Just like that? How am I to trust yeh?"

Domitas gritted his teeth. "Would you prefer I placate and pander? Would that make it easier to digest?"

"He is not a recruit or one of your officers, Dom. Go easy."

"Go back to Shadowsedge, Renette. I can handle this."

"Clearly."

Stalking closer to the rex, who stood at least a span shorter, Domitas craned his neck toward him. "You are not the only king on this chessboard, Rex Crey. Any player can be . . . removed."

The man's eyes widened in understanding.

"As the admiral of the Symmachian fleet, I must carefully weigh and consider every move with every pawn, knight, bishop, rook, queen, and king." He let the snapped cadence of those pieces crackle between them for a tick. "You are one of many. The role I play is dark and daunting, but I am up to the task because I know the endgame. And it will not be gained with pretty words and ego stroking."

He shouldered in, let his span unfurl and gust air into the rex's face, enjoying it when the Hirakyn sucked in a breath. "What of you, Crey of Greyedge? Are *you* up to the game? Or do you yet again choose your selfish endeavors?"

Crey worked his jaw. "Darius—" Eyes wide, he rubbed a hand over his head. "That's why yeh brought him." Awe speared his expression. "Yeh . . . *Yeh* wanted him here. To . . . heal me."

"Aye, to readjust your foot to the path you originally chose." Domitas shifted away and let his gray-black wings fan out. "A Lady recently said you were too important to lose."

"The same one who met me in the raider camp?"

"No, but having two of our kind appear to you should force careful consideration about refusing this path. There is no easy way, no guarantee of life in either course. But how would you be remembered? As one who hid on his gilt throne, or one who gave all for the people he ruled?"

Again clenching his jaw, he slowly nodded. "With honor."

Renette appeared in the in-between. *"We need to talk."*

"Give me a few minutes and meet me in my quarters." To Crey he gave a long look, then extended a device. "I support your choice. If you have need of me, press that." He folded from the room.

Back on his ship, Domitas knew the time stamps would not record him as having left. They'd show no differentiation. He flicked off the screens and exited his office.

"Admiral on the bridge!" the XO barked, bringing the bridge crew to attention.

"As you were." Domitas went to the array and eyed the latest intel. "What do we know?"

"A handful of Interceptors have slipped through. Three destroyed, sir." With practiced flicks of his wrist, Dimar brought up reports and intel. "They're running sorties, but those that made it through are stranded."

"Send them coordinates for one of the camps." Domitas nodded. "I want the Two-one-eight ready to drop on my word."

"Understood, sir."

He clapped him on the shoulder. "You have the con, Dimar."

"XO has the con."

He exited and made his way down the concourse to his quarters, which were notably large and nicer than anything the other officers, crew, or staff of the *Cronus* were afforded. Entering, he didn't bother with the lights and went straight for the anchored bar. Tugged open a door and removed a shatterproof bottle containing amber liquid. He poured some into a glass.

Arms slid around him from behind, warmth seeping into his spine as a minty trill coated the air—the same fragrance that also said she'd blinked out the tech. "You always were so grumpy and stern."

He set his arm over hers as he took a swig. "And you too outspoken and insistent." He cocked his head in concession. "But compassionate."

"Mm," she said, her cheek to his back. "Tigo would disagree on that last one."

He stored the liquor and faced her, wrapping his arms around her. "It was his way to disagree with us about everything." He smiled at the Faa'Cris who had decimated his will against marrying. "Hello, wife."

"Hello, husband."

"I assume they are not happy you have come again."

"I did not ask," she said with a shrug. "It has been too long . . ."

"I agree." He traced her face. Kissing her. Diving into that kiss. Later, as they lay abed, he stroked her shoulder. "They are excluding me from intel and directives regarding Drosero."

She lifted her head and rested her chin on his chest. "TSC? If they're excluding you, how do you know?"

Domitas stared at the ceiling in the darkened quarters. "Crey said the Irukandji have established a city and government with Symmachian help."

Now, Renette sat up, hugging the sheet to herself. "That is a problem."

"I begin to wonder if Drosero has a prayer to win this war."

"How could you not know about this? You have satellites—"

He groaned. "Let us not fight—"

"But you are tasked—"

"And it is *your* planet, where the Ladies have anchored for centuries. How can *you* not sense it?" He propped himself up on his elbow. "Irukandji are carved, craven creatures. Eleftheria marked them—that darkness has a very distinct fetor. How has it been missed?"

She hung her head, and it tugged at his heart. Little moved him, mastered him. Except Renette. And right now, her expressive violet eyes were clouded with uncertainty. "I do not know. Only one answer comes to mind: that creature, Xisya. I sense she is closer than ever before to Shadowsedge, but . . . Dom, *the* war is upon us. *They* are returning and there is so much to orchestrate, so many things that must go right. The odds are . . . unfathomable." She rubbed her forehead. "Every time I think we are gaining ground, I look up and we are leagues away from where we should be. It feels . . . hopeless."

"How can you say that? Of course it—we must. There is no 'trying.' If we do not, we become extinct."

"He . . . he is well."

At the reassurance of the medora's safety, Kersei smiled, uncertain to what end the kyria had come to visit. The close call in the skies had been a sabbaton past. "Of course he is."

Isaura gave her a wan smile and swallowed. Set a hand to her belly where Marco's child grew. "I . . ." She moved to a chair and perched on its edge. "I fear it, every time he walks out the door. Every time we are apart."

"That he would die?"

Green eyes rose to her. "Or that I will." She shuddered.

Startled, Kersei considered her and those haunting words. "I pray none of us are removed from this life any time soon." Yet, she must admit—never would she forget the bells pealing throughout Kardia. Word flying through stone and shadow of his ship being targeted.

"I am sure his close call must have been frightening for you." Sitting on the thick rug in her chambers, she lifted Xylander and nestled him on her lap.

"Terrifying," Isaura admitted. "Had it not been for the dreamscape, I would have run all the way up the mountain myself."

"Not in your condition," Kersei said with a laugh, then frowned. "Dreamscape?"

Isaura smiled, quiet settling into the room. "I discovered one day while he was yet gone that I could . . . hear him. At first, I thought myself merely dreaming or imagining it. I thought myself going mad as my ma'ma had, but then he answered my questions!"

"That sounds like Lifespeech—a Faa'Cris gift." Kersei bounced Xylander in her arms, watching the winsome beauty. "I wonder how you were able to access it."

"Dusan believes it was because of our baby."

"Truly, it would take a unique, powerful bond to access Lifespeech. I am glad you have it."

A nervous smile danced on her lips. "An unexpected gift to be sure."

What did she want? Why had Isaura come to her? Kersei had no doubt of what Marco thought of her, though she did not deserve his censure. Was the kyria here to dole out more?

"I would talk with you . . ." Isaura lowered herself to the floor beside her, sliding a finger into Xylander's fist, drawing his blue-eyed gaze.

He locked onto her, eager as he tried to pull her finger to his mouth. Gave her a toothless grin.

"I come as a friend." There seemed a great weight on Isaura's mind—and shoulders, which drooped beneath the silk and gossamer bodice—something heavy weighting her eyes. A lingering sadness. "A friend of our medora."

"Considering his reproof, I fear you may be in the wrong rooms."

"I am not." Defiance flushed through Isaura's eyes. "Though he is medora and his words require no explanation, I would perhaps . . . fill in some gaps." Seated on the rug, she ran her hand over Xylander's sandy blond hair. "Our children are cousins, and I hope they will be friends." She met Kersei's gaze. "Great friends."

"I as well." Unless Marco made good on his threat to banish her.

"I pray"—there again rose that specter of grief through the kyria's delicate features—"he will watch out for Aeliana."

Who was that? "Ael—" Kersei gasped, looking to the kyria's round belly. Kersei angled her head. Knew Marco had detected the baby would be a girl. "A girl! Is that what you will call her?"

"While Dusan was yet gone, the Lady told me that would be her name. We are agreed that we love it."

"A very pretty name for no doubt a rare beauty."

With a faltering smile, Isaura worried the lace trim on her sleeve. "Shortly after Dusan returned, we discussed certain matters. It was then we . . ." She adjusted herself. "It is my hope that you would agree to be Aeliana's Benefactress."

Kersei started. They had not exactly been friends, and to bear such a title was one of the greatest honors in the realm, as she would be guardian over the medora's daughter. Over the princess. "I . . ."

"I realize it is a great duty and responsibility to bear such a burden, however, it is not without benefits. Not only would it ensure Aeliana will have a woman to guide her, protect her interests, but it would also secure your future, as you would need to remain close enough to watch over her." Her mannerisms seemed nervous and jittery. "In earnest, it would please me greatly if you would agree. Despite our rocky encounters."

Shocked that such a topic was discussed, Kersei gathered her wits. "I would be honored, my kyria. Consider it done."

Isaura's features brightened beneath a smile and relief. As if some weight had lifted from her shoulders. "You do me a great service."

"This is all well and good, but you will not need me to fulfill such a role. I am sure of it." At each turn Kersei had treated this beauty poorly, yet Isaura always came back the victor. "Isaura the Gracious."

"What?"

"That is what you should be known as. Ever have I seen you offer grace and be gracious when others—myself included—have been anything but."

"I do what anyone would do—"

Two sharp raps hit the door seconds before it flicked open and Myles barked, "Make way for Medora Marco."

"Oh!" Face brightened, Isaura kissed Xylander then began the arduous task of rising from the floor.

Marco entered like the storm that he was. He lit on Isaura struggling to her feet, losing her balance as her last trimester size made standing a challenge, and he rushed to assist. "Careful." He cupped her elbow. "You should not be—"

"I hoped for you to rescue me, and my scheme worked." Isaura took the hand he offered and leaned into him. "I am glad you are come. A moment ago, I told Kersei that we had agreed to ask her to be Aeliana's Benefactress, and she has consented." She flashed him a smile that rivaled the sun. "Is that not excellent?"

Hand at the kyria's elbow, he indicated to the door, where the aged onetime iereas waited, hands clasped before him, head down. "Ypiretis and I have need of your assistance."

Faltering, Isaura produced a practiced smile. "Of course." She inclined her head to Kersei, and sadness once more rimmed her green eyes. "Thank you for letting me have time with Xylander." She again swiped his mop of sandy blond hair and cheek. "A handsome Tyrannous with their blue eyes."

Marco's scowl darkened and struck Kersei. "Duchess. We beg your leave."

With a wistful smile, Isaura stepped around Marco, pressed her lips to Xylander's downy head, whispered something—was that a tear again?—and hurried from the room.

Holding her son closer and more than a little disconcerted with the kyria's obvious grief, Kersei stared after them. What was that about? Only then did she realize Marco yet stood near.

His eyes blazed. "It would do you good to realize the mercy she gallantly pours out regardless of the betrayals done her."

Heat scorched the back of her neck beneath yet another of his reproofs. "I am well aware—"

"Think beyond yourself. Do not again let the kyria sit on the floor."

"I—"

"I thought better of you once. Clearly, I was mistaken." Marco stalked from the room, his gaze never leaving the retreating form of his kyria. The exchange, his pointed words, destroyed any hope that he would ever turn his favor or friendship in her direction again.

"You are angry, Dusan?"

"You entrapped me, Isa."

Startled at the accusation, at the idea that he thought her capable of ever doing something underhanded, she had to fight the tears. Concern bit at the edge of her weariness. Isaura was so tired of it all—the fear, the conflict, the tension that ate up the air in the lower passages that felt more dungeon than home. "We agreed to name—"

"We *discussed* it—briefly," he countered. "Before anything can be—"

"Then you would change your mind?"

Dusan snapped his head down, lips taut, and exhaled heavily. "I did not say that."

"Mayhap not with your words."

Brooding, Dusan paced the length of the stone room that was his makeshift solar.

She knew he would not understand her dealings, the way she would prepare . . . but neither did she want to discuss what stirred within her. "I thought you and Ypiretis needed to speak with me."

Dusan ran a hand over his head. "He is coming." Did he miss having longer hair to hide those beautiful eyes? When a knock came at the door, he nodded to Kaveh and Theilig, who allowed the kindhearted iereas entrance. Lips still flat with irritation, Dusan resumed his pacing.

She ached for him, for the turmoil churning through him. Though he would not speak openly what tormented him, she could sense it as clearly as he could smell her Signature.

"I will return." Dusan strode out.

Isa deflated a little but kept up the mask of strength as she turned to Ypiretis. "You would speak with me?"

He shuffled forward and pointed to a chair. "May I, Your Majesty?"

"Of course." In truth, her aching back would be glad for the chair, so she joined him by the fire. "This must be urgent—"

"Urgent? No." He seemed chagrined.

"Pray, then why did he so hastily remove me from the duchess's quarters?"

Bushy eyebrows rose, then fell. "You are too intelligent to have asked that, my lady."

"Being overtired, I have not the heart for politicking."

"This is not about politics." He looked up through those thick brows at her. "This is about you."

"Me?" she balked.

He gave her a sympathetic smile. "Why did you name her Benefactress?"

How deftly he homed in on her machinations. "Dusan and I agreed it was a good choice, as she is the mother of Xylander, the only other heir." Yet she would defer, unwilling to discuss her motivations for any of the many pieces she was putting into play. "Why has he sent you? Is it to chastise me?"

Ypiretis swallowed his smile. "Aye, that was his intent, but I have another mission, Your Highness."

Dusan intended her to be reprimanded. It pained her, yet she would not be deterred in what she felt must be done, prepared.

"I have noticed certain . . . measures being put in place. Plans . . ." His muddy brown eyes held hers. "Preparations for your death."

Her heart jarred. How could he possibly know? She swallowed but said nothing.

"What makes you think that is your fate?"

Could she have an ally in this aged iereas? Would he betray her confidence and share the words she spoke with Dusan?

"What is said between us, stays between us."

Sensing a tendril of an alliance, Isaura chewed the inside of her lip. "Dusan's vision . . . Before we bound, he told me of a vision he had." It hurt to recall. Hurt to remember that she was not in it. "Of him and Kersei . . . with their . . .

sons." She lifted her jaw. "He told me he feared that vision meant my death. And in light of circumstances, I—" She swallowed again, her throat thick with emotion. "I do not know if it will come to pass, but I would prepare for it. Protect Aeliana, since daughters cannot rule and that vision—if true—shows Marco will have sons."

"It may not be my place to speak," he said quietly, "but I have become aware of a royal decree that has been given to the Council, declaring all heirs—sons and daughters—will be in the line of succession according to birth order."

Isaura blinked. "Truly?" Her hand was on her belly before she realized it. "Dusan did this?"

The door flew open and Dusan returned, head down, stride intent and decisive. Thoughts plagued his handsome face, twisting his brow into a knot.

"Why did you not share with me that you would change the line of succession?"

He stopped short, his frown deepening, before his gaze slammed into the iereas. "It was not for you to divulge."

Ypiretis dipped his head, unperturbed. "Forgive me."

"I did not want to do you injury, make you think that . . . after what I shared about the vision that I . . . that the writ . . ." Dusan huffed. "We are in an impossible war. If she survives and we do not, there will be no doubt of who takes the throne."

It was startling, a relief. No matter what happened to her, at least their daughter would be heir apparent. "Thank you for protecting Aeliana's future— as much as we can. Of course, I would have it that we both survive and live to see our daughter marry Vorn's son."

"If she wills it, so do I."

Plied by the softness of that answer, she stepped closer. "Do you think I will die in this war, Dusan?"

He looked down, his expression tormented. His hand slid to his brand arm. "I know not. In truth, my greater fear has been of my own demise. Regardless, what the future could be for our daughter . . . the thought of this slaughters me." His voice shook beneath the restrained emotion. "Failure feels very near and very . . . powerful."

"The outcome is not yours to decide, Dusan. That belongs to the Ancient alone."

His smile wavered. "Alas, despite our every effort, even if we survive it, I fear this war is designed to be one of torment." He sniffed. Nodded. "Perfectly but painfully true: it is a war of torment."

There were things he had given up on long ago: the hope of peace in the wastelands, seeing the raiders run into the Sea of Tribute, Marco rejecting warmed cordi, and . . . love. Deliontress had convinced him that any such notion was for the young and for those who . . . well, were not him.

Ixion strode the lower passages, somehow once more having taken the longer route, the route that led to a certain lady's quarters. The absurdity of it! She was nearly half his age. Yet she had endured more than people twice his age. Maturity and wisdom were gripped in her right hand tighter than the manriki he mastered.

Mnason played in the dimmed passage, a straw dummy a dozen paces from the door that stood open. The boy hopped up, feet shoulder-width apart. He wore a leather vest today. Where had he gotten that? Crisscrossing his back, a baldric with two sparring swords. Wood swords were a poor substitute and twice the weight of longblades. At least the boy would have a strong back when he graduated to steel. Why did he have yarn tied around his . . .

Ixion staved off a smile, realizing the boy had even tried to imitate the binding of his hair.

The seven-year-old should be out with the other children, playing in the bailey. Most his age—mayhap a mite older—attended the Kynigos housed in the walls, learning their tactics for scaling walls and skimming rooftops. But this lad . . .

Arm up, Mnason swung a manriki overhead.

"What is this?" Ixion demanded gruffly.

Mnason jerked, sending his weapon thunking into the wall seconds before Commander Theilig rounded the corner.

The broad-shouldered man startled. Widened his eyes.

Mnason cried out, distressed that he had nearly struck a regia.

"Shame." Ixion planted a hand on the boy's shoulder. "Truer aim and you could have delivered this regia of his head."

Theilig gave a mock scowl. "After my head are you, little master?"

"N-no! Sir." He stood stiff and straight. "A m-mistake. Elder Mavridis startled me."

"Ah, but see?" Ixion growled. "A good Stalker or regia is never distracted by the unexpected. Would you not agree, Commander?"

After a moment's hesitation, Theilig nodded. "Indeed." He shifted his attention back to Ixion. "Have you knowledge of Lady Kita's location at the moment?"

Something in Ixion twisted. Burned with venom that leached into his clipped reply. "Not here."

Theilig raised his brows and his hands, placating. Smiling. Did the man mock him?

"Nay, I am here." Entering the passage from another doorway, Kita pierced the tension. "Is there a problem?" Her voice was like honey and yet as effective as a knife to carve a path through this line he had drawn. Brown eyes considered him, then the regia.

Theilig smirked. "My lady, the kyria asks for you." He gave Ixion a long, knowing look. Taunting. Then snapped a nod, pivoted, and strode from the passage.

Kita's quizzical gaze followed him out. "What was that about?" She turned to him, shifting a pile of linens in her arms.

"Nothing." Except the regia mocking Ixion. "Too full of himself and the position he holds."

Kita eyed him and nodded, slipping into her chambers. "Ah, so much like you."

He scowled. Did she mock him, too? He had thought—

"Stop scowling. It makes you look formidable."

"That is not a bad thing," he said, stepping toward her.

"It is if everyone is afraid of you."

"That is not a bad thing either." He peered into eyes so like the amber warmth of the setting sun. "Unless it is you."

A flush rose through her cheeks. "I do not fear you, Ixion."

"Nor would I have it so." He touched that inflamed cheek and liked the way her eyes fluttered. Not even Deliontress had reacted so. "How do you fare this rise?"

She leaned into his touch, then cupped his hand there. "Better now."

His heart jammed against his ribs.

Her small hand smoothed over his hair and traced the plaits that hung down his neck and over his shoulders. A marvel that she never lingered on the scar that bisected his face. "I may be wrong, but you did sound . . . jealous just now."

Many times he had thought to take the kiss she seemed to want, to offer, but he would not sully his name or hers. No matter how much he wanted it. "What reason have I to be jealous of that pup?"

"He's younger."

"Youth is no replacement for wisdom."

"And handsome."

"You have called me that before."

She smiled demurely. "He is very strong."

"Have you seen me behead a raider?"

Now she grimaced. "Though you might find that . . . attractive, to a woman, it is gruesome."

"But it is strength."

She sighed. "So you will not admit to jealousy."

"Again I say, what reason have I to be? Is that where your attentions are set?"

Earnestness coated her features. "You know where my heart is. But you have also said you will not set petition."

"It is unwise. The war—"

"The war is an excuse, Ixion."

"The war could end us all."

"Mercies! All the more reason to—"

"Focus on a solution. A way to protect our world and people. To make sure you have a home after this—"

"My home burned to the ground with my husband."

He grimaced. "I meant Prokopios."

She shook her head. "I have no home there. The family I thought I had in Trachys is gone. There is naught left for me—I am alone."

"You are not." He shifted nearer, wanting to apply a salve to that wound. "But rush not into this so blindly, Kita. I am old."

"You are perfect."

Now his face heated. "You deserve better, younger—"

She surged upward on her toes. Pressed her lips to his.

Ixion froze. Rigid, he tried to extricate himself. Undo it. But . . . it was done. She had kissed him. Honor—

Her arms encircled his neck, mirroring the way his arm coiled around her waist, as if with its own mind to claim her. Winch her to himself. His mouth hungrily taking possession of the passion she offered. Her lips were soft, her curves full and right.

A clearing throat yanked them apart.

Ixion jerked around, swiveling Kita behind himself, his thoughts sluggish in the aftershock of their shared passion—until he saw who had come upon them. "Mar—my medora."

Expression hard, Marco tucked his chin. "If you would excuse us, Lady Kita. I must deal with my man."

"Please, Your Majesty," Kita said as she stepped forward. "I . . . It was me. I kissed him."

Marco's eyebrow quirked. "I believe it takes two to kiss, especially in the manner just witnessed. I respect your claim of guilt, Lady Lasdos, but no man should let a woman assume guilt—"

"And I do not!" Ixion snapped, furious he'd been so dull-witted and hadn't intercepted Kita's attempt to clear him. "She is naïve—"

"Nay, I am not!"

Marco held up a hand, silencing them both. "The kyria is in need of her lady's maid. Please do not keep her waiting."

Embarrassed, Kita ducked. "Aye, Your Majesty." She glanced at Ixion, then scurried away.

Marco swung his disapproval to Ixion. "Is it my turn?"

"For what?"

Gaze dark despite those icy irises, he considered him. "My turn to demand you set petition."

Gulping guilt, Ixion felt the pummel of anger beating him for his weakness. For what Marco threatened. "You know—"

"When you discovered me with Isaura, you said honor *demanded* that I set petition. To protect hers and mine."

"Aye, and you begged me not to do it. Said it was not right." The same could be said of now, when he would only fail Kita as he had failed his first bound. As he had thoroughly failed Isaura and abandoned her to the wastelands. Failings that fueled his constant need to be fighting, moving, protecting.

"Convenient that you recall this now that you wear my boots." Marco's hands now hung at his sides. "What of Kita? Who is to watch over the kyria's lady and protect her from untoward advances? As she has no family, as she resides in my house, in my realm, the responsibility—"

"I will set petition," Ixion gruffed, disbelieving he had uttered such words, but neither would he be rushed into it. "*After* the war." *If I survive.* There was little chance, considering what they faced.

Marco studied him, then pursed his lips. "Not good enough. Set petition now—"

"Nay—"

"The binding can come afterward." Marco stalked closer, ferocity in those icy eyes. "Set petition this day and claim her and the boy, or I will demand you be bound by nightfall."

Ixion's cheek twitched as he glared down the Kynigos who had become a medora. "What is this? Revenge? Since you returned, ever has there been a darkness about you."

"Is this you trying to weasel your way out, by now impugning your medora? First you let the lady assume guilt, now you blame me." Head down, brows tight, Marco homed in on him. "Either we live by honor or we do not."

Properly reprimanded, Ixion could not argue. "You speak . . . truth. But you also said a woman should never be forced to bind—that she should have a choice."

Marco laughed. "And you think this is your out?"

Ixion ground his teeth.

"Did you forget how she kissed you? Nay, you will not escape this one, Ixion." He nodded. "Set petition."

"We are here, at war, I have no ring—"

"A gift from House Tyrannous." He remained implacable. "So . . .?"

Stiffly, Ixion nodded.

"Good."

It was settled. Kita would be his, which both excited and terrified him. "That was cruel."

Marco arched an eyebrow. "Well I know the feeling—"

"Nay. It is not the same. I failed Isa's mother. I know nothing of tending a woman or family."

"Then you will learn, as I have had to do. And your new life will be fulfilling, a chance to alter that legacy."

"Why did you force this? You know what is coming, the darkness we face."

"Aye, better than any man or woman here." Marco started down the passage slowly. "All the more reason to sprinkle some happiness into it. I would encourage you to reconsider waiting until after—"

"Nay." Ixion balled his fists. "I cannot believe my own foolishness. Letting myself get trapped like that—by the both of you!"

Marco laughed. Eyed him. "In earnest, *she* kissed you first?"

With a groan, Ixion rolled his shoulders as if he could undo all this. "I had yet been telling her why we were not a good match when her lips were on mine."

"There was more than just her lips in that kiss," Marco chuckled.

"You are correct in challenging me, but . . ." Ixion ground his teeth. "I abandoned one woman and here I stand forcing that life upon another."

"I was told by one I trust more than myself that you needed to be . . . encouraged in that direction, so I do not believe anyone is forcing Kita to accept you."

"What—? Who said this?"

"Since my return, Isa has spoken of the whispers between you and Kita, stolen moments and touches, that it started shortly after my kidnapping." Walking again, Marco side-eyed him. "She asked me to encourage you."

Ixion stopped, glancing back in the direction they'd come. "Isa? Isaura said this? She . . . approves?"

"Your daughter *conspired*, Ixion." Marco laughed. "You would find excuses even to your grave to avoid setting petition. You are a man of war and justice. Used to fighting, protecting your entoli via Stalking." He paused in the hall, closer to the ground level. "And must I remind the onetime elder of Prokopios that her honor must be defended? It is your duty to do so, mine to ensure it is done." He slapped Ixion's shoulder. "If she brings you joy, then it is your right—your duty even—to pursue that. To hone it."

"You speak as if it were a weapon."

"Aye, it is. A weapon against dishonor and one to protect your family's name and line."

"The thought of dishonoring her . . . pains me." Pushing back the daunting realization that he was officially bound, though no writ had been drawn or signed—it had been voiced to the medora, and that sealed it as solidly as any parchment and signet—he focused on a new point. "You sought me out?"

With a grunt, Marco roughed a hand over his face. "Considering the bombardments and knowing it will only get worse as more Uchuvchi fail, I think we should send the elders and ladies north."

Ixion whipped to him. "Send them away? To the Medoran Range?"

"Ypiretis told me of a cave system there."

"Aye, it protected Kalonicans almost a century past," he said, considering the possibilities. "Neither Isaura nor Kersei will go—"

"Both are levelheaded enough to see that going protects the future of the realm and its people."

"I fear you underestimate—"

"No." Marco's voice echoed in the passage and he paused. "I need them to go. They must. I need Isaura . . ."

Ixion saw then the agony churning through Marco. Through his son-in-law. "You want her to be safe."

Misery coated a young face that had endured so much, including beatings and enhancements. "If Isaura dies, our child dies. I cannot lose them. Cannot"—his nostrils flared—"*will not* let that happen."

"I share the burden. The thought destroys me."

Marco ran both hands over his close-cut hair. "She is my very air. Without her, I can't breathe. Nor would I want to."

Though he had suspected a deep connection between this young man and his daughter, now more than ever, Ixion feared the future.

"You disagree that he should set petition?"

"Nay." The way Isaura drew out that word belied her hesitation. "I fear Kita may think he only sets petition because you demand it."

"I did demand it," Marco said with a chuckle. "But not in the way you suggest, and if you will recall, you are the one who said to encourage him."

"Encourage, aye. Not—"

"I only helped Ixion see what was right. Nothing was forced." Marco stretched his neck, hating the high collar of his ceremonial garb. "We are not guaranteed a tomorrow. Well am I acquainted with a warrior ethos that would starve pleasure, deprive oneself of love, fearing it would distract or compromise effectiveness." He framed her face, memorizing her features, her expressive eyes, and her compassion. "More than ever before, I know its importance. Your love carried me through the darkest time. I would have every regia, aerios, machitis, or man know it. We are better for it."

Appreciation ebbed and flowed through her efflux, which also carried another note. One he could not seem to allay no matter what he tried: concern.

"You are sure he . . . is accepting of this."

"I am."

Catching his forearm where the brand warmed beneath her touch, she smiled at him. "It is only . . . Mavridis . . . he does not take well to being cornered."

All too aware of where her hand rested, he withdrew his arm. "You doubt me?"

"I doubt *him*," she said. "That he would agree so readily . . . it is so contrary to the man I know."

"You knew a father. Kita knows a man. There is a great difference. Already Ixion voiced his fears that he will fail her as he did you and your mother. He goes into it with great thought, I assure you."

Isa nodded, her concern slowly abating.

"The bigger question, the one that does give me pause, concerns you."

She started. "Me?"

"Are you ready for a new ma'ma and brother?"

Her laughter carried them into the dinner hall, which was populated with but a few: Kynigos and aerios, a few nobles, Ypiretis and his apprentice Duncan were seated near three Sebastianos—Galen, the sister Danae, and the elder Bazyli, who was locked in a tense conversation with Daq'Ti.

The instant they realized their medora had arrived, chairs and boots scraped as they came to their feet.

With Isaura on his arm, Marco strode to the head of the table, where Ixion was seated with Kita opposite him in a resplendent lavender gown that was more extravagant than those she usually wore. No doubt Isa's doing.

They stood before the gathered. "Before we eat, I would beg your mercy for a special occasion. There is little to celebrate these days—"

"Save your return!" Theilig barked, eliciting a chorus of *Vanko Marco, Vanko Kalonica!*

Marco lifted a hand to quiet and encourage them back into their seats. "I appreciate your fervor, but this night is not for me." He indicated to Ypiretis, who came forward with a parchment that had been drafted, signed, and sealed in the short oras after the encounter between Ixion and Kita. Whispers of "petition" murmured around the room. "As you have guessed, a petition has been set for one under my protection." His gaze found the object of the writ. "For Lady Kita Lasdos." He appreciated the surprise in her eyes that flicked to her hero. "Speak now, you who sets this petition."

Chair thumping back, Ixion stood again. "I do, Your Majesty." He was formidable, fierce in his Plisiázon attire, yet a strange vulnerability skated through his gray eyes. "At your approval, sire"—he nodded to Kita—"I would claim as my bound the Lady Kita. Her son Mnason will be named my heir."

Gasps and shock radiated through the small hall, swiftly followed by an uproarious applause. Even as Marco detected the thick relief and gratefulness of Kita, likely for the protection and provision regarding her son, regia and aerios stood.

"What say you, Lady Kita?" The question was not a part of the legal ceremony, but Marco would give her voice.

Embarrassed, Kita inclined her head, tears brimming. "Of course, I would be honored."

Shouts went up as the Stalkers converged on their leader, congratulating him and offering the lady their well-wishes—and some offered her teasing regrets.

Regaining his seat, Marco reveled in the joy that thickened the air here. It had been too long since he had feasted on that scent in such large scale.

"You're pleased with yourself."

Marco smirked at the master's voice during the celebrations later in the evening. "Am I pleased with myself? Mayhap. But with this"—he indicated to the dinner that had now become dancing and merriment—"much more so." He sipped his cordi, gaze sliding to where Isa sat talking and laughing with Lady Danae. "Laughter is a rare commodity these days."

"The duchess is noticeably absent," Roman said.

"I had not noticed." Marco shouldered away the galling point and redirected their conversation to the present. "It is good for them to remember what they fight for."

"What happened in the square—"

"Curse the reek," Marco hissed, slamming down his goblet. "Leave it."

Roman's eyebrow winged up. "What she did—"

"Was rob a man of his will, just as Khatriza did in their enhancements on the Draegis. It's repulsive!" Boils, he would not endure this any longer. He started for the side door, noting his First converge on him.

"Y-your Majesty."

"Not now." The nervous efflux swam in from the left, slowing Marco as he recognized the scent. "Walk with me, Duncan."

"Uh . . ."

Marco looked to the teen and saw he was not alone. A very blonde, very pretty girl shifted awkwardly beside him. "What? Would you set petition as well?" His lame attempt at humor shocked both young people.

"No!" Duncan nearly yelled. "I . . . I only . . ."

The girl flushed as red as an unripe cordi. "I . . . I am not of age. My papa—"

"Your papa what?" General Sebastiano joined them, his large hand resting on her shoulder. The girl nearly leapt out of her skin, as did the jittery apprentice.

Ah. "This is your daughter, Bazyli?" Marco asked.

He kissed the girl's temple. "Yalena is my second eldest."

How had Marco not known this? "Your father is an asset." He should've quit this party and not altered his course. He looked to the apprentice. "You had need of me?"

"Yes, sire. We did—er, I mean—"

"Excuse me, General. Quickly, Duncan," Marco urged as he started walking. "I have matters that need attending." *Like finding a way to release the agitation making my skin crawl.*

"The caves, sir. Ypiretis asked me to scout them, and I discovered something amazing."

"Yes?"

"The touchstones, sire."

Marco's gaze even now struck one mounted on the wall. "What of them?"

"The caves hold large deposits of the ore."

Frustrated with the kid's inability to get to a point, Marco slowed. Looked him in the eye. "Duncan."

"Right." He held up a hand. "Since I've been working in the *Qirolicha* helping coordinate efforts with our Interceptors, I learned about its power core."

Marco pinched the bridge of his nose.

"Hurry," Yalena urged.

"Daq'Ti told me the drone ships have a system that uses the same type of power core."

Marco started backing away.

"I-I think the touchstones could be refined to replace the power core."

Marco stopped. "Say that again."

"The core—"

"You think we have a way to power those ships?"

"It's been my theory that this is the real reason Symmachia wants Drosero. Touchstone energy is both efficient and clean. Refined, it could power—"

Marco snapped a gaze to where Bazyli was still standing. "Did you hear? What do you think?"

Bazyli shrugged. "His knowledge far outweighs mine, but if it is true . . . we might win this war."

"Not sure I'd go that far, but we could survive it."

"But, Your Majesty," Ixion edged into the conversation. "Even if we could refine"—he glanced at Duncan, seeking confirmation on the word—"enough in time, how would we get ore to the ships? Are there not hundreds?"

"Agreed. The effort would be enormous and time consuming, not to mention Symmachia would do everything in their power to prevent us from refueling." With a grunt, Marco nodded. "But the *Qirolicha* . . ." He clamped a hand on Duncan's shoulder—a stream of pure blue streaked through the youth's pupil. "Duncan, I want you to take Daq'Ti, as well as Ramirus"—he looked to Bazyli again—"and go into the caves. Survey the ore and prove that what you just said might be possible."

"M-me, sire?"

"It appears you are the only one here with big enough brains. Mayhap you have long outgrown 'apprentice.' You are officially our chief science officer."

Brown eyes sparked, pride effusing from the boy. "Y-yes, sire!" He pivoted away, remembered himself and spun back for a quick bow, then darted off.

Yalena rushed after him, but her father caught her arm. She squeaked, half anticipating the interception.

"Stay with your aunt," Bazyli gruffed.

"But Papa—"

"Your. Aunt," he growled. "Go."

With a curtsy, she skulked toward Lady Danae and Isaura.

"There is a natural affinity between her and Duncan," Marco said. "No harm—"

"He's a skycrawler."

Disappointed with the prejudiced term and attitude, Marco cocked his head. "Who may just be our salvation."

"Admiral, you have a wave from the *Macedon*, asking about ordnance failure."

Tapping his comms, Domitas wondered how Baric had connected the dots so fast. "Understood. I'm en route back to the bridge." He spotted the black-and-green light armor of an Eidolon thudding toward him and nodded to the commander as he fell into step. "With me, Commander."

After a curt nod, Trent "Slice" Keeling joined him on the lift to the bridge. They rode in silence, then Domitas stepped out, aiming for his office.

"Admiral on the bridge!"

"As you were." Detecting an assault of excitement that buzzed his senses, he diverted to the con and looked to the Comms specialist. "Get me a channel to Baric." He stood over her station as she got the wave set up and handed Domitas the headset.

"Admiral."

"What's this about ordnance failures, Baric?"

"We've noticed an unusually high rate of ordnance failure that we've sent down to orbit. What actually launches breaks up in atmo."

"What's Engineering saying?"

"Not much. They can't figure it out."

"Human error?"

"Not to this extent."

Domitas grunted. "We're not having any issues here. You're ineffective without ordnance, so get it figured out." Heart light for the first time in a while—that'd been a brilliant suggestion by AO—he nodded to the XO, who had a spirited excitement on his fair-skinned face. "D'you find something?"

Dimar looked ready to combust, but then he hauled it into line. "Possibly. We're double-checking and comparing data."

"On?"

"That weakness in the net."

"In my office." Over his shoulder, he said, "Slice, with me."

The doors to his enclosure opened via biometric reading. "Illuminate." He strode to the desk, punched in commands until the array rippled in the air between them, then stuffed his hands on his belt. "Give it to me."

Dimar stepped toward the display and tapped a sector until it filled the space the entire planet had occupied a moment ago. Six ships hovered there. Five red, one orange. "On routine patrol, another Rapier noticed this delta ship's energy rating wasn't running at the same level as the others. He buzzed them for a closer look and reading."

Chest tight, Domitas eyed the commander. "And?"

"Well, the other five deltas fired simultaneously. Destroyed our Rapier."

Setting aside the fact that one of his pilots had been killed, Domitas skidded his gaze back to the array. Keyed the control on his desk, zooming back out some. "And how many times have the ships fired on our pilots before?"

"None since we ceased attacks."

Domitas rubbed his jaw.

"Pack protection," Slice offered. Though short, the guy made up for it in instinct and ethos. In every test and certification, he'd outstripped everyone else by a mile.

"Exactly my thoughts."

"We did this op on Criem, one of the moons here in Herakles, and there are these massive wild wolves—criemwolves. Unlike most dog packs that will attack and kill a wounded member in order to protect the pack, criemwolves came in droves when one of my guys shot one in self-defense. They came out of the woodwork to defend the injured member. Lost Maralson, like somehow they knew he'd wounded their own." He pointed to the array. "There's a wounded wolf in the pack."

"And the others saw our pilot as the threat."

"Removed the threat." Domitas had another level of respect for these deltas that had swarmed in to protect Drosero.

"Agree with that, but I think we're looking at something more," Dimar muttered.

"Like?"

"They've never been so reactive with firing. Responsive, yes. But I think . . . I think they're facing a net-wide problem."

Domitas straightened. "Come again?"

"They've been up there weeks. Without refueling."

"So has the *Cronus*," Slice argued.

"But we have large fuel stores," Dimar said. "While it's true we know nothing about the way they work, I think the delta ships have depleted fuel reserves."

"Find out how many other ships have similar levels to the wounded wolf we stumbled upon."

"Aye, sir." With a crisp nod, Dimar exited.

Domitas pressed a panel, and the glass walls went opaque. A blue glow traced where wall met ceiling. He leaned back against his desk and crossed his legs at the ankles, eyeing the array.

"Worries you," Slice said, squaring his stance and tucking his hands under his armpits.

Domitas sighed. "It does." The weakening array meant Drosero's vulnerability would be exploited sooner. All he could do was delay as long as possible. He roughed a hand over his face, then shifted his attention. "So, what happened out there?"

Slice inclined his head. "We tracked that ship you sent us after."

Weeks ago, even before the sphere-craft had arrived, Dimar had delivered some intel he'd picked up—the launch of an unusual ship from the *Chryzanthe*. As fleet admiral, Domitas was required to clear any ship deployed, but he'd had no knowledge of this one. Which annoyed him. Endangered fleet ops. When he'd asked Baric about it, the captain denied any such launch. Even when presented with an image of the ship.

"Nobody saw you?"

"No, sir. Stealth capability worked well."

"Where'd it go?"

"Tracked it as far as Sicane, then lost it."

"Lost it?"

"Yessir. There one blip, gone the next."

What in the Voids? "Did they go to the planet's surface?"

"Scans of the surface revealed no ships—in fact, nothing. No ships, infrastructure, or life." Slice shrugged. "Which is what we expected, but it doesn't explain where the ship went."

"Destroyed?"

"No debris or chemical signatures to indicate something of that magnitude." He shifted and set down a flex screen and nudged it across the desk. "Thought you'd want to see this, sir."

Dom lifted it and scanned the image. Saw something in the upper right corner. He zoomed in and stilled. Glanced up through his brows at the commander. Then studied it again. He wanted to ask where this capture had been taken, but the stars and the giant brown planet hugging the bottom quadrant told him. "Signature?"

"Symmachian, sir."

He knew that for Void's sake. "*Specific* signature, Commander?"

"Two-two-five."

Domitas bit back a curse. Arkin Cleve. The team under the thumb of Baric. The team that'd had it out for Tigo and the 215. This meant . . . "D'they see you?"

"Impossible to know for sure, but since we came up on their aft and threw our shields up as soon as we caught the signature"—he shrugged—"hope not."

"Pretty thin hope."

"Agreed."

Domitas moved around his desk to the chair and dropped into it. What was an Eidolon team doing around a dead planet on the outer reaches of Herakles Quadrant? An Eidolon team controlled by Captain Zoltan Baric . . . who was in the very clutches of Xisya. There was something there, something he was missing . . .

What the Voids was Baric doing this time? And tasking Tascan elites to run his errands . . .

"Want us to return to Sicane and take another look?"

It'd take weeks to get back out there, but he did need to know what Baric was up to in the outer reaches. It'd taken months to soothe alliance egos when it was discovered he'd built the *Chryzanthe* essentially in Heraklean space. But with the net possibly starting to fail here . . .

Air shimmered and rippled behind the commander in warning of Renette's incoming. The shredding of time was not noticeable to those without the ability to fold, so he wasn't worried about Slice seeing it, but he needed to clear the deck.

The commander shifted, anxious for an answer.

"No." Domitas squinted. "Get your team up to speed on life and cultures on Drosero."

"Sir?"

He leaned forward and threaded his fingers into a fist. "They're a non-tech planet and you'll need to blend in down there."

"Down where?"

"Isn't Aimes an ordnance specialist?"

Slice frowned. "She is, sir."

"Good. Briefing at 0400." He jutted his jaw to the door. "Dismissed, Commander."

TRYSSINIA, HERAKLES

Everything had changed. Drastically. Diametrically. It wasn't just the juicy bit of intel handed him by AO—

Tigo sniffed. AO, short for Ancient One. A truer moniker had never been bestowed.

Unbelievable. Ridiculous. Head in his hands, Tigo sat on a knoll overlooking the small mining town. The one AO had ruled at some point in the man's nearly timeless existence.

Tigo lifted his gaze to the star-riddled canopy of black. Up there, you'd never know how this planet struggled. From this view, it was no different than any of the other dozen planets he'd landed on as an Eidolon.

Eidolon . . . If he was this thing AO mentioned—Do'St—was his skill as an Eidolon *his* doing, or had it been wired into him? Did it matter as long as he did the job well?

"My head . . . is going . . . to explode."

"Well, don't let it because I have no towels to clean it up."

Although Jez's words were meant to be humorous, he just wasn't sure he'd ever laugh at anything she said again.

"Sure you will."

He growled and punched to his feet. Turned away. Maybe he should stay here with AO. Learn how to block her from his thoughts.

"Please . . . don't"—she pulled up sharp when he spun at her—"go."

He faltered. Had been ready to blast her for reading his mind. But she wasn't doing that. Or was she? "Augh!" He balled his fists. "I *hate* this, Jez. Hate it."

Sagging, she lowered her gaze. "I know."

"Why, because you're reading my thoughts?"

"No, I'm reading your body language, hearing the anger in your words. Anger that is not like you, Tigo."

"What *is* like me, Jez? Because I suddenly have no idea who I am or what I'm doing here. What I can do on my own and what was some . . . magical, supernatural part of my bloodline."

"I didn't want you to find out this way—"

"But didn't you?" He sidled up to her and angled his head. "Why else would you bring me to AO?" When she didn't answer, he knew he'd nailed the target. "You wanted me to find out."

"I . . . I was forbidden from speaking it, and you needed to know the truth, but I imagined more conversation, less accusation and hatred."

"Needed to know information that would turn me against you?"

Her caramel eyes held his for a long second. "Did he?"

Tigo bounced his gaze to the rocky ground beneath his boots. "Honestly, I have no idea. Right now, I can't make sense of anything except that." He pointed to the canopy of stars above them. "*That* makes sense to me. It's where I belong. Where things make sense. Flying, fighting, mech-suits, PICC-lines . . ." He clenched his fists again. "I miss it."

"Because that's what you love, Tigo—fighting for the innocent." She touched his arm. "No matter what you have learned, it does not change who you are."

"Doesn't it, though?" he challenged but then flicked his hand in the air. "Never mind. Let's just . . . get out of here. It's making my nerves buzz."

"Clever." Roman glanced around the hastily erected, makeshift quarry. Nodding his approval, he met the gaze of the young genius responsible for this discovery. "How is the collection and processing going?"

A half dozen machitis were using pickaxes to extract the ore, another handful were hauling it to a conveyor that delivered it to a cauldron.

Duncan motioned back down the cave system toward the entrance. "It would be better if the ships were smaller—they could lift a load and get it to the processor faster. But we work with what we have."

At a pile of raw touchstones, Roman crouched and lifted a chunk of grayish-tan rock. Turned it over, noting the energy radiating off it, the very subtle but unique metallic scent. "Duncan?" He pushed to his full height as he shifted to the prodigy. "How is it you discovered the connection?"

The youth hesitated. "I—" He pointed to the Draegis. "I was with Daq'Ti in the crescent ship, down in the main engine compartment, and I . . . I don't know—it just came to me as we tried to figure out alternatives to the core."

Angling aside to avoid a cart of ore being led up the incline and around the narrow corners to the processing area, Roman grunted. "Just came to you."

"Yes." Duncan frowned.

Was it mere coincidence that this young man made a connection between the two fuel sources that had a similar scent? Did the teen have a latent ability? Was that why Marco had kept him close?

"Forgive me, Master Hunter, but there is much work to be done . . ."

Roman inclined his head, watching the young man throw his every effort into the harvesting of the touchstone ore, watched him even suggest a change to the way the machitis were loading it, which would save time. "Daq'Ti, how long will the net hold?"

"The ships are very low, another died even this morning, but no gap in net." Daq'Ti shrugged. "Net will fall in seven rises of the sun, maybe a little more. Then too few ships to hold."

"Will they be able to refine the necessary ore fast enough to extend the timeline?"

Daq'Ti looked mournful and spoke so Duncan would not hear. "Not easy to measure. Likely not."

A waft of air sent that note across Roman's receptors again, once more pushing his attention to the prodigy. Back to the Draegis, who stood at the pile, aiming his weaponized arm at the rock. The scent he anak'd . . .

Roman drew up straight. "What are you doing?"

The boy grinned. "He's softening the rock, making it easier and faster to chisel out." He shifted between them, taking readings, entering them into a flex screen, then moving on.

That scent was unique. So unique he'd only detected it from one other person. "Daq'Ti, can you tell me of this weapon you bear?"

Weariness pushed down the man's shoulders. "Regret . . . I asked Xonim to leave it, but it makes my heart black. I tell Uchuvchi to release it, too, but he say no."

Roman narrowed his eyes. "Marco."

Daq'Ti trilled with a slow nod. "It is not good." He lifted his arm. "The more you use it, the more it wants"—he thumped his chest—"this. Me."

So this . . . *this* was what he'd been detecting from Marco since his return. "You say it is not good?" The rash decisions, the quick anger, the impulsiveness . . .

Forlorn eyes pulsed at him. "It can only destroy—the enemy and the wielder."

KARDIA, KALONICA, DROSERO

"You must leave this place and come with me."

At the pronouncement from the corner where there had been only supplies and shadow, Kersei startled. Lifted her gaze from preparing the foodstuffs for the city and stilled at the form who had appeared. "Ma'ma."

"What are you doing in the dungeons stuffing baskets with bread and cheese when war is at your door, Child?"

"Taking care of our people," she ground out, tying off the ends of a cloth to hold the staples together. One bundle for each family. "As any good Kalonican noblewoman would do."

"What good is food if they are dead? If you do not inspire the men to lay down their passivity and pick up the courage of war?"

"Courage of war?" Kersei scoffed. "It does not take courage to war. It takes courage to seek peace. Father always said that."

"And is this how you stand your ground against Marco?"

Kersei stilled, her heart pounding. "What know you of that?"

"Nothing that passes beneath the Heavenlies is missed."

"Well, that is patently untrue."

"Just because we do not interfere in the affairs or wars of men—"

"Again, untrue." Swallowing hard, she turned and smoothed a hand down her omnirs as she tried to remember what she was supposed to do next.

"This is for sergii to tend, Kersei!"

"If there were sergii here to do it, I would leave it to them!" Her voice echoed across the low ceilings of the belowground kitchens. "Fear drove them out of the keep and into the hills. Few remain to tend chores and children."

"Children and chores are not meant for you, heir of the *Trópos tis Fotiás* and a Lady!"

Even at that, Kersei's brand flared with heat and purpose. Absently, she curled her arm toward her bliaut. "You raised me in Kalonica, not Deversoria and now choose to tell me I do not belong here or helping the people."

Ma'ma lifted her chin. "Have you spoken with Mr. Haltersten since you gave him the Touch?"

"That encounter earned me a rebuke from the medora and—"

"Faa'Cris do not answer to men."

Kersei sagged with a heavy sigh. "Would that I had your wings and armor to protect me from remonstrations, but I do not."

"Your clypeus is yet there, waiting for you to remember it."

Kersei faltered. Sniffed. "Now you would have me abandon my people and join you, who will not help the very people you lived among."

"This is not our war, Kersei."

"But it is mine!" she snapped. "And I am bound to this mortal ground and this existence within Kardia. As such, I will carry out my duties as the daughter of Elder Dragoumis and honor . . . the crown."

"The crown? Or Marco?"

"They are one and the same."

A sly smile touched her ma'ma's face. "Not in your heart, Daughter."

The same heart thudding at those words. "What do you want, Ma'ma?"

"Speak to Haltersten—"

"Think beyond yourself for once."

His words ringing in her ears, she tensed. "I will not."

Anger speared her mother's visage. "Because of Marco."

Kersei lowered her gaze, sighed as she moved to another table and started wrapping cheese in cloth.

"Marco acts out of fear, not wisdom."

"I may not have the wisdom of the Ladies, but even I could tell that."

"He could be Corrupt."

"Speak not"—Kersei's breath hissed from her—"those words again." Her chest rose and fell unevenly. "You know he is not. Marco is the Progenitor. In this war, he will—"

"If he does not make changes, all may be lost. Prophecies do not supplant will, and Marco is seceding his will to a dark influence."

"And did you not just tell me you do not interfere in the affairs or wars of men, yet there you stand trying to force me to interfere? By supplanting the will of another, no less."

Her mother sighed. "Nay, that is not so. Speak to Haltersten."

"As said, I will not. Besides, Haltersten is mustering and training a militia. Last I heard, he was south of the city with his band of fighters. It is said they are arming and training every person who comes into camp willing to fight, man or woman."

A fact she had been both pleased and relieved to learn. Admittedly, what transpired between her and the brigand frightened her. A fearful curiosity slowed her work. "What is it, Ma'ma?" She looked at her own hand that had pressed to the man's chest. The same one as the brand. "What did I do?"

"It is an uncommon gift—only seen in a rare few Faa'Cris." Ma'ma was at her side . . . her presence familiar with her brown hair and brown eyes. Kindness tucked beneath severity. "What did Eleftheria speak to you at the Temple? Remember?"

How could she possibly forget that moment or Her words? "'Daughter of Nicea, chosen wielder of light, you will awaken what lies dormant in the army that gathers. The days will be long, the heartaches endless, the battles cruel, and your enemies merciless, but remain strong.'" It seemed a mockery of what she felt. Strength was not close to what she had experienced since Darius fled this existence and Marco reviled her.

And yet . . . Kersei stilled, widening her eyes. "Haltersten started a militia . . . He is yet recruiting." Her heart stuttered. "I Touched him and he . . . he gathers an army." An incredulous laugh flitted through her chest.

"And you stand between life and death, between the Living and the Dead. As defenders."

Kersei sniffed and wiped tears she'd only just noticed. "Defenders." From the shelves against the far wall, she gathered more baskets. "What are we to defend? How am I to defend *anyone* against skycrawlers? They vastly outnumber Droserans, and their technology is obliterating all we know and . . . love."

Ma'ma caught her branded arm, making it flare so fiercely that Kersei yelped.

Her ever-present guardian, Myles shifted in place by the door, hands going to his longblade.

"*We* outnumber them. *We* out-wield them with weapons not limited by technology or time," Ma'ma snipped.

"Neither Ladies nor Droserans are immortal. *We* can die just as they can," Kersei bit back. "And faster, since they have weapons that reach from the skies and burn our lands and either blow our people up or turn them against one another as they have done with the Irukandji and Hirakyns. And Marco speaks of these Draegis coming from another star system, who have arms that turn people to ash. That, Ma'ma, is what we face. That is why I feed the people, because there is naught else to be done!"

"Why, Child?" her mother grieved. "Why have you so wholly forsaken your inheritance?"

"Forsaken it? I have only just learned that there was one, but what is it?" She thrust her arm forward. "Besides this brand and the Touch, which I have no idea how I did, what have I inherited?" She returned to the preparations. "I was raised within stone walls with two sisters, both of whom are dead. Raised by a ma'ma who chided me over my omnirs and unruly hair, who rebuked me for my earnest yearning to fight and spar." She slammed her hands on the table and glowered at her ma'ma. "You could have been preparing me—"

"I knew what would come and wanted you to have peace for as long as you could."

"Ignorance is what you raised me in. So if there is one to blame . . ."

Nicea Dragoumis lifted her hand even as her entire form shifted into a glorious illumination of weaponry and ferocity. "You are right," her voice echoed. "I have failed to train you in war as Rufio and Darius did. However, what is in us, our nature, is not taught." Her hand reached to Kersei's chest. "It is imbued."

Even as Ma'ma's warm touch settled over her breast, Kersei expected to be struck down. Or feel some ignition as she had at the altar on Iereania. Instead, she felt . . . nothing but the pressure of fingers. The touch of a mother, of a Faa'Cris that was warm and minty.

Ma'ma's eyes glowed with understanding and . . . mischief. "It *is* within you, Kersei. When you are ready, you will not need an instructor. Or a Touch." She motioned Myles forward, and he came willingly. She held out a hand to Kersei. "Come here."

Panic lit through Kersei. "No."

"Do it, Child!"

"Nay, I will not." More panic drilled at the thought of leaving that imprint on Myles. She heard Marco's rebuke. Saw and felt his disgust. "No."

Ma'ma caught her hand.

"*No!*" Kersei thrust herself backward. "Stop it!"

Ma'ma grinned up at her.

Up.

Ma'ma was looking . . . *up* . . . at her?

Kersei glanced down and discovered her toes dangling above the stone floor. Only then realizing she was not on her feet. A strange, powerful ache ran down her spine, and her brand exploded with fire and . . . intent. Something in her periphery startled her—feathers.

She cried out and dropped, barely breaking her fall. Heart crammed into her throat, she gaped at Ma'ma, who smiled as Kersei rounded—wings sweeping the table clear of the baskets she'd prepared. "Augh!"

"Slowly, Kersei," Ma'ma said. "Draw them into your clypeus."

"What? I—"

"What goes on here?" Marco jerked, gaping at her.

Blood and boil! Why did he have to show up now, of all times? She faltered, panicked.

"Kersei, seek peace!"

With Ma'ma's voice ringing in her head, Kersei stilled. Heard herself whimper. She felt her wings hit a shelf and cupped her hands over her face, fighting the tears.

"Into the clypeus," Ma'ma intoned in her head again. *"Calm and roll. Say it to yourself."*

Seek peace. Seek peace. Kersei drew in a silent breath. Calm and roll. Calm and roll. She rolled her shoulders. Sensed the wings retract, folding into her clypeus. Even as she straightened, lowered her hands, and sensed Marco's revulsion once more, she felt a new courage steal into her heart.

Out of breath, as if he'd run all the way down here, Marco stared between her and Ma'ma. His now-silvery eyes locked onto hers. "What . . .?"

Shoulders slumping, she let her hands hang at her sides. Knew he hated her, what she was—Faa'Cris. Knew because she could smell his hatred. "I . . ." She shrugged, fighting back tears. She indicated the tables, noting the disarray of the pantry. "I have been preparing food to take to the people." That's when she noticed Ma'ma was gone. Of course. Start this instruction into Faa'Cris existence, then vanish when Kersei made a fool of herself.

"Kersei." His voice was gruff, his brows knotted. "You had . . . wings."

She stood before him, feeling . . . naked. Wicked. Confused. "I know you hate the Faa'Cris . . ."

Marco stepped back. Scowled. "Leave the bundles for the aerios to deliver. You . . . stay within the walls."

"It is more important than ever for us to be seen. Isaura understands this—"

"The kyria is not the medora!"

At the bark in his tone, she stilled. In other words, *his* say was final. Though irritation slashed Kersei, she bit her tongue to keep from speaking against him. Everything in her wanted to assert she was no longer a girl to be commanded, but she would bite her tongue. Bide her time. The Ancient had tied her fate with Marco's. She must trust that. Would trust that.

He pivoted and started for the passage.

"Did you have need of me?" In earnest, why did she speak?

He stopped short. "No."

"Then why . . . why come to the kitchens? It is not a place for a medora."

"Nor for a duchess." He seemed to look behind her. "Or a Faa'Cris."

She did not miss the sneer in his voice as he named her kind. Again, she had to keep her mouth closed to avoid throwing some pithy remark his way, but even as she did, she felt heat crawl through her brand.

Marco's gaze shifted to his arm, which he rotated, and then he stood motionless for several long seconds. "Leave us," he commanded the guards.

Tension coiled around Kersei's middle. "I have not Touch—"

"I came down here because . . . something strange flared through my brand. I . . . felt . . ."

Kersei's heart jolted. "You felt that?"

His left hand went to his sleeve, as if to lift it. Brow forever tangled in a scowl, Marco did not move. Did not look at her.

Being alone with him was not appropriate, and truly, she feared Isaura coming upon them, but what harm was it to speak to him? "I . . . I can still feel"—she dared not say she felt *him* or he would flee—"*it*, the . . . connection. O-of the *Trópos tis Fotiás*."

Beneath those dark, brooding brows, Marco's eyes slid to hers. What he did not speak writhed through his features—misery. "What else?"

What was he asking? This . . . No. He could not possibly be insinuating . . .

"*Think not* that I seek attachment or attraction," he growled. "That's not what—" He clamped his mouth closed. Whipped around and started for the door, but again stopped. His hands fisted. "Stay in Kardia." Without another word, he was gone.

So was her clarity. Her confidence. Both Ma'ma and Marco had spoken ominous words.

"My lady?"

Kneading the knot at the base of her neck, Kersei moved toward the rear wall, putting her back to Myles. She did not want anyone to question her confusion or the stricken expression she undoubtedly wore. Or the hurt or . . .

With a heaving sigh, she tilted her head to the ceiling and fought for composure. Every time she convinced herself all those feelings for Marco had been quelled . . .

"Kersei."

Her spine rippled with fight at her ma'ma's tone. "Now you return? When he is gone and you need not contend—"

"P-please, Your Highness," came a nervous voice from behind.

"I am no kyria," Kersei said, rounding to find Belak with another man, and behind them, her ma'ma. Could they see her?

"I beg your mercy, my lady." Demeanor one of subservience, Belak bowed, eyes and head down. "I brought my brother, Owik. He has had some . . . trouble. We beg you to Touch him."

"I . . ." Lips parting, she eyed Ma'ma for explanation or direction. *I have no idea how I did it.* How was she supposed to tell them that?

"*It* is *within you, Kersei,*" Ma'ma said through Lifespeech. "*This is what*

Eleftheria freed in you at the Temple—the ability to heal the adunatos—"

"I will not do this! Marco was right. It is wrong to remove a man's will."

"Think you he knows more of our ways than I? That is not the way of the Touch. It does not remove another's will. It frees one from doubts and darkness so the desires of his true self can be made."

Considering the men, Kersei weighed the words. *"It sounds like a play of words. Does not it mean the same thing? If I change something in him, then have I not altered his will?"*

"You have not. His will is his own. Haltersten could return to the tavern and ale, lose himself. You see Owik before you, his will seeking help—your help. There will be those who will not accept the Touch. They are steeped in their darkness and enjoy it. Most men—and even women—when choices are before them, their decisions are filtered through doubts, through their past, which colors their choices with fears, wounds, grievances . . . Those filters, better named tethers, prevent them from finding truth, freedom. Are they altered? Aye, but only inasmuch as herbs provide flavor, water sates thirst. The Touch is a healing. A restoration."

Kersei let her gaze drift back to Belak and his brother but spoke with Ma'ma still. *"I have had no training. I know not how to . . . do it."*

With a serene smile, Ma'ma slipped forward and motioned Owik closer, then nodded to Kersei. "Touch him."

So he can see her. Kersei could not help but recall the ferocity of Marco's response, how fiercely he objected, and she did not want to anger him further. "Ma'ma, it is not—"

"Hand to his chest." Ma'ma lifted her arm by the wrist and guided her.

Rigid, uncertain, she allowed the direction. Pressed her palm to his scratchy wool tunic.

"Now, repeat after me," Ma'ma said to Kersei. "Will so chosen is answered this day. Via my hand and the Ancient's Touch, breathe and shed the weights that have held you captive." She inclined her head.

Bouncing her gaze between the man's eyes and chest, Kersei repeated the words, tense in anticipation of the same reaction as Haltersten.

He suddenly sucked in a gasp. Clutched his hand over hers.

Unnerved, Kersei jerked it back and held it to her own chest, and appreciated when Myles shouldered between them.

Owik gaped at her, his expression one of amazement. Tears coursed down his face as his knees gave way, depositing him on the stone floor where he sobbed. "Mercy, mercy!"

Disbelief pushed Kersei back a step. Turned her away from the display, which seemed entirely too private and raw. She felt more than saw Ma'ma step closer. "I . . . it worked." She shuddered an airy laugh. "I— Wait!" Concern laced her. "The words—I cannot remember them." Jerking her gaze up, she saw not pride on Ma'ma's face, nor a smile, but rather a flat, disapproving cast. "Remind me, please, so that I might be prepared next time."

"No."

"I must know them, if I am to—"

"Child, how can you be so dull-witted?" The words were cruel but classic Nicea Dragoumis. "The words were not for his benefit, but for yours!"

Kersei blinked. "What?"

"There is no magic prayer or potion for the Ancient's healing, Kersei. Only will and trust. Blessedly, He has chosen you to be a vessel for healing His people, and your willingness beneath His guiding is all that is required."

"But . . . I *spoke* the words. And they worked."

"The words merely calmed your own fears and insecurities, allowed you to let His power flow." Ma'ma tilted her head. "Once you spoke them, did you not anticipate the healing Touch?"

Kersei scowled. "No." *Yet did I not?* "Aye."

Now, Ma'ma did smile. "Willingness and trust. That is all the Ancient seeks. There is no more perfect—"

Claxons trilled through Kardia, the stones ringing with a panicked alarm.

The fetor of fuel was so strong, foul. Stirred something oily and black in his gut.

Marco's brand warbled, warming. The weapon stung, responding to that renewed heat from the threat the clanging belltower warned. Marco swiped his thumper. "Roman, what's happening?"

"Too many drone ships are failing. Twelve to fifteen Symmachian fighters got through before the net could reestablish. Interceptors incoming!"

Heart in his throat, Marco pivoted to Hushak. "Where is the kyria?"

"In chambers, sire."

"Symmachian fighters incoming."

"But the net—"

"Failing." Marco glanced at Theilig. "Get the women out of Kardia. To the caves in the mountains."

"Understood, sire."

"Do you? Because with you goes all that is left of Kardia—the heirs. Fail and who knows what will stand on these cliffs in the days to come."

After a curt bow of his head, Theilig sprinted off in the opposite direction, his steps echoing loudly . . . and mirrored by a set of incoming boots. And an odor of anger and readiness.

Roman rounded the corner and stopped short. Though he looked ready to make a pronouncement, he stilled. "You know."

"Go with Theilig to protect Isaura and Aeliana."

"No, my skill—"

"Is needed protecting my wife and child!"

"I must help with the fighters. *You* should remain—"

"I am Progenitor. By that very name this fight is mine!"

Roman scowled. "What is the stench roiling off you, Marco?"

The heat of the brand flared under the accusation, but he would not be delayed. "Anger? Readiness? I know not. Only that it is whatever they made me to be."

"They?"

"He."

Roman's eyes glinted. "Marco—"

"Bah!" He waved off the master hunter. "No time."

The master hooked his arm, brought him around, gripping tightly over the vambrace where the weapon seared its readiness into his flesh. "This is not you."

Marco wrenched his arm free and a burst scorched the wall beyond Roman's head. "This *is* me! It is what they have named me—Progenitor."

"That weapon is eating your adunatos—"

"Enough! You are needed in the Command bunker, and I am needed in my ship." He pivoted and started down the passage, gradually picking up speed and half expecting the master to face-plant him into the wall at any second.

The regia stayed with him until they reached his chambers, where he made quick work of shedding his Droseran attire. Set aside his vambrace, tugged off the jerkin. Fist coiled, he flexed his forearm muscle, the skin taut and blackening around the embedded weapon. It no longer seemed smooth like stone. Now, it had a sort of pocked effect, the surface like . . .

Ash. Lava.

Lavabeast. Marco's pulse spiked.

What have I done?

He thought of his first encounter with the Draegis, with Daq'Ti . . . The monstrous black Lavabeasts swarming the *Prevenire*. Killing with prejudice any living form that was not them. *What . . .?* Was he becoming . . . *them?* Breath staggered through his chest, fighting its way up his throat, but got stuck as it warred with his head.

Movement nearby startled him back into action. He jerked his arm to his chest, pressing it close so that none would see.

"Here." Ixion stood holding his tactical vest that would help him plug into the ship. "Interceptors are launching. Vorn has reported engagement in his sector." A bevy of nerves roiled off his First.

His sector, two kilometers above Jherako. "Then it is in ours, too."

"Aye . . ." There was more.

"What?"

"He does not know how we will survive."

"That is not promised to us." Marco tensed as Ixion tried to tuck the tube around his arm and secure it to the shoulder mount, where it would plug into the PICC-line when necessary.

The Stalker firmed his hold. Met his gaze. Lips taut. He dragged Marco's arm down and threaded it through the tube. He undoubtedly saw the change to Marco's flesh, yet said nothing. "Ground operations are ready north of Lampros City, a klick away. Isaura, Kersei, and Xylander have their regia and a few Stalkers with them as they head to safety in the caves."

"Kita and Mnason?"

"With Isaura."

Marco nodded.

His First hesitated. "It would seem both our hearts are heavy."

Heavy? Marco did not feel heavy. Unless that meant laser-focused with a mission. Bloodthirsty to see the enemy in a heap of ash as they had done across many a system. "I want them obliterated."

Ixion clasped forearms and caught Marco's shoulder. "Seek peace, Marco."

That fire again ignited, not only his gut, but the brand, the weapon. "No," he growled. "The hour is not yet come for peace."

Uncertainty flickered through Ixion's gray eyes.

"We war!" With that, Marco and his entourage stalked through the stone passages, empty of laughter or warmth. Haunting silence gaped as he moved past the gathering hall, the chambers that had held Kersei and her newborn.

In what felt like seconds, he was climbing into the cockpit of his Interceptor, doing preflight checks. Verifying the ship was flight and combat ready. When he had final clearance, Marco eased the fast-attack craft through the tunnel. Came up north of the cliffs of Kardia, the *Qirolicha* a painful witness to Drosero's severe disadvantage against Symmachia and the Draegis, who had not yet even reached the Quadrants.

And already they were outnumbered. They had to take down these Symmachian fighters. Live another day.

Marco keyed his comms. "Aetos Actual away."

"Dusan . . ."

Somehow, Marco felt her call, felt that she was on the ground, looking up as his ship shot higher. *"Guard the others, get them to safety,"* he said, trying to refocus her—and himself. *"I know it's not fair—you protected them while I was gone and must do it once more."*

"The caves? We agreed not to be separated again."

"And we are not. How can two who are separate speak?"

"I love you. Hurry back."

"Already working on it." He banked right, detected a fetor to his left. And

the right. Muscles taut, he entered the treacherous dance across the skies to avoid ordnance. "This is Aetos Actual. Enemy contact."

Instrumentation lit up. Alarms blared across the holo array.

"Xanthus Four en route to intercept," comm'd Galen Sebastiano.

Irony at its best—Marco had coldcocked the young pup on the *Kleopatra* when he'd attempted to stop Kersei from leaving with Marco. Would he truly protect Marco now? "Putting bygones behind us, pup?"

"Not at all," Four returned, "but not letting these skycrawlers win takes precedence."

Marco almost smiled as he banked and pulled some hard g's to evade the Symmachian fast-attack crafts who were on him now. Sparks *tsing'd* off his wings and canopy as he dove hard and fast away from the two fighters.

"Command, Aetos Actual is under heavy pursuit. Scramble more fighters to—"

"Negative," Marco growled as he navigated the skies and found a way to pull up hard and drop behind one of the fighters. He unleashed a barrage of pulse cannon fire.

It lit up like one of the two moons that kept Drosero well lit even in their darkest hour.

Dodging the one he still hadn't evaded, Marco focused on eliminating him. It took a few more sharp maneuvers and pulling more hard g's, one so tense that his PICC-line automatically activated. He hissed as the line shot cold venom into his veins to protect him against the gravitational forces. Neck-in-neck with this fighter, Marco grew aware of the tension radiating through his limbs and remembered what his flight instructor on Kynig had taught him—to relax into it mentally while tensing his muscles to keep the blood pumping to his heart and brain. Let the ship show him what it needed. He settled into the seat and let it cradle him.

Then he saw the opening he needed. Dipped to port.

Crack! Tsing! His wing tapped the other craft as it attempted to duplicate the maneuver he'd used to eliminate the first one. The fighter lost a wing. Went into a spiral dive. Marco veered up and away.

"Aetos Actual, you have four more heavy fighters coming at you."

"Sounds like they know who they're targeting."

Marco twitched. "Maybe I need to break atmo."

"Interceptors are space capable, but the fuel isn't there," came Jubbah Smirlet's warning through comms.

Jaw clenched, Marco wished he could look up through the black to wherever that creature was. Nothing would fuel his fury more than eliminating her.

"Aetos Actual—two coming in hot and fast—"

Trusting his receptors and instincts, Marco veered off and banked around, finding himself in a head-on with a Symmachian craft that was ahead of the others. One thing about Symmachian fighters—they all fought the same way. Same tactics. Which meant they were predictable. A shiver rippled through him and competed with the fire of his brand. He cocked his head, trying to shake the discordance. "Xanthus Four, ready to chase down some diabolus?"

"Thought you'd never ask, Aetos Actual."

"This is Xanthus Six," came a panicked comm. "Lost engines . . . right wing . . ."

A dozen more Droseran ships went down, followed by twice that from Vorn's fleets. An hour and too many lives lost. Another hour flying doubled the casualties.

WorpWorpWorpWorpWorp!

"Proximity alarm," the system warned.

A jolt radiated through the ship. As if someone had hooked Marco's chest. Stopped him cold. His body thrust forward then ricocheted—but not by much, thanks to the harness.

Silence gaped through the craft. Marco scanned his displays. Felt the emptiness of the moment. "Curse the reek!" Even as he felt gravity yank him downward, Marco scrambled to restart the ship. He'd heard about these modified EMP blasts—targeted. How in the Void had Symmachia harnessed that to Interceptors?

He was falling fast. Too fast. In a spin. Cold.

Head whipped and thoughts frenzied, he closed his eyes. Went through the protocols to get the ship operational again. These EMPs were temporary—wouldn't fry the ship. Only disable it long enough for it to drop out of the sky. Loss of environmentals made it cold, a feeling that trilled into his bones.

His ship whorped back to life even as the wastelands rushed at him, taunting him with a rhinnock who grazed unwittingly. Thrusters fired. Interceptor rattling hard, angry over what he'd put it through, Marco pulled back on the throttle. Veered off to port and skyward.

"—rco! Marco!"

"Here. I'm here!" he said around a ragged breath as he pulled away from the death dive and let his systems and body catch up. Even when they had, he felt something . . . wrong. He searched the sky, his instruments, his—

"They've got a modified EMP on the dreadnought they launched from."

"Yeah, figured that out. Thanks." Shaking his gloved hand to put some warmth back into it, Marco realized it was more than that. The chill—

"Aetos Actual, you have heavy fighters coming your way."

Screen alive with the ships bearing down on him, Marco whooshed eastward, toward the Kalonican Sea. "I know, I know—they're on me. Taking fire!"

Sensors were alive with readings—both Interceptors and Rapiers.

"Marco."

Roman. Marco almost let out a breath.

"They're targeting you."

"Enlightening," Marco bit out. Cold. So very cold. Why? Was he over Iaizon? The colder temps might wreak havoc on the Symmachian ships. Of course, their older, lesser fighters would have a harder go of it. But the tundras of Iaizon might be the best place to crash. Lower the casualty rate. That wasn't the reason, though. He . . . Maybe he should thump—

"Marco." Roman's tone was borderline condescending.

Ever since he'd lifted off, Marco had felt like a man standing in a swarm of locusts that were trying to eat his flesh off. Xisya wanted him dead.

She wants more than that.

The fighters swarming him . . . keeping him busy . . .

Marco hauled in a breath. "No!" Suddenly, he knew. Knew what this was about. He jerked down, angled the ship to see the ground through the canopy, but he was getting too far away. Heart jammed in his throat, he pulled up hard and spiraled around back toward Kardia.

He keyed his comms. "Roman." Marco's veins pulsed, sending an icy finger down his spine. "They're distracting me—all the fighters." He narrowly avoided a collision with a Symmachian. Cursed as he banked down and back toward the sea, searching the capital.

"Aye," the master hunter growled his agreement.

"They're going for Kardia—Isaura!" Sick to his stomach, Marco cut his engines, let the ship drop. "Get them off me."

And just as the locusts again swarmed, a barrage of Interceptors was there, peppering the enemy ships, pulling in and diving around the ships as Marco fell away. With enough distance between him and the fight, he hit the thrusters and shot toward Kardia.

Panic churned and pecked at his focus. Fire coursed, chasing off that col— "Cold." Heart alive with panic, Marco reached out. *"Isa . . ."*

Emptiness filled the dreamspace.

"Isa." Why wasn't she answering? This felt very different than before, when he returned from Kuru. *"Isaura!"*

Marco fought off one last Symmachian who'd managed to tail him, and unleashed his fury on the skycrawler, sending his ship tumbling through the sky, over the cliffs, straight into the sea. "Kardia, Aetos Actual RTB. What's going on down there?"

"Repeat, Actual?"

"The kyria—make sure—"

"Sire, reports are coming in—Eidolon in the castle. And Irukandji."

Marco cursed. Skipping the tunnels and base, he came in faster than he should've. His Interceptor skidded into its landing and slid to a stop next to the *Qirolicha*. He flicked off his harness and punched open the canopy. Hopped out. Used his parkour skills to slide down the still-hot ship.

Even as he regained his equilibrium, he heard the belltowers peal and shoved his receptors wide open, searching for her. Screams ricocheting throughout Kardia, yanking him onward.

He stumbled and caught his balance, only then seeing the bodies of regia strewn across the courtyard. Sprinting, he lifted his gaze to the heavily damaged walls of Kardia. To the westernmost entrance that led to the lower reaches. Still intact.

Boom! Boom-boom!

The concussion of a bomb vaulted Marco into the air. He landed on his back, vision black. Hearing hollowed. The acrid smell of burning metal and flesh thrust him back into action.

"Isa! Isaura, answer me. Please!" Marco raced for the entrance.

Aerios and regia rushed toward him, swords drawn. Their faces melted into relief when they recognized him. "Four Eidolon—we killed two but lost the others, sire!"

Marco turned, his gaze trekking over the façade, windows that now only had one arc. Turrets slumped in agony. The walls dribbling stones down into the gardens, burying horses and sergii alike.

He knew not what threw him forward, but his thoughts finally caught up as he pitched himself down the dozen steps into the lower reaches, following her scent. Lavender and white oak. Soft, beautiful. "Isaura!"

Not soft. *Faint.*

Panic punched through him as he plowed through the passages, shoving aside one haggard person after another. Following . . . Where? Where did her scent go?

You are too panicked. Calm yourself.

Breath staggering through his lungs, Marco stretched his neck. Rolled his shoulders. Pressed on. Heard shouts and coughs around him. Regia ordering people aside. Her scent called to him with a note that . . .

Marco stopped short.

Cold. The chills in the ships. The feeling of being near Iaizon. It was not the atmosphere he felt but . . .

Absence.

"No," he breathed even as he threw himself at the stairs to the left. Scrabbled over the marble floor littered with rock and debris. A line of aerios blocked the hall that led up a flight to the library and . . . nursery—and they yielded without word as he barreled through.

Chin down, eyes and receptors homed, Marco stalked forward, all too aware of the strident scents, the ash warring with the anaktesios. Panic warring with it as well. The assailing, suffocating grief.

Cold. Why was her Signature cold?

Wading through the passage felt as if he slogged through muck, each step impossible. Each inch torture. Each breath arduous and infuriating. Aerios were facing him. Unmoving. Eyes down.

He clamped his jaw and stormed deeper into the castle and its darkness.

A beleaguered, familiar face emerged from the dust and haze—Theilig. The man pitched to the side and vomited.

Marco threw himself around the corner and rammed into the aged iereas. "Ypire—"

"Sire," the man choked, sidestepping Hushak the Stalker who slumped against the wall, knees gripped as he sobbed. "Do not—"

A thrumming swelled in Marco's head, his heart. A fury. A searing ignition of light and power that sent the iereas sliding across the hall and thudding into the wall.

Marco reeled around. "*Isaura!*" he roared, his voice bouncing back at him.

Somehow light flared ahead.

And stole his breath.

In the middle of the passage, hair in disarray, Kersei knelt in dark omnirs and a blue, flowery bliaut before a mound. Bloodshot eyes rose to him, widened. She let out a mewl and turned her head away.

"No," Marco croaked, rejecting what his receptors told him. What the void around his heart and adunatos screamed. Breathing a chore, he forced his gaze to the mound of tapestries and blankets before her . . . only then realizing the light he had noticed was not truly light. It was Isaura's golden hair splayed over the stone, grabbing the torchlight as it always had.

A garbled noise reached his ears as he saw her face. Ghostly white. Lips gray. His mind assembled the pieces it had formerly rejected. Kersei's omnirs were not red . . . they were covered in red. Blood. She held Isaura's arm . . . bloodied. Black blankets and dark tapestries covered her from the chest down. Saturated in blood. Isaura's blood!

"No!" With a strangled howl, he staggered forward. "Isa." He dropped to all fours. "Isa. Isaura," he pleaded. Caught her face, desperate for her to look at him. "Isaura!"

She blinked.

He choked back a sob, vision blurring beneath the tears. "Please!"

"Du . . . san," she wheezed, eyes fluttering.

"I'm here, I'm here," he said, drawing his legs under him. "My aetos, I am here." He pushed aside the heavy tapestry that weighted her. It was too heavy for her to rise. That was all.

"No, my medora." A bald man dared catch his hand. "Do not—"

"Release me!" Marco thrust him off, and the man flipped backward beneath a blast that surprised, but he cared not. Returned his whole attention to Isa. "I am here. It will be okay." He just had to get her out of here, so she would be safe. They could fix whatever injury . . . "My love, come. It's not safe here."

"Marco, please!" Kersei's voice was ardent but broken. "She . . ." Her brown eyes were pools of ebony beneath unshed tears. "She is . . ." A sob wracked her.

"Away!" he snapped. "Get away, Kersei. Leave us." He bent to gather Isa up. Help her—

She grabbed his face, her hands slippery against his beard. "Marco! *Do not* move her." Her chin trembled just as her words did. "She is dying."

"No." The word was empty. Like the dreamscape. Like her Signature. He glanced down, finding . . . emptiness. It yawned, taking the whole of his heart and adunatos. "Isa . . ." He slumped at her side. "Isa. Isa, no! Do not leave me. I forbid it!"

Lips moving without sound, she blinked. Those glorious green eyes found his. Glittered for him as they always had. "Du . . . sa . . ."

He moved in, hearing the shouts to clear the hall. Feeling . . . hating . . . *resenting* the emptiness. "Isaura," he said, with a deep, agonized moan. Hot streaks slid down into his beard.

Her hand somehow found his, slick with her own blood. "Mer . . . cy." A red stream slipped from between her lips and she coughed. Choked. Blood squirted.

"Isaura, I'm here." He would be strong. For her. "It's okay, we'll get you to a lectulo. Th-the *Qirolicha*. Or a Lady. They will help—"

"No . . ." The word struggled from the back of her throat as those long delicate fingers closed over his. Squeezed—a touch so light he almost didn't feel it. She grunted, her eyes sliding closed and pushing free a tear. "Sorrry, Du . . . san . . ."

"No," he growled. "*No*, you will be okay." He bent and kissed her face. "I need you, Isa. You are the calm to my storm. The light to my darkness. Th-the Lady will help."

"No." She again struggled with the word. Shifted and coughed.

"Isaura, be still. The pharmakeia . . ." Marco felt something against their hands. Saw that she held another—Kersei's. He frowned. Then refocused on the pharmakeia, who slumped against the wall, his stench one of regret and despair. "Do something! Save her!"

Misery haunted dark eyes. "There is . . . nothing I can do." His chin dimpled and bounced as he fought tears. Shook his head. "I beg your mercy."

"No!" Marco barked. "No mercy, you simpering fool. Help her! Stop the—"

"Dusan."

So soft a whisper stilled his warring breath. He jerked back to her. "Isaura . . ." This could not happen. Not to her. Not Isaura. "My aetos . . ."

A crooked smile wavered across lips that had spoken lifegiving words, challenged him, startled him, loved him. "Wings . . ." She smiled at him. "Love . . . her." With a soft grunt she slid her blood-slickened hands over his—and Kersei's. "Peace . . ." Her face twisted as she cried. "I . . . love . . . you. Thank . . ."

When she did not finish, he searched her face. Her Signature yet bathed his receptors, but faintly. He slipped a hand beneath her head. Bent closer. Pleaded quietly with choked words, "Don't leave me." Tears stung, running hot and fast over his nose and beard, silently dropping onto her face. "Please—I beg you." He slid his arm around her and pulled her into his arms as they lay on the slick stone. "Isaura, please! This life has nothing for me without you."

She did not move. Did not speak.

He buried his face in her neck. "Please! Please, please." He strangled a sob that wormed through his chest, pulled her closer, wanting to protect her. Keep her here. Yet he felt her Signature fading . . .

Her body relaxing.

Strength leaving.

Breath slowing . . .

"Noo," he begged, not caring how he sounded, how he cried out that word in a way that warbled and whined. Tears defied him as she did. Though his anger rose to the fore, he wanted her to know one thing: "I love you." She had known so much pain in her life, and in the last cycle, she had conquered it all. "Fly, my aetos. Be free."

The last wisp of her note slipped past his receptors with her final breath.

Never had she seen or heard such a terrible thing. Her heart rent in two, watching Marco curl Isaura into his arms and lie with her as she died, both of them soaked in her blood. Kersei huddled to the side, sobs wracking her. It had all happened so fast. One minute they were in the tunnels and closing the door, the next they realized Mnason was not with them. Even with her swollen belly, Isaura had rushed back to the castle without concern for her own welfare.

Unable to move, finding it abhorrent to leave Isaura's body or Marco, who could not let her go yet, Kersei sat against the wall. Tears returning every time she looked at the ashen face of the Moidian beauty.

Marco's groan and sob reverberated through the darkened passage, so horrible and agonized that Kersei could not bear it. She tightened herself into a ball, sobbing quietly with him, for him.

Was it minutes or oras later, she knew not, but he finally released her. Eased back as he stared down at her, hand on her shoulder. "What happened?"

He did not growl it. Or speak as a demand. But there was a latent ferocity in his question that terrified Kersei, forbade her from speaking. She looked around for another to speak the terrible truth but realized they were alone. No doubt Theilig had forbidden anyone entrance, and Ypiretis had gone to check—

"What. Happened?" Marco's voice was hoarse . . . and angry.

Sniffling, Kersei straightened to answer. But even thinking of it shoved tears out again. "She . . . um . . . Mnason was missing . . . I turned to ask Kita where she had last seen him, and . . . I heard a shout. Looked back down the tunnel opening and saw Isaura hurrying across the lawn. Cetus behind her . . ." She chewed her lower lip to stop crying. "It happened so . . . fast. So chaotic. I raced after them, and we all quickly realized there were raiders in the house. Theilig was fighting that one"—she bobbed her head toward the dead raider who lay in shadow and his own blood—"when another appeared.

Isaura and I tried to get Mnason to safety. Kita and her son managed to slip away, but . . ."

Kersei cupped her hand over her mouth amid another sob. "I . . . I heard . . . this . . . noise . . ." Recoiling as the memory washed over her, she strained to speak, her throat raw and her heart bludgeoned. "It was so . . . horrific. When I glanced back . . . I s-saw . . . a javrod . . . It went right through her."

Marco pushed to his haunches, touched Isaura's hair and face again, then stood. Stared down at her fallen form. "So, this day Symmachia has ripped from my hands . . . *everything*. My love, my heir . . . hope."

More tears rushed in, but then she heard his words. "No." Kersei struggled to her feet, wavering, her boot, sticky from blood, slipping on the floor. She steadied herself. "No, Marco. The baby—"

His gaze snapped to hers, those eyes fierce and cold, daring her to speak.

"Isaura . . . sh-she knew her death was certain, but she said the baby had a chance. She begged us—the pharmakeia to save her." She choked another sob. "The only way to do that . . . It meant they had to . . ."

"Cut her out."

The way he said that, emotionless, hollow, startled, made her lose the battle against her tears, remembering Isaura screaming, agony all she knew in her final moments.

"Aeliana . . . lives?" He sounded so raw, vulnerable.

Oh, that she could hand him this one saving grace. "I . . . know not. The other pharmakeia took her to a clean, quiet place to work on her. She was so very tiny. So frail."

Those words seemed to ricochet through him, then he knelt again beside Isaura. Scooped her into his arms.

"My lord—"

His scowl seemed like shards of glass as he skewered the regia trying to stop him. He lifted his love into his arms. Pressed his cheek to her head where it rested against his shoulder, whispered something, then stood and carried her down the hall.

Legs and courage weak, Kersei trailed them. They were halfway down the hall when Mavridis rounded the corner.

The powerful Stalker hauled up when he saw his dead daughter in Marco's arms. With a strangled shout, he staggered back against the wall. He dropped his head to his chest that rose and fell raggedly amid his anguished silence.

They continued down the passage to their chambers, and Ixion Mavridis joined them. In his private quarters, Marco strode into the bedchamber and laid Isaura on the bed. Drew the coverlet to her chin and sat at her side, holding her hand.

Unable to remove herself, to leave him in this state, Kersei perched on a settee, and Ixion stood on the other side of the bed, arms crossed, chin tucked, as he gazed down upon his dead daughter.

"Duchess?"

Numb with grief, Kersei twitched to the side and found Kita there. She rose and caught the woman's arms. "The baby—"

"Would you come?" Isaura's lady's maid pulled Kersei just outside the door. "I must speak with you."

Kersei moved through the small crowd that gathered in respect of their fallen kyria. "Did she . . . Is . . .?" She could not bring herself to speak it. Losing the babe as well would destroy Marco.

"I beg your mercy to be so blunt," Kita said quietly as she tucked her head, looking at her with meaning. "We need a wet nurse."

Surprise leapt through Kersei, and though she felt a tinge of embarrassment, there was a notable truth. "Then she—"

"Does she live?" Marco's strident voice demanded from the room.

They both looked back through the crowd to where he still sat at Isaura's side, his back yet to them, his grief evident.

"For now," Kita said quietly. "She . . . the pharmakeia has tried all he knows, but she is struggling."

Poor thing had been cut from her dying mother's womb. Grateful the woman did not openly mention what she sought, Kersei nodded to her. "Come. Let us—"

"What good can Kersei do?" Marco asked. "She is not a pharmakeia."

At his challenge over her summons, Kersei lowered her gaze and hesitated, then looked over her shoulder, past the regia and Stalkers. "I yet nurse Xylander . . . It is thought, mayhap, I could help Aeliana."

There was barely a twitch before he gave a dull nod. He seemed so rigid, so barely composed. On the verge of collapse. Or mayhap rage. She knew not which burned hotter in his veins, but she sensed the next few rises would determine his course, and she ached for him. He had not had time to process anything, not even the death of his beloved, and his daughter was yet in distress. Desperately, she wanted to go to him, promise him he was not alone in his grief. Hug him. Assure him Isaura would not be forgotten. But her niceties would be rejected, of that she was certain.

So she made her way to the makeshift medical area where the pharmakeia and two nurses hovered over the tiny form laid out on a thin blanket on the table.

Her heart cinched at the little thing, nearly two months early, arms and legs flailing as the pharmakeia pressed one device after another to her bare chest. With a huff, Kersei snatched a cloth and blanket from the side table and strode across the room. "Are you mad to leave her so exposed when she is so new?"

"Duchess, I am well able to take care—"

"No wonder she struggles." Struck by the tininess of the babe, who was not much bigger than her hand, she swaddled her up and tucked her close, fingering the downy black hair. Though the babe quieted, her eyes—was that a hint of green?—did not focus as she stared into the air. It was as if she saw nothing.

The pharmakeia huffed. "Her lungs are underdeveloped and her—"

"Kita, find the master hunter and ask if he might have a means to supply extra oxygen to the babe." Kersei looked to the pharmakeia. "And now, some privacy, please." Uncertain why she felt irritated with the man, she was glad when he left with his nurses. Settling into the only chair in the room, she wasted no time adjusting her bliaut and setting the babe to her breast.

Though she nuzzled, the babe did not latch.

Kersei pleaded with her as she tried again. "He cannot lose you as well, little one. For him, I beg you do it."

But once more the babe lay listless in her arms. As if she, too, were in shock. As if she knew what had happened to her mother. Throat thick and eyes burning, Kersei thought of what had been said about this babe, this . . . "Daughter."

Oh mercy. Tears welled stronger, realizing if Marco's daughter was also one of Eleftheria's Daughters, she had felt what happened to Isaura. She knew. It was there, imprinted on her adunatos.

"Ma'ma," Kersei called around her own tears, which landed on the cheek that should have had two more months within her mother. Two more months to develop. *"Ma'ma, please!"*

"What is it—"

"The babe!"

"We are aware Aeliana is born."

"She needs help—your help." She again smoothed a hand over the downy head. *"I fear she may not live as she does not thrive. She knows, doesn't she? She knows her mother—"*

"It is impossible for her not *to know when they shared the same body."*

"Can you not heal her? Somehow? Please—Marco cannot lose another. The loss of Isa . . . I see it already in his eyes. Losing his daughter—"

"Seek peace, Kersei. The child has more in her than we could ever provide. Feed her. Care for her."

"I would, but she will not latch." Squeezing tears off, Kersei stared at the little baby in her arms. So much smaller than Xylander ever was. So fragile . . . so . . . quiet. "I beg you, Aeliana . . . eat."

She swiped her finger along the cheek that should have been fuller when she made her entrance into this cruel world. "Which merely shows you to be a fighter already." Kersei raised the babe and kissed her cheek. Whispered, "You will never be alone. I swear it." She knew not why she made the vow, but the words were as fiery and Lady-breathed as anything that had come from Kersei.

"Please . . . eat. For him. He knows it not yet, but he needs you, little one. He will need the reminder of her that you are. He will need to see Isaura in you, to help him remember. Help him grieve . . ."

For that was what Xylander had done for her, helped her grieve his father's loss. Yet each day she saw pieces of Darius in her son, though he was yet only a few months, and those kept his father alive in her heart and thoughts.

"Thrive," she whispered. "It is the best weapon against an enemy bent on destroying us. So, thrive, Aeliana." As she lowered the babe to her breast once more, she teased the side of her mouth, encouraging her to latch.

Kita returned with a small bottle and a mask. "He said to put it near her mouth and nose." The lady's maid set the metal bottle on the chair and set the plastic mask near Aeliana's face, then excused herself to afford them privacy.

Kersei felt the cool air and wondered if it might interfere with—

With a small, shuddered breath, Aeliana turned and opened her mouth. Hands bunched at her throat, she latched. Suckled.

A tremulous laugh forced out more tears. "There . . ." Relishing the newborn's hair and soft skin, she caressed her. "I knew you would fight. You are *his* daughter. How could you not?"

TSC-C *CRONUS*, DROSERAN ORBIT

The bombardment was going well. Maybe too well. But Domitas had measures in place and prayed earnestly what he detected from the planet was not accurate. Even as he wished it, he had not one but two very unexpected visitors that threw up the security halo in his office.

Domitas came to his feet, chest swelling with pride. "Son."

"You need to stop the attack on Drosero." Tigo's eyes blazed. "Now."

"I'm good, thank you," Domitas sniffed. "How are you?"

"Billions of lives are at stake and you want pleasantries?"

Indignation flaring, he shifted his gaze to the Faa'Cris at his son's side. "I see you're rubbing off on him."

Rejeztia lifted her chin. "Tigo has ever been your son, Do'St."

"It's pretty scuzzed finding out everyone you thought loved you or respected you has been lying to you the whole time."

Wincing at the truth of his son's words, Domitas side-eyed Rejeztia.

"He needed to know."

Tigo frowned, looking between them before focusing on Domitas again. "Can you explain something to me?"

The way he said that tightened Domitas's clypeus, because it wasn't a question the way it'd been presented. It was a challenge. Enough years in the Navy taught him to offer as little as possible up front. Besides, Tigo was notorious for thinking the worst of him.

His son leaned in and pressed a hand to his desk. "I don't get it, Admiral. Months back on the *Macedon*, you handed me key intelligence. Helped me escape." He folded his arms and cocked his head. "But I also know you were in private meetings with Baric and Krissos and other officers who are leading the charge against Drosero. When you gave me that disc and I watched it, I thought—you know, maybe I've got him wrong. Maybe my dad isn't the diabolus incarnate." He stretched his jaw. "Yet! Here you sit on this dreadnought attacking a planet that has no hope of protecting itself."

Domitas dragged a hand over his head and beard. On this ship or any other, he had never openly spoken of his duplicity out of fear that, despite his measures to secure his home and offices, he might be heard. Found out. He would be branded a traitor, guilty of treason. Which he didn't care about, but those judgments would stipulate his removal from Command. And that he did care about because it would prevent him from being in place when the time came to do what would have to be done. Remove him and there was a gaping void in the war.

"*Stop* the attack." Brown eyes sparked with conviction. "Tell me you know there is no honor in destroying a people who have no hope of defending themselves against the armada. What glory is there in the annihilation of a race that is weaker and less advanced?"

"That is your mistake," Domitas said, temporarily shelving that his son thought this of him, "believing anyone in Tascan Command cares about glory or honor." He stabbed a finger at the obsidian surface between them. "I am not here to gain more medals or accolades."

"Then what are you doing here, running sorties against them?"

"Decades have I spent working myself into this position, denying who I am, what I stand for." He stared at his son. "All to bring us to this day, this hour—that we can be the protection of that planet."

Tigo faltered. "I . . . I don't understand."

"While Baric may have put pretty words to speech to convince Tascan Command to move against this planet in order to gain the elefthanite for the jumpgates, the real reason—as the three of us know—is a prophecy. Xisya told them the ore is more powerful in fueling the gates, but from samples we've taken during excursions to the planet, it can't possibly be true."

"Then tell them and pull out! Go back—"

"Back where? I'm not leaving this engagement! Besides, it's useless to talk to them. They're spineless, consumed with their greed to expand power and line their accounts with more soleris."

Irritation dug hard between his shoulder blades. He considered the man his son had become. His only son. Eidolon commander faster than the majority of his peers and those who had come before him. An unfathomable instinct in combat. And that dogged, take-no-slag personality that made him a leader.

And a Do'St.

"You are angry because your own efforts have been ineffective in a war that still rages." Domitas paced the office. "A frustration I know far too well." He directed himself back toward the two. Stood behind Tigo, recalling the day he'd chewed out the 215 for their activities involving Marco and the

Droseran girl. "You've stepped onto a path," he said to the back of his son's head, "that has reached from centuries past. Affects the paths of not just your friends or this planet, but all of the Quadrants." He ambled around his desk. "Have they told you that?"

"There is little I don't know."

Domitas chuckled. "I'm glad to see you are man enough to acknowledge you do not know everything."

"I'm not here for father-son bonding."

"You never were." He cocked his head to the side. "Do you know why you are innately perceptive?"

Tigo held his gaze, almost in challenge.

Domitas went on. "I am—as Rejeztia just named me—Do'St. We are an ancient race as powerful as the Faa'Cris—"

"Jaigh already told me. And Jez."

"But did either of them tell you that you're one as well?"

For the first time, Tigo flinched. "I . . . assumed . . ."

"You were the first Do'St born in two hundred years, Tigo."

The kid shrugged, his eyes sparking. Though he smiled, his disgust filled the air. That and derision. "So." He bounced his shoulders. "When do I get my medal?"

Domitas relished his attitude. Classic Do'St. "When you survive the Progenitor's War."

"No one will survive," Jez hissed, "if this family reunion doesn't end." She angled to Tigo. "Remember why we are here."

Annoyance cloyed against his pride over Tigo. "I see the Faa'Cris still haven't learned that Do'St are not their puppets to be commanded."

Tigo slid his gaze to Jez. "Give us ten minutes alone. Then return—"

"You don't need her to be able to fold." Domitas shouldered in. "Have you found your span yet?"

Tigo stilled, eyeing him, uncertain. Scared, according to that efflux. "I . . ." He focused on the Faa'Cris. "Please. Ten minutes."

After shooting Domitas a glower, Rejeztia spread her wings. *Do not corrupt him, Domitas.*

"You and your Sisters far exceeded any damage I could do."

"That is not what I meant." She folded away.

Alone now with his son, Domitas wondered at Rejeztia's meaning. Was it possible she really cared about Tigo?

"Why do I not have a sister?"

Domitas cringed. He looked down and exhaled heavily. Of all the questions . . . "The accident that laid me up for several months when you were ten—"

"Metraxis 12. Epic tragedy."

"Took the lives of my entire team, but I survived to finish the mission."

"If you hadn't hit the facility overtaken by renegades, thousands would've died and a key fuel source for operations in the sector would've been lost. The fleet cut almost in half. It's why they gave you command of the fleet. You were the hero of Tascan Command."

Domitas felt his cheek twitch. "My team wasn't the only thing lost . . ." He stretched his neck. "I was heavily irradiated. And though I recovered, my ability to produce another heir remained . . . compromised."

Tigo considered him, eyes so like Renette's staring back. Hard. "Was it your ability or your will that proved uncooperative?"

"You mean did I cheat your mother out of a Daughter?"

Tigo didn't falter.

"No matter what you think of me, I did not cheat Renette of anything. I loved—*love*—your mother. And while the Faa'Cris now despise the Do'St, our kind are not without honor. In fact, it is a hallmark."

"Then why do the two races hate each other?"

"Difference of opinion on when and how to intervene. Do'St returned to the surface to be among those we were tasked with helping, while the Faa'Cris hid. Grew ever more secretive and deceptive, all in an effort to protect themselves against men who lusted after more than just the beautiful creatures they were."

"Is Marco a . . ." Tigo flicked a hand between them. "One of us?"

One of *us* . . . Pride swelled through Domitas that his son had already claimed his identity as one of their bloodline. "Sadly, no, though his mother is the Revered Mother." He angled his head to the side. "I expected more anger, resistance to this knowledge."

Tigo moved to a chair and sat. "Being the admiral's son taught me long ago that anger of that kind and its counterparts—bitterness and resentment—are useless in effecting change."

Domitas could not help but smile. "After you were a hellion."

"Couldn't let you off scot-free."

"So that's why you became an Eidolon."

"Becoming an Eidolon was the only way to change what I hated."

He took the chair in front of his son, a trill of excitement racing through him. "That is the very essence of being a Do'St."

The air warbled beneath his anger. "To the situation at hand, I want your word, *Admiral*, that you will cease operations against—"

"That I can't do."

"Why? What—"

"*Look* around you." Finally, his son seemed to have grown a pair of ears. "Get your head out of your butt and look around you, Tigo. What do you see?"

Brown eyes flickered to the door, the glass, where it lingered long enough to have taken in the crew. "Bridge."

"Yes. I am the admiral, not just of this dreadnought, but of the entire fleet." He growled, giving himself permission to speak of it. "*Think* what I must do. What it takes for me to maintain this position—why would I be willing to command this fleet, when—as you deftly pointed out—I helped you escape, I aided the Kalonican prince."

Tigo hesitated. Recollection rippled through his young, intense features. "Mom . . ." He blinked. "When she brought me to you at home, she said you had to remain in Command." Now as his gaze roamed the office, then the bridge, he was processing information. Assimilating it into the recollection he'd just had. "Xisya . . . the war . . ." His gaze hit Dom's again. "You're here . . ." He looked at the desk, the arrays. "Strategically."

Domitas drew in a breath and considered the efforts, the subtle sleights of hand over the years. "I may not be able to control them, but there is something I do control . . ."

Tigo stilled. "You mean to use the *Cronus* to defend the planet."

With a sigh, Domitas nodded.

"Then why haven't you stopped the attack on Drosero?"

"Being a double agent is risky enough. I have to do just enough to stay in power and as much as I can to protect that planet. Right now, what's saving Drosero is a sudden and pervasive ordnance failure on a few of our ships, all blamed on a software error." Domitas grunted and stroked his beard. "Truth is, I . . . I sense Xisya has an ace up her sleeve, and I will do whatever I can to stop her endgame. Though it may seem I'm on the wrong side of *this* war, I must remain here to be on the right side of that one."

Tigo studied him now, his expression fierce as his gaze roved face, beard, uniform, finally comprehending the volatility of Domitas's position.

"Understood." He swallowed. "I'm . . . sorry."

"Never apologize for doing something like what you just did. You saw what you believed to be a wrong and confronted it. That's the very nature of the Do'St, Tigo, though I know you don't want to hear it."

"Actually, it's nice to hear."

Domitas startled.

His son shrugged. "It explains a lot."

"It should." Never had he been so proud. "Now, let me show you something that will help your Droseran friends and prove what I've said. Who I am."

Deep below the once magnificent halls of Kardia, Ixion stood watch over his medora, who sat alone in the dim, musty crypt, staring at the contraption Daq'Ti had retrieved from the grounded *Qirolicha*. A lectulo, Marco called it. Sealing Isaura's body within would keep her preserved until she could be properly buried. Though touchstones lined the small chapel, darkness seemed to have an edge this rise.

Never would he forget coming around that corner and finding Marco carrying her from the passage where she had been slain. Where Aeliana had been miraculously saved. The pod rested atop the stone dais with Marco on a bench before it. Bent forward, elbows on his knees, one hand over the other and pressed to his lips, he sat silently. Had for the last several oras. Never rallied. Never spoke. No weeping. Just empty staring.

Behind him, Ixion grieved, too.

How things had changed: the man who had once begged Ixion not to force him to marry Isaura now sat brokenhearted before her corpse. This man struggled with change, with decisions thrust upon him. Ones not of his making or plans. Yet he had confronted them all. Lived and conducted himself with honor. It had done Ixion's heart good to see how Marco had loved Isaura and she him. Yet, she had been robbed of the life she had earned. Even as kyria—a title none had dreamed she would ever hold—she had not been treated as she deserved. Many loved her, but there were enemies bent on her destruction.

As her death proved.

Ancient, I beg your mercy for not being a better father to her.

She was greatness in an unassuming smile. Gentleness with the ferocity of a rhinnock. A ruler with the shrewdness of a sage in the youthful beauty of a woman who stole a hunter's heart.

"How long has he been there?" came a quiet whisper from behind.

Ixion glanced over his shoulder to Marco's uncle. "I found him here last eve shortly before the tenth bell."

The master hunter let out a soft groan. Shook his head.

No doubt he was taking in scents as the Kynigos were wont to do. Processing them, he likely knew better than any what Marco was feeling, thinking.

"What do you detect?" Ixion did not doubt that a plague of death and grief drowned this castle and the Kynigos receptors.

Roman planted a hand on his shoulder and squeezed. "Get some rest. I'll stay with him."

Ixion should be annoyed at the unanswered question. It spoke of disrespect, but he knew Kynigos were men of few words. Men who sought honor at all costs, yet their emotional wells ran deep.

The master stalked past him. Past the handful of hunters and regia positioned along posts and in shadows. Silent, respectful. But close enough to protect him. Hypervigilance was the name of the game after Kardia had been infiltrated and cost them the life of their kyria, his daughter. *My sweet, strong girl . . .*

Concern etched itself into his thoughts as the master approached his hunter. An uncle to his nephew. The closest thing to family Marco yet had, considering his other uncle was steeped in treachery.

Eyes dry and heavy, Ixion yielded his position, nodded to the regia, who had just changed shifts an ora gone, then started out of the crypt. He climbed the steps and trudged toward his quarters. A soft, gentle laugh pulled him around. Down the stone passage, he saw the light of a touchstone dancing out of a room. The voice—Kita's—drew him toward it. He stopped outside, peering into a room that had been converted into a nursery. Mnason slept on a cot in the far corner, and the infant prince, Xylander, lay on a blanket on the floor.

In a rocking chair, Kersei held the newborn princess. She met his gaze and smiled. "Elder Mavridis," she called quietly. "Would you like to hold your granddaughter?"

His heart lurched, and he moved faster than he had in many oras. Crossed the threshold and stood before her—*his granddaughter*. When the duchess gently lifted her into his arms, he froze. "I fear I will drop her."

"You deftly handle those blades and manriki," Kita teased, "so it is doubtful you will mishandle so precious a life." Her delicate fingers tucked aside the blanket that yet concealed the babe's face.

Small. "How can she be so small?" Wonder speared him. "I see Isa . . ." His eyes burned. Felt his throat thicken. "Aeliana . . ." A bud—she was a bud waiting to bloom.

"I believe she has her mother's eyes," Kita said. "She will change much, but I do hope she fairly resembles Isaura."

"In manner and appearance," Ixion grumbled a laugh as he lowered himself to a chair, staring at the tiny bundle. "What has Marco said of her? Is he pleased?" He sniffed. "Of course he is—she is his daughter."

When only silence met his query, Ixion glanced at the two women, who both seemed to have lost their voices and joy, gazes firmly fixed to the stone floor. "He has not come," he guessed with a sigh. "It should not surprise—I only just left him in the crypt." Around a yawn, he again feared dropping his granddaughter. "I should go . . ." Yet he remained a half ora, sitting and staring at the miracle Isaura had fought to remain alive to make happen. "It is time."

"Then, allow me to see you to your door," Kita said, shifting the baby from his arms back to Kersei's. "I would speak with you."

Out of his depth—both with the babe and with the woman he would be bound to soon, Ixion inclined his head. "Duchess."

"Elder Mavridis." Kersei moved to a bed and sat with the babe, staring at her so fondly.

Kita slipped her hand through his arm as they walked. It was nice—though strange—how comfortable she now seemed with him. He felt awkward of a sudden, alone with her, no other nearby as they reached his quarters.

She unthreaded her hand and pressed both palms to his arm, which she held in place. "I . . ." She met him with those soft eyes. "I am so sorry for your loss, Ixion."

His throat tightened. "Isaura leaves a great void in this world." He gnawed his lip to keep his chin from trembling. "It did not deserve her." He sniffed and wiped a hand under his nose. "I . . . I am grateful to the Ancient for Aeliana. I feel we yet have a small piece of Isa."

"Indeed. I look forward to watching her grow, telling her of her mother."

Ixion's eyes burned. He cleared his throat. "I should rest."

Kita nodded. "First—well, we are aware that these times are difficult, and I realize you have much on your mind with the war, with being advisor to the medora. As such . . . I would not have you worry about me. About a commitment you were pushed into." She removed the ring he had set there a few days past and placed it in his palm, curling his fingers over it. "When this is over—"

"No!" Fisting the ring, he caught her shoulders. "Do this not to me, Kita."

Surprise widened her eyes and parted her lips.

"I . . ." He nearly choked on the words, on restraining them. But there was naught for it. "I need you. Need the promise of us, of a future."

Her eyes glossed in the low light of the touchstones.

"I beg you not to undo what is done, what Marco demanded of me but was borne of my deep regard for you." He touched her cheek, cupped it. "Please, Kita. More than ever, knowing not what tomorrow might bring, I would have this—*us*. I need this, our future. You. Your . . . love."

A tear slipped free. "I feared you only complied with the medora's wishes—"

"Let there be no doubt. What I take is only the beginning, and I recognize what I have done." Once more, he slid the ring on her finger. Kissed it and her hand. Pressed her palm to his face. "If you will have this old, ragged Plisiázon."

She leaned into him, inappropriately, but blessedly wonderful. "Have you seen yourself lately, Stalker? Heard the way sergii fawn over you?" She tiptoed up and kissed him. "And you are mine."

"I pity you, Lady Kita."

"Pity?" she scoffed, then sobered. "It does seem amiss that we harbor this joy after Isaura's death, in the midst of affliction and pain." She peered up at him. "Do you not fear it will touch our lives again?"

Meaning she feared he would die, that she would lose another man she loved. "Mayhap, but at least we have once more known joy."

"Aye." Her gaze turned back the way they had come. "She fears for him . . ."

Ixion's brain struggled to catch up. "Who?"

"Kersei. She fears for the medora—he has not seen the baby."

"He will," Ixion assured. "In time. He has been dealt a terrible blow." He steadied himself, his own raging heart. "I struggle with the grief, the anger, the guilt . . . so I can only imagine what . . ." He bit down on the swell of emotion. Struggled to restrain it, to—

Kita slid her hand to the back of his neck and pulled his head to her shoulder. Wrapped him in a hug.

Cracks formed in the dam around his heart, ready to break. "I miss her," he sobbed, choked it off. Pulled out of her arms. "Beg your mercy." He shoved into his room and slammed the door closed.

And the dam broke. A sob wrenched from his throat. She was gone. His daughter. The one wrong he managed to turn around. She had made him proud. Her beauty spoke to them all, not the blonde hair or green eyes, but the pure heart and insightful mind as she stepped into a role none had prepared her for.

He growled through the cruelty that had robbed him of the greatest joy he had in life. "I failed you, Isa." He slumped against the wall, the room dark, empty, and cried.

It was hard enough to shoulder his own grief, but the pain clawing its way through the walls of this fortress was suffocating. Teeth gritted, Marco could not move. Had not moved. Cared not for the numbness that had settled in his legs and back.

A shadow fell over him where he sat before her body. Dimly he registered someone speaking his name.

She was gone.

Roman crouched at his side. "Marco. The net has sprung leaks. I'm sorry, but your people need you. We need you in the air."

He turned away. *"Isa . . ."* How many times had he called to her through their dreamscape? *"Isa, please . . ."* It was futile. He knew it. But he could not stop himself. Vainly hoping she would somehow answer. That because of their connection, the Ladies had snatched her up into their bosom and kept her alive.

"She is not here, Marco."

The walls around him hazed into a gray shadow that suddenly yielded its heaviness to the light of the Faa'Cris before him. "Mother." He stood, and though he knew not if those in the crypt could see him do so, he moved a step nearer to the elegance of power and might. "Where is she? Let me speak to her."

"Marco, you know she is gone."

"You could have saved her! And you did nothing!"

"We do not interfere in the—"

"Then by all that is holy and within me, I will give you war." He pivoted, then yanked back. "Seek peace? I think not! Peace is a fool's errand." He slapped his chest, then lifted his branded arm. "Vanko Kalonica! I *bring war!*"

Tucked into a cave on the cliffs of Kardia, far below the ruined castle, Tigo sat by the fire and stared out the opening to the night-darkened Kalonican Sea. The surf thrust itself on the jagged rocks below, haunting the cave with the raw power of the breaking waves. So much had changed. He wasn't really even sure who he was anymore.

And for the most part, he didn't care. He just wanted to protect this planet. No idea why. Just knew it was what he had to do.

Was that because of being a Do'St? His mom being Faa'Cris? Why couldn't it just be because he was Tigo Deken?

Scuz that. The whys and wherefores didn't matter. What mattered was standing up for those who couldn't defend themselves. Drosero needed help. He had two powerful bloodlines coursing through his veins. What good was that if not to save a planet?

"You should rest."

Jez's soft voice intruded from where she lay on a blanket pallet behind him. "Can't."

She was at his side so suddenly, he jerked.

"Gah! I hate that. Be normal—come up like a normal person."

She smirked. "That would bore you."

"At least my heart would still be working." Legs up, he hooked his arms over his knees and watched the foamy wakes racing each other back to the sea on the rocks below the cave. Even now, he heard the familiar whine of an Interceptor scream overhead. They had decided to wait until morning to visit Marco. Going in now might get them killed.

Jez nudged his shoulder, leaning into him. "Why can't you sleep?"

He lifted his gaze to the sky, barely visible from his vantage in the damp cave. "Everything. Sitting here, thinking about all the lives that are about to be lost to this insidious war." He huffed. "All because two sects couldn't work out their differences."

"That's an oversimplification."

"I know."

"I have never known a time when the Corrupt did not exist, but I grieve what happened. I long for the peace in the Tellings. For the brand of Marco and Kersei to be . . . real."

He shifted, frowning at the beauty beside him. "You don't believe in the prophecy?"

She breathed a laugh. "Oh, I believe. I only meant—I want what it says will happen to be real—now. To be in effect. For the Corrupt to be vanquished, peace restored, lands and peoples healed."

With a grunt, he nodded. "Knowing what the armada can do . . . knowing that this planet is as backward as they come . . . what hope is there? It seems so impossible."

"I understand, but if we trust the Ancient, if we believe His words in the Tellings, then we have no reason to doubt."

"Jez, come on," he muttered, just needing some space to explore his dark thoughts, "think how outnumbered and out-tech'd the Droserans are."

She gave a slow nod. "I know, but either the Ancient's word is true, or it's not."

"What if the person who recorded the Tellings was wrong and we have false hope?"

Leaning back against the cave wall, she gazed out at the waters. "Then it is implied that the Ancient could not overcome an inept person and right what was wrong. And that is something I will not accept. He always finds a way and vessel to deliver His truth."

"But—"

"Always." She turned and held his gaze, not to be fierce, it seemed, but to show her conviction.

He clenched his jaw, frustrated. Irritated. "I'm not sure who I am anymore."

"What we face is enormous," Jez said, kneading her temples. "It's normal to question and doubt, but do not let it distract you from the path."

"It's . . . maddening. So many things are wrong, upended. I can't even imagine what it's like for Marco, to lose the woman you love to this war . . ."

She considered him, and an intense sorrow crossed her features. "You're right. And as a hunter, Marco has an incredible empathetic connection because of the anaktesios—the ability to smell emotion—just as the Faa'Cris do—and the Do'St. The loss is unfathomable." She shook her head. "This is part of why we must go to him. Help draw him back from the darkness trying to consume his adunatos."

Tigo frowned. He was supposed to draw another man back from the darkness stealing into his own life and overtaking him?

"What you are sensing in yourself is not darkness, Tigo. It's the absolute justice of the Ancient."

"It feels . . . dark. Heavy."

"It *is* heavy." She shrugged. "And dark, in the sense that it is painful and difficult." She hooked her arm around his and leaned against him. "But I know you will bear it well."

"Wish I had your confidence."

She rested her chin on his right shoulder and peered at him. "Who you are has not changed just because you now know you're Do'St. You are still Tigo. A warrior in every sense. A compatriot. A protector." Her mahogany features softened. "*That* is Do'St, though I know AO would have you believe your kind to be the diabolus."

"He blamed that lie on the Ladies."

She seemed chagrined. "We started it, but many Do'St perpetuated it, lived up to it. Became it."

Tigo chuckled. "So now you're saying I am the diabolus?"

"No," she said, catching his chin and turning his head to face her. "You could never be that, Tigo. It's not in your adunatos. Warrior, yes. Guardian, yes. But not violence for the sake of violence. Not bloodlust."

"Are you just trying to make me kiss you?"

Jez looked away.

"This is when I want to do violence . . . when you tease me then retract any connection between us."

"I don't want to distract you from your path, Tigo. Your purpose is too important. Too many depend on what you need to do."

He frowned, studying her wide eyes, her full lips. "What're you saying . . .? What purpose?"

"To help Drosero."

He sniffed. "I was worried you were going to say there was a prophecy about me."

When she didn't smile or deny it—or scoff—he felt his gut tighten. "What aren't you telling me?"

"Nothing. I just—"

"No." He stood, thoughts sliding and slamming against one another. "There's a prophecy, isn't there? It's why you took me to Deversoria. It was never about being in love with me."

"When did I ever speak *that*?"

"Well . . . never, but— No." He splayed his hands, as if manipulating a flex screen to turn it off. "No, you're not distracting me from this. It's why you've given me the cold shoulder. Why you kiss me like nobody's business one second, then you're a frozen fish the next."

She drew back, her head angling. "I beg your mercy?"

"Holy slag. There *is* a prophecy." He shoved his hands over his hair. "That's why nobody told me off in Deversoria. That's why you left with me. Stayed with me." He sucked in a breath and flashed his palms again, bracing himself. "Okay, just give it to me."

Her ebony brow tangled in a knot. "What?"

"Am I going to die? Is . . . is that why you don't want to give in to what you're feeling for me? Because you know I won't be alive much longer?"

"Tigo."

Okay. So he was going to die. Yeah. Great. "How am I going to die? At least let it be glorious, since I don't have a choice."

"You always have a choice. Prophecies are not written to steal wills but to foretell the actions of the Chosen who let the Ancient use their lives."

Tigo drew up sharp. Stared at her. Couldn't breathe. Then huffed. "So there *is* a prophecy." He nearly choked.

"Enough, Tigo. We need to talk with Marco. In light of his loss, he is losing his way."

"You're Faa'Cris, why don't you just jump in and even the score?"

"If we entered every war between men or countries or even planets, where would it end?" She rubbed the center of her forehead. "But . . . we do need to deliver the intel Domitas provided and get Marco to focus on defending his people, not revenge."

"It's unfair, considering Isaura's death, that he has no time to grieve."

"If he does not refocus, many more will die."

Tigo balked. "Slag. I'm going to die." He roughed his hands over his face. "I should've seen this coming. That's why you came with me—to be with me when I die. Y-you didn't want me to die alone."

"At the rate you're going, who's not to say I didn't bring you here to kill you myself?"

He stilled.

"Oh mercies." She laughed. "You are too easy."

He frowned, thoughts ricocheting. "I don't understand."

She framed his face. "For such an intelligent man, you are often so blindingly, achingly slow." Shaking her head, she peered into his eyes. "Tigo, there is no prophecy that does or doesn't say you're going to die."

"B-but you and my mother said I was Chosen."

"We are all chosen. We *all* have a purpose." She laced her arms around his neck. "Mine is to be with you."

"In the cave where you're going to kill me."

She smacked the back of his head.

"Ow!"

KARDIA, KALONICA, DROSERO

The strangest of sensations wove through her chest and pulled Kersei into the passage. She stood there, cradling little Aeliana after an early-morning feeding, and scanned the dark hall.

Voices scampered over the stone, and she retreated into the shadows, hand slipping into the pocket of her omnirs and closing around the collapsible javrod. Since losing Isaura to those foul raiders, she dared not expect anything but trouble. In fact, she should return to the nursery—

Heat flared through her brand with such sudden ferocity, Kersei nearly yelped. She shifted Aeliana to her other arm and shook out the fire. Which told her—

Marco.

His tall familiar shape swung around the corner with power and determination marking every step he made. Securing his vambrace, he focused on his forearm, but there was a strange thickness to his arm that made him struggle to thread the clasps. Barking orders to the dozen or so with him, sending some off to the tunnels to take to ships, others to the outer walls to guard against raiders, he had not seen her. Had not smelled her.

Which betrayed his distraction.

Then that icy gaze snapped to hers.

Froze her. Stole her breath.

Glowering locked on her, he stalked onward as he crossed the great hall, unyielding, his broad shoulders swinging with his strident movements. No acknowledgement of her beyond that glower. Then his gaze dropped to the bundle in her arms. Hope thrust itself between her hesitation. Believing he would come to her, she angled Aeliana in his direction. Thought she saw a shift in his intensity for a fraction.

But it vanished just as fast.

Did he not care about his daughter? He had yet to see or hold her.

"Your daughter," Kersei spoke above the chaos around him. "She needs you."

Marco tucked his chin. Lowered his gaze. Swept past her.

"Please, Marco! She needs her father."

How could he not want to see Aeliana? She was beautiful and precious, so little. All that remained of Isaura . . .

Roman paused next to her. "He is at war," he murmured. Tucked Aeliana's blanket and touched the little cheek of his great-niece.

Once again, she found Marco, now donning a helmet as he climbed the steps out of the lower reaches. "Clearly. Are not we all?"

"No," Roman said, the word but a breath as he touched her shoulder. "With himself."

The warning in his words, the painful truth of them, what they could mean, pulled Kersei up a level to the dusty remains of a chamber that yet had an intact window. Moments later, she watched the ships take to the sky. Watched as Marco climbed into the ship he'd zipped in on when the keep had been attacked. He settled in the cockpit and his gaze somehow found hers again. There was no faltering. No . . . feeling. Nothing but a cold, hard expression.

The brand fired again, and hissing, she looked at her arm. Sensed not just rage—which would be justifiable—but also . . . darkness.

Alarm trilled through her. "Marco . . ." she whispered.

"My lady."

Startled at the voice and sudden intrusion, she turned. "Myles."

His visage softened. "I have orders to take you to the tunnels."

"The tunnels . . ." They had yet been heading there when Isaura went back in search of Mnason . . . and died. Kersei peered out the window to the last ships leaving the green.

"My lady, the medora has ordered you removed to the mountain shelter.

With the heirs." His corded arms flexed as he motioned her across the room. "We must go—at once."

"Aeliana is too fragile," she said, even as she started toward him. "It is too dangerous to take her into the musty tunnels. Her weak lungs need the dry warmth offered here."

Myles glanced at the babe but did not alter course. "She is Medora Marco's heir, and he would have her safe."

He has not even seen her.

Confused, Kersei went below. Not to comply with the order, but to afford herself time to think, to find a way around this. "I must speak with the pharmakeia. It would be foolish to take Aeliana into the tunnels in her fragile condition."

Myles said nothing as he escorted her to the chambers where Danae was already packing.

"This is foolish," Kersei muttered.

"Give care how you speak against your medora," Myles said with more than a little warning in his tone.

She knew he was right, but . . . "She is too small, too weak. Think what he would do if she caught pneumonia and succumbed."

At this—finally—Myles hesitated, flinched. "I beg your mercy, but I like my head attached." He shook said head. "I will not defy Medora Marco. Not now."

Kersei slowed and looked up at the burly guard. "What do you mean?"

He roughed a hand over his reddish-blond beard. "Well you know the medora has always been intense, but now"—he shook his head—"he is . . . fearsome. Downright intimidating. Something about those silver eyes . . ." A shudder ran through the man's burly frame. "I dare not cross him. As well, he is my medora and I will respect him for that alone."

Strange. She had never heard anyone speak ill of Marco before. Yet his words mirrored the uncertainty and confusion that had riffled through her moments earlier. "You are right. He is our medora," she conceded.

She sighed and laid Aeliana in the small cradle in the corner, grateful when the wee one did not stir. Even as she checked on Xylander, still so soundly asleep that he snored around his chubby cheeks, she struggled against the weight of the times.

Straightening, she started toward her wardrobe. "Myles, would you please retrieve a large basket—one that babies can sleep in, mayhap one we could sling over our shoulder for the journey?"

He inclined his head, ducked out of the room, and returned moments later with a reed basket. "We are out of time, so I hope this will suffice."

Flustered, Kersei nodded. She moved toward the babes and hesitated. Who should she carry? Xylander was her son, but she felt a powerful protective instinct over the newborn who fought for every moment.

"Could you carry the princess?" Danae whispered. "I . . . It frightens me to be responsible for her. She is so fragile, and she is . . . *his*."

Something akin to grief tugged at Kersei, hearing the fear in her cousin's words. Though she wanted to offer encouragement that Marco was not to be feared—*"You have nothing to fear of me"*—she understood the meaning. The change. The man who had husked those words to her a cycle past was not the same one who ordered them into the mountain.

"Of course." She passed Xylander to Danae with a practiced smile, then turned and bent toward the cradle.

Blue-green eyes fastened onto hers. Though only two days old and a preemie, she had a keen, startling awareness.

"Hello, little one," Kersei whispered around a smile as she gathered her into her arms. She followed Myles into the hall and faltered when she found more than a dozen regia waiting. The warriors snapped to attention, their readiness ever present. Leading them out, Myles nodded to the regia as he passed, Kersei and Danae following with the babes and noticing the way the regia flanked in a protective perimeter.

She glanced down at the Kalonican heir. *They are here for you . . . He cannot bring himself to look upon you, but you are what is most precious . . .* Delicate fingers splayed wide and rested over the blanket as those tiny eyes focused on Kersei. *He should know you. I wish he would . . .*

Light glared through the hall as they reached the top of the stairs and wound toward the door to the garden. Another half dozen regia stood there, waiting.

A powerful build broke from the entourage, and for a tick, her heart jarred, thinking him Marco.

"Duchess." Roman so strongly favored his nephew, it gave her a glimpse of Marco in twenty years, though she believed the medora to have an even more favorable appearance. His hand rested on her shoulder. "Wait a moment—there is heavy engagement overhead."

As if confirming his words, the walls and floors trembled beneath a concussive blast. Behind her came the sound of dribbling and cracking.

"Our fighters will draw the enemy away to ensure you and the heirs make it safely to the wall."

"How? Symmachia knows Kardia is the seat of power. Will they not singularly target us?" As they had when they killed Isaura?

His somber gaze told her what he would not speak. "We will soon have you to safety. Be patient." After a nod, he returned to the door and tapped something into his vambrace.

Marco. Marco was drawing them away. It was the only explanation for why the enemy would be lured from the castle—if they knew he was in one of the ships. She hurried forward and caught his arm. "Do not let him sacrifice himself."

Sad eyes met hers. "We both know there is little to stop Marco from doing what he sets his mind to."

"Ever were you his master, his mentor. Guiding him, instructing him. Have you no voice now? Do you not care for him that you would let him be so foolish—"

He lifted her hand from his arm and held it. "Think well the words you speak against Marco in this hour, when all are looking to him. Guard them. Guard him." He set a hand on the blankets in her arms, as if pointing her attention back to the babe. "Guard her."

"I have every intention of doing so."

Something played in his eyes that made her feel so very vulnerable, as if her heart splayed open. In truth, was it not her own body betraying her to one who could read emotions the way warriors read body language in sparring?

"Skies are clear!"

Roman shouldered into the door and thrust it open. "Go—run! Do not stop until you are in the wall."

Marco dipped the craft straight into the path of the oncoming fighter, locked for a head-on collision, firing. When the craft returned the barrage, Marco zipped back and forth, still holding course. At the last second, he pulled hard, darted straight up and away. Above him, he could see the Uchuvchi ships, no longer able to hold the net, strafing the incoming tide of Symmachian fighters.

It took no effort to anak Aeliana. Her scent so clear and distinct and with him like a warm cloak. So powerful, much more than in the days when she was still in . . .

Isaura.

Bloodied. Choking. Dying.

Fighting the wave of grief, Marco growled. "Augh!" Slammed his fist against the canopy.

Sparks and rumbles against his hull warned he not only had the attention of the fighter but by the fetor of fuel, at least two. Good. He shot southward, away from Kardia. He noted Kersei's scent doused in frenetic fervor, and even fear. A second later, it was muted, but not so much it could hide from him. They were in the tunnels.

"Aetos Actual, you have heavy focus."

"Copy that," he comm'd, redirecting his thoughts back to the engagement. "My stench is filling their nostrils, and I wouldn't have it any other way." What was the worst they could do to him? Kill him? It would be a mercy.

Teeth gritted, he focused on maneuvering. Fighting with wit and the millions-denarios ship that wasn't half as conducive to evasive maneuvers as the *Qirolicha.*

Why hadn't Symmachia yet nuked them? Wiped Droserans from the face of the planet. Had it not been for the safety net of the Uchuvchi, they would've already, he was sure.

Or . . . they want something . . . Something from this planet . . .

Crack! Pop!

Alarms screamed through his cockpit. A small fire on his tail fin. Marco put the Interceptor into a roll and pulled up hard, aiming straight upward. Sensors were bleeping and screaming at him, but in a few minutes, the fire was deprived of oxygen and snuffed out. Engines faltered. And he was falling back toward the planet.

Weapons' fire sparked off the ship.

Marco brought the nose up and over and felt the ship shudder and then rip to life once more. He bolted around, unleashing a barrage of fire at the Symmachian ships. Though he should bank away to avoid the debris, he knew doing that would cost precious seconds. Possibly let this vermin leave his skies to fight another day.

Not happening.

He plowed through the fiery debris, metal clattering over his hull, yet inflicting no real damage. He locked onto the other ship. Fired.

The enemy lit up and came apart.

After bringing his ship around, he shot back toward Kalonica, the thrill of victory sweet . . . and short. Always too short. "We need to get out of atmo and take down that dreadnought."

"You know well we don't have a powerful enough ship or weapons," came Vorn's voice from Command.

"Then give me a ship I can fly up their noses," came the voice of Galen Sebastiano, who had proven a fierce and effective pilot.

It wasn't that simple either. "They have shields," Marco said. "What of the *Qirolicha*? Is it ready yet?"

"Negative," said Rico. "Even if it were, we have yet to refine enough of the touchstone fuel. That's a no-go for now."

He banged the console around him. Keyed his comms. "Criemwolf."

"Go for Criemwolf," Vorn replied.

"Secure channel."

"Okay, Aetos, we're secure."

Marco roared back toward Kardia, and habit had him reaching for her again. Isaura . . . He growled and banged his head back against the rest. That thread where her Signature had always met his hung hollow and empty. A void. Jaw clenched, he closed his eyes.

"Aetos?"

Marco sniffed. Cleared his throat. "I know Jubbah isn't my biggest fan, but I'd like him to come to Kardia. Help us get the *Qirolicha* retrofitted for the touchstone fuel."

"The ship you returned on? I thought it was damaged."

"Daq'Ti's been working on it, but if we can get her space-worthy again, we might have a prayer of dusting these maggots."

"I'll get him there."

"Copy."

"Aetos?"

"Yeah?"

"Sorry . . . about your queen. She was unparalleled."

Marco gritted his teeth.

"I hear you have a daughter now."

The babe . . . He'd seen her in Kersei's arms . . . so impossibly small . . . Too small. Like she would die. Two months premature, what chance did she have of surviving? He just . . . couldn't. Couldn't touch her. Couldn't open himself to another death. It was better to detach himself now.

"I would talk to you about a wedding for our children in a couple of decades."

A glint near the horizon jerked his attention back to the fight. "If I survive this battle. Aetos out."

Over the next several oras he picked off Symmachian fighters who were entrenched in their tactics. Ones he had memorized, anticipated. The fetor of their fuel gave him ample warning. He would stay in the air and fight as long as he could.

But the *urp-urp-urp-urp* of his low-fuel warning forced him to ground. "Aetos Actual RTB for refuel."

"Copy that, Aetos Actual. Prepped and ready."

Even as the comms silenced, Marco saw four new fighters tear into the sky and head his way, providing protective cover for his landing. He set down and gave a thumbs-up, waiting for the team to refuel his fighter, anxious to get back up there and continue the fight. Dangling from his control was the amulet . . . yet sticky with her blood. He reached out and touched it. Felt his chest constricting. Remembered the first time he'd seen that carved into its center was the *Trópos tis Fotiás*. He had touched it where it sat at the hollow of her throat . . .

Isa . . . My aetos . . . His eyes burned.

"Augh!" He jerked his head up. Banged it against the headrest again.

Realized his Interceptor hadn't been fueled. He glanced to the side. No workmen. He keyed his mic. "Base, this is Aetos. Where's my fuel?"

"No more sorties today, sire."

"Says who?"

"Marco." Rico had a commanding voice. Always had. "You're not going up for another twenty-four. You know flight rules."

"Those rules are for training, not combat." Marco frowned. "Stop protecting me and let me do my job!"

"Stop being petulant," his advocate said, his voice matter-of-fact. "You need rest. You haven't slept, and you've been running sorties for hours. Your ship needs maintenance, rearmaments, and refuel. That takes time."

"Then give me another ship. The enemy isn't taking naps. Neither am I."

"Come in, Marco. I command the airstrip and you will not be cleared for flight."

"What will you do? Shoot me down?"

"I'll throttle your ruddy neck, *then* disable your engines."

Marco punched his console several times.

"Feel better now?"

He cursed. Felt the rage rushing in to devour him.

"Now?"

Unplugged, he hit the canopy release, snatched the amulet, and hiked himself over the side. He dropped to the ground with more than a little spike of pain up his right leg. Amulet fisted in his hand, he yanked off his helmet. Stalked toward the underground system. What was wrong with them? They wouldn't stop Symmachia by sitting on their butts. What did Rico think he was doing, grounding him?

"Augh!" He pitched his helmet across the road with a shout.

Air and scent around him evaporated. Sucked into a vortex. Light exploded. Marco vaulted backward, sure the enemy had finally made it past the Uchuvchi strafing to find the base. He crouched, shielding his eyes.

Air rushed at him, violent and chaotic, sending a squall of . . . *Minty lavender.*

What the reek?

He dared look, stunned to find glimmering armor wreathed around a dark-skinned female warrior. Faa'Cris. He recognized this warrior . . . knew her from somewhere, though his mind refused to make the connection. The man at her side, hand falling away from its grip on her sword arm, was easily known. Even without the heavy mechanized armor of an Eidolon.

"Tigo." Receptors speared with the minty aroma, Marco unfolded himself from the crouch. Struggled as the woman's glorious form morphed into one he did recognize. "Jez." He detected the stench of surprise from the crew and glanced between the newcomers. Wondered what they were doing here. Prayed they were not now to be named enemy. "You missed Symmachia by at least a hundred thousand klicks."

Jez squared her stance.

Void's embrace. He really did not want to war with someone he'd thought to call friend—but why would a Faa'Cris be here? His brand tingled.

Her gaze traveled from his rolling helmet, which had hit a wall and spun back toward him, to his hand, then his face. "Have we interrupted something?"

He was done being lectured by women who thought themselves superior. "Smart to ditch the Eidolon uniforms. Might mistake you for the enemy." He pointed toward the sky. "Not sure if you've noticed, but our planets are at war with each other."

Jez lifted her chin. "We must speak with you."

With a huff, Tigo shifted around her. "Excuse Her Superior Mightiness, but we have been to Tryssinia. Then Symmachia—not as Eidolon. That rank no longer weights our shoulders or consciences. Last we visited with a certain fleet commander in orbit over us. Now, we are here as . . ." He eyed Jez, then lifted a shoulder in a lazy shrug. "Honestly not sure what we are anymore, but we have intel I think you'll want."

"Much has changed since last we saw one another."

Tigo followed Marco into the tunnels, stretching his neck at how strangely familiar they were to the ones in Deversoria. He couldn't help but wonder if the network of caves here—used by the Kalonicans for their ships—wasn't on some other plane like Deversoria. "Right? Last time, you were a hunter absconding with a warrior's daughter, a fugitive."

"Absconding." Marco sniffed. "You Symmachians always have a unique way of seeing things."

He smiled as they entered a room set up like a simplified Command center. No high tech or systems, and it was . . . strange. "Yet here we are—you are a king."

Marco's jaw muscle jounced as he looked to the ground.

"And I . . . well, I guess now *I* am the fugitive."

"Your father still hunting you down?"

"Actually . . ." Tigo glanced at Jez as they were offered seats around a long table. He tugged out a chair and lowered himself onto the wood, taking in the faces and names of the men who filled in around them. A handful were, no doubt, guards here to protect their king. The others . . . advisors, he guessed. "We need to catch you up on things. Showed up at first light, but you were already in the skies doing your thing."

Jez widened her stance, refusing a seat. "As such, we have no time for pleasantries." Her eyes glowed violet as she looked to Marco. "Progenitor, we come because the tides are shifting. Your enemy is winning and will soon overtake you."

Marco's cheek twitched beneath his light beard. "Unlike the Faa'Cris hiding in their precious underground city, I am here—aboveground—fighting for my people, and I do not need a Lady to tell me we are losing."

Tigo stood with a nervous smile. "Sorry. She's not real good with diplomacy."

"Never met a Faa'Cris who was," a broad-shouldered man said as he joined them, his voice deep and edged in annoyance.

"And you've met many?" Tigo wondered, confused at the confidence in the man's words.

"Roman," Jez bit out, "your dislike of the Ladies has long been known. Color not this discussion with your disgust."

Tigo cleared his throat.

"Remember, don't mention his wife," Tigo said to Jez via Lifespeech.

"But she—"

"Don't mention her."

"Why?"

"He's bleeding grief all over the place. Touch that wound and he'll never work with us."

"That may already be the case. He blames the Faa'Cris—"

"My uncle is not alone in his disgust," Marco said, grabbing a mug proffered to him by a man with braided white hair and swords crossed at his back— Ixion, if memory served. After tossing back a swig, Marco wiped his mouth. "Say your piece, then be on your way. We have a losing war to fight."

"You have a spy among your ranks."

Marco slowed in lowering the tankard to the table. "And the name?"

"The admiral did not know, only that this individual has been feeding intel to Tascan Command about your militias, troop movements, tactical plans, and . . . your location." Tigo adjusted his stance. "If I recall . . . there was a man from one of the clans involved in the attack that cost Kersei her family."

"Rufio."

Another fierce-looking man—were they all as scarred as fighting dogs?— broke in. "I cannot believe we are blood related. My mother and her family have disavowed him." *What was his name? Bazi? Bazil?*

Bazyli, Jez said, her voice in his head exasperated.

Marco seemed focused on one thing. "My location . . .?"

"The admiral believes," Tigo said quietly, "it was this person who supplied information, play-by-play of your movement that led to a certain attack."

"You mean," Ixion growled, "that this person is responsible for Isaura's death!"

Marco seemed to grow in height and fury.

"If guilt is determined," Ixion said, "we could place the deaths of thousands on this person's shoulders."

Marco narrowed his gaze. "You mentioned troop movements, yet our troops and militia are unimpeded."

"Only because the TSC views them as insignificant." Despite their differences, Tigo had always felt a kinship, a connection with this onetime intergalactic bounty hunter. He may not wear the Kynigos cloak anymore, but he still had that stiff brooding mastered. "It is how Symmachia has gained such an edge over you. We have technology, weapons, ships, but—haven't you wondered why the fleet so perfectly targets every location? Or why they haven't pursued trying to destroy that unique ship you are retrofitting?"

Now Marco scowled. "They want it."

"You know there are already Eidolon on-planet. I would be very careful about who gains access to that ship."

Those eyes, which Tigo would've sworn were blue before, now had an icy edge. Cold, hard. Still trained on Tigo, the king angled to the side and whispered something to a brawny, much taller guard.

Only . . . he wasn't a guard, was he?

"That's him," Jez said via Lifespeech.

A few sputtering heartbeats later, Tigo still had no idea how to respond. If Jez was right—and she'd rarely been wrong about things like this—then this was the alien who'd come back with Marco. *"I guess your kind are wrong again—I see no violent beast prone to depravity."*

"Looks are deceiving."

"But he has the ear of the king, which we do not, so play nice." Tigo jutted his jaw. "He came back with you."

Gaze sharpening, Marco stepped through his guards and indicated to the tall alien. "What do you know of him?"

Palms out, chin down, Tigo demonstrated his intention to converse, not throw accusations. "Only that he returned with you on the ship that sits by your fortress."

Marco flicked his gaze to Jez. "You unnerve Daq'Ti, yet you are like the one he lives to serve."

"Meijatsia," Jez said.

"Bloodbreaker," Ixion muttered from behind Marco with more than a sneer.

Wait. "What?" Tigo eyed Jez, her visage still enlightened and shimmering and—well, he'd just never get used to how terrifyingly stunning she was in this form. "Who is that?"

Inclining his head, Marco ambled nearer. "You may have known her as Eija—she was on the *Prevenire*."

Tigo balked. "Seriously? From HyPE?" He squinted at Jez and deflated. *"You didn't tell me she—"*

"It was not relevant."

"Daq'Ti saved us from his own kind," Marco continued. "Eija set off a chain of events with her Touch, one event being a total rewrite of his DNA, which brought about a transformation in him that defies words. He was once a creature who looked more like lava over a fiery skeleton than what you see now. His kind have weapons that reduce people to ash. In fact, at least one of our crewmembers was obliterated by his men. I should have every reason to fear him, yet he has proven himself far more worthy of my trust than the Ladies." He gulped more of the drink, then narrowed his gaze on Jez. "Would you not agree? It is, after all, your kind who are responsible for what happened to his people."

"We are not on trial here."

"Aren't you?" Marco cocked his head. "You banished the Corrupt, so they fled to Tryssinia and there, poisoned the waters. Then they were thrust even farther away and ended up in a system where they found another race of men to control." He sniffed. "Faa'Cris . . . said to be so beautiful and inspiring, yet all I see in your wake is death and destruction."

There was going to be bloodshed. Tigo cringed, waiting for Jez's blow . . .

"Our—" Jez stretched her neck. "We have failed," she said quietly, humbly. But she hadn't yet surrendered her enlightened form, and that was interesting. Or terrifying.

Tigo wasn't sure which. Maybe both.

"All these things," Jez said, "are why I have walked the Quadrants with Tigo, seeking a way to help Drosero—"

"*Help* us?" Marco scoffed. He swallowed the last of the drink and slammed down the mug. "A day late, *Faa'Cris*." He had a wicked curl to his lip. "You had the chance to do that years ago, yet you cowered in your caves and kept your power and miracles to yourself. Chose few men to bed and left the rest floundering in a Quadrant that hated us. You're out of your eternal mind if you think we'll fall prey to sweet words just because you flash that armor and swing that sword—"

"You are right."

Marco stared at her. "I'm done." He motioned toward the door. "Let's g—"

"Your anger, Progenitor, is wrongly directed."

"Right, taunt the angry man by bludgeoning him with your truths."

"He is angry at the wrong people."

"But . . . is he? Completely?"

Now Marco laughed. A soft, empty laugh. "I think not." And that's when Tigo realized what he was seeing—or rather, what he wasn't seeing. This man, the hunter who'd spirited the pretty warrior's daughter off Cenon, had been raw intensity packaged in a black cloak and intrepid determination.

But that was not who stood before him. Not this time. This man was . . . bitter . . . jaded.

Marco shifted his gaze to Tigo with the barest of nods. "Thank you for the intel about the mole. We'll address it."

That sounded a lot like he'd kill the mole, but who was Tigo to say what punishment should be meted out to someone who jeopardized an entire planet?

"The Progenitor is diverging from the path."

"Quiet," Tigo hissed through the Lifespeech. *"I told you to let me talk to him."* He moved forward, not surprised when the guards angled in to protect their king. "Please, Marco. Wait. There is more." He lifted his hands half in point, half in surrender. "Please—we have started badly here—you and I both know the Faa'Cris are out of practice with tact and humility, but I will not leave Drosero until this battle is done. I would join your efforts."

Marco studied him for a long second, as did the others—his uncle, guards, the alien . . . who leaned in and said something to the onetime hunter.

Tigo must make him listen. "It is a sad tale that you listen to an alien from an enemy civilization that has spent its existence snuffing out people like us but will not hear me out."

"It is," Marco agreed, apparently understanding via the anaktesios that Tigo truly meant it in the manner which he'd spoken it. "In times like this, quickly does a man learn who is a friend and who is an enemy."

"Point taken, but I would hope you would reserve judgment now and allow me the chance to prove that I solidly fall into the 'friend' category."

MAHATUR, KURU SYSTEM

"It's been three *weeks*!"

Reef planted his hands on his belt and watched her hobbling across the yard in the dark, doing reps of various exercises to get back in shape after she'd broken a rib when they'd crash-landed into the hillside dwelling. "And you're still limping."

"I'm not," she countered—and immediately lost her balance. Stumble-shuffled to the stone wall that hemmed in the property. She slumped on it and growled. Banged a fist against the rocks.

"Careful," Reef said, folding his arms. "You did that once and your wings deployed."

She glowered at him.

He lifted his hands. "Hey. Just sayin—"

"Well, it doesn't help."

"Fine. Whatever." Reef stalked toward the door and hustled down into the earthen home. Cold bit into his bones, and he cursed the day he'd grabbed Eija, trying to keep her from leaping off that *Qirolicha*. He raked a hand through his hair, hating that it was too long to stand in a high-and-tight. Might just make like Marco and shave it off.

"You're too soft on her." Chief worked through his pull-ups, using a bar he'd set into the jamb of the pantry door.

"I'm nothing on her," Reef bit out. He turned toward the door. No. Didn't want to look at her. Also didn't want a lecture from the chief. He was freaking scuzzed. "She's a Faa'Cris—a Lady. What I do or don't do does not even matter to her."

"Oh, I think you've got that entirely backwards." Shad emerged from the pantry with a sack of grain. "Eija needs you more than ever, now that she's aware of her true identity."

"That doesn't track."

"Everything she remembers about herself is upended, and you have been with her on both sides of that."

"So have you," Reef huffed, then saw Shad's look. "Yeah, don't even go there." He rubbed his chest, only then noting the burn. Remembering . . . "Slag."

They both eyed him.

With another huff, he again shoved his hair back. "Help me get her back on her feet . . . er, in her wings—whatever—so she can do what she needs to do, and we can bail on this Voids-forsaken planet."

"And how do you plan to do that?" Chief had a challenge in his words. He dropped to the ground, wiped his face and chest, then slipped into a shirt. "What ship are we going to use to get out of here?"

Reef slumped onto a chair and held his head in his hands. "I have no idea. I just can't . . . I can't do this anymore. My skin is crawling."

"Can't do what?"

At the sound of Eija's voice, he popped to his feet. "Nothing." Since she was blocking the exit, he headed to the storage room. Not because he needed anything but because he had to get away from her. Away from this burn in his chest. He yanked the door closed and slumped against a shelf that housed crocks and tubers. Palming the wood, he felt that burn again. He drew his chin down and lifted his shirt. Peered at the imprint thrumming with heat and a very faint glow. "Slag," he muttered again.

"What's wrong?"

Dropping his hand from the shirt, Reef shoved to his feet. "How—" How had she gotten in without him hearing the door open? He eyed the wood barrier. Still shut. Catch in place. Slanting her a glare, he gritted his teeth. "Not fair."

Expression soft, she came toward him. "You're angry."

"Wow, is that your impressive supernatural skills of deduction there?"

She frowned, hurt rippling across her features. "What did I do to deserve that?"

"Nothing." He headed for the exit.

Though small, she was fast and determined, stepping into his path. "Reef, what's going on?"

"Just a bad day. Ready to get back in action. Tired of sitting around." He rubbed his knuckles and made another move for the door.

"Liar." Her hand landed on his chest.

Fire stabbed straight into his bones. "Augh." Beneath her fiery Touch, he crumbled to a knee.

Eyes wide, Eija jerked back. "I . . . I'm sorry." She swallowed, gaping at him. "What—"

Reef seized the moment. Punched up and grabbed the door. Yanked it open, his breath still trapped in his throat. Ignoring the two in the house who stared at him. The taut expression of the chief. Wary concern from Shad quickly pushed to the person behind him. He pitched himself across the living area. Up the earthen steps. Grabbed the iron handle, his legs weak, head throbbing.

Reef was done. Done listening to Eija. To commands. To everyone telling him what to do, what not to do. He broke into the open again, the icy night a refreshing smack in the face. His trapped breath finally vaulted free. Coughing, he stumbled over the yard. Wavered. Felt dizzy. Dropped onto all fours by the stone wall. He felt like a rabid animal with drool sliding from his mouth, but he didn't care. Just breathing felt an agony after that blast she'd spiked through his chest.

"Hey." Chief's word was more grunt than voice. "You okay?"

Holding his chest, Reef slumped onto his backside, stone wall digging into his shoulders as he dragged his gaze up to the chief. "No idea." He massaged the burn. Ambient heat from the mark swelled against his fingers.

Chief eyed the spot he rubbed. "D'you take a blast?"

With a snort, Reef almost laughed. "Something like that." He shook his head. "I . . ." What had he gotten himself into? Why had he been so hot for the candidate who got it all wrong? "Wishing I'd never—" The pain swelled again, like a hand reaching up from the pit of his stomach and closing around his lungs. Groaning, he gripped his pectoral and strained against the fiery agony.

On a knee, Chief rested his elbow on the other. Reached over and tugged Reef's shirt aside. "What the scuz?"

"Yeah," Reef wheezed as the fire subsided. "Asked the same thing." He lay on the frozen ground, looking up at the gray, overcast sky.

"What's that from?"

Man, it'd have been a whole lot easier if Chief had met Daq'Ti, seen what happened to him. "Eija."

"*What?*"

Hauling himself upright, Reef kneaded the muscle around the imprint as if that could ease the burn. "She . . . she did the same thing to one of the beasts that hit the *Prev*—remember?"

Chief frowned, his angular face hardening. "Guess our pods had already jettisoned."

"Right." Reef huffed. "One tried to kill her—she shoved him. Palm met pectoral. Next thing we know, BeastieBoy was following her around like a lost puppy, obeying her every command."

"Slag," the chief muttered.

"It gets better. The Draegis *changed*. Went from that black-lava hulk to a nearly normal-looking man."

Chief stared at him. No cursing. No frown. Nothing.

"His name was Daq'Ti. He helped us escape and was on that ship with Marco when it jumped back to the Quadrants." Reef eyed the spot again. "So what I want to know is, if something in her reverted *his* DNA and made him into her personal warrior and guard and altered his appearance . . ."

"What the scuz will it do to you?"

With a halfhearted nod, Reef looked down. "Exactly." His gaze slid across the yard. Spotted dark shapes coming up the road. "Company." He struggled to his feet.

The chief slid his arm up under Reef's and helped him back to the house. Reef stumbled down the steps, surprised at how weak his legs felt. It reminded him of being a young Marine and struggling with land legs after a long space deployment. Then he heard the sniffling. Glanced to the table.

Eija was lowering her hands from her face, eyes red. Cheeks wet.

Voids. He didn't do tears. Jaw clenched, he moved to the table and dropped onto a chair as they heard the chief talking to whoever had been on the stone road.

A minute later, he returned, bolted the door. Hands stuffed on his belt, he clicked his tongue. "Slag, if I ain't still reprimanding recruits."

"Rhinn," Shad chastised softly as she went to his side.

"Ah." Silencing her with an upheld hand, Chief cocked his head. "I know you're always telling me I'm too gruff, but that's exactly what's needed here, and this is a Command situation."

"No." Though her throat sounded hoarse, Eija had no hesitation in her words. "This is not a situation for Command—it's humanity."

"Humanity," Reef scoffed.

Her gaze flicked to him and her brows drew up into a knot. "I . . . I can't explain why . . . or how I . . . *it* happened." Those brown eyes he'd always liked glossed with tears. "But I am sorry. I never intended—"

"Do. You. Know"—Reef told himself to calm down, come down a notch from ballistic—"what is going to happen to me? I mean, the Touch rewrote Daq'Ti's DNA, morphed him into a human."

"It didn't morph him into a human. He already was one, just . . . corrupted," Eija said. "The *Ovqatlanish* does not change essence or rewrite genetic code; does not turn a dog into a cat. It is a cooperative transformation—"

"Cooperative?" Reef scoffed.

She drew in a breath, sadness creasing the lines around her small nose and mouth. "As with Daq'Ti, it only works on those willing or yearning for a transformation. Recall the Draegis on the dreadnought who were impervious to my Touch. It amplifies your gifts, your true qualities—"

"The only thing"—his voice echoed off the low ceiling—"it's amplifying is pain."

"Hey." Chief glowered. "Keep it down if you don't want to get put outside the wall."

"I might prefer that to this." Reef narrowed his gaze at her, wondering when he'd stood. "I don't get it—I had your back. I've *always* had your six, even at the Academy."

"I know."

"Then *why*?" He jerked up his shirt. "Why do this to me?"

She covered her mouth.

"Yeah." He thrust down his shirt.

"C-can we have a moment alone?" Eija looked to the chief and Shad. "Please."

The chief glanced at Reef, hesitating, asking if that's what he wanted.

Reef rolled his eyes and turned away from her.

"We need to head off some rumors anyway." Chief motioned Shad toward the door, then nodded to them. "Ten mikes. Remember—don't draw unnecessary attention."

Reef returned to the chair, not really wanting to listen. Definitely not wanting to talk. He bent forward, elbows resting on his knees, when he heard the door latch. Quiet steps returned and he saw Eija standing in front of him.

"I . . . I don't know how to say this without you thinking this was my idea, that I did it on purpose."

He hung his head. "Can't possibly get worse than it already is."

There was subtle crunching and a floral shifting of the air. When she didn't say anything, he opened his eyes. Found Eija on her knees, peering up at him.

Slag, she was beautiful.

No, this was just fallout because of what she was. He didn't really like her. She wasn't his type. Too lower class.

"*That was never important to you.*"

Reef jerked up and back, shoving himself out of the chair. "Wh-what was that?"

Eija's freckles seemed to darken beneath a blush. "It's . . . Lifespeech. A way Faa'Cris communicate with . . . each other."

Feeling the need to massage that imprint again—could he ever do it hard enough to rub it off?—he gaped. "I'm *not* one of you."

Without moving or a sound, she was suddenly standing before him. "I know. But because of the imprint, I can share my thoughts with you, and vice versa."

"How . . .?"

A smile wavered on her lips. "I will explain later, but for now, we should go. Our presence is causing trouble for the chief and Shad, and we must give consideration to them." She drew in a sharp breath, gaze darting to the door. "Someone is here." She held out a hand. "We must go. Trust me?"

"Not in the least." But he heard the door latch *shunk* free. Caught her hand. Felt the world tip and fade to gray even as hooded men edged into the house.

"Sire. Commander Sirroc's Interceptor was shot down this morning. He's dead, sire."

Marco faltered at the door to his hub, eyeing the blue-eyed Xanthan, Galen Sebastiano. The death of the flight commander put them down one more competent fighter pilot and ship, but it also meant a gap in leadership. "Guess you've been promoted."

The younger, tenacious brother of General Sebastiano and Elder-in-place Jencir Sebastiano twitched in surprise. "Sire?"

"Are you not next in the chain of command?"

"I—" Galen stiffened as if that javrod he'd sparred with had been shoved down his spine. "Aye, sire."

Marco nodded. "Get up to speed with Mavridis and the others." Leaving the regia at the door, he entered his hub where Tigo waited, and loosened the choke of the collar on his flight jacket. He wanted to remove it but wouldn't risk anyone seeing his arm. "We're dropping like flies."

"It's amazing you've withstood the bombardment this long."

"We would've been long gone if the Uchuvchi hadn't showed up and formed that net."

"Who are they?"

"Came back from Kuru with me."

"Brilliant move on your part," Tigo said, walking the hub and taking in the space.

"Would that I could take credit, but I had no knowledge the pilots had hitched a ride with me on the *Qirolicha*."

"The net ships are drones, yes?"

Narrowing an eye, Marco considered the danger of discussing that intelligence. "How do you know that?"

Tigo lifted a hand. "Let me allay your fears—I am not the spy I mentioned earlier. The heat signatures coming off those ships don't indicate life."

Marco grunted. "The pilots were in the *Qirolicha*—the crescent ship yet on the lawn. They plug in just as Xisya did to me on the *Prevenire*."

A nervous efflux came from Tigo as he glanced around. "Is this the extent of your accommodations?" he asked, changing the topic as if they had been talking about the weather. "You are a king—I had bigger quarters on the *Macedon*."

It was an exaggeration, considering Marco had a sitting area, small kitchen, bathroom, and bedroom in his suite. "What need have I of more? I eat, sleep, war." He stood between Ixion and Daq'Ti, while the hunters and other pilots eased into chairs at the opposite end. "Speaking of—you intrude on my rest. Be quick."

Tigo's expression tightened. "You and I have much in common, Marco, though I know you would argue it. Both our mothers are Faa'Cris."

"In that, we had no choice."

In a cockeyed nod, Tigo went on. "Both have been lied to most of our lives about our identities."

At the refreshment table, Marco poured himself a cup of steaming cordi from a steel carafe.

"We are both embroiled in a battle for the existence of innocents who depend on us."

"Last I heard"—he took a sip of the citrusy concoction—"you were a fugitive and your father was in collusion with the very alien who dug ports in my head and chest, forcing me to pilot a ship back to her system so her spiderlike sisters could return to destroy humanity."

Tigo nodded and sighed. "You are right. At least, that's what my father and the Faa'Cris arranged for everyone to believe." He grunted, then groaned. "There is so much to tell, yet I know your men are in the skies battling it out in an impossible engagement that they will not win. You will not win."

Marco took a nice long sip, watching the onetime Eidolon over the rim of the mug.

Tigo folded his arms. "My father's so-called collusion with Baric and Xisya is a long game to keep the left hand from knowing what the right hand is doing. In fact, I just learned that my father is no normal human—he is Do'St, the male equivalent of the Faa'Cris."

Marco barked a laugh in disbelief, but when the pup didn't join in, he sobered. "There is not—"

"A belief perpetuated by the Faa'Cris to drive the Do'St farther from them and mankind."

Both Tigo and the Faa'Cris seemed earnest. "As if there is not enough turmoil with just the one breed manipulating the worlds."

Hands fisted before him, Tigo hesitated. Then lowered himself into a chair at the oblong table. "I could not agree with you more. Shortly after seeing you and Kersei to Iereania, I . . ." He looked over his shoulder to the door. "Jez took me to Deversoria." He rubbed his knuckles, face twitching and contorting as he thought through things. A storm. His scent roiled with irritation and frustration. Admiration. Agitation. "They have fallen so far from their purpose. And they know it."

Attention and irritation flared, Marco sharpened his gaze on the guy. "Fallen." He moved to the table. Set his mug down. Palmed the surface. "The *Fallen* of the Faa'Cris are responsible for countless lives lost, innumerable destroyed societies, cruel, debilitating plagues—as seen on Tryssinia. All caused by the Corrupt, as they are called in Kuru."

Tigo nodded. "My word was poorly chosen. I lost someone very close to me—"

"I lost my wife!"

The man flinched, his shock at the tone and grief at the truth wobbling in the air between them. "I know . . ." Brown eyes met his. "Truly, I am sorry. Isaura's death is a great loss for all. It rang through the Heavenlies. There are no words—"

"No." Marco's heart hammered in his chest, as if each thud pounded the missing heartbeats from Isaura on his ribs. "There are not." He pivoted and started for the door. "This is a waste—"

"I know I swim tricky waters here," Tigo said as he again stood. "But I *am* an ally, Marco. I know well what it is to feel as a puppet in the hands of a master who doesn't care the toll he takes on the one whose strings are pulled."

Frozen one reach from escape, Marco gave him a sidelong glance. What did he mean?

"My first officer and another of my team were both manip—" Tigo growled. "Out of my head, Jez!"

What the reek?

Tigo stretched his neck. "Sorry. She . . . we . . . we're connected. She can hear my thoughts if I am not careful, and she freely inserts hers into mine." He ran a hand over his cropped hair. "It's maddening."

Instinct had Marco reaching across the Voids to Isaura again. To hear the singsong of her voice calling him "Dusan" just one more time. To hear her laughter. Her sage thoughts. Ache constricted, slashing grief through his bruised and battered heart, the emptiness reminding him of her absence. Her death. *Meni xominga qaytaring.* Return me to the lady . . . He understood so deeply what Daq'Ti felt. He leaned against the wall, bracing against the memories, the loss. The hollow existence without her.

"Forgive me." Tigo's words were quiet. "You . . . had this with Isaura?"

Somehow Marco managed a nod.

"I beg your deference for intruding more, but how? Isaura was not Faa'Cris . . ."

"Our baby tethered us," Marco croaked out, throat tight against memories he did not want to recall, "made it possible for me to talk with Isa when I was trapped in Kuru. She brought me home." He fisted a hand, staving off a squall of torment. "And they killed her. Stole into Kardia and killed her."

So much blood. Her gargled words . . . her Signature fading from his receptors . . .

"Then ally with us, Marco. Help me stop Baric and Xisya. If we can help rout the mole exposing your weaknesses, I would be glad to volunteer. If we do not set aside our wounds, our entire civilization will be lost."

"I do not need you to tell me that when pilots are dropping from the skies—"

"I might have a way to stop that." Tigo held out a hand. "But I would barter that information for a few more minutes of your patience."

"Patience I do not have . . ."

"Then I'll be as brief as possible." Tigo nodded. "Symmachia allowed Baric to conduct Xisya's research with the intent of strengthening their reach into Herakles and beyond. After seeing the Engram and what it did to Kersei, we can both attest to the fact ethics and oversight were not top priorities."

Needing a diversion for his roiling gut, Marco dumped back the lukewarm cordi and poured more. Tried not to think about Isaura and her custom blend of cordi that he'd become addicted to. Tried not to think of all the little things she did to make his life better, to make him smile. Reek, he missed her laughter.

". . . members of Tascan Command quickly realized they were losing control—of Baric, the research, and the armada."

"Too little, too late."

"Those who opposed anything related to the jumpgate project . . . vanished. However, while there are still those loyal to Baric, there is a great number who are not, including my father, who has played friend to the regime responsible for the ships in your orbit."

"Again, too little, too late. You say your father is on our side, yet is he not on that ship, bombarding us?" Marco tightened his jaw, anger bubbling. "And before that, he stood by and allowed that chamber? The jumpgate?"

"We were first told of the Engram project five years ago." Tigo was all business as he delved into the history. "I discovered it'd been in the works for over a decade. Like the gates. Regardless, Tascan Command is entrenched, and even if they managed to yank his budget and funding, Baric has private-sector funding to build more gates across the Quadrants, including this one. Not sure if you're aware, but a gate is about to be operational over Cenon, and there might be another near Sicane. So neither he nor the gates will go away any time soon without drastic action."

"How have they let him run so rampant and beyond the Tertian Space Coalition's own Quadrant?" Marco's attention flicked toward a concern that his heart would not let him release: the traitor, whoever he was, had Isa's blood on his hands. It stirred a thrum in his veins—the brand. Or the weapon. He wasn't sure the distinction mattered anymore.

"They're afraid of Xisya, only because it will impact their credits accounts."

"They named me Progenitor, said I was to start this war, and though I have the anger to do it, I have few weapons. It is a losing battle—you have seen what little we can do. Our resources are already stretched thin and it has only just begun."

"That's why Jez and I are here."

Marco glowered. "Never again will I accept anything from the Faa'Cris. I am done with their edicts and superiority. They left me to fight this war alone and did nothing to protect Isaura when those savages invaded our home and slaughtered her!"

"I understand—really—but do not categorically exclude me," Tigo said, holding up his hands. "Please. The Faa'Cris may have stayed in their caves and hidden from reality—*enough, Jez!*" Fury reddened his face, which made Marco wonder if these two were having a not-so-silent battle via the dreamscape, or Lifespeech as the Faa'Cris called it.

Tigo huffed. "However, the Do'St *have* been working across Kedalion and Herakles to rally aid to Drosero. Though few in number, they have recruited what they could of techs, pilots, and scientists to assist."

"Scientists?" Marco balked, feeling that hungry fire in his arm again. "You speak as if you hold the answer to this war, yet you are not connected to our reality: we are *at* war. We fight. Bombardments have destroyed the fortress and Pyres-know-what across Kalonica and the southern continent. *Scientists* do us no good—they require labs and time, of which we have none. We need ships, pilots, weapons!"

Tigo tucked his chin. Smirked. "Tell me, have you wondered why the bombardment has not been worse? Ever question why this non-tech planet has not been obliterated by the armada that is ten times your better?"

The guy definitely had his attention now.

"That's because those scientists that you don't need? They've developed a sensor-linked code that sends a hyperfocused EMP blast to any dispelled armament with a Symmachian transponder and—"

"That's great until Symmachia takes down the device."

Tigo held up a hand, continuing. "—are so infinitesimally coded into the core system that makes it virtually impossible to find but also has an anti-tampering measure that destroys itself before they can realize it's not alone in the core. Then consider the EMP device itself, built of a technology that conceals itself and its emissions to avoid detection, both electronic or visual."

Surprise stilled Marco. "I am . . . impressed." Stunned. "Reek." He ran a hand down the back of his neck, realizing if that hadn't been in place, Drosero . . . gone.

"Then hang on to your rhinnock boots because it's about to get better. I've confirmed with the admiral a mission to erect EMP towers across this continent that will protect you when that net fails completely."

"We've been working on mining ore to refuel those ships."

"Then this could buy you time to do it." Tigo gave a satisfied sigh. "I know it is only a beginning, but these measures might even the fight out a little. Allow the volunteer armada to pick away at the Symmachian ships in orbit."

"Which we desperately need." There was one hiccup Marco could not embrace. "Does this in any way involve Faa'Cris?"

"I . . ." Tigo thumbed over his shoulder. "Jez—"

"*Her* I accept."

Head cocked, Tigo frowned. "Sadly, no—this is the Do'St and myself. A few others."

"Then I am grateful for your help."

Tigo squinted at him. "Would you really risk your people to avoid working with them?"

"They have shown themselves entirely selfish. Helpful one instant, nonexistent the next." Like when those Symmachian fighters drew him away. Like when Isaura was impaled by the raider.

"He is especially hard toward the Faa'Cris."

"You have only yourselves to blame." Tigo entered the chamber they would use for the night.

Jez pulled him around. "How can you—"

"*Think*"—Tigo flicked fingers to his temple—"what he is going through! His wife was just murdered by the dogs Symmachia sent in . . . all in a war coming to fruition simply to end a centuries-long argument between two Faa'Cris factions."

"You oversimplify, Licitus."

Tigo slid toward her. "The only time you use that derogatory term is when I hit the tender mark on that cold heart of yours."

Her expression slipped and slid into contrition by the powerful hand of hurt. She stepped inside their alcove and turned to him. "I sensed much concern from you during the conversation. Did you feel Marco was confrontational?"

"Not entirely . . ." Tigo tossed his ruck on the bed in the nearest room, then turned and scratched his head. "Mostly, I felt he wasn't himself. He was cold, hard."

"He's a Kynigos, trained—"

"No. I met *that* man on the *Macedon*. Saw his intensity and focus." He tucked his hands under his armpits. "No, this Marco . . ."

"His wife just died."

"Yeah." He frowned, thinking. Wondering at the change. "No. No, there was more there. Something . . . dark."

Jez drew closer, angling her head. "I detected that, too," she said in a soft voice, "but could not make sense of it. I find it intriguing that you could sense it as well."

"I think we were right to separate and let me speak to him alone." He grabbed a cup of water. "He and Isaura used Lifespeech when he was in Kuru."

Her eyebrows winged up. "How—"

"He guesses because of the baby Isaura carried."

"Aeliana," Jez whispered, her face awash with grief. "I cannot imagine what it must be like to have a *potior* ripped from that channel through which Lifespeech forges its connection. The empty hollowness . . ."

"I think you're understanding on a level I can't. What do you mean *channel?*"

"There is a connection that forms between two preferred persons—potiors—and it . . ." She framed her face and whimpered. "I would not will that loss on anyone. It is impossible to explain with words."

"Please. Try." He had to understand what was happening in Marco if he was to continue to advise and help him.

Jez nodded, her caramel skin rippling with emotion. "You sense not only what I say in Lifespeech, but what I feel when I say it. Yes?" When he nodded she went on. "Through that same channel that is forged between us, you can throw me a warning, a thought, a smile . . . and you *feel* it. I feel it. But it's not just a superficial thing. It's instantly deep and grounding. In a sense, it drives your direction, your path. Now imagine that I am gone, but the channel remains. And you reach into it to tell me something only . . ."

"You're not there."

Another nod, this one smaller, sadder. "It would be like walking an empty, dark hall—for eternity." She shivered. "I would go mad."

"I'd *be* mad." Tigo tried to imagine it. And now that she explained its immediate depth upon being established, he realized that even though he at times resented her mental intrusions, he could not fathom how voidlike it would be to have her gone. Dead. Dealing with it day after day. "And angrier with every passing day."

She frowned. "Why anger?"

"Because you were taken from me and I am yet forced to live without you." Though Tigo felt as if he were reading Marco's adunatos, he also realized his own feelings regarding this were just as sharply aligned. "*That* is what I sensed in him—anger, resentment. It would explain his rejection of the Ladies."

"How is it our fault?"

"Nobody saved his wife. And that anger I sensed? It's only going to grow and build . . ."

"Likely it will be factored into his role as Progenitor . . ." She chewed her lower lip and considered him, as if wanting to say something.

"What?"

She looked down. "Did you notice his arm?"

"The brand?"

Her brow wrinkled in thought. "I am not sure it is his brand alone. I detected something more, something sinister."

"In that case"—he gave a cockeyed nod—"I pity those who cross him."

It seemed Jez may truly understand this time.

"Vorn can wait. We need to stay and help Marco."

"Agreed. We must try to guide him so he is not lost to whatever this is." She paced in the small hub. "You know, maybe this isn't our responsibility. I mean, the Progenitor is said to be the rage of the Ancient against those who corrupted his children."

Tigo recoiled. "Don't even try to tell me the Ancient had Isaura killed just to make Marco angry in readiness for this war."

"I only meant that the Ancient will use the anger borne of Isaura's death. It is as any wound—we ache, heal, then learn and grow. Through that, we are able to help others."

"But Marco's pain is inherently worse because of the potior loss, right?"

She gave a slow shrug.

"Don't ever volunteer as a counselor."

"Why?"

He couldn't help the mocking laugh.

"You may think as Faa'Cris I have no feelings, but you have a terrific way of wounding me, Tigo."

"Yeah? Well, when you're feeling better, the Ancient will have something to use."

Grief hung over the encampment like a dark cloud. As the hours passed and Kalonicans settled in, moods were low as they processed what had happened, what sent them fleeing into the mountain. Most every family had been affected by the bombardment that stole so very many lives and homes.

Standing outside the tent she shared with Kita, Danae, and the children, Kersei hugged herself, too aware of what had been lost. Isaura . . . Oh, the heaviness her death left in her own heart. She scanned the regia set in a perimeter around the tent, which was comforting but seemed too little, too late.

Though nowhere near as grand or luxurious as Deversoria with its soaring caverns, magnificent structures, river, or occasional sky opening, the cave system was large and accommodated the hundreds who had set up home here. Tents consumed the far side, and people used sheets to divide sections into living spaces. One would never know the encampment was belowground if they did not look up or consider the stone walls. Though a chill hung in the air, which was damp from the little stream that wound through the center of the vast chamber, there was no breeze. The air was still and . . . suffocating.

Kersei lowered herself onto the nearby trunk. Watched the people talking, children laughing and playing games. Amazing, the resiliency of her people. A little girl of no more than three hugged a doll. The blonde hair reminded Kersei of Isaura . . . who would never see her daughter laugh and play. Darius would never see Xylander do the same.

So much loss . . . Tears burned, the ache raw all over again.

Distant booms rattled the stone overhead, dribbling pebbles and dirt onto heads and tents. Thunder pervaded the day. Hearing a whimper from within, she returned to the tent and checked on the babes. Brushed dust from the blanket that protected a sleeping Aeliana. Back at the front, she noted her own vibrating nerves that would not allow her to settle. How went the effort aboveground? What of Marco?

Myles negotiated his way back to the tent with two steaming bowls of stew. What was he doing with those when they had dried meat and bread here?

Myles stopped to talk with an older man who held something up to him. Myles's stolid gaze traveled the distance to her, and he nodded to whatever his elder was saying. He pushed from his haunches and continued his trek back.

Broad-shouldered and brawny, he wore his red-blond hair cut to the shoulder, his beard neatly trimmed. He was kind and the people respected him. *She* respected him—had since before Rufio gave permission for her to spar.

He trudged past the regia and handed her a bowl. "Thought you could use some sustenance."

Ohh, the thought of warm broth to chase off the chill enticed her. "Very kind of you." She cupped the bowl in her hands and appreciated the heat that spilled into her palms. She settled once more on the trunk and eyed him as he lowered himself to an upturned crate. "How are the people doing?"

"Tired, beleaguered," he said as he ate the first bite. "Yet they are all glad for the efforts of our medora."

"Are not we all." They ate in quiet for a few moments, and she prayed earnestly the children would rest well, despite the resonance of war vibrating the walls and ground.

"How are the babes?"

"Thankfully, sleeping." She smiled at him and froze when he smiled back. "What is this? A smile from the ever-fierce aerios, Myles?"

He chuckled, and she noticed how the color of his hair made his eyes seem more blue. Kind. Which warred with the ferocity of the man she'd taken on with the javrod.

"You do well with them. Incredible, taking care of two infants. It must be like twins for you." His face went crimson. "I mean—they are much work."

"Indeed." She laughed, knowing well that was not what he meant. His implication was that she nursed two babes. "Truly, it is exhausting. I cannot recall being so . . . depleted." She lifted her half-empty bowl. "Sustenance such as this is much appreciated."

Smiling down at her, he nodded. "It is my pleasure . . . princessa."

Ever had he called her that. "I was not a princessa until Darius."

"I am acquainted with Mistress Kersei, daughter of Elder Xylander." He gave a nod. "Well we all knew the imp who insisted on sparring—"

"*Imp?*"

"—and refused to accept any answer other than 'begin' from Aerios Minos." He set his bowl to his mouth and drained it.

Kersei gaped, then laughed, wishing she . . . Well, why not? Bowl cupped, she lifted it to her lips. Ma'ma would butcher her backside for such behavior. But Kersei did it, sipped the broth, and nearly moaned at the strength that seemed to fill her bones. When she lifted it away, some spilled down the side of her mouth and chin. She yelped to keep it off her bliaut.

Myles barked a laugh. "Never have I seen such a mess made. You need more practice."

She giggled, setting aside the bowl as she retrieved a cloth and cleaned her face. "'A lady should ever be the picture of propriety, Kersei. Back straight, chin up . . .'" She wilted, leaning onto the trunk. "Those were days of innocence and abandon, though I did not know it." She hugged herself again and sighed. "I do miss it."

Adjusting his position, he folded his arms. "I do not."

"No?"

"Things were different then. We were different."

"How could we not be after all that has transpired?" She followed a mother chasing her two children back and forth over the little stream, laughing and making quite a scene. "Never would that have happened in Stratios Hall."

"I would say not," Myles said lowly. "She is a villager. You and your family were nobility."

"There is also the difference of the times. Now, I think it much needed to dispel the pall of grief." She would defend her own upbringing, however. "Yet it does not speak that we should be without humor or spirit."

"Oh, do not think you missed any of that last part."

Kersei balked, then laughed. "I concede you are right." She wiped her hands.

Myles suddenly hopped to his feet, taking her heart with him.

"What is the matter?"

He drew up sharp, his head inclined at a figure who approached. "Elder Mavridis."

Scowl perpetually in place, Ixion stormed toward them with two Stalkers. His hard gaze shifted between them, his misunderstanding plain. "Return to your duty, Aerios." It was an intentional demotion from Myles's rank of regia and personal guard. "I would have word with the duchess." He motioned to the tent, waiting for Kersei to enter.

Rattled, she ducked inside. Hurried to the bassinets where the children lay—gratefully still asleep. "Myles did nothing untoward, Sir Ixion."

His gaze avoided her as he glanced at the bassinet. "How are they?" His voice was as steel on steel.

"As well as can be expected," she said.

He stood over her. "I came to deliver word that Kardia is lost."

Kersei felt her own sadness amplified. Grief rushed down her spine and pooled in the pit of her belly. "And the city?"

"Crumbling. The remnant are heading south to the Plains of Adunatos."

So near Stratios . . .

"The man Haltersten has rallied a militia. We sent machitis down to join them." Ixion touched Aeliana's blanket, his expression softening for a tick. "Plisiázon will come to escort you and the children deeper into the caves."

"Deeper?"

"Raiders were discovered prowling the mountain, no doubt seeking a way in."

At this, dread contaminated her grief. "I . . ." She rose. Felt the collapsible javrod in her pocket. "Are there more regia or aerios to go with me? I . . ." Her gaze fell to the children. Kalonica's heirs. "We must protect them."

"Aye," Ixion growled. "I fear your guard has become too comfortable. He is not on his guard."

"What? Myles has—"

"He did not see my approach until I was yet upon him. It would do well to reassign—"

"Please. Let him remain. I confess even my guard is down—weariness has made me slow-witted." She brushed away an unruly lock of dark hair. "And . . . admittedly, ashamed."

"We have all known that feeling. You are in grief and exhausted. It is understandable." His gray gaze radiated his meaning. "Learn from it. This war will not let us linger in the mistakes."

"Of course." She smoothed her hands down her omnirs. "However, a concern yet touches my thoughts—both heirs are with me. If I am discovered or set upon . . ." She looked up at him.

"Mayhap we should split them up."

Kersei stilled. "I . . . am not sure that is an efficient course."

His eyes narrowed. "Why?"

She tilted her head in a nod. "We would need another wet nurse"—she noted how his face reddened—"and I hesitate to increase our number with someone we do not know."

Ixion grunted, eyeing the babes, but she did not miss that his gaze lingered longer on the dark-haired head. His granddaughter. "Agreed."

She turned and met his gaze, considered a question she would not ask anyone else. "How fares Marco? You say Kardia is lost—it must be a terrible burden on him. When I left, he refused to see Aeliana and seemed so . . . vengeful."

"Are not we all after this savage violation by the skycrawlers?"

"But there is more, Ixion. I sensed it. The brand . . . we have had a connection since Iereania, despite all else that has transpired, and I felt"—dare she speak it—"darkness. Do you think he is given over to it?"

"It does not matter what I think—"

Kersei caught his arm, and he flipped that grip in a lightning-fast move that snatched her breath. "B-beg your mercy. I only . . ." She swallowed, hating the fear he gouged into her courage. "Your thoughts do matter, Ixion. He listens to you."

"Nay, he listens to no one at the moment. That weapon . . ."

Kersei's heart started. "Weapon?"

Ixion shifted back. "I should go."

"Please, no." Squaring her stance, she shifted in front of him. "She is your granddaughter, Ixion, and he is her father."

"Before all of that, he is my medora. And his will is mine to obey."

"Of course." She glanced at the baskets even as a tiny fist thrust upward and a cry of protest rent the air. "I must . . . tend the princess since you have disrupted her nap."

"The Stalkers will be here soon for escort," Ixion graveled. "When you are ready to go deeper into the caves, speak it."

Heavyhearted, Kersei lowered herself to Aeliana's side. Eyed Xylander, who could probably sleep through the entire Symmachian bombardment if she let him. When she refocused on the princess, she wilted in relief to find her eyes fluttering closed again. A mercy.

Heel of her hand to the bridge of her nose, Kersei fought tears. Worried over Marco, over the fate of Kalonica and Drosero.

"Ma'ma . . ." she reached through Lifespeech. *"I need help."*

But there was no answer. No help. She must stand on her own.

Eija folded from the home of Rhinn and Shad into a cold, dirty street. Buildings jutted up on either side, the stench of waste permeating the setting. Trusting the anaktesios that allowed her to emerge here, she rolled her shoulders and scanned the dim surroundings. They must be on the same side of the ice planet as the village they'd just left, but the thicker, warmer air said they were farther north. Warmer by maybe ten or fifteen degrees. Still brittlely cold. Despite the blackened street being pocked with patches of snow that seemed more mud than frozen droplets, at least here her clypeus did not ache from the bite of perpetual winter.

With a hard grunt, Reef held his knees and glanced around.

She had to ignore the sympathy for him that rose through her and focus on what she'd sensed when they corporealized.

"Is it my imagination or is it warmer here?"

"Yeah," she whispered around a shiver, her breath spiraling in the air between them.

"It's like a heatwave. We should shed some of our clothes."

Unwilling to waste a glower on him, she worked through the scents. There were the normal ones of life in a decently populated town, but there was something more. Something unsettling. Made her probe the dark passages before she started forward.

"Okay, not liking the look on your face." He straightened, his six-one form hovering over her. "What's wrong?"

"I . . . don't know."

"Huh. Another miracle—Eija Zacdari doesn't have the answer."

"Quiet," she hissed as shadows ahead shifted and morphed into three large men.

"I don't need this thing on my chest to figure out those guys are trouble." He huffed. "Couldn't you have picked a less hostile environment?"

She flicked her irritation at him. "There was little time to plan. I just followed the scent."

"What scent—detritus?"

"Human."

"I think I'm offended."

The three advanced, shoulders wider than any human's and breathing louder. Then that scent warbled toward her like heat plumes in a desert. It assaulted her receptors and—

"Ugh," Reef grunted. "That . . . I *am* offen—" He sucked in a hard breath as the glory that rose off her illuminated the three. "Draegis . . . but not."

"Hybrids!" Eija shouted, throwing her glory at the beasts, searing their eyes. Blinding them. Thrashed her wings at the nearest.

Reef reached for a weapon he didn't have. "Slag."

Aiming at the sidearm strapped to the hybrid, she fired, eliciting a monstrous roar as the bony part of her span cracked against his leg. The weapon skittered free as he stumbled but kept advancing.

Whirling to attack the others, Eija felt a heat blast race across her secondary wing, scorching the feathers. "Augh!" She spiraled in the air and struck two simultaneously. Before touching down, she saw Reef slide beneath her and dive for the weapon.

With her longblade, she released a beast from his torment. Let him fall into that Eternal Embrace. Had no time to savor the victory. Thrust her boot into the second's chest and raised her sword again.

Reef was energy and rage as he engaged the third, firing and searing its already blackened body.

The roar of pain was deafening—the shot infuriated him. Both arms powered up.

"Two? They have *two* weaponized arms?"

Worried for Reef, Eija knew she had her own beast to slay. She refocused— the sooner she delivered this one of its suffering, the sooner she could assist Reef. Silently she prayed the Ancient would guard Reef and protect him until—

Superheated air volleyed at her. The wake seared her hands and heated the hilt of her sword. Teeth gritted, she could not lose her blade, so she flipped into the air and tightened her grip. Felt it stinging her palm. With a growl, she hovered over the beast. Two-handing her sword, she gusted upward, then folded her clypeus back, essentially dropping right into the beast.

Red eyes pulsed—surprise. Anger.

A guess. With no scent, it was impossible to know.

But she drove the blade straight down into his shoulder. Felt the moment his life fled this cruel existence. She deployed both spans, the sudden expulsion cracking in the air, stunting her fall seconds before her boots thudded against the icy, cobbled road.

Spinning around, she snatched the dagger from its scabbard.

The other beast had Reef pinned beneath his weaponized arm, trailing a fiery wake along Reef's neck as he pulsed several short blasts. Not the one-shot ash-maker. This was taunting, cruel.

"Augh!" Reef buckled . . . bucked. Screamed.

A strange noise riffled from the beast.

The sound startled Eija, stilling her for a split second, her stomach churning as she realized what was happening. The beast was laughing. Mocking the pain he inflicted on Reef.

They wanted to play dirty? So be it. No mercy.

Eija barreled into the hybrid. Pitched herself and it past Reef, into the wall. Channeled every bit of fury and righteous anger that existed in her straight at the beast. Holding him, she folded. They emerged on the other side of the building, and she slammed him into the rock barrier. He dropped to the snow-covered cobbled road.

On her knee, she thrust her hand at him. Through him. Palm melting down into his back, reaching for his adunatos.

His howl of anguish and rage echoed through the night, ricocheting off the metallic bars that covered windows and doors. Off the bell that hung in the cloister of what looked like a temple or Sanctuary.

Eija focused the righteous purity of her Touch and shoved the creature back into the Void from which it'd been born. She stared down into its slitted eyes as the red pulsing slowed . . . stopped. It deflated beneath her touch, but still she waited, daring the thing to tempt the Ancient's anger once more. Even as she pulled her hand free with a sticky, hot slurping, she heard the thud of boots behind her.

Reef skidded up to her. "What the . . ." He swallowed, gaping. "Slag, Eija."

She pushed to her feet, stretching a kink in her neck and folding her clypeus away, sensing his shock. "He found pleasure in harming others. There is no mercy for his kind."

"No," Reef said, pointing behind her. "I mean . . . *them.*"

Eija shifted around and found men, women, and children pouring from buildings, alleys, hesitation and fear guarding them as they ventured closer.

A nearly bald man held a hand up to the rest, staying them, then stepped out a few paces. "Are . . . are they dead?"

People with their expectations and hang-ups . . . Not her forte. Eija shifted, hoping Reef would take the lead. But that's when she noticed he was cringing, his hand reaching—then not—but then reaching again to where the beast had burned him.

"Your neck!" She gaped at the burn, his flesh slick and glistening in the moonlight.

Reef shrugged her aside, stepping toward the villager. "Yes, they're dead."

Relief fluttered on the chilled air. "Y-you are sure?"

Eija glanced down the length of her body—now fully human again—to the ground where what remained of the beast lay. Though she grieved the death of a living creature, she did not grieve the end of such a monster.

The man shuffled closer, his gaze never quite meeting Eija's. "May I see . . .?"

Had he come to gawk and revel? "You take pleasure in the pain of others as well?"

Reef scowled at her.

"Forgive me." The man's voice was small as he hunched. "These beasts have terrorized our town for the last several months. None have been able to vanquish them. We have had limited success against the Draegis, but when she delivered these three to our gate . . . we were lost." He indicated to the other villagers. "We hid in our homes, and when that became futile, we went into the sewers."

"But we heard them howling and came out to see what happened." A woman inched nearer, her face alight. "Truly, you must be blessed."

Reef shifted his gaze between Eija and the people, then frowned. Touched his neck.

Eija huffed. "Your ne—"

"Leave it. I'm fine." He moved toward the locals. "You said someone dropped these things at your gate?"

"Y-yes. Xonim." The woman lifted her hands plaintively. "They bring the beasts to harvest our sons, kill some of us women. Convert the men."

Hands firming into fists, Eija felt anger churning through her gut. "I may not win this war, but neither will I let this evil go unanswered. I will end as many of them as I can before *my* life is ended."

"Um, hello with the ending lives thing? Remember that mine is sort of wrapped in yours." He winced. "Kind of want to avoid the whole apocalyptic ending, if we can." Eyebrows winged up. "Deal? Give this the old Academy try?"

BELOWGROUND MOUNTAIN ENCAMPMENT, NORTH KALONICA

She fit in his hand, Ixion's long fingers framing her little face. Tiny eyes stared up at the powerful man who held her, talked quietly to her. He bent forward, pressing his lips to the downy black hair, his white hair sliding forward and curtaining them. So terribly small and fragile in the palms of such a powerful, intimidating man, Princess Aeliana lay content and quiet. A sabbaton old, she should still be in the warmth and security of her mother's womb.

Standing outside the new tent set deeper into the cave system and trying to busy herself, Kersei surreptitiously watched the exchange between the Stalker and his granddaughter. Though the journey from the Plains of Adunatos was not easy or short, he had ventured in to visit Aeliana on several occasions. Each time Kersei afforded him solitude, but she could not deny the curiosity, surprise, and admiration she felt as she watched the way the intimidating Stalker handled the premature infant with such care, whispering to her and stroking her tiny cheeks.

In battle, he had a lethal elegance with which he confronted his enemies. In many respects she had considered him a hard man, hard to please, hard toward others. But here . . . with the princess . . . she almost could not reconcile it.

What would Marco be like with Aeliana? The ache jarred through her chest and constricted again. Would he ever visit her, hold her? That, too, was hard to reconcile. Marco was not a hard man. Nor cold or cruel. But clearly he was too wounded by the loss of Isaura to face their daughter.

Aeliana needed him. He needed her. He could find healing with the little one who had survived the violent way in which she had been thrust into the world. Kersei wanted to storm to wherever he was holed up and shake some sense into him.

Someone behind her sucked in a breath.

Kersei started and glanced over her shoulder. Lady Kita had returned from washing linens and now stared into the tent. "How long has he been here this time?"

"He arrived shortly after your departure."

"This whole time . . ." Lady Kita's smile was evident in her words.

"Never did I imagine he could be so tender," Kersei confessed.

"Oh, there was no question in my mind. I had seen and heard his exchanges with the kyria."

It was difficult to imagine this sweet, caring woman who had tended the kyria could be convinced to bind with so rough-edged a man, yet women had little voice in petitions when they were set. Had she been herded into it?

Kita's gaze settled once more on the fierce man. "He had so hoped to rebuild his relationship with Isaura . . ."

The words forced Kersei's gaze back to the tent where the first squeaks of protest from the princess spirited from the dim setting. "Would it be too bold of me to ask—but your binding with the elder . . . is it a love match?"

Kita smiled. "Did you not hear?" She sniffed a laugh. "Most of the regia have, I'm sure."

Kersei frowned.

"Aye, there is a . . . match between us. Mayhap it has burned brighter than it should. The medora happened upon us in a small moment of . . . indiscretion. And as Ixion did to the medora in Trachys, so the medora did to Ixion."

Kersei recalled when Darius had returned and shared the tale. "He demanded your honor be protected."

Kita brushed strands from her face with a tremulous finger. "I . . . I would never force his hand, but I also . . . Elder Mavridis is such a man . . ."

"Aye," Kersei laughed. "He is such a man. You need not say more."

Touching her arm, Kita seemed distraught. "Oh, think not poorly of him. He is fastidious about protecting Kalonica, but I have truly never known a greater man."

I have.

"Do not fear that he would force binding on me . . ."

Amused at Kita's defense of Ixion, Kersei nodded. "Thank you for the reassurance of his character, but in that regard, there was little concern on my part. The medora would not have chosen him as his First had he been of ill repute."

Kita studied her for a moment. "She was intimidated by you when we first arrived at Kardia. Did not even want to get out of the carriage. Isaura so feared that she could not measure up to you, that she would be rejected."

Words lodged in her throat at this story of Isaura, Kersei could only blink.

Were the words meant to wound? As an accusation, an indictment against her sense of nobility and pride as onetime princessa? No . . . the reference was to Kersei's connection to Marco, their love smothered in the ashes of this war.

"Isaura had the last laugh there, did she not?" Kersei managed. "After all, in an unfathomable period of time, she mastered the hearts of all Kalonica." *And Marco.* "I greatly admired her."

"And now, you nurse her child."

Kersei shifted. "By the mercy of the Ancient, I am in a condition to give aid to the princess, and it is my honor." A demanding shriek came from the tent, pulling their gazes inward, but it seemed necessary to offer one last reassurance. "Isaura and I may not have been friends as you were, but I will do everything in my power to honor her legacy."

"Thank you for the reassurance. I so feared Aeliana would not live . . ."

Swallowing, Kersei nodded. "As did I." She smiled and gave the woman's hand a squeeze. "Thankfully, our fears were unfounded."

"Are you done gossiping?" came Ixion's growl from inside the tent. "My granddaughter needs something I cannot provide."

Sharing a laugh with Kita, Kersei slipped inside. "I thought you would never let go of her."

"That thought crossed my mind as well." He shifted the crying bundle into her arms, then smoothed a hand over Aeliana's dark hair. Bent and kissed her head. He took a step, then stopped and touched Kersei's shoulder. "From the deepest parts of my being, thank you. Thank you for what you do for her."

Flushed by his gratitude, Kersei adjusted the princess into a better hold. "As told to Lady Kita, it is my honor." *Keep her alive for Marco.* "And some may recall that Isaura named me Benefactress, so it is also my duty." She managed a smile. "One I am also honored to fulfill."

But Elder Mavridis did not leave. Or move. He remained there at her side, gaze on the rugs that warded off the chilly air.

She angled to look up at him, wondering what—

"Has he been here?"

Oh. Her heart tripped over the question. Relieved someone else worried about that, yet feeling ill for the answer, which seemed a betrayal of Marco, she gave a quick shake of her head. "I am sure he will. He has much to tend."

"Aye, and Aeliana is one of them."

Kersei could not argue. "It is my earnest hope that he will come . . . because while she is a delight of a babe and cries little, I worry she somehow feels not only the loss of her mother but . . . of him."

Ixion bobbed his head. "I sensed it, too, while holding her. She is *too* quiet."

"The kyria told me that when Marco was in Kuru, he could detect Aeliana's scent." She peered down at the angelic face that scrunched but then smoothed out. "Mayhap she can detect his as well."

"A possibility we cannot know. Regardless, Isa is gone and a daughter needs her father." Forlorn, he again touched her thick downy hair. "I learned that too late. I will not let him make the same mistake."

He ducked out of the tent, and regia snapped to attention as he strode away with his Stalkers. But she feared his words were merely that, because Marco would not be forced into something he did not want to do. Then there was this path his boot had been set upon—a heavy, dark one. Worry had dug into her bones that he too eagerly embraced that darkness.

Comfortable on the pallet, she set Aeliana to her breast. The little one hesitated, then finally started suckling, as if she did not want to be bothered but knew she must. Or perhaps a noncommittal acceptance that the one who nursed her was not her mother. "You need him, do you not?"

Green eyes fastened onto hers. Marveling at the little beauty, she cupped Aeliana's head where it lay in the crook of her arm. Ignored the heat of the brand in her arm but noted a current of emotions rushed through her: Loneliness. Fear. Sadness.

Is that you? she asked the little one. *If you called him home as they claimed, I cannot put it beyond you to send me your feelings via the anaktesios.*

With a twitch, as if shrugging off something, Aeliana stopped nursing. Shuddered a sigh as her eyes closed. And . . . she slept. As if relieved someone finally understood her situation.

But that was absurd. No doubt Kersei transferred what she imagined the newborn felt.

Danae slipped in with a cranky Xylander. "He rejected the porridge, and I fear he is jealous for your attention."

"Much like his father was." Kersei sighed, a bit drained and ready for a nap. But she must feed him. She laid Aeliana in her bassinet, then nursed her son, who guzzled as if the well would run dry—and it just might.

He conked out, a stream of milk sliding down his ruddy face.

Though she tried to hold back her laugh, she could not. It was classic Darius—even the snoring. Fresh tears sprang to her eyes, suddenly seeing so much of his father in his round cheeks. Hugging her son close, she savored the sweet smell of him, kissed his cheek, then laid him down for a nap.

Sitting back on her knees, she shoved loose curls from her face. Eyed the corner pallet, greedy for a few hours' rest—and it pulled a big yawn from her.

Something rolled toward her from the entrance, catching torchlight and tossing it in her face. Her javrod. She looked up and saw Myles standing there, a crooked grin splitting his beard. "No," she groaned softly and shifted, rejecting his invitation to spar. "I would rest. Thank you." Odd, how she felt not the tempest that had constantly driven her to spar, to be among the men. She glanced to the sleeping babes and smiled. Felt a peace she had not known since . . . well, ever. Curled on her side, she cuddled Xylander and rested a hand on the princess's bassinet. Marveled at how her priorities had changed.

Brooding, they had often named him. Now, they named him cold, ruthless.

Let it be.

The northern flight base on the easternmost edge of the Medoran Mountains had become their home. Gathered around him in the small room that served as a command base were his First and his most trusted advisors of both Kalonica and off-world, including Roman, Theilig, Bazyli, Daq'Ti, and a handful of Stalkers and other high-ranking officials. And now the two newcomers. There were others—commanders of the infantry, flight commander Galen Sebastiano—aerios, regia. Roughly a dozen. All discussing strategies for troop movement, how to best work with the civilian militia led by Haltersten—which was rumored to number over ten thousand now—and how to rout the traitor who had done so much damage to their fight.

Fight? No, so much damage to the realm via the loss of the kyria.

Isa. Agony corkscrewed through his chest again, twisting his heart and lungs. Stealing breath. Stealing his will to reason or be reasonable. They would pay. Die.

Heat rose from the weapon, and Marco drew his arm closer. Swallowed. Not out of shame. He had no shame of his weapon-arm any longer. It was a means to an end. An end he'd bring to the traitor.

Fisting his hand, he rotated his forearm. Felt the tightness of his flesh, which had hardened from wrist to elbow. A small price to pay for such empowerment, such a resource to address . . . so much.

"Sire!"

Marco snapped up his attention to the general who stalked across the room.

"Word from Duncan and Daq'Ti."

Hope charged to the surface.

"The mining is going much slower than anticipated," Bazyli reported. "Duncan is not sure they can have enough refined to be of any benefit."

Reek! So much for hope. Marco roughed a hand over his face, anger writhing through him. Would nothing go right? He glanced at his weapon-arm again, fisting and unfisting his hand. Recalling what it was like to be plugged into a ship. Hating it. Yet invigorated by it. So much of him did not want to be plugged in to the *Qirolicha* ever again. But if he must, he must.

Marco looked to the general. "Tell Daq'Ti and Duncan to do what they can and keep me posted."

"Daq'Ti said he can do little more with the ore refining—Duncan has what he needs—so he went south with the Uchuvchi on the ground to join the militia."

Uncertain he liked that, Marco had little choice. He homed in on the master hunter, who no doubt anak'd what churned in Marco, so he chose to head it off. "I would ask a favor, since I know you to be light of feet and have command of your scout."

Dark brows narrowed over blue eyes, and there was a silent war there. As if he debated whether to call Marco on the issue. "Of course."

"Go to the tunnels. Find Aerios Myles and bring him here. Since I would not have Kersei and . . . the children unprotected, make sure to set guard over them before returning. If needed, I will find a replacement."

"A replacement?" Roman drew back, staring at him. "You would test him?"

"Long has he been a bit too attentive toward the duchess." He sensed the master's concern, not just over this suspicion of Myles. "Will you do this?"

The master hunter considered him. "We both know what I detect from you, Marco, but aye. I will do this. I would also speak with you when I return."

Talk was cheap. "Go." He urged him out the door, then turned to the regia who closed it. Extended his hand. "Theilig."

The regia grasped it as their eyes met, face and neck marred with healing injuries from his efforts to save his kyria. "Majesty."

Noting the light in his eyes, Marco nodded. "Secure the doors. Nobody leaves without my explicit word." He rounded and met a hunter. "Ariesteides, aid Theilig, if you please." He joined the gathered. "For those of you who have not yet met him, I would introduce Tigo Deken, onetime Eidolon commander—"

"Symmachian?" Galen balked.

That efflux was strident, likely compounded by the feelings of many in the room.

"Should you see fit to doubt him," Marco said, aware of his rage over the discoveries made in the week since Isaura had been brutally murdered, "I would mention that were it not for his assistance, the duchess and I would never have made it off the Symmachian warship months past. We are here, and I am medora, thanks to his efforts. Disrespect him, you disrespect me."

Galen's mouth tightened as the air swam with morphing effluxes.

As the Signatures settled, Marco resumed introductions. "With him is his former lieutenant, Jez Sidra, who in fact is"—he slid his gaze in her direction but refused to meet her gaze—"Faa'Cris."

Now both admiration and attraction trilled in the air, and Marco wanted to punch some people. Clearly they did not realize that the Faa'Cris were directly connected to and responsible for the disaster they found themselves in.

"They have brought intelligence deemed vital to our efforts in this war and the attack that took Isaura's life." He stepped aside with a nod to the commander.

"Thank you," Tigo said, positioning himself at the center of the room. "I realize most of you would likely enjoy putting a few blades through me, but I appreciate your forbearance. It's hard to talk with holes in my abdomen."

Silence met his attempt at humor.

"It is true I was an Eidolon commander, and if Symmachia can get itself together, I would readily return to duty. I loved being an Eidolon, fighting for justice, truth, and the innocent who could not fight for themselves."

Slow, mocking clapping began with Galen, then filtered through the ranks. "Are we supposed to be impressed?"

"Well, I kind of hoped you might be." Tigo smirked, then sobered and squared his stance. "My father is the admiral leading the assault on Drosero—"

"Now, I'm impressed," Galen taunted. "Imagine the ransom."

Tigo's first moment of hesitation tugged at Marco's mood. "I . . . What?"

The air snapped and crackled. Gusted in Marco's face, shoving a minty lavender across his receptors seconds before Jez stood behind Tigo in her winged form.

The men shuffled, scattering from her. Fear had nothing on their admiration of the Lady.

"Yeah." Tigo smirked at her. "Not helping me win trust."

"Enough!" Marco growled. "These two are my guests, and as such you will treat them with respect."

Tigo shifted on his feet. "I get it—I'm the last person you want to believe. So don't. Believe the intel I brought. Check it out, verify it. I really don't care what you think of me, as long as you give the information legitimate consideration."

Though no one answered, Marco detected that, despite being disgruntled at taking instruction from a Symmachian, they were just as anxious for help. "Perfect segue." He peeled from the corner, balling his fist as his mind settled squarely on the intel he'd uncovered . . . with Tigo's help. "First order of business . . ." He swiped a hand over the stubble that was more beard than scruff and nodded to his First. "Ixion, line them up."

Without a word, the Stalker arranged everyone into an arc.

Marco paced, annoyed that he could not simply anak this solution. "It has come to my attention that there is a traitor among us." He walked the queue, taking in every machitis and hunter. Staring into their eyes.

Was it wrong to revel in their nervous effluxes?

"Someone here sold us out. Put the lives of every man, woman, and child in Kalonica at risk." Pulling up, he scanned the line once more. "This person is responsible for the death of our beloved kyria. My wife. Isaura the Gracious, as she has been dubbed. That murderous traitor will pay."

"How will you know the traitor without proof?" Ixion asked.

"Curious, Mavridis," Marco said coolly, rolling his shoulders as the stiffening in his arm seemed to spread even more as he stood in this room, "that when introducing your new medora to the wastelands you defended desert justice, but now that I would rout a betrayer whose hands bear Isaura's blood, you question me."

Ixion held his gaze. "I would avenge Isa's death as readily as you, but I recall a young medora uncomfortable with desert justice, asking 'what about the courts?'" His gray eyes probed him. "We have courts . . ."

"We have a medora," Marco snapped, "who is the final say in all matters of law. Is he not? Am I not?"

Jaw muscle bouncing beneath his white beard, Ixion gave a slow nod. "You are, my medora."

"And sadly, there are no courts left standing, thanks to this war, the raiders, and our traitor. So we must deal with this now." Marco extended his hand to him. "We are agreed?"

Ixion took it reluctantly. "Agreed." In his eyes radiated that pure light, hot.

Relieved, Marco gave him a nod, backstepped along the line, and caught the shoulder of the next man. Stuck out his hand. "Kaveh."

The regia set his palm to Marco's. "Sire."

Grateful to find that pure light again, he patted the guy's shoulder and sidestepped. "Hadrien."

"Majesty . . ."

They shook hands.

Pure.

Marco kept moving. Few knew of the *Orasí*, the gift from the prophecy that gave him a glimpse into the adunatos of a person, and he had not mentioned it in an age, thus the confusion riddling the room. Today, however, it was his guiding beacon.

Next . . . "Cetus."

Clammy and trembling, the man's palm settled against Marco's. And . . . what was this? The light not quite . . . bright and blue. A bit blurred. *Just like Crey's.* But he would not name Crey a traitor, and he had seen more corruption in other eyes.

"S-sire?" Cetus stammered, his face white now. "I—I am not—I would *never*—"

The door opened and Theilig called, "Sire, the master hunter—"

"Let him enter." Marco stepped aside, watching between the shoulders of General Bazyli and his younger brother as Kersei's guard entered behind Roman. "Myles." He indicated to his left, then waited, anticipation humming in his veins. "Thank you for coming." The heat vibrated and thirsted, arousing that heady sense of . . . power. Retaliation.

Myles took in the line of men, nodding to some he had served with. "Sire, I am concerned about being away from the heirs."

Away from Kersei, more like. "You do not trust my instruction, Myles?"

The man stiffened. "No—that is, I meant no slight. Only that circumstances and this ora are difficult—"

"My wife is dead, I would seek to find her murderer, and you seek to instruct me?" It hurt to breathe, to restrain the weapon, heat wafting from it.

Myles dropped his argument, arrogance, and gaze.

Angry, Marco extended his hand.

Despite being startled by the offer, the aerios accepted and shook it.

The light was there, strong. Though tinged slightly orange, it spoke of poor choices, not betrayal. Not the traitor he sought. Why did it so disappoint him?

"You are trusted with the care of the duchess and the heirs, are you not?"

Myles squared his shoulders. "Aye, my medora."

"And that would mean protecting them in every regard from any threat, foreign . . . or domestic."

The aerios faltered, quickly searching his face. "A-aye, Majesty."

"What form of discipline would you impose, Regia Myles, on a man who would think to take certain . . . liberties with a member of House Tyrannous? What would you say I should do to such a man?"

Myles darted a gaze to Ixion, who stood with his hands clasped. "I . . ."

"Should the punishment be severe?"

The aerios swallowed. "Aye, my medora." His voice was so small it did not seem to come from this burly warrior.

"Mm." Marco twisted the family ring on his left hand as he paced a circle, then slid his hand over the hardened weapon. He caught sight of Jez, no longer in wings and armor but in more common attire. "Lady, what is your rank among the Faa'Cris?"

At this, Myles startled, his efflux flinging straight into terror.

"Triarii Rejeztia," she said, her chin lifted.

"And what is the punishment in your city for a man who would take liberties with a Lady?"

"Exile," she said. "Or death."

"M-my lord," Myles stuttered, going to a knee. "I beg your mercy."

"Beg, Myles, but there will be no mercy. Not this day." Marco paced, determined to set the example. "Your saving mercies are your own actions. Though you were attracted to the duchess, you did not move on her. Yet that distraction put in jeopardy her life, her son's life, and that of my"—it hurt to say it—"daughter."

Thick shoulders sagged.

"Because we are gravely short on sword arms in this fight against Symmachia, you will report to General Sebastiano for reassignment. Theilig."

"Sire," the man called from the back.

"Can I trust you to oversee the protection of the heirs and duchess?"

"Aye, sire! Vanko Kalonica!"

Marco stood over Myles. "Be grateful we are short on fighters, aerios. You are too skilled to lose at such a critical hour." He pivoted to the man who had resented his intrusion into Isaura's life on the plains of Moidia. "Hushak."

With a slow incline of his head, the man shifted on his feet, his efflux rank with nerves. "Medora Marco." The irritation that radiated from him over being examined seemed fitting for a Stalker. "I am sorry for your loss, sire."

The man's apologies surprised. And grated—because someone, likely in this room, had been behind Isa's death. Was this a distraction?

Marco didn't want to touch him. Wanted to walk away. But he must. He needed to know if this man had somehow bought his way into favor with Symmachia. He stuck out his hand. "Thank you for your service to her . . ." Why was it so hard to say her name? Why did it stir a fury and the heat of the brand?

Why did it charge black rage through the weapon?

With a stiff bob of his head, Hushak clasped his hand. "An honor, sire."

A light tinged with yellow . . . a little fury to go with that honor, apparently. Marco could relate.

Hushak again shifted. "All is well, my lord?"

Still processing what the *Orasí* declared, Marco nodded. Stood before Bazyli.

The general offered his hand. "My liege."

Grateful for the ready manner of his general, Marco accepted the handshake. Pure, of course. "Thank you, Bazyli." He struggled to refocus himself as agitation grew, going from one man to the next without discovering the traitor. It was possible the man was not even here, but he would clear those of his inner circle before exploring beyond these. Next he faced Bazyli's little brother. "Galen."

"My medora."

A hollowing out of the air rang in Marco's receptors, seemed as steam against the brand. He narrowed an eye as he opened his receptors. Extended his hand.

Galen's lighthearted manner glitched. He tensed. His palm met Marco's— so light. Lifting quickly.

Shock ricocheted through Marco as the light bled orange, then red. Like a trap sprung, he clenched his fingers around Galen's. Slid into the man's personal space. "What is this?" Marco demanded, shoving into the traitor, a move that carried them back until he heard a crack as the guy's spine struck the wall. His forearm found the soft tissue of Galen's throat.

"No-no!" His blue eyes widened. "No, my lor—"

"*You!*" Marco roared, pushing his full weight in. Saw the rippling of the weapon's power. "You killed her!"

"No!"

"My lord." Ixion rushed toward him.

Marco shoved harder, wanting—*needing*—vengeance for Isa. "You told them where to target. And they killed her."

"N-no. They—"

"This is not proof," Bazyli shouted. "Give him a chance to—"

"—they weren't supposed to kill her."

Enraged, feeling justified, Marco answered the call of the weapon. Reared back. Aimed. Fired.

Blue eyes widened beneath the sudden explosion of flame.

It registered with Marco what he'd done. What it meant. And he drew the weapon down, stopping short of incinerating the whole of the traitor whose betrayal cost Isaura her life.

Bazyli gave a strangled cry as he caught his brother's dying form.

"Who convinced you to betray your realm?" Marco demanded quietly, feeling the wake across his arm. Wanting the name revealed.

Galen grunted, his gaze struggling up to Marco. "Ru . . . fio."

As Tigo had suggested.

Jaw tight, fury burning hot amid the shocked and terrified effluxes in the room, Marco raged at who had sold them out. Who had killed Isaura. Would the man's perfidy never cease? "For your treachery, Galen Sebastiano, burn with the diabolus."

Shock rooted Ixion to the stone floor on which Bazyli knelt over his dead brother, no tears shed. Fist to his bearded mouth.

What madness was this?

The door slammed shut behind Marco.

Ixion glanced there and found a half dozen aerios missing even as the master hunter shoved through the door, calling after the medora.

Touching Bazyli's shoulder, Ixion knew he must follow Marco. But he did not want to look at him or speak to him. Was afraid of what he'd say.

The general stood. Looked to Ixion. "How did I not know?"

Ixion gave a tight shake of his head. "Do not blame yourself."

"I must!" Bazyli barked. "My *own brother*—in league with the Symmachians against Marco and our homeland. He betrayed us, killed our kyria!" Grief rolled through his northland features. "I am sick and angry and . . . know not what."

"Grief needs time—"

"*Grief*? Nay, I am livid. My own brother!" Face red, he shook his blond braids. "I knew him to be petulant and self-righteous, but *this*? Our father taught him better! I tau—"

The scream of alarms severed his words. They darted out into the passage. Stalkers, regia, hunters alike raced for the bay where the ships were berthed.

"What is this?" Ixion demanded of an aerios who rushed past, donning a helmet.

"Skycrawlers! They're dropping from the skies in suits of armor and are even yet entering the tunnels."

His heart jammed, thinking of his granddaughter's frail body. "Where is the medora?"

"Already in the air. Heard he's headed north to that entrance."

Ixion released the man to get underway, then debated his best course of action.

"North," Bazyli said as if reading his mind.

"Aye, but we will never reach the tunnels in time."

"We can help with that."

They pivoted and found Jez and Tigo there.

"You have a ship?" Bazyli asked. "Where?"

"Not a ship," Ixion said in unison with Tigo, knowing the Faa'Cris intended to transport them. "No, thank you."

"You will never reach them in time, as you have said. Is your pride so deep that you would risk your granddaughter?"

Ixion tensed.

"No," Bazyli said, catching his arm. "Please—help us save them. If the Symmachians see Marco use that entrance . . ."

Jez moved closer, even as she transformed. "Stand close."

BELOWGROUND MOUNTAIN ENCAMPMENT, NORTH KALONICA

The *thwap* of the javrod in her hands reverberated down her arms. Kersei gritted her teeth and glided forward, advancing as she snapped the rod low.

Crack! The rod struck hard and true against her sparring partner's shin. "Augh!" Thorolf hopped aside, holding his leg up, his shin likely throbbing.

"I . . ." She thought to apologize, but was it her fault he was slow? And where was Myles? Why had Roman taken him away? "Mayhap it is good to rest." She inclined her head. "Thank you for the challenge."

He grunted. "I am little challenge for you, Duchess. Your skill with that weapon is known across the realm."

"Your praise is overgenerous, but thank you. I would honor the Lady who gifted it to me."

"I thought Ladies used moon discs."

"It is an ancient weapon for them. The Lady who—"

A low rumbling spirited through the tunnel from the opposite direction, followed by shouts and screams.

"To your tent, my lady!" The aerios all but pushed her forward as two hunters bled from the shadows and joined Thorolf, Caio, and Belak in rushing her back to the tent where Danae and Kita stood, holding the babies, Mnason stuffing his wood sword into his belt.

Kersei took her son from Danae and checked on the sleeping Aeliana in Kita's arms. "What has happened?"

"We do not know," Kita said. "No one will tell us—"

The air shifted and mint speared the tent.

Before them stood a group of four—Jez, Tigo, Ixion, and the general.

Though Kersei tried not to cry out, Danae did not master herself, her screaming greeting the Faa'Cris and warriors.

"Jez! Tigo!" Kersei rushed forward, shifting Xylander so she could hug the Lady. "It is a joy to see you, but what do you here?" As her gaze connected with Jez's, she knew her joy was short-lived. "Trouble has found us."

"Much." Ixion went to Kita, the tenderness oozing from him so very strange.

"Bazyli," Danae gasped, then hugged her brother. "How are—why is there blood all over you?"

General Bazyli hesitated, belatedly looking at his tunic and noticing the stains. "I . . . We must talk." What torture crawled through his normally stoic features!

"Later," Ixion barked. "Symmachians are breaching the tunnels. We vacate at once."

A scream split the air, drawing their attention to the disarray of the encampment center as people raced here and there, gathering children and belongings. Pulse weapons fired on the far side.

"Move. Now," Ixion ordered, thrusting them out of the tent.

"Where are we supposed to go? Already we have been moved in deeper." Kersei set Xylander in a wrap and strapped it to her chest. "Where is Myles? Why did you—"

"Myles will not be returning." Ixion's jaw flexed. "Now, let us—"

The side of the tent collapsed. The throaty sound of a blade cutting canvas jerked her around in time to be enveloped by the falling fabric. It surprised how heavy the material was, weighting her. She tripped, her boots tangling in the chaos. Even as she landed on her hip, she heard Kita cry out amid mingling screams from Danae and Mnason. Grunts and the clang of weapons sent terror shooting through her veins.

"Help them!" Ixion shouted.

Beneath the heavy material that ensconced them in darkness, Kersei rolled to her side, hand protecting Xylander who grunted his disapproval of being squished. Her hair tumbled free of its binding. Fell into her eyes even as she spotted a gleam of light to the side and crawled toward it.

"Duchess," Ixion said, hauling Kersei to her feet and giving her a once-over. "This way."

Three dead raiders sprawled amid the chaos of tent material and bedding.

Even as he drew her to the left, away from the bodies, she scanned the encampment. Saw not only raiders, but three Eidolon in metal armor. Her heart sank, and she scrambled to keep up with Sir Ixion as General Bazyli fell in behind. Picking her way over rocks, she noted Kita struggling to keep Mnason close and hold Aeliana.

"Come." Kersei tugged back the wraps that held a fidgety Xylander. "Put her in here. I can handle them so you can manage Mnason."

"It is too much," Kita argued.

A blur from the side made her cringe and duck, curling inward toward Kita and the babes to protect them.

The shriek of steel on steel as Bazyli met the threat made her heart spasm. "Hurry," she whispered, helping the woman slide the tiny newborn into the bindings. She deliberately tugged up the edge and folded it to hide what was within, shielding the children.

The terrible sounds of crunching bones. Flesh sluicing around a blade.

The attacker howled.

Cupping the babies close, Kersei turned away, sought Ixion. He vaulted into the air over one raider, who raised a Symmachian weapon at him. Ixion's arms snapped in opposite directions as he landed, and the raider's head slid from the in-motion body. Beyond him was the whirlwind of two Stalkers confronting a slew of blue-marked raiders. The sight pushed her hand to the pocket of her omnirs, and she drew out her javrod. Better to be ready than emptyhanded.

Gloriously, Jez was in the middle of it all, delivering death with her sword. Never far from her side, Tigo parried and deflected in tandem with the Faa'Cris. They protected each other and addressed the enemy with a fluid partnership that was both beautiful and terrifying.

And then she saw him. Marco. Intensity amped, eyes ablaze as he bolted at a Symmachian. Zigzagging up onto the wall in a corner and whipping his legs at the enemy. Knocked the guy in the head. Snapped it back. Sent him to the ground. His weapon came out of nowhere, and he seared a massive hole through the man's chest. Even as he confronted another, he couldn't see the one coming at him from behind.

"Mar—"

He was already in action, swinging around with a pulse weapon that severed the raider's neck. Pivoted and killed the other raider. Of course, he was Kynigos—the scent warned him.

The deaths were righteous. Needed even. But there was something . . . feral about his actions. His intent.

Her brand writhed and churned beneath Aeliana in her arms.

Marco . . .

He growled and aimed at another raider. And another. The look on his face. Nostrils flared. Brow knotted. Lips curled . . .

A heaviness settled in her middle, one that seemed to cast a pall over her whole being.

From the side, a raider dove at her. Xylander and Aeliana strapped to her chest, she whirled, flicking the javrod. It lengthened even as she felt the air stir. Instinct shoved the sharp end to her right, and she felt it connect with sinew.

A howl wracked her eardrums as she extracted her weapon and spun as she'd been trained, arcing the rod around. She struck his temple. The raider gaped, dropping to the ground. "Kita!"

The woman emerged from a large rock, cradling a rigid Mnason, and rushed to her.

Kersei stumbled toward Kita. It was strange to find themselves without guards, all hands needed in the fight. "Go! Go, go!"

"Danae—we were separated." Kita peered over her shoulder.

As they negotiated the melee, Kersei searched the chaos of men battling and women hurrying for safety. "There!" Across the encampment, Danae was among the other women slipping into the escape tunnels there. Crestfallen, Kersei realized there was no way to reach them. "This way."

They snaked around one tent after another toward the most northern tunnel. Kersei adjusted Aeliana in the wrap, securing her more in a cradle position. Xylander protested, clearly too crowded, but there was nothing for it. "Shh," she whispered, trying to reassure him.

The terrain rose and fell, forcing them to assist each other toward the black maw of the passage ahead.

"Are you sure, my lady, that you know where it leads?"

"I saw aerios coming and going. If it is not an exit, at least we can hide until things settle."

But even as Kersei looked to the entrance, she faltered at strange glowing symbols warbling in the shadows. Mind racing, connecting those marks with the raiders, she backed up. "Back," she hissed. "Hurry before they see us."

Kita shifted and dropped back several feet. She scampered around a pile of boxes.

Whoosh! A tent ballooned out as it collapsed, the posts sticking up at odd angles. Its collapse had dislodged crates and a barrel from a stack.

Kersei faltered, realizing her path was blocked. No. She glanced back, praying the raiders had not seen her.

Greedy, crazed eyes met hers.

Jerking around, Kersei looked across the way. Saw Kita panicking, her face alive with terror. *Ladies, help me!*

Balking, Kita froze for a second. But then she drew up sharp, wheeled around, and sprinted off.

Shocked to be so wholly abandoned, Kersei tested the surrounding routes, rocks jutting up around her. Had she maintained her training, this would have been no hard task. But nursing two babes had left little time for anything except naps.

Weak. *You are weak!*

Her legs ached and already she wanted to just sit down and rest. An impossible and unrealistic thought. Forcing herself to keep going, she slipped through a crevasse that formed a passage, using it to hide her movement. As it narrowed, she collapsed and pocketed the javrod as she advanced.

Behind her came the soft pad of feet.

Unable to turn in the narrow space, she ignored her hammering heart and peered over her shoulder. Her heart jarred in her chest. A raider—small but ferocious all the same—slunk toward her with those writhing marks and leering eyes.

Crying out would do no good, so she strangled it. Shoved her hair back as she gripped the sides of a smaller crevasse and dragged herself up over the boulder. Snarling and snapping teeth drew closer. A whimper escaped as she felt the slightest of touches at her calf.

Protect me and these children.

Pulse jouncing, she climbed over one boulder and down another. Chastised herself for not getting after her training sooner. The specter of defeat and exhaustion demanded her surrender, making her limbs and courage tremble. If she surrendered, the children—

"No." It was her responsibility. She took it seriously. Though she thought to drive the Touch into this savage, she did not want it that close to the heirs.

Eyeing the next juncture, she grunted at the climb. Could she do it? There was no choice—she must. This fight was about more than herself. Hand on the wall, guiding her, she reminded herself that these two strapped to her depended on her being smart, quick, and unyielding. Thinking of the babies made her glance down as she wended through the tunnel. Cocooned in the wrap, the two were sound asleep, nestled against one another. She let out an incredulous laugh—and drew up short. The passage ended in front of her. Obsidian blocked her. No way out.

"No." Palming the surfaces, she swallowed hard. Bit back another whimper. Hustled back a half dozen steps to . . . where? Where could she go when surrounded by granite? Hands to the cold, damp stone, she followed it.

A snarling filled the hollowed recesses, snaking around her. Constricting.

Please, Ancient—

Even as she called out to him, she saw the raider.

Blue marks swirling in the constricted space, he was much larger than the last one. And seemed to own a lethal power as he lowered his head and peered under a thick brow.

"Mercies," Kersei whispered. Hauling in a breath, she stilled, her hand going to the bundle at her chest. Thought of his bulk. The narrowing space. If she could just . . . She sidestepped into the thin gorge.

The thing lunged at her.

Kersei screamed, shrinking back as it wedged in, reaching toward her. Angling her shoulder to protect the heirs, she groped for her javrod. Felt the raider's hot, rancid breath skate across the rock to her. Fire lanced her shoulder, and she dropped the javrod.

Kersei watched it clatter down and land out of reach. No! Even if she slid back down, the space was too narrow for her hand. There was nothing for it. She was defenseless.

Frantic, she shoved and pushed, trying to free herself. Get away from him. The snarling. The spray of spittle.

Choking back tears and a sob, she shriek-growled as she pushed herself out the other side. The pain was terrible. The babes wailed, making her ache and fear she was killing the very ones she would protect. She struggled, felt her bones threatening to crack. All at once, she pitched backward, stumbling, surprised at the sudden freedom granted her. She landed on her backside, then scrabbled upward. Only then noticing the raider . . .

He raged and thrashed, stuck.

Seizing the small—likely temporary—victory, Kersei scoured the small chamber for an opening, but only found more of the oppressive black walls. Boulders. Stone.

Where, where, where?

Was there no mercy to be had? She must get out, find shelter and—

There! A cleft that delved into another narrow space. Bones aching, babes still wailing their protest, she realized it was her only option. The raiders were too determined. Thankfully, she had not confronted an Eidolon. Praying the others were faring better, she wedged in. Climbed. Scaled up and—was that another tunnel? She threw herself in that direction, careful not to bang the babies' heads as she negotiated the space that was ever-shrinking. Tightening. Rising. She planted a foot—and it wedged in. She shoved up and felt her foot sink into the space. Pinch. Squeeze. Gripping her ankle solidly.

Oh no.

She caught the upper ledge, arcing her spine away from the rock to protect the children. But failed. Xylander's head struck the hard surface. He let out a peal.

Foot stuck, she tried to pull herself up. But the rock held tight. Dropping back down, hair in her face, she pressed her other toe against the rock and worked to free her booted foot.

A flash of heat, and rock disintegrated nearby.

Kersei yelped and jerked her gaze to the side. To the yellowed teeth as the raider slid in like a serpent. She eased her hand to the javrod—only to remember it had fallen. She braced herself and angled the babies away from him.

He aimed and fired.

Another superheated blast skimmed her face.

With a scream, she ducked. Gritted her teeth. Shoved once more to free herself.

A second raider appeared from the other side. Lunged in.

"No!" Kersei shouted, shoving with her weapon hand.

Slamming into her, the raider met her hand with his full weight. She heard a distinct crack, even as heat spiraled from her brand, down her arm.

Light exploded, searing her eyes.

Kersei squeezed her eyes shut, realizing the Touch had released again. She knew not how. Did not care how, only that it had. But she dared not look away from the raider for long. He'd kill her, kill the children.

But when she opened her eyes, Kersei couldn't make sense of what she saw. The Irukandji fell away, shrieking. Screaming. Writhing. Blue marks overtook his body. Swarmed and filled every portion of his skin—arms, neck, face—until another light burst erupted.

She gasped as ash rained down.

Trembling, she felt both traumatized and relieved.

In the small chamber, three raiders paced back and forth like wild dogs, looking from the spot where their compatriot had stood to Kersei wedged in the rock with crying babies.

Arm dangling at her side, exhausted and defeated, Kersei cried. Leaned her head to the side and braced herself, even as the tears blurred her vision. She gritted her teeth and tried again to yank her foot free. No good.

Something dribbled into her hair from above. Kersei looked up, stunned to find a raider hovering above her, wedged in the cleft where it widened over her head. Another to the right where the first had been reduced to ash.

Panic clawed at her. Wholly trapped. Unable to defend herself or the children.

A shot seared her shoulder.

She screamed and bent over the children, hiding them. Hugging them. Desperate that she had failed to protect them. That they would all die in a tunnel—

Thud! Crack!

Grunts and thumps ensued . . . but no strike to her back or head. No life-ending pulse fire to her. No daggers. No feral snarling. Crying, she looked up. Nothing there. Over her shoulder—

Visage dark, sweaty, and mottled with blood, Marco released a volley of fire straight at the raider's chest with a growl of his own.

Cradling the children with one arm as she supported herself with the other, Kersei leaned against the rock, trembling from exhaustion and adrenaline. Relief. She watched Marco as, back to her, he looked around, bloody sword in one hand, a dagger in the other, searching for more raiders.

Apparently satisfied they were safe for the moment, he scaled the rock to her. "You are well?"

"Thanks to you, alive."

"Come," Marco said roughly. "Down from here."

"I . . . cannot. My boot is stuck."

His gaze struck hers, and she would vow there was irritation in the way his cheek twitched beneath that beard. Sliding his weapons into their sheaths, he made quick work of reaching her. He leaned down and she felt his touch against her calf. "Shift your weight to the other leg."

"I already tried that."

"Do it."

With a huff of embarrassment, she complied and used her arms to support herself as she angled to the side. Muscles strained and she shook with the effort.

Marco turned her foot. "I must release the laces."

Humiliation was her name. It was inappropriate for him to do this—if they were in any other situation. Here, it was necessary.

"Turn your foot toward me and pull."

She complied, and after a couple of tugs, it came free. Slumping with relief, she leaned back. Felt her limbs failing her.

Aeliana let out an ear-piercing scream.

Marco's gaze shot to the swaddling, where her tiny little fist thrust free of the wrapping, and through that sliver, her face shone. He sucked in a loud breath, frozen.

Daring not to move or speak, Kersei knew this moment was crucial.

He had never seen her. Never touched her. His hand lifted to the downy head. Fingers brushed the hair so gently, so slowly that it did not seem he moved at all. Was he breathing?

Kersei held her own breath.

Aeliana quieted beneath her father's touch and squinted up at him.

"Marco!"

At Ixion's shout, Marco blinked, as if a spell had broken. His gaze met hers. Wonderment glittered in his eyes, but to a greater degree . . . torment. Anguish.

Kersei touched his warm forearm. "I know what it is to lose your bound and have a child as a reminder," she whispered. "It is painful, hard, but beautifully healing. She needs you. And I think you need her."

"Are they well?" Ixion called as he hiked toward them, expression taut. "Is she—"

"Safe." Marco's brittle tone echoed in the small space as he angled aside and allowed Ixion to help her down. Once on the cave floor, he shifted behind the Stalker. "Get them to safety. I'm going to see how our people fared." He slipped back through the narrow entrance.

Ixion met her gaze and her own grief was mirrored there. His mouth tightened, and he lifted a hand to indicate she should precede him through the passage.

Finding the way easier now that she was no longer being chased, she soon limped into the main chamber again. A few paces away, Marco stalked among the fallen tents, pausing to speak to Bazyli, who nodded tersely and headed for an exit.

"You must get to safety as well, sire," Ixion said loudly, emerging from the passage behind her.

The people nearby looked up from tending wounded and restoring order to the encampment.

Marco came to a stop but did not turn. He cocked his head, flexing and unflexing his hand. His brand arm—it'd been warm there and hard. Was he wearing armor under his tunic? Strange. Was it not more effective above the clothing?

Aeliana let out another shriek, startling Kersei. "She cries for you," she said quietly as realization spread through her. It was a bold statement, an accusation. In truth, it was not the babe alone who cried for him. Though her ankle was sore from being trapped, Kersei hobbled to him. "She has not cried thus since her birth. She has little will to live and barely eats, but she cried when you were near. With your touch, she quieted." Though Kersei tried to look into his eyes, he stared into the camp. "Not only does she need you, she *wants* you. Her father."

His icy gaze slid to her as animosity tumbled off him. "Which should I set down to coddle the child? My sword or my dagger?"

"How about your cold heart?"

His eyes widened almost imperceptibly.

Aware of the people around them, she worked to keep her voice low. "She is your daughter!"

He shifted to his First. "Mavridis, remove the duchess and heirs to safety."

"What care you if we are safe?"

He grew a couple of inches, his eyes cold and hard above the sigil that had once defined who he was and signaled his mettle.

"Where is your honor, your character—"

"Mavridis!" Marco barked.

"Aye, my lord." Ixion touched her elbow, using his body to press into her space, forcing her aside. "This way, Duchess." He guided her to the others, past the carnage that turned the stream red with blood. "This is not the way to get through to him."

"Clearly," Kersei bit out, limping to protect her ankle, which still throbbed. "You said you would speak to him."

"I have," he growled. "He is not easily moved, and if you have missed it, he has good reason for his absence in the war that threatens our lives." He paused, facing her. "Let us ensure the heirs survive, hm?"

She wilted as he nudged her along like some petulant child told to go back in the house. Glancing up from her shuffling feet, she found Ypiretis coming toward her.

Silently, he took her arm, as much supported as supporting, and the two of them made their way to a cluster of overturned crates.

"I could use your wisdom." She lowered her voice as they sat, unwilling for others to hear her speak against the medora. "Marco is distracted and foul. I fear—"

"His focus is on this war."

"How—"

"He is named Progenitor." He lifted her brand arm. "You were there when the Lady spoke it to him. Now you must trust that he is doing as he must to fulfill his role."

"It is not the warrior in Marco that gives me pause, Ypiretis. There is more—a heavy . . . darkness. Each time I encounter him, it is worse."

Wizened eyes narrowed. "I . . . have noticed it as well."

Flooded with a mixture of relief and anxiety, Kersei slumped, one hand on each of the babes still bound to her chest. "It is so hard. I fear we are losing him."

Ypiretis nodded. "I share that fear, but I do not think talk will adjust Marco's focus. And in truth, there is little said of the Progenitor after this war."

"So we are to just leave him? When we sense this? Are you in earnest? Should not his closest friends and allies share their concern? I do not understand—always you have been so understanding and intuitive regarding such things."

"I am out of my depth, Duchess. We have entered a territory previously unknown to man. Neither of us can know what it will look like. The Progenitor was to instigate this war. He has done that. What will come next, what it will do to him . . . we cannot know. Pray for him. It will make the days ahead easier."

Kersei drew up. "No." She shook her head. "No, I don't accept that. As such, I do not care for ease. I only want him to survive this. All of us."

"Neither is that promised."

"Truly, are all men so cold and heartless?"

"Search the tunnels!" Undeniably, that cool fragrance unique to skycrawlers flooded his receptors. Marco signaled his Brethren who had fought here. "Symmachians dare intrude on our lands even now! Roman yet battles in one of these tunnels. We go to his aid."

Even as he started forward, he thought of . . . that tiny, fragile face peering up at him. So small. Terribly fragile. Yet so very complete. And beautiful. Radiating that floral-minty aroma that had guided him home.

Ahead, he spotted the Faa'Cris. "A favor, Triarii Rejeztia."

Her jaw tightened as she pulled to the side to listen.

"I know you are here to fight with us, and I am grateful, but with the fall of Kardia and Symmachia in the tunnels, I fear for Is"—reek!—"*Kersei* and the heirs. Please. Take them to your city beneath Drosero."

Jez considered him and glanced to Tigo before meeting his gaze again. "I am not sure the Ladies will allow me to return ther—"

"Do this or I will end my life right here."

"Threats are weak—"

"A promise." He tightened his jaw. "Am I right—Aeliana is one of you? A Daughter." When she did not argue, Marco knew he had solid ground on which to base his demand. "Do it. Or her death and mine are on your head."

"You quite vociferously demand the protection of a daughter you will not claim."

His heart pounded on his ribs that she might deny him. Yet he would not beg.

"Kersei will not go. She is a Lady—"

"Then Aeliana. The Faa'Cris named her. Let them claim her."

"*Claim* her?" Jez shouldered in, somehow seeming much taller than his own one-point-eight meters. "Do you realize what you speak, Licitus?"

It meant she would be safe, live. "I do."

"No." Tigo stepped in. "Do not do this, Marco. You will regret it."

Jez glimmered in the pale light of the tunnel, then lifted her chin. "I will take her to Deversoria—"

"No!" Tigo balked, panicked.

"—but not permanently. Only until the Revered Mother decides it is safe for her to return to you."

His pulse sped at that. The Revered Mother . . . *his* mother. He nodded. "Thank you."

"Do not thank me," Jez said fiercely. "This is a decision you will regret, but it is for her safety, so I yield my objections."

He nodded and started down an alternate entrance tunnel, noting Cetus and Ramirus falling into step with him. Odd, but the farther he ran, the heavier he felt. A half klick more, and the air cooled in the narrowing tunnel. Ahead, scents grew thicker, more numerous. "Ready yourselves."

Almost as the words left his lips, they rounded a corner into a cave a little larger than the ballroom had been in Kardia. The melee of bodies and swords. Snarls from raiders. The acrid scent of burnt flesh from pulse weapons.

Marco assaulted the nearest enemy—a raider leveling a pulse pistol at the back of an aerios—by hiking up and driving the heel of his boot into the center of the man's back. The raider went down and Marco landed, snatched up the pistol, whipped around, and aimed. Fired.

The blast incinerated the man's head.

Faltering, Marco frowned, hesitated. He had fired the Symmachian weapon, but that was too much damage for the pulse blaster. What had done that . . .? His gaze turned to his weapon-arm. He eyed his sleeve—burned away. The vambrace smoking but intact. The weapon . . . glowing. He hadn't intended to use it, yet it responded to his . . . thoughts.

A rabid scream came from his left.

Marco pivoted, crouched, feeling the wind stir as another raider vaulted at him, narrowly missing the blade the savage aimed at his throat. Even as he rolled aside, he aimed his arm at the raider. Contracted the muscle. Fire burst out.

The savage was now but dust.

An uncanny awareness spread through Marco of the pleasure he felt at seeing these monsters reduced to ash.

Yet . . . am I not the monster?

Had not Draegis used these against the *Prevenire* crew and been named beasts? Though a modicum of shame struck him, he was glad for the exacting weapon.

Awareness lit through him—he was not the only one who'd noticed the unusual results of his engagements. He couldn't draw any more attention. Besides, his arm ached, felt stiff. Angling around, he tucked the Symmachian pistol against his shoulder and scanned the cave.

He didn't miss the way Ixion and the others glanced at him as they fought off the raiders.

Pulse blasts suddenly filled the cavern. A dozen laser sights leapt and danced in the darkness.

"Eidolon!" Tigo shouted. "Take cover!"

Where? There weren't any large rock formations like near the encampment. This place was open and wide with a large pool of water.

No . . . They had no recourse. No way to defeat this many, and if the Symmachians kept coming, this place would become their grave.

Wait . . . Marco scanned the ceiling all the way to the tunnel opening. "On me!"

With his vanguard, Marco darted to the perimeter. Tic-tacked along the wall until they reached the side. "Target the opening!" He flexed his wrist, then pointed at the ceiling. Willed hard for a full volley. Heat coursed through his arm. He quickly clenched his fingers into a fist and released the shot.

It struck the ceiling. The cavern trembled beneath the blast.

But didn't yield. Then the men fired pulse weapons they'd taken from the dead, released a barrage. The ground shook and rattled, as if it were angry with them. He sent another volley, doing his best to not get distracted that another dozen or so targeting beams stabbed the dark tunnel. He fired another volley. And again, the ground rumbled harder and louder until, with a roar, the tunnel collapsed, drowning shouts and snuffing out those laser sights.

Marco swiveled, targeting within the cave now. They'd not only blocked off more enemy from encroaching, but cornered the enemy already within. Now to neutralize them all.

Heat shot through his shoulder, slamming him into the cave wall. He caught himself and rotated, seeing only the backs of Ixion and an aerios as they provided protective cover.

Firing at a raider, Cetus neared him. "You okay, sire?"

"Besides being shot?" Marco held his injured arm—thankfully not his weapon-arm—to his stomach and climbed to his feet. Sent off a blast in the direction from which he'd been shot.

"Formation Orion." Ixion's instruction carried through the cavern.

Marco moved into position, as did all others warring for Drosero, effectively fighting their way into a circle that they would tighten, shrink, as they battled.

"Okay, okay!" an Eidolon said, his mechanized voice ringing off the stone walls. "We're trapped and surrender. We are at your mercy."

The fighting died down, his men glancing around, unsure what to do. Marco angled around to stand before the handful of remaining Symmachians. "You come to our planet, where you are not wanted, where a treaty states you are not welcome. With suits that hide your faces and give you a ridiculous advantage, you wield weapons that are far advanced to force us into submission." At this, the Symmachians glanced at one another— and despite the heavy armored suits, their irritation and frustration could be detected—then removed their helmets. "And you speak of mercy?"

"His name is Bedth, commander of the Two-two-eight," Tigo said. "He's as dirty as Cleve and Baric."

"Baric." Rage spiked through Marco. "No mercy." He turned and fired at the commander. Then the woman in the mech-suit next to him, while the vanguard eliminated the other two—another Eidolon and a raider.

Gasps and scents around him rifled in the cavern. He sensed their shock. Disgust from some. Relief from others. But mostly, he caught their uncertainty. About him. When he rounded, he found Ixion watching him intently.

"More desert justice?" Ixion's efflux was drenched in anger, disappointment. Not quite revulsion, but not far from it.

"No," Marco said calmly. "But for them, for what they have done, there is no mercy."

Ixion craned his neck forward. "There is always mercy," he said in a low, raspy tone. "Always, Marco."

Gaze traveling the men, who were dispersing yet remaining close enough to hear, Marco felt a preternatural calm. "From Marco, mayhap." He met Ixion's gaze coolly. "From the Progenitor, no. There is no mercy." He focused on the men, knew they needed direction, encouragement. "They come to our world, seek to change it," he said in a ringing voice. "They care not who they kill in forcing their will upon us. I was set in this place, in this time, not to placate or pander to false illusions of their peace—which, do not mistake, is subjugation of our people. The Ancient named me Progenitor, not to make them feel good or show weakness. I was set in place for one reason: to give them war!"

"Vanko Kalonica!"

"No!" Marco shouted. "Vanko *Drosero*! This is about more than us. It's about this planet. About free will. About not allowing slippery tongues and offers of comfort and convenience to steal our freedom. Our very lives!" He turned in a circle, appreciating the way they grouped up around him. "When they seek peace, give them war!"

BELOWGROUND MOUNTAIN ENCAMPMENT, NORTH KALONICA

"Here, Duchess. Remain within for now. Rest with the babes."

Incredulous, Kersei gaped at Sir Theilig, knowing Marco, Ixion, and the others still battled to push raiders and Symmachians from the tunnels. Yet . . . pains were making themselves known. Ankle throbbing. Head pounding. Scrapes and cuts. Exhaustion.

"Please." Face, beard, and hair splattered with blood—evidence of the intense fight he'd waged in the caves—Sir Theilig reached for Xylander and motioned to a small tent. "You will be safe within, my lady."

They were supposed to be safe at Kardia, but it had been destroyed. Safety should have been here in the caves, but the Symmachians and raiders yet found them. Attacked.

"Safety is an illusion," she whispered, smoothing a hand along the tiny frame of the princess nestled in the wrap once more. Thought of how Marco had frozen, realizing what he had protected. His daughter.

"Your reticence is understood," Theilig said. "But be assured, my men and I will stand guard as you rest and give that ankle some care. It might need to be wrapped."

"Nay," she said wearily. "I think just some time off it will help."

With care, he set Xylander in a basket within the tent, then held out a hand to her.

Though she thought to reject him, Kersei could not deny the aches and pains. But did not all here have those? Aye, mayhap, but none else nursed two infants. She managed a smile, accepted his help, and hobbled inside. Loosening the wrap, she extricated Aeliana and laid her next to her cousin. "What of Ladies Danae and Kita?"

Hand on his sword hilt, he cocked his head to the right. "Both are tending wounded."

Kersei shifted, searching the scattered crowd, whose faces were lit by touchstones. "I should contribute to—"

"Rest, my lady," Theilig insisted firmly. "As the medora ordered. He placed you in my care, and"—a shadow of deep sorrow crossed his eyes—"I will not fail him again."

Pausing, Kersei searched his countenance, reached for his arm—what mattered propriety in the face of such pain? "I am sure he would not—"

"I lost the kyria." Torment writhed through his beard and worn visage. "On my life, I vow I will not lose you as well."

How her heart ached for him. "He does not blame you. No one blames you."

The weight only seemed to increase on his shoulders. He stepped back. "You do me a kindness I do not deserve, Duchess. Rest. Please. The babes will demand your attention soon enough." With a nod, he stepped out and dropped the tent flap.

A lone touchstone glowed softly beneath a cheesecloth, throwing just enough light for her to find a place on the pallet to lie down. She shifted around and set her spine to the back of the tent. Tucked a blanket under her head and another beneath her ankle, which was glad for the reprieve of bearing weight.

She reached over and drew the basket closer, peeking in at the children. Aeliana's little chin worked as she suckled in her sleep, cuddled into Xylander, who was on his side, his balled fist resting on his cousin's shoulder. She hoped they would always be close. Depend upon and defend one another long after this perilous war they would not remember, thank the Ladies.

With her toe, she nudged a blanket over the touchstone. Light gone, the outline of two men—Theilig and one of his men—in front of the flap cast long shadows on the tent, likely by firelight. She closed her eyes, and sleep ravenously claimed her. Dragged her deep into its heavy embrace.

A scritching yanked her awake.

What was that?

Heart racing, she first noticed the campfires must have been doused, as no shadows danced on the flap. Distant chatter reached her ears. That must be what had wakened her. She released her captive breath. Told herself to go back to sleep. Mayhap they would be on the move soon en—

Something pricked her hip. She yelped and reached for the spot. Glanced over her shoulder—her head colliding with a masked face. She tried to scream, tried to shout, but realized neither her limbs nor her mouth worked.

The tent flap flew backward. Theilig rushed in.

A weapon slid past her face. Aimed at her guardian.

Nooo!

Theilig must have seen the weapon—his eyes widened—but he charged forward.

A blast flashed past her face.

Seared into the regia's chest as the Symmachian hauled Kersei and the babes into the darkness.

Sheltered by the locals, Eija sat at the table with a cup of warm tea, staring into the fire. "Are there Uchuvchi still here?"

"You saw what I did," Reef bit out, tearing off a chunk of bread. He chewed it and slurped the tea.

Indeed. After the sonic boom-style propulsion of the *Qirolicha* that had them vanish in a blink, a swarm of Uchuvchi drones lifted off and blinked out of the system as well.

"But you were with Marco when I wasn't—you saw that facility. The ships that took off. Did that seem to match the number of pilot pods you saw?"

"Slag, I have no idea." Reef frowned, scratching the back of his head. "There were . . . a lot. But there were a lot of ships that left, too. Not sure I can count that high."

"*Think* about the pods—they're hooked into towers. In the hybrid facility, there were easily a hundred to a hundred fifty in each tower. About twenty towers—"

"I was a little distracted by Vaqar eating Marco's lunch and Daq'Ti turning human."

"He wasn't turning human—he *is* human. He was healing."

"Holy mother of Baru," he huffed, slamming down his tin cup. "I give up. You have all the answers, so figure it out." He stood and started away.

"Where are you going?"

"Saw what looked like a pig pen. Think I'll muck it. Doesn't reek as much as what's in here."

Eija rose to her feet. "What does that mean?"

With a dismissive wave, he continued out the door.

Surprised at how much that hurt, considering all she had done, who she was, what she had accomplished . . . She had expected—

What? For him to fawn over you?

No, but at least a little respect. She nodded to the owner of the hostel and followed Reef into the stable yard. Out here, the air trilled against her clypeus with warning. Had something happened to Reef? Her heart gave a start, but then she spotted him through the barn and house on the other side, bending over, then straightening near a fence, on which he dangled his arms.

She sighed and headed over to him, determined to explain what he had misunderstood. As she moved between the buildings, her mind flicked back to the encounter with the hybrids. The villager's ominous telling of a dozen Xonim. Their word for the Khatriza.

A chill swept through her and pinched the ridge of her span at the thought of so many nearby.

Voids! What could she possibly do against that many? Once more, she was on the street after the encounter, hugging her knees—figuratively speaking, of course.

I am Faa'Cris. This is why I'm here. Why I was sent out.

Picking up the crumbs of her courage, Eija pushed herself into the open to talk with Reef. He had always been a good sounding board. He'd believed in her from that first day at the Academy.

Now he stood looking out at the snowy plain that seemed to stretch to the horizon where another community—*is that Shad's village?*—was discernible by only the barest specks of light. His hair had grown a bit from his normal high-and-tight. But his athletic build had leaned out—fighting for your life did that to a person.

Yet, he was still Reef Jadon. Eidolon. Smart alec. Master of sarcasm.

Mine . . .

Jarred at the thought, Eija drew in a quiet breath. There was a dichotomy in her own essence now, having the memories and direction of the young Symmachian Shepherd competing for a chance on the *Prevenire*, the ship to make the first-ever hyperjump.

What fools they'd been. And since then, she'd regained her existence as a Faa'Cris. A wealth of knowledge and experiences . . . and yet, somehow they paled to her time as simply Eija.

Because of him.

The sound of his voice nearby startled her, making her still. Had he seen her? Called out and she missed it? Eija took a step forward—

A softer, sweeter voice halted Eija's advance. Where—

There. In the shadow, leaning against the shed. A girl their age—Reef's age, actually, since Meijatsia had centuries on her limited experience as Eija—

talked to him. She did not have to anak to catch an attraction assault that spiraled from the girl.

Surely, Reef would see through it.

He snickered. Shifted and took a step closer to the girl, his words too quiet to hear. But his scent wasn't quiet or difficult to take in. He was attracted to this . . . this inconsequential villager!

Fists balled, Eija stood rooted in place, as if the tendrils of this insipid place had tethered her to its soil, forced her to watch this absurd—

Reef laughed.

More attraction spewed from the sniveling girl of loose morals, out alone in the dark with a complete stranger. Repulsive!

The weak fool moved nearer to the girl.

Eija felt a wake of heat rippling over her. Knew she could easily end this girl just as she had the beasts. Bore a hole straight through that linen tunic. Singe that blonde hair.

Reef's scent wavered. He did not turn, but his Signature shifted. Changed. He knew . . . knew she was watching this play out. And he did not even look at her or don some contrition.

Hurt clamored against presumptions . . . assumptions. *He's supposed to be mine.* The anger both confused and compelled her, demanding satiation.

Yet . . . it was wrong. Yes, she was Meijatsia, Bloodbreaker, but that was a vengeance doled out against the enemies of the Ancient. Not a girl aroused to jealousy and anger over . . . over a Licitus!

Calling him that did not alleviate her pain. Not even close. In fact, it fueled it. She growled as she stomped back through the village. Down an alley. Away from the street where she'd killed the beast—the reek was yet there. Past the square. Toward a road that would lead her out of this foul place.

"Xonim!"

Eija tucked her chin, not willing to be bothered. Needing space to clear her thoughts and empty her anger.

"My Lady—please!"

Lady? Eija glanced over her shoulder and found the bald villager who'd first braved approaching her after she killed the beast. She hesitated.

No, no. Keep going. They don't need or deserve—

"Please, do not go out of the village at night. Their senses are keener, sharper in the open plains, so they prowl them."

Eija faltered and looked toward the road, the pinpricks of light on the horizon beckoning her across the void. The terrible thing of it was, she wanted to go. Even considering the danger. "Are there a lot of them?" Were they part of what she was here for? Part of her purpose?

"Xonim," the man said, his voice nearer. "You can go out there, fight them, but you do not have to. Rest, stay in for the night."

She turned and met his gaze, found him standing much closer. "But they are what I am here for, what I was sent to deal with."

"Sure," the man said kindly, almost in a fatherly manner, "but you warred once today. You look fair exhausted. Please, come inside. Eat, rest. War in the morning." Now there was a smile playing around his eyes and a quirk to one side of his mouth.

Too used to the taunting and being the brunt of jokes on Symmachia, Eija stiffened. "You mock me."

"No," he said with a laugh. "I only meant—fighting is always there. Always waiting for us. But we can choose when to engage . . . or disengage."

"If only I were afforded that luxury," she murmured, once more eyeing the horizon. *Escape. Do what you were sent here to do.*

But Reef . . .

Had chosen his path. Now it was time to choose hers.

But had she chosen it? Well, until she saw him with the girl.

No, it was a selfish thought. She had given herself to the Ancient to do with as He would. Now that the situation had worsened and the days grown hard, did she dare decide she was too tired to fulfill the mission? Quit when she had given her heart and life to Him?

Sure, he could find another to complete the mission. But had she started this journey only to have it finished by another?

Conviction laced through her, threading a band tight around her lungs.

Yes, there were times the Ancient used multiple people to perfect the task—and in a way, He was doing that very thing with this prophesied war. He had Marco in Drosero fighting for his people, and in that realm of influence there were a half dozen or more individuals vital to his path and countless others affected by his decisions.

Then there was Miatrenette's admiral, buffering things as best he could against the traitorous, self-absorbed captain who had given his adunatos to Xisya . . . who had killed Conalestrata—Patron Alestra, as Eija had once known her.

Overwhelmed by the enormity of it—through all the threads weaving and running through life, through this grand scheme called war, their paths had been guided. Choices offered. Missions accepted. Lives impacted. Was it easy?

She sniffed. Where would be the fun in that?

It was . . . incredible, beautiful, a reminder sorely needed in the most testing time of her existence. Her knee found the hardpacked road, and she inclined her head, recalling her training. Tenets learned as a hastati.

"When innocent blood drenches the parched lands around Deversoria, the rocks will cry out."

"So spake Magna Domine," she had intoned with the other hundred hastati who had taken a knee, their unified voices echoing down the long field of the training coliseum.

"In that time, war will come and the Ladies will emerge," continued Resplendent Iisil.

"So spake Vaqar."

"But after men's bloodlust depleted their adunatos and before their greed drove them to depravity, Magna Domine received her Daughters back into the earth."

"Laborare pugnare parati sumus," Eija voiced into the cold night air.

"M-my Lady?"

The bald man's plaintive words turned Eija, and she peered up at him around the face shield that left her eyes visible. Only then did she realize she had unfurled her enlightened form during her recitation of the vow. Wings dusted the ground. Armor smoothed along her body. A weapon settled in her hand. It had been so natural, a part of her that she loved. Regret dug away at the complaints she had lobbed, the whining in self-absorbed pity.

Forgive my distraction, Ancient, for having my eyes on me and not on You. I am Your servant and blade.

"What did you say?" His face tangled in fear and worry. His scent, too. But then, these people had mastered cowering and fear because of the malignant Corrupt, who had leeched their weakness and lust for all things craven into the Lavabeasts, the hybrids, the so-called nursery.

Eija pulled herself erect, only then seeing Reef slinking closer.

His shoulders were hunched, his head cocked. Uncertain, wary. Why would he cower?

She shifted her attention to the villager. *"Laborare pugnare parati sumus."* She slid the sword into the scabbard at her back. "To work, to fight, we are ready." Recalling how he had tried to convince her to rest tonight, she lifted her chin. "I appreciate your words, sir, but the time for sleeping has passed. In fact, I have done it for too long." She inclined her head, spared Reef a glance, knowing well his decision already—the air reeked of sadness and reticence—then gave him an acknowledging nod. A farewell.

She faced the horizon and started walking, choosing not to exert her span quite yet. Their time would come, too. For now, she would remember the girl named Eija who had lived so simple a life, though she had been convinced—

"Not much for goodbyes, are you?"

At Reef's voice chasing her, Eija tried not to show her shock—and failed. Though her feet nearly tripped her on the snow-covered road, she kept walking. "Goodbyes are meant to make us feel better about parting ways, but at this point, there is little to feel better about."

"No," he countered, "goodbyes are a courtesy, a sign of respect and consideration."

She adjusted her vision to the distance. "I considered . . . and respected your decision to remain."

"My what?"

"There is no time for games, Commander. I am not offended that you chose the infant female."

"Infant."

She shrugged. "Comparatively." After all, Meijatsia had centuries on the girl who was, what, eighteen? Twenty?

"Then you are not just an old maid, you are an ancient maid . . ." His eye narrowed and he lifted a shoulder. "Okay, that didn't work."

Pulling up, she looked at him. "Reef, my purpose demands I confront the darkness plaguing this system. Long ago, I accepted my role, what was asked of me. It is not pleasant, and it does offend those with more delicate sensibilities, but I will set my blade to the throats of these creatures to ensure they cannot make it back to the Quadrants."

"Wait, are we back to the Bloodbreaker thing? Because I thought we'd moved on."

Eija paused. "There is no moving on. Not for me. And you—it was clear by your Signature that your interest in the infant—"

"That really amuses you, doesn't it?"

"—convinced you to remain here. Perhaps you have even wrapped that decision in a noble quest, that you will help protect her and her people."

"And why is that bad?"

Why did it hurt so much that he did not argue it? "In truth," Eija admitted with a sigh, "it is not. They need help. Their hands have forgotten how to hold a sword, their hearts how to hope for a different life."

"What of you?"

She frowned at him.

"Has your heart forgotten how to hope for a different life?"

The question was tender and affectionate, but very misplaced. "You are an Eidolon, a champion for the people. One who wants to see them victorious, who wants the innocent protected. I mean, that is why you became an Eidolon, right? Or was it for the cool weapons and mech-suit?"

"C'mon, you gotta admit the mech-suit is serious slag. Tier One—"

Eija turned back to the horizon.

"Hold up." He skipped a step and caught her arm. "Okay, yes. You're right about me. I fight for people and do it with cool toys."

"I can no more change who you are and the cool toys you love"—she managed with a light smile—"than you with your brown eyes and charming manners can alter who or what I am. Or what I . . . do."

"I know." Reef stepped closer. "When I saw you kill that beast, I knew . . ."

"Knew what?"

A half smile wavered through his lips. "Mostly, that I made a promise to you—"

"When?"

"Okay, maybe it was a silent promise, but I made it." He palmed his chest. "Here. I am with you, Eija. Till the end. And if the end comes and we're both still alive . . ."

What was he saying? That he was with her, even though he knew she was the one to deliver death to the Corrupt? To slay the enemies of the Ancient? That he would still feel that attraction toward her? "Reef, when this is over, I will still be Meijatsia. That—I—will not change."

He nodded. "Knew that, too." He touched the side of his mouth. "Let me ask you—there's no escaping this destiny of yours. Is there?"

Reluctant to answer, her mind flicking back to seeing him with that girl near the fence, she took longer than necessary in shaking her head. "No, not that I can find. And if I do find one, I will destroy it. I cannot let the Khatriza and their spawn reach the Quadrants. Even though I plan to decimate the facilities, if there's even a remote chance they could find their way out of here, I have to destroy it."

A smirk that bordered on a frown now bled into his handsome features as he peered down that long road. "You were right"—he spoke to the road—"I plan to come back here. Yeah, Frelisse is pretty and sweet, but—don't get a big head that you were right about this, too—she's a child." He shrugged and shook his head. "I've seen too much. Done too much to be good company for anyone."

Eija struggled to extract his meaning from those words. He'd said he would return to this village, yet he wasn't coming back for the naïve girl. "I don't understand. Are you returning for her or not?"

"I committed my blade, as it were, to you."

She smiled. It surprised, despite deciding to move on without him, how badly she wanted to *stay* with him. It could work—once she destroyed the labs, the Lavabeasts, the spawn, the hybrids . . .

Wait. Did this mean he . . . cared about her? Loved her?

"After that, I think it's best if we go our separate ways."

His words snatched her breath. "*What?*" She jolted. Straightened. Turned toward the road, her heart pounding. "Right." Two paces down, she found she couldn't move. Her vision blurred. Fool that she was—

"Please—it's . . . it's not what I want."

She pivoted to him. "Isn't it?"

He tugged up his shirt and showed her the handprint on his chest. "Blame yourself, Meijatsia. *You* changed me. Altered who I am. And I . . ." He shook his head again, swiping a hand over his mouth. "I find that I have no stomach for this anymore. I would do anything to go back to who we were, two dumb HyPE Shepherds who only worried about Tascan codices and piloting the *Prev*. But we can't," he growled, pointing to her mark on him. "I'm *different* because of you, and I'm not just talking about this scuzzing imprint. I don't want to have to war at your side, but I will. I won't leave you alone out there. Thankfully, that's something about me this mark hasn't changed."

Heart breaking, hope dying, she shifted out of his reach. Lifted her hands, trying to get a bead on the insanity erupting through her chest. Anger and hurt and sadness and relief—every fathomable emotion slammed into her then. "Foolish me, thinking you were going to ask me to stay with you, say that you loved me."

"I do!"

"You do not know the meaning of it!"

"Love knows when to let go. When the wild thing it has attached itself to will only die and grow frustrated in the simple life that is now presented for the taking." He angled closer. "I would do anything, Eija, for me not to have to war at your side. For you not to be Bloodbreaker."

"I am a fool," she said, jabbing the heels of her hands to her temples, "to think I had finally found a man who could see around my dark role. To think I could ever have that love my Sisters speak of, that some have with the Do'St and great men."

"If you hadn't Touched me, I'd probably be all over this, begging you to believe me." He rubbed the spot where her hand had left an indelible mark. "I *do* love you. But I feel . . . violated. I know you say this would not have happened if I did not want or accept it, but . . . you didn't ask me. And this—us . . ." He shrugged and lifted his hands. "It's unfair to ask it of me, to watch you . . . war." He put a palm to his chest. "I became an Eidolon to help people, not slaughter them."

Her eyes and cheeks were wet. "You think I like being the Bloodbreaker?"

He shifted in, tenderness in his gaze. "I know you don't. But as you said— it is who and what you are. You accepted it—still do. And I won't be the one to cause you to fall from your purpose."

Her vision blurred as she tried to hold his gaze.

"I am with you to see this through. And never doubt—I will always love you. But this path—it's yours alone, Eija." Head tilted, he kissed her. Let his lips linger there, then lifted his lips to her forehead. "You are amazing, and it is my honor to know you."

She clutched at him, hugging him tight. Crying. Not because she was sad. But because she knew he was right—the path was hers alone. It was too dark, too heavy a burden. She would never will it upon him, not even a wisp of it. And he was also right . . . their paths would diverge.

Tonight. Now.

Eija kissed him back, tasting her tears as she did. Framed his face with her hands, even as she unfurled her enlightened form. "Seek peace." And she stepped into the role and place where she would do what Meijatsia did best—deliver death.

"Set aerios and machitis—as many as you can find—to guard these entrances. It is the only safe haven we now have for the people." Gathered with his men among the horses and wagons left at the north end of the tunnels, Marco wondered many times in the last few oras why Tigo had stayed, but he would not argue it. All able-bodied persons were needed in this darkening ora.

Ixion stuffed his gloves back on. "Pray, was the cave-in of the southern openings complete enough to leave them unprotected?"

"Nay," Marco said. "Though I anak few Symmachians remaining close by. We have pushed back the threat here." He turned to Roman. "Have you word from the other sectors?"

Face streaked with dust and blood from the engagements within, the master hunter looked grim. "Vorn reports Hirakys and Jherako are overrun— they, too, have gone underground. The wastelands devoured."

Marco frowned, preparing to deploy his receptors further afield, when another scent pulled on his attention. Like so many other Symmachian stenches, yet . . . different.

"Their attack is comprehensive," Roman said. "Rico thumped and said Symmachia has spread their attack wide—Avrolis and Giessen fell fast and hard in the last few days."

"I am stricken," Kaveh muttered, as he nursed a shoulder wound from the cavern engagement, "at the speed with which the fortress of Kardia fell. It has stood for centuries! Since I was a boy, I remember looking upon the spires and turrets, dreaming of being an aerios within those walls. Now 'tis in ruin."

"What is stone against pulse cannons?" Tigo noted.

"Nothing save an instrument to crush those within." Marco's thoughts were weighted by the memory of the raiders dead in the halls of his home, killing Isaura . . . Galen's complicity.

"Surely, we will rebuild." Kaveh seemed to need reassurance. Hope.

"Surely." Marco spoke more out of sarcasm than expectancy of a new fortress. But it seemed to rally the men, and he would not begrudge them it. Even if he had no heart for the thought of *after*.

And there it was again, that strange note.

Roman grunted, nodding to the sky. "Jubbah's mercenary fleet says activity in orbit has increased. Formation has changed. Guess they're switching tactics."

While there was little fear that the Symmachian ships would enter the atmosphere, dropping more Rapiers or Interceptors . . . that was more likely than Marco cared to consider. Now that the realms of Drosero were reeling, the occupation would begin.

"We must find a way to stop them from sending down more troops or ships," he muttered, half to himself. To Roman, he said, "And the state of the net?"

"Failed."

"The Uchuvchi went south?" Ixion asked Hushak.

"Aye," the younger Stalker answered. "The aliens did well in training, though they tired quickly, so we worked on techniques to aid them. General Sebastiano took them with him to check on troops and militia."

"The death of his brother spurred the general into a fury," the aerios muttered.

"No," Marco countered. "That Symmachia stole his brother from him is what fuels the general. His focus is now completely on eradicating the vermin." Even as he finished his words, he detected a sharp scent from the master hunter. And disapproval.

Frustrated with that smell, Marco held up a hand, anak'ing the peculiar odor again. "What is that . . .?" He noted Ramirus and Ulixes catching the scent as well.

"Hm." Roman shifted, angling his head up slightly, his eyes narrowing. Nostrils flaring. "I detect it as well."

Ixion glanced around. "Symmachians are making sure little remains with which we can rebuild—there are fires across Lampros City and up into the mountains. A league of the Altas Silvas is lost, thanks to those savages."

"Rest assured, we will return the favor," Marco growled, coming off the wagon he leaned back against. "But . . . no, that's not what I'm detecting." Rolling his shoulders, craning his neck forward, he hauled the scent deeper, into the back of his throat.

Two scents rose to dominance. One he yet did not recognize, though its very foreignness chilled his adunatos. The other . . . "Symmachians! With me!"

Ignoring the shouts of protest from Ixion and—was that Tigo?—Marco vaulted into a waiting saddle. He spurred his destrier into a full gallop, racing west, the scent building, stiffening. A strange vibration danced over his skin as they rode across the spine of the most southern peak of the Kardia Mountains. Exhilaration spiraled as he felt the scent growing stronger, clearer. The cool, piney scent he'd come to associate with skycrawlers firmed.

Anger made him push the destrier harder, the terrain challenging them with its rugged resistance.

Something niggled at the back of his mind. But the vibration along the hairs of his arm pulled his attention away. He refocused on the anger, on heating the weapon-arm so it was ready to fire. As he rode, branches snagged his sleeves and the wind chafed his face.

Ixion surged ahead, his torso flat over the horse's spine, navigating the heavily treed slope with skill and experience. His white braids bounced and seemed a beacon.

Challenged to keep up, Marco lowered his body more, trailed his First.

Ixion straightened on his mount and pulled the destrier around to a stop. "There!" He pointed through the trees.

Following the direction of his gloved hand, Marco adjusted his Black to see what he indicated. Greenery and massive trunks blocked his view, so he nudged the destrier aside more, squinting hard. Finally—between two trees and behind that, where a dense copse bent beneath the wind, something metal caught his eye.

"What is it?"

Tall and glinting, the contraption jutted up among the trees, its dimension thicker than a century-old pine. It soared skyward, likely cresting the canopy and into the clear.

"Unknown," Ixion grunted. "Definitely not Droseran."

Marco considered the thing. "Tigo mentioned a tower . . ." To create an electromagnetic pulse. Squinting up, he wished he could ask the Symmachian if this was what he meant, but . . . EMPs required significant energy, and the generator had to be big enough to accommodate the blast. "This can't be it. Not big enough."

"I am ignorant in this matter," Ixion admitted. "However, until we ascertain the truth about it, we should make sure they aren't doing something to harm Kalonica."

"Agreed." This could be Drosero's secret allies, but if it were not . . . then they had a problem. Or . . . what if Tigo had it wrong? Could Marco risk everything on the word of one man? In the maze of betrayals, who was to say Tigo was not the one being betrayed? He would not put it past Symmachia to attempt something like that to overtake the planet. The repugnant arrogance that they would come to Drosero and inject their will and edicts on a people who had chosen decades past not to yet embrace technology infuriated.

Around him formed up his vanguard—Ixion, Roman, Hushak, Kaveh, Ramirus, Ulixes, and other aerios—and barreled toward the tower. As they crested the rise and started down, Marco eyed the path sparsely populated by machi trees and fire elms. Then he saw an Eidolon in full mechanized armor hauling a long, thin piece into place.

Marco swung his arm up and aimed. With a twitch of his fist, he released the volley—not at the Eidolon but at the tree behind him.

It sizzled through the air, singeing leaves and branches as it struck the trunk. Branches cracked and fell, narrowly missing the Eidolon and his two compatriots. Hushak blurred behind the mechanized trio, vaulting over and hauling one into a stranglehold, manriki wrapped around the neck.

The third Eidolon pulled two pulse pistols, aiming one at Hushak and the other at Ixion. "Stop! Stand down and identify yourselves!"

Shouting erupted. Two aerios with javrods flanked the pistol-wielding Symmachian.

Furious, vindicated, Marco readied his weapon again, aimed—

"Friendly!" a mechanized voice barked. Seeming frantic, the first Eidolon released the metal he held. Raised his mechanical arms. "We're friendly! We are here—"

"Aye," Ixion growled, noting the others taking up position around the Symmachians. "On our planet. Attacking."

"No!" The leader pointed to the device. "I know how it looks—"

"Enough talk!"

Something shimmered and coalesced between them and the Eidolon. In a blink, a legitimate shield, not the nanite-composed armor, protected the Symmachian. Jutting out from it . . . Jez. Fully armored.

"Stop this." She paused, looking from man to man, waiting for weapons to be lowered, tempers to cool.

As one by one the others stood down, Marco reined in his anger with great effort and took a step toward the Faa'Cris. "Did you finish the task I gave you?"

"I neither obey nor answer to you," she said, then lowered her chin.

From behind her stepped Tigo. "Marco, these men are the ones I told you about—this is the EMP tower."

"Shouldn't it be . . . bigger?"

Tigo almost smirked. "You're right—EMPs are enormous and more tsunami-like than laserlike in their ability to neutralize, but with special shielding, the towers will focus the EMP into a focused electromagnetic field. Since EMPs do not continuously emit the charge, sensors will detect and neutralize later ship arrivals with repeated pulses."

Marco crossed his arms and smoothed a hand over his beard. "I like that. Except—"

"Most Droserans have limited knowledge of technology," Ixion grumbled, seemingly annoyed he wasn't understanding or tracking the conversation. "What . . .?"

"This tower is a part of a system that, essentially, will disable their ships," Marco said.

"How does it differentiate between their ships and ours?" Hushak asked.

"It can't." Marco stared at Tigo, probing his scent and wondering what his light looked like now.

"So, our ships would be disabled as well?" Hushak's Signature radiated sadness, defeat.

"This is not the problem you think it to be," Roman spoke.

"How could you suggest that?" Hushak shifted and glanced around. "We only accept technology to have it ripped—"

"It is good," Marco snarled, "because it levels the playing field."

Tigo nodded, smiling. "That was my father's intent."

Studying Marco, Ixion edged closer, with his scent bending toward understanding. Excitement but with a tinge of uncertainty. "Then . . . this would mean we are no longer outmatched by Symmachia's technology."

Hushak frowned. "They still have the"—he motioned up and down the Eidolon team—"metal suits. And weapons."

"All of those require energy, and once the four towers are activated, they'll be ineffective. In fact," Tigo ventured, "I wonder if Tascan troops would be at a *dis*advantage because they don't know this land, its idiosyncrasies—but worse, they have never had to live without technology. It will be a massive adjustment."

"Which will put them off their game," Marco said. "And give us time to strike fast and furious." Yes, he liked this a lot. "When will this be operational?"

Tigo glanced at the Eidolon, whose face shield cleared. "Slice?"

The Symmachian nodded to a panel—an electrical panel. "Best estim—"

"Won't the EMP neutralize the towers as well?" Marco asked. "Is this a one-shot deal?"

"No," Slice said. "The towers are lined with a material and software that, together, shields them from the neutralizing effect."

"Do the ships have that?"

"It would require an inordinate amount of the material, and that much would make the ship too heavy." He patted the side of the tower. "These don't have to fly."

Marco eyed the metal structure, pleased to finally have something go right for the Droserans. "Before it goes live, we need to be sure our ships are on the ground."

"I'll send word to Command," Roman said, tapping his thumper and shifting aside to talk quietly via his comms.

Could these towers help them win the war? "This will force them down," Marco said, considering the ramifications. He nodded to the Eidolon. "Will those suits work?"

"Nothing electrical will," Slice said. "The pulse will take out standard mech-suits. Our suits—we're a Tier One team—have all the upgrades. It won't affect ours."

"Are there other Tier One teams?" Ixion asked.

"Wrong question," Marco muttered. "*How many* other teams have protected suits?"

"Three . . . currently deployed." Slice held his gaze. "Here."

Cheek twitching, Marco heard what he didn't speak. "How fast can the suits be upgraded?"

Slice's expression tightened. "Too fast."

"Material and tech upgrades take a week to upload, then they'd have to run diagnostics, get aligned with the Eidolon wearing it," the female Eidolon said, nodding to her commander.

"In this war, with the way they're hungry to seize this planet," Slice said, "they'll skip all that, deem it a waste, even if it does protect the Eidolon."

"So it won't protect them?" Ixion asked.

"It's possible without those measures the suits might be susceptible to pulses or have a hiccup in their firing mechanism or PICC-line." Slice lifted an armored hand. "Anything could go wrong . . . or nothing could go wrong."

"Unless . . ." Tigo said, his brow knotting, then smoothing as a smile slid into his tanned face. "Unless someone uploads some sort of virus that would make the suits susceptible, particularly their environmentals."

Slice nodded, grinning. "Alter their O$_2$ ratios."

Marco patted Tigo's shoulder. "I like it." The scent of confusion pulled him around to his men. "Mess up the air they breathe and you force them from the suits. If they want to live."

"Come out of the suit to live, only to die." Ixion eyed Marco with an appreciative smirk.

Marco nodded, ready to have some advantage in this war. "Do it, Tigo. They wanted this planet, and now they'll see what it's made of. Force them to ground and we'll bury them in it."

That night as they sat around a campfire, eating and grabbing some sleep—a luxury they had not had in over forty hours—Marco gritted his teeth against the burn in his arm. Not the brand burn that thrummed and writhed with its own life. But this new one from the weapon that had burrowed in his bone and marrow.

Seated on the ground and propped against a downed tree, his boots stretched toward the fire, Marco kept his arm against his abdomen. Somehow, it seemed to sate the thirst of the flame. Would that Daq'Ti were here so he could ask if this was what he felt every day. All his life. For Marco, it was new, painful, distracting . . . That was, when not actively engaged in a fight. He hoped the Draegis was faring well with the troops and militia.

"I detect much turmoil in you, Marco." Roman's words were neither a chastisement nor a benign comment.

"So much for not anak'ing the Brethren."

"We are far removed from those strictures this day." He settled beside him. "Would you not agree?"

"Mm." In fact . . . "It feels a lifetime." Marco angled his head. "What of the Kynigos?" He glanced across the small camp and spotted Ramirus, Ulixes, and a few others. "How many are left?"

"Too few," Roman sighed. "Besides myself, I know of only one other master who is not captive or dead. I have been working to compile a census. A vain attempt in the middle of this war."

Was not everything in vain at this point? At another fiery twinge, Marco flexed his fingers.

"How is it?" Roman asked, jutting his jaw at his arm.

Marco stared into the fire a few meters away and said nothing. He had thwarted this conversation with everyone else and only felt comfortable talking about it with Daq'Ti.

"How did it happen?"

That pulled Marco's gaze to his uncle's. "Don't you know?"

"I know what rumors speak."

With a grunt, he again looked to the fire. "They enjoy the rumors, especially when it involves the supernatural. Truth—ugly, painful truth"— he pursed his lips—"not so much."

"They look for hope. Mayhap that weapon on your arm provides it."

Rolling his arm over, Marco eyed the bulky part that his sleeve covered. From his bicep down was now thick. "They would not enjoy it if they watched their friends and peers being reduced to ash in front of their eyes."

Roman cocked his head and leaned forward. "What do you think they see when you use that weapon?"

Jarred by his tone and question, Marco frowned. "What do you mean?"

"You, Marco." Roman planted a hand on his thigh and angled toward him. "Numerous times you have incinerated people with that thing. You." He gave a cockeyed bob leaden with disappointment. "It's . . . horrific."

"Would you have me let them live to kill one of our own?"

Blue eyes probed. "You're defensive."

"I'm being chastised for doing what was prophesied about me."

"No chastisement, nephew, and no—this was not prophesied about you." Roman's voice softened. "Are you aware of or considering what that thing is doing to you?"

"The only thing I have *considered* is its effectiveness." A lie meant to stave off this interrogation.

For a long moment, Roman studied him. "It's as if you have no understanding of how it's taking over. What it's doing to your Signature— the acridity of it. And," he said with a sigh, "if I'm not mistaken, it has grown since you first returned."

Refusing to look down again, Marco balled his fist. Tensed.

"Your anger—"

"Is great!" Marco snapped, pulling his legs up and shifting to the log. "My people and our planet are under attack. My wife is dead! Our existence is in jeopardy because two supernatural factions decided they couldn't get along. And *I* am tasked with forcing them to end this campaign of hatred."

"Aye, you've said that a few times."

The apathy pouring off the master ignited something in Marco's gut. And arm. Alarmed by the implication, he tightened his fist. "After all I have said, you only whine over a device that allows me to even the score a little."

"I would ask you to weigh the cost, Marco." He planted a hand on his shoulder. "You are not only one of my hunters but my nephew. My blood. And I would not see you lost—"

"I know where I am. Fighting this war as I figure out what being Progenitor means."

"It does not mean this," Roman countered firmly. "What the prophecy foretold has been completed: you instigated this war. We are in it, fighting. To assume you must end it is faulty. Progenitor means instigator, not end-bringer. Too great a burden do you take on your shoulders"—blue eyes shifted to the embedded weapon—"and arms that you were never intended to bear."

Marco pushed to his feet. "I will make no apology, as I do everything I can to free Drosero from this dogfight and avenge Isaura's murder."

"Break camp. We ride out in an ora."

At the Stalker's shout, Tigo watched the men snap into motion, stowing gear and preparing horses. They'd woken to find Marco had taken a couple of guards and departed in the night. Now . . . what was Tigo supposed to do? Stay with the 210? Or with Marco's men, which meant he had to mount one of those massive black horses? That was something he'd never learned. Admittedly the destriers they bred intimidated him, and that was a rare occurrence.

"Ixion." Was it rude to use his first name? They had a lot of archaic rules here . . . "Uh, sir."

Though the same height, the man turned that scarred eye in his direction and seemed to look down on Tigo. Somehow, the moonslight managed to stab between the trees and make his white hair and braids glow. "You ever ride a destrier, skycrawler?"

There it was. "No."

"Hm." Ixion pitched a ruck over the back of a horse. "The Great Blacks are mighty and shrewd. They do not tolerate incompetence."

"I think you and our medora have that in common with them," the burly man in the green jacket said with a smirk, sliding Tigo a wicked glare.

Clearly not welcome. "I . . ." He glanced to the 210 and—gratefully—Slice gave him a nod. "I'll stay with the Eidolon for now."

Ixion paused in readying the horse. "If all skycrawlers are so easily thwarted, this war will be won by first rise."

Voids. The man had no qualms about shredding him. "I would slow you down. That is all I meant."

The man's face probably never cracked a smile, but it sure seemed there was one there now.

"Have you ever flown an Interceptor?" Slice challenged the Stalker.

A spark hit Ixion's eyes as he started toward Slice. "No," he said in a low, tight voice, "but then I've also never tried to slaughter an entire planet just to show I know how to prey on the weak."

Slice jutted his jaw, which seemed a small move in that mech-suit. "Neither have I." He tossed down his helmet. "Do any of you realize what will happen to us when they learn we've done this? Betrayed our own people?"

"Probably better if we die with downworlders," Lieutenant Valtira Hesse muttered. "A worse fate would be if they forced us to live here among those who measure strength by the size of their horses."

"Stand down, Lieutenant. That is an order." Tigo looked to the Stalker and faltered at the man's ferocity. The dark hour did not help make this man appear reasonable. Slag, he was some kind of vicious.

Her gaze barely shifted from the Stalker's. "Aye, Commander."

"I know you think of us as the enemy, that it is hard to believe we are different from those who are attacking, and I get that. But I vow—we are not your enemy." He noticed the other Droserans and sigil-marked Kynigos arcing around the Stalker. "I would ask you to trust us, but that is probably a bridge too far."

"So Symmachians do have brains," Ixion snarled.

Hesse growled and twitched.

"Valt," Slice snapped. "Grav down."

Tigo knew there was no use trying to make amends. No time to prove themselves to these men. Not tonight. Maybe their actions over the course of this war would convince these men. "Once Slice gets the towers working and the EMPs deliver your real enemy to your battlefields, you will see who we are."

"Hmph." Ixion stepped back, his expression one of extreme annoyance. He shouldered past Hesse and returned to the horses.

"Why on earth do they hate us when we gave up everything to risk putting this scuzzing system in place?"

"Because"—the master hunter shouldered in—"Symmachia murdered his daughter." His blue eyes seared into each one of them. "Their kyria—queen."

Tigo stilled. "Isaura . . . was Ixion's daughter?"

Refocused but with a scowl now, Roman nodded.

"For the record," Slice said, "our reports state the Irukandji were responsible."

Roman sniffed. "Before Symmachians touched this soil, those blue-marked savages were barely clear-headed enough to find their next meal. But within a year of the incursion into the southern part of this continent, those raiders are organized and spurred to attack a realm that has long kept the peace. It is no coincidence."

For a long second, Slice studied him, then nodded. "Agreed."

Roman smirked—and in that moment, even with the darkness, he so resembled Marco it was unsettling. "I care not if you agree. What has happened on this planet is nothing short of evil." He turned toward the horses.

"Palinurus," Slice snapped.

The master hunter stopped, shoulders hunched, head tucked. Then, his tall frame roiled, rounded.

"What're you doing?" Hesse squeaked the question radiating through Tigo.

"Speak quick, Commander," Roman said, sliding his gaze and anger over his shoulder. "I was your staunchest ally here. Now my patience suddenly grows thin."

Slice thudded forward and held out a flex screen. "Proof that me and my team are not the enemy here. Thought you should know."

Curiosity was a beast that drew Tigo closer. "What is it?"

After a glance at whatever Slice had discovered, the master hunter shoved at Slice. "When was this?"

Tigo eased in and peered at the image. His gut tightened at the familiar chamber—an Engram. Balled in the corner, a bearded man with long, dark hair silvered with age threw himself at the wall, tic-tacking the corner. Twisting and collapsing in a heap. Wailed. Climbed onto all fours. Hit the wall again. It was hauntingly clear he was trying to get out. Over and over, hurting himself each time.

"Right before we left, a friend waved that." Slice looked down, his shame and frustration over the situation evident. "He's not the only one either."

Eyes widening, Roman leaned in. Growled, "There are more Kynigos there?"

"I don't know how many, but yes."

Roman squared his shoulders and advanced, the anger rolling off him barely constrained. "What. Ship?"

Slice winged up an eyebrow. "That's the *Argus*. It's in orbit."

"Krissos," Tigo hissed.

The hunter looked skyward and took in several long draughts. "Yet, I cannot anak him."

"Chambers are sealed. No sound, no smell." Slice lifted his hands in surrender. "No . . . nothing."

"Wrong," Roman gritted out, grabbing the ring of Slice's mech-suit where the helm locked into place. "There is a *person* in there. A human. Tortured for no reason other than *he* can smell your filth."

Slice held the hunter's gaze, unflinching, and raised his palms. "You're right."

Roman seemed to find himself then, releasing Slice. "You do your kind proud, Commander." He held up the screen. "For this, if ever you need a nose . . . you have but to wave me."

As Roman stalked toward the horses, Slice let out an audible breath. "Slag," he whispered. "I thought I was about to be vented."

"You and me both!" Tigo huffed a laugh to expel the tension that had tightened his chest. "They are revered but not known for being gentle or—"

"*Tigo!*" Jez's voice reverberated in his head. "*Are you en route?*"

He faltered at her strident tone. "*Not yet. I'm—*"

"*What about the Droserans?*"

"*Mounting up.*"

"*Send them south.*"

"*What? Why—*"

"*Do it! They've taken Kersei and the babies!*"

"Holy mother of Baru," he muttered. "Master Hunter! Ixion!"

On their Blacks, they came round to face him.

He darted there. "Go south. At once—"

"*I'm worried about Marco. He is—seems . . . fallen. I cannot reason with him, so I'm with him. We took an Interceptor and left. If the fleet sees our ship—*"

Tigo pointed to Slice. "How far did you get on the EMP?"

"Just needs a few more lines of code and activation."

"Get it done. Now! Whatever it takes." He glanced at the Droserans again, and his attention fell on a monstrous riderless Black. "Slag . . ."

"Too much ale, Commander?" Ixion growled.

He was going to regret this. Wondered if Jez could stop in and pick him up. Quick exfil without ending up saddle-sore. But no, it sounded like she needed to stay with Marco. "I need to go with you."

Ixion crossed his arms and considered him for a second. "Mayhap you should ride like a child, behind me," he taunted.

"Or as a woman—in front," a Kynigos sniggered.

"As insulting as that is, I may need to. I don't know how to command a horse."

"You do not *command* a horse," Ixion said. "You respect—"

"Yeah, yeah. No time." He indicated to Slice. "We can't let any craft leave—"

A ship screamed overhead, drawing their gazes skyward.

"Scuz me," Slice muttered. "That's a Rapier! Where did it come from?"

Holy . . . is that who took Kersei?

"You know what that means," Valtira warned.

"Yeah," Tigo muttered. "Likely Cleve and the Two-two-five. Apparently Marco is in another ship, giving chase." He flicked his attention to Slice. "Stop the Rapier from leaving Droseran airspace."

"What's wrong?" Roman demanded. "What does the ship matter that you are—"

"They've kidnapped Kersei and the heirs."

"South, where?" Ixion demanded.

"Some plains where they're amassing—"

"That's two days' ride. We won't make it in time."

"Their ship would," Roman suggested.

"Aye, but is he not about to cripple all ships in the air?"

Roman grunted.

"Here's the plan," Slice said, even as he worked the flex screen. "Valt, fly them as far south as you can in our ship. It's not an Interceptor or Rapier— we had too heavy a load—but at max speed . . ." He tapped frantically, then nodded. "Should make the plains."

"Flying does us no good if we do not have Blacks once we get there."

"Missing the point, downworlder. Our ship can take you and the beasts. Need to secure them in case there's a rough landing. If you weren't going with the horses, you'd make it farther faster—"

"We appreciate the help," Roman said.

"Horses flying," Ixion muttered. "There has to be some prophecy about that."

"If there's not, the Iereans missed a great opportunity."

"Let's go," Hesse said. "We have a twenty-minute hike down to the ship."

"Oh . . . slag." Slice froze, fingers poised over the flex screen. "Slagslagslag."

"What?" Tigo stopped and glanced back. Saw his friend's face. "What's wrong?"

Wide eyes met his. "Infantry." He scrambled toward the tower. "Go, now! I'll give you as much time as possible, but I need to shut down all tech before this planet gets slaughtered."

"There it is!" Marco banked hard right, taking the Interceptor out over the bay and opening up the throttle as they streaked across the sky after the lightning-fast ship. "How did I not detect them?"

"If I'm right," Jez said from the copilot seat, "that's the Two-two-five. He's Baric's personal scum."

"Xisya," Marco hissed. "She's how you Eidolon were able to avoid detection when you intercepted us on the *Kleopatra*."

"It's a serum. They fed it into our PICC-lines."

Arm thrumming, he prayed he could stifle it long enough not to jeopardize their flight. They weren't in atmo, but flying this high and fast without flight suits . . .

"Marco," Jez said, her voice preternaturally calm. "I sense—"

"Not now, Sidra." He tucked his chin, focusing on the ship. "I let you in that seat for a reason. Not a lecture. Do your job."

Zipping south now, the Rapier went low over the desert.

"Why aren't they going back to the *Macedon*?" Jez asked. "Those ships are designed to break atmo in record time. Why's he dusting trees?"

Marco growled. "He's taunting me."

"Let him," Jez said. "The longer you keep him engaged down here, the better chance Slice has to get the EMP activated."

Which was good. But also bad. "We'll go down." He frowned at her. "Kersei and my daughter will go down, too."

"They won't let them get hurt."

"You can't control how a ship crashes."

"That ship can," Jez said. "We, however, might not be so fortunate."

"You reeking metalnecks."

"That's a riot coming from you, since you have a PICC-line, too. And we both know that, while I served for a time as Tigo's lieutenant, I am Faa'Cris." She flashed her violet eyes at him. "I won't let either of us die."

"And yet, I am not comforted."

"I fear there is little that will comfort you now."

Marco glanced at her just as her gaze left his arm. "Ah." He grinned. "Don't like it when others have as much power as you do?"

"That is not power, Marco."

He grunted. "Tell that to the last raider I dusted." On the array, he saw the Rapier veering higher.

"He's going to make for orbit," she said. "Drop back."

"Back?" Marco balked. "But we—"

"He's arrogant. Has nothing to lose. If he thinks you aren't keeping up, he'll either come around or slow."

It was good in theory . . . "That's a dangerous gamble."

"One we have to take since we need him down here when the EMP goes off."

Hardened resolve unwilling to let him yield, Marco stayed on the throttle. He focused on the array, the bleeping warnings that said systems were straining.

"You say you hate Xisya—"

"Say?" he barked. "I live it with every fiber—"

"Wrong. You *are* her."

Marco jerked. "*What?*"

"That weapon embedded in your arm—"

"It attached to the brand. Chose me—not like I had much say."

"It chose the light in you, to feed off it, but where did that weapon start? Who created it? What is it feeding on that it's growing, overtaking you?"

"How do I know?"

"You *do* know. Daq'Ti—his kind—would warn you against this thing."

"Don't pretend to know him. When Eija went to heal him, he told her to leave his weapon." Odd, how his conscience barely pricked at what he omitted—the Draegis's urging that it was not good, to let it go. "Don't get all holier-than-thou on me, Faa'Cris. This weapon has served me and Drosero. I will use it and the anger it stirs in me to wipe out every Symmachian—"

"But that's just it. The *Trópos tis Fotiás* is not about Symmachia. It's about the Khatriza. You are so focused on this present, temporal threat you have forgotten Xisya and the queens."

"No," Marco countered, his voice low and anger thrumming, "*you forget* that this war you Ladies started impacted people. Altered people. That is what I fight. For you to loose your hold on us, all of us. It's what Eija is fighting."

"You pretend to know Eija, but Meijatsia exists for one purpose—to bring death!"

"Augh!" Marco felt his arm vibrating and heating, like his temper. "Can't you Ladies just exist without being death or the blade? Be *people*."

"Would you have Vaqar just be a person? Would you have your hunters just be men?"

"*Yes!*" Marco shouted. "Then that vile creature would not be killing the Brethren by harvesting our gift for her putrid sche—"

"Look out!"

Proximity claxons rang through the ship. Marco shoved the Interceptor into a dive to avoid the collision that the Rapier threatened. "This idiot's arrogance is going to get him killed."

"You or him?"

Marco glowered. "Lady or not, I really don't know what Tigo sees in you."

"Same."

He came around and glided out over the Kalonican Sea before he swung back in behind the Rapier that was heading out toward the fire gorges. "You said they wouldn't let them get hurt . . ."

Jez side-eyed him. "I did . . . but—"

Marco flicked up the firing cap.

"Wh—*no*! You can't."

"You said—"

"In a crash—they'd be protected. But that's a Rapier—a totally different craft than this one. If you hit too close to the nacelles, it will ignite."

"Quite a design flaw."

"There aren't many in the Quadrants who will fight us, so they weren't worried. Besides, that ship is built for speed, not for combat."

"So I just need to *not* hit the nacelles . . ."

"Marco, please. Don't."

"He'll toy with me all day if I don't end this." He slowed the engines and let the ship coast, deliberately aiming for the fire gorges.

"This is too dangerous—"

"Quiet," he said, smiling as the Rapier came around to find out what was wrong. Marco locked in the firing solution. He had to believe the targeting was accurate—

His thumb swept the weapons launch control. *Don't let this be a mistake.* He applied pressure.

Twang! Thunk!

He slammed forward. His five-point harness yanked him back with incredible velocity, even as a deathly silence hollowed his hearing. His neck and back ached, as did his shoulders and gut where the harness had stopped him from colliding with the bulkhead. He groaned, barely conscious. His head pounding. He reached for the controls. They were stiff. Wouldn't move. No power.

Haunted by the deafening silence as they plummeted, Marco tried the emergency restart. No go. "Get us out of here."

Silence met his shout.

He strained to look to Jez. Her head lobbed forward, blood at her temple. What had hit her?

"Jez! Wake up, Jez!"

No response. Okay . . . so they were going to die. No way they'd survive if he couldn't even coast the ship down. The gravity pulling on them felt vicious. Vengeful. Good. Death . . . was good. Tired of fighting the weapon, he would be free. With Isaura . . .

My aetos—

Aeliana. Marco flinched. "Jez!"

With a groan, she shifted.

"Jez!" With no readout, no warnings, he had no idea how close they were to the ground now, but the ship wouldn't fall infinitely. And disoriented as he was, he *could* smell the earth stronger. "*Jez!*"

Light flashed. Death. It came for him. His insides felt like they'd been ripped out.

And it made him angry. Jerked him upright.

He stumbled. Boot skidded on rocks.

Wait. His boot couldn't skid if he was dead. Or if he was on a ship.

"Marco! Snap out of it."

He blinked and light exploded through his field of vision. "Augh!" Squinting, he looked at Jez then beyond her, to the raging fire gorges.

Boom! Thud-thud-boom! Crack!

Marco ducked even as the concussion of a blast brushed against him. Pushed him a few steps. He pivoted back to see a burning hulk of wreckage. "Was that—"

"Yes."

He pivoted to Jez, whose wings were still deployed. With the facial helm, the injury to her temple was no longer visible. "You okay?"

"Headache."

"Same." He shifted around, scanning the gorges and wastelands. "Where did their ship land?"

"It hasn't yet," Jez said, nodding to the south.

Marco spotted what she indicated to—the ship glided and dipped. "Does it have power?" No, even he could anak that it didn't. "How . . .?"

"It is not visible from here, but Rapiers have a canopy that deploys to prevent a hard crash. I assume it activated when they lost power and altitude."

"Let's go!" Marco hopped into a run.

"I can take us," she said. "It'd be faster."

He skidded to a stop, hesitating. "Not as fun."

"Or as tiring."

He hated putting his life into her hands again. "That . . . moving from one place to another is . . . unsettling. But when we get there, I will need my strength to kill the Symmachians."

"You mean to rescue Kersei and the babies."

"One is a means to the other."

"O Antiqua, accipe omnem libertatem, memoriam, intellectum, arma, ac voluntatem. Omnia mea, quae habeo, et foveam, dedisti mihi. Omnia tibi trado tuo duci. Sufficit mihi gratia tua et amor. Haec mihi da, et nihil amplius posco."

Heart still broken, Meijatsia stepped from the fold into higher reaches of the final facility after clearing the other two. She had slid into her entire purpose in this system. Though she did not dread what was to come, it grieved her—and the Ancient—that any should perish.

It was what must be done, so she whispered the *Sanctateum*, trusting the prayer of self-dedication to align herself with His design.

As she rose, deliberate intent adjusted her focus from Reef to the facility, to the thrum of electricity, the quiet gurgle of tubes feeding life-sustaining nutrients to the pods, and the rattle of machines that were the delivery mechanism. Amid it all coasted a hum of nerves from the Mahaturan guards. But there was another, sharper note stabbing the cold, sanitized air. One she recalled from Daq'Ti and the Draegis who greedily accepted the Touch.

Her presence on this upper level had not yet been detected, but it would be soon.

She eyed the columns of pods stacked so deep they seemed to stretch for infinity. But there was an end. Physical and metaphorical. Not all these were hybrids. Some here, even in their dormancy, longed for release.

All betraying one truth: they had been put on alert because their queen anticipated Eija's return. With the wisdom of the Ancient, she knew how to end this. It would be neither pleasant nor easy. She took no pleasure in what she must do to prevent the senseless attack happening in the Quadrants, all so that the Corrupt could attempt a coup on Deversoria.

No, this was not about the coup. This was about punishment. Knowing the Faa'Cris had favored Drosero and the Quadrants, the Khatriza wanted to make the favored hurt, bleed. Die.

The irony was that what the Khatriza attempted to do in the Quadrants was what Meijatsia had been tasked with here—annihilation. In many respects, the two paths were eerily similar.

Yet not the same. Even now, she grieved for these altered beings, though she would not stop until their eradication was complete. If she did not fulfill her responsibility, the creatures in these pods would follow their programming and seek out another queen, jeopardize more innocents. Cycles of destruction without end.

Meijatsia strode to the main control port and eyed the small round connector filled with djell that had two industrial hoses going in different directions. The left one drew gelatinous liquid from a tank and filtered it through the right into the pods. She hurried to the tank and spun the hatch handle, turning off the feed.

The roar of engines died down, telling her she'd succeeded—which also meant her time was limited.

Claxons grated through the facility.

"So it begins."

She darted back to the port and threaded her hand into the bubble. Knowing the Khatriza would quickly figure out her location now, she closed her eyes and freed what the Ancient put into her.

It surged down her arm and stirred the thick djell as if it were water. The purity of the Touch rushed through the hose and into the thousand-plus veins branching out to the pods.

"I know you are here," trilled the shrill voice of the queen watching over her nest of children. This was how the term *nursery* had come to be, as perverted as it was, considering what the Khatriza sought to do. "You were foolish to return. Now, this will become your grave."

As she had learned to do as a hastati, as she had during her days as a triarii, Meijatsia let her gray-black wings sweep in and cocoon her. "*Ab hac ad proximum, vade in pace.*" Infusing her Death Touch into the liquid, she whispered another prayer, sending the creatures from this life to the next in peace.

A great throng of chaos and vibrations rattled the columns, such that she expected it to collapse. The sound of hissing and draining pervaded the column. Within a second, it fell silent. Deathly silent. The pods now empty. This batch of hybrids vanquished.

It'd worked. Relief rushed through her with a potent dose of pain.

Shrill to the point of piercing—so painfully that ears might bleed—the queen shrieked.

The sound sent Meijatsia folding to the next column as she whispered the *Poenitentiam*. "Cleanse my sword and hand that I might do Your will and stand pure before You." She spun the hatch handle. *"Custodi cor meum, ne desperem in caligine."*

"Bloodbreaker!"

Hearing her legendary name screamed as the system shut down on this level, too, she darted to the second system port. The war had begun.

Even as she plunged her hand into the second trough, she sensed a shift in the air. Caught the rage of the Corrupt. No, Meijatsia must not be distracted. Only focused. There were three more of these columns, and billions of lives depended on her success.

Pulsing the purity through the djell again, she repeated the sending words: "From this existence to the next, go in peace."

Vibrations this time came with a few errant howls of agony that seized the softer side of her adunatos, but she had dedicated herself to the Ancient's path.

She folded herself away from this one—and anticipating the Khatriza would be at the very next one, she skipped that one. Went to the next. Spun the hatch handle to turn off the pumps.

Searing acridity slammed into her a split second before the Khatriza did.

Head cracking against the steel tank, Meijatsia tasted blood. She snapped around and struck with both wings and blade at the Corrupt. Saw a spray of black blood splatter the rails and tanks, but the elongated head merely bobbled as those pike-like appendages stabbed back.

One speared her shoulder. "Augh!" Meijatsia folded herself to the trough. Protecting her injury, she used her sword to sever the hose. Struck her hand into the trough. Whispered the words as the Death Touch pulsed from her.

The next attack came with no scream or shrill warning—only the rustling air and the acidic fetor that was the Corrupt.

Meijatsia cracked her outer wings at the attacker. The bony tips found soft flesh.

A shriek erupted even as the hybrids in these pods were delivered from their cruel existence.

Exhausted, shoulder throbbing in pain, Meijatsia folded herself away. Two left. She had to pick—and went back to the one she'd skipped.

And stepped into an ambush of Draegis and hybrids. A fiery volley tried to sever her wing. She shot into the air and from this vantage knew she couldn't alight there again. But as she hovered, something registered that hadn't before. The fifth column of hybrids . . . the pods were grayed out. Dark. Her gaze struck the third. A faint thrum of bluish light with shadowy forms within. These . . .

"No," she breathed. She dove for a closer look and verified the pods were no longer active. They had been when she'd come with Reef. Right? She thought back, the images flashing in her mind's eye. Yes, all pods in this sector had held a hybrid.

Now, they were empty. Several hundred missing.

From behind erupted another attack scent. She rolled aside, narrowly avoiding the pike aimed at her chest. Spiraling, she folded herself across the facility to deal with the third column. Expecting the queen to meet her there, Meijatsia unfolded *in* the tank. Vicious djell cocooned her.

Beyond the steel, the Khatriza roiled in confusion.

With everything in her, she shot the Death Touch into the djell even as she struggled for air. She probed the djell and felt the thickness of scents vanishing. Her lungs ached, burned, but she refused to release herself until they were all gone. Split-second panic thrust the djell up her nose. She choked—and forced herself to not breathe, not cough as the last scent evaporated.

Again Meijatsia folded—not within the facility. Instead she stepped out, stumbling, her legs and lungs aching as she collapsed onto all fours on a cold, cobbled road. Coughing, she felt her lungs struggling. Her stomach heaving.

"*Eija!*" Boots thudded toward her.

She vomited the djell onto the ground, its blue hue strangely luminescent in the night.

"Slag," Reef muttered, avoiding her sticky goo. "What—"

"They're gone," she said around a burning throat, more djell coming up, gagging her. "Hundreds."

"Hundreds what?"

"Hybrids."

"Voids." He huffed. "But what happened to your wing?"

Eija grunted and frowned at him. "What?"

"Your wing—it's . . . dragging."

Peering over her shoulder, Eija only then felt the excruciating pain in her clypeus. "Augh!" Tears rushed down her face, strangely warm over the djell that seemed inevitably cold.

"The feathers are singed and there's . . . a hole."

Shoulders aching from the injury and weight, she moaned and had to work hard to realign her thoughts. "I . . . I'm not important. Stopping the—"

"You scuzzing me? You're the *most* important one because only you can destroy them."

She groaned, trying to tuck her span, but the damaged wing screamed its objections. Growling through the pain, she forced it away. "I . . . I don't know where they are."

"Pretty sure I do." Reef helped steady her. "At least, it would explain that."

Smearing the djell from her face and eyes, she squinted at him. "Explain what?"

"That." He indicated to the blanket of stars that lit up the night.

Only, it wasn't stars. "Ships," she murmured, a knot forming in her throat. "Oh no." She struggled to get to her feet. "No no no. We can't let that happen." Wavering, she bit against the pain.

"Hybrids?"

She nodded. "The queen must've released a column when she realized I could destroy them."

"That looks closer to a half million, maybe three-quarters . . ." Reef glanced up at the happenings in orbit. "Loosed on humanity? That's extinction-level."

Terror swept through her. The thought of the ships making it back to Herakles or Kedalion . . . "They can't jump. I can't let that happen."

"Can you still . . . fold?"

She stopped and frowned. "Yes, but with my broken wing, I won't be much good. And I am not even sure—"

"Take me."

"Where?"

"To one of those ships. I'll take it over and fly it into the gate."

"Are you out of your skull?"

"Obviously." Resolution carved a hard line through his handsome face. "Do we have any other options? Can you do anything with your Faa'Cris abilities?"

She whimpered, hating how high the odds were stacked against them. "Little now. With the pods, it was simple to neutralize them using the djell as a conduit. Easy once I got myself out of the way." She peered up at the fleet in readiness, the Sentinel glowing brighter with each second. "I could fold into the ships and shut down the engines, but that'd be one by one. I'd never get them all in time."

"Like I said, put me on a ship. I'll fly it into the gate."

"No way. You'd die."

His expression tightened. "After earlier, I was already dead." He waved to her. "C'mon. Send me up. I'll be the—what'd they call Marco? Uchoo-choo."

"Uchuv—" Eija gasped. "That's it!" She straightened. "There are pilots still on Rohilek. We'll send them through the gate, too."

"But the ones who wanted to go already went, remember? The others chose to stay."

Eija sagged, but only for a moment. "I have to talk to them, convince them. Things have changed since Marco left."

"Okay, but first—put me aboard one of the ships. I'll take control and target the gate. Maybe between me, the Uchoo-choos, and the ones who already went, the Quadrants will have a prayer."

Though Eija faltered, she removed herself from this fight and allowed Meijatsia to slide back into place. Gritting her teeth, she angled her wings back and caught Reef's arm. "This may be a one-way trip for both of us."

"Figured."

With an internal shriek of pain that rivaled the Khatriza's howl, Meijatsia folded herself and Reef onto the small craft nearest the gate—and slammed into a wall, his added mass terribly straining her injured clypeus.

Groaning and curling his legs to his chest, Reef met her gaze. "Nice landing."

Fire had nothing on the blaze in her underwing. She struggled to her feet, glancing around. "Aft engine room."

Standing, he stretched his neck. "Go." He nodded. "I've got this." He was already scaling the ladder to the upper deck to reach the cockpit.

Meijatsia's knees buckled. She fell against the bulkhead. Teeth grinding, she held her arm to her chest and strained back upright. Eyes burning, growling through the agony, she folded.

And emerged—collapsed.

The air was different. Lighting flickering. Craning her neck, she tried to get her bearings. Control the pain. Dragged herself upright. Staggered forward. Saw that this section of the pilot pods was empty.

"He said you would come."

Meijatsia jerked to her left where the voice came down a long passage, a man following it. "Who?"

"You must hurry," he said, hustling toward her. "Xonim has returned."

Her heart stuttered. "She's *here*?"

"Two."

Two Khatriza? Shaking her head, she had to focus on getting the pilots to help. "We need the Uchuvchi. Hybrids about to jump through the gate."

Concern scratched at his elongated eyes. "To destroy the Progenitor?"

"Yes." Mouth dry, she tried to swallow—and it forced a cough. Which spasmed through her clypeus. With a cry of anguish, she slid against the wall, barely able to keep her feet.

"You are injured."

A feral shriek echoed through the building.

The Uchuvchi widened his eyes and sucked in a hard breath.

"She knows I'm here." Meijatsia pushed off the wall. Sweat dotted her brow and upper lip. "How many Uchuvchi are left?"

"The reconsidered"—he motioned to the left where pilots filled the narrow hall—"are ten and two. Others reject offer."

That was all? Not great, but it was better than nothing. Dizziness wove through her, and she closed her eyes. Took a breath. "My friend is in a ship up there right now and will try to destroy the Sentinel. Stop the hybrids from leaving. If he fails, you must go through with the fleet. Destroy them. Destroy any that make it through. Clear?"

The Uchuvchi inclined his head. "We serve, Xonim. We pilot."

That shrill noise radiated down the corridors, raising the hair on the back of her neck and making her clypeus ache.

"Come." She stumbled down the main passage and let them follow. "Wait." The pain was making it impossible to think clearly. "You . . . you need a ship because you're drone pilots, right?" Djell! She rubbed her shoulder where the wing hung heavily askew. "I can't get you up there."

"We go to base ship." He tapped his temple. "Drones humming ready."

Skittering seemed to vibrate through the facility.

Meijatsia forced herself to shut out the pain and straighten. "Go. Get your pilots up there, and I'll stop her."

Wary and frightened, the Uchuvchi stared at her as they wound their way around her and out to the ships.

Sword out and sizzling, Meijatsia faced the threat, felt the purity invigorating her.

"Wounded," the Khatriza trilled as she launched herself forward. "We will eat you, Faa'Cris."

Amazingly, the agony fell away. Meijatsia curled her wings around her and spiraled upward, feeling the razor-sharp claws rustle her feathers. She hiked her legs up and shot back down—less work for her damaged wing—blade driving down into the spindly-legged creature. The shriek died as Meijatsia hit the floor, rolling, her span crumpling beneath her weight. She cried out—instantly knew it to be a mistake.

Another Khatriza flew at her.

She flipped over—too late. Felt the searing claw slice her abdomen. "Augh!" Forcing her uninjured wings to compensate put strain on the impaired one, but at least it moved her out of striking distance. She landed, her boots sliding on the floor slick with Khatriza blood.

"You are dead," the Corrupt shrilled.

"Not yet." Meijatsia regained her stance and allowed the blade to once more slide into her grip. *"Reef—sitrep."*

Slag-scuzzing-voids! What was he thinking? Commandeer a ship?

"Yep. Almost there." If "almost" included being seriously slagged.

Heat warbled and seared Reef's neck. Again? Didn't these dogs have any new tricks?

The Lavabeast pinned him to the hull, weaponized arm powered up, trilling his serenade of death.

Hearing the subtle shift in the weapon's resonance, Reef anticipated the volley. Hooked the beast's legs. Using the full weight of his own body, he flipped the thing.

A blast volleyed out.

Reef ducked, feeling that wake trail over his shoulders. With a roar, he slammed his boot into the three-eyed Lavabeast's head. Again. And again, until the thing wasn't moving. "If I had my mech-suit, you'd be black gruel, pal." He snatched the pulse pistol from the beast's leg holster and ended him. He wasn't one to kill in cold blood, but he also couldn't have the thing coming after him or alerting the pilot.

Panting hard, he grabbed the bulkhead and pitched himself down the gangway that separated him from the cockpit. A few steps in, he spotted a hatch. Glanced in as he kept moving. Stopped cold. Backed up and peered through the reinforced window. "Voids!"

Stacked three high and at least fifty lockers deep along the gangway . . . hybrids.

"Scuz me," he muttered. What—

The ship canted. Weight lifted.

They were moving!

Okay, sort out the hybrids later. Get to the bridge, take control, find a way to cut environmentals to the pods. Weapon up, he sidestepped toward the cockpit. Felt his core clench as the Lavabeast at the helm seemed to blend with the dark. If he missed and somehow didn't breach the hull, the thing would kill him.

Then don't miss, genius.

Aiming, he steadied his breathing. Slid his finger along the—

Something plowed into his back. Knocked him into the bulkhead.

A roar came from the cockpit, even as Reef scrambled back onto his feet, wondering what hit him. He shifted and his boot kicked something. He glanced down. "Ei!" Where had she come from? Must've folded—

Fiery heat erupted from the cockpit again.

Reef yanked backward and swiveled to protect Eija's fallen form on the deck. Wanted to take a wild shot at the beast piloting the ship but couldn't risk damaging the arrays. He'd need those.

Fun times.

Blasts scorched Reef's arm. "Augh!" He swiveled and pitched backward, believing Eija too low to be a target. He slid along the hull. Whipped out. Fired.

Even as the Lavabeast's head splattered, Reef shoved himself forward. Fired again, aiming down into the torso, so he didn't inadvertently hit the vital engine systems. When the trilling stopped, he climbed into the cockpit. Eyed the chair with the biomatter of the Lavabeast gooping up the pilot's crash couch. Groaning, he grabbed what he could of the dead Draegis and hauled it out. Then he angled into the couch. "Ugh." Even his pants now felt . . . sticky.

"SENTINEL JUMP INITIATED."

At the mechanical voice of the ship intoning the sequence, Reef jerked his gaze to the array. Saw the ship's system powering and trajectory veering toward the red circle to the right. Probably the Sentinel.

Fingers sliding over controls, he worked to alter the trajectory. Even a fraction would be enough. But as he reached for the course alignment, he felt hard g's. A pinch at his neck.

"Eija!"

She wasn't strapped in!

He lunged forward—but the auto-restraints dug into his shoulders. Yanked him back against the couch. White exploded across his field of vision.

KALONICA, DROSERO

The Rapier was landing in one of the gorges—thankfully, not one of the fire gorges. Marco stood with Jez atop a ledge, watching as it settled, anak'ing the Signatures. "Five Eidolon," he said.

"Standard," Jez noted.

He angled his head, watching the canopy float down and settle gracefully atop it—right over the upper hatch. "Kersei is stressed, but . . . unharmed. Not sure where—"

"Aft, likely in the quarters on the lower deck."

Marco grunted. "A guard with them."

"So four on the upper deck," Jez said. "Probably trying to find a way to power back up."

"Need to pull off the top canopy access hatch."

"Why?" Jez gave him a smirk. "I can get us inside. We grab them and exfil. Agreed?"

Why did he keep forgetting they could do that? "Stop wasting time and"—the air and light changed—"let's do—"

Marco jolted, realizing he now stood inside the ship. Disoriented.

The Faa'Cris was several steps ahead. Had an Eidolon in a choke hold and put him down for a nap.

"Marco!" Kersei leapt up from a bunk. Hugged him, but then jerked back. "I—I beg your mercy."

"The heirs—get them and go!" Jez instructed, even as the rear door slid open and an Eidolon appeared.

As Jez dealt with the newcomer, Marco started forward. Kersei shoved blankets in his arms. He scowled but instantly recognized the weight he held. Glanced down. Saw the tiny eyes and round face. *Mercy . . .*

In a blink, Marco noted the ground just beyond the baby was no longer the steel deck of the Rapier but the gravel and sand of the wastelands. He faltered, stumbled, still gaping at the green eyes locked onto him. Eyes that held him in a fist-hold of condemnation . . .

Floral and minty. And for the first time since anak'ing that Signature in Kuru, he could name it—wild rose and peppermint. An odd but beautiful fragrance. The two did not inspire by name alone, but combined, they hung in the air long after his receptors first anak'd them.

Unable to move, to speak, to function, he stared at her. *My daughter.* So tiny in his hands. Pure and sweet. Jet black hair framed her olive skin and those green eyes. So like . . .

Isa.

Aeliana twitched, her eyes locking onto him again. A smile flashed.

Isaura's laughter trilled through his heart. Blonde hair soft against his hand. "Dusan—"

The ground beneath him collapsed. He shifted. Felt himself falling. "T-take her." Boots grinding in the rocks, he tensed. Shoved the baby toward Kersei, but her arms were full with her own son. He pivoted, thrust the infant at Jez, who, for some reason, was on a knee. "Here. M-my shoulder . . ."

Heart thundering, he turned away. Hated himself for the lie. Dragged a hand over his mouth. "We . . . we need to find a way to the plains where the others are converging." His brain spasmed, shaking off the weight. He blinked at Jez. "Y-you can take us."

She looked up at him dully. "No."

He angled in. "Anak the air, Rejeztia. What do you detect? I'll tell you what—raiders, Symmachians. Ships downed. And you would leave us there? To what end? To be captured again? Killed?"

Her eyes seemed to slip out of focus and back. She rotated her shoulder and revealed a heavily singed wing. "I need time to heal."

"Reek!" Marco balked. "What happened?" Finally focusing on her, he saw blood stained her temple.

"The Eidolon fired as I folded." She struggled to her feet.

They were out in the middle of the desert with no food, no weapons, and no ship. "We have to find shelter." He eyed the ladies, both with babes in arms. But the way Jez stared down at Aeliana sent something crossways through him. His arm itched and his brand burned. No, not the brand—the weapon. He had a strange compulsion to fire at her. Which was ludicrous— she was injured. Was on his side. Held his child in her arms.

Aeliana.

Her face, her smile, those green eyes . . . blurred with Isaura's.

Struggling for a breath that did not hurt or remind him of Isaura, he cleared his throat. "I . . . I'll be back." Two steps out, he faced them. "Wait here." Didn't want them following, him somehow ending up with the child in his arms again. She . . . rattled him. Upended his world. Reminded him of what he'd lost. What had been ripped from his hands. Scarred him.

"Mer . . . cy." *Blood slipped from between her lips and she coughed. Choked. Blood squirted.* "Sorry, Du . . . san . . ."

He stumbled, knee scoring on the rock as he climbed to a higher vantage. Pushed up again. Shook his head. Scrubbed at the sides of his head. "No." He cleared his throat and thoughts. Feet tangled.

"Wings . . . Love . . . Peace . . . Thank . . ."

He tripped. Landed on his hands and knees. Growled. Gritted his teeth. Clenched his eyes. Growled again, letting the fury course down into his brand, through the weapon. Released a volley into the ground, which rattled and plumed dust in his face. Dust in his eyes and mouth, he twitched away. Coughed.

Served him right. Pushing onto his haunches, he hung his head. Forced his thoughts to focus—on the danger. On the war. On getting out of here.

But he failed. *Isa . . . Oh, my aetos . . .*

"Marco."

Stilling, rubbing the side of his eye, he stared at the ground. "Leave me. I just need to scout our options."

Kersei was at his side. "I know not what I detect from you, but truly, it gives me grave concern."

He frowned. "What?"

"Darkness. The weapon, I don't know," she said. "I am worried about you."

"I do not need your worry. Just your—"

"Obedience?" she snapped. "You are better than that, Marco Dusan."

Balling his fist, feeling another thrum of fire course across the brand, Marco glared into the dirt. "I am medora and have asked that you remove yourself to safety. Is that so hard to understand?" The snarl in his own words sounded cruel and demeaning, and he wondered why he did not care.

Kersei stared at him, her chest rising and falling unevenly before she expelled the writhing breath. "You do not frighten me with your commands and orders, but your cold rejection of your beautiful daughter, aye. That *terrifies* me—for you, for her." She touched his arm as she knelt beside him. "Did you see her smile?"

See it? He had *felt* it. The collision of her innocence with his chaos. With that barrier he'd erected to keep himself going. To keep himself . . . sane.

"That is the first smile I have seen from Aeliana."

"She is newly born."

"Aye, but neither does she cry. For the most part, she simply lies in my arms as if she would rather die."

We have that in common. Yet the words gouged his barrier.

"She is failing and *needs* you."

"She will have to wait."

"If you ignore her, she may die, Marco." Her touch firmed on his arm. "Please. I know you would not will that." She paused . . . "How did you ever grow so coldhearted? She has lost her mother—"

"Aye!" Roaring, he thrust upward, throwing off her hand and making her stumble backward. "I lost her, too!"

Lips parted, Kersei sought purchase on the rocky ground, caught herself.

"The only person that mattered to me! The kindest, gentlest of souls to ever exist on this accursed planet, and because of me—she is dead! Slaughtered!" Roiling, he shoved his gaze outward, away. Far distant. And what he saw, trapped his breath in his throat. "Kersei." Pulse rapid-firing, he stared in disbelief at the plain. "Go back—down."

"Marco—"

"Now!"

Finally her gaze followed his, and she pulled in a hard breath.

Stretched before him, across the wastelands and far into the flatlands . . . Troops. Hundreds . . . *Thousands*. Ships downed, expelling their human contents. Symmachians staining the Droseran terrain.

The war had come to ground.

Terror shoved Kersei down the slope, rocks and dirt giving way beneath her boots. She all but fell onto the ground below, pitching forward.

Marco hauled her up and propelled her onward. "This is why I told you to take her to Deversoria. Do you wish death on them?" he growled as he stormed toward Jez. "The plains are crawling with Symmachians. Thousands! If you had done as I asked, Kersei and the children would be safe. Never in danger. But you couldn't follow one simple command."

Breath trapped in her throat, Kersei stood stupefied as Marco raged at Jez. A Faa'Cris. A Lady. This man she had once thought to love, to spend her life with—what had happened to him?

An absurd question—so much had happened—yet he was a man of honor. Was.

It seemed the man who had hunted her and swept her off her feet on a transport ship died with Isaura in that hall within Kardia. The one before her? She knew him not.

Storm moving across her face, Jez seemed to grow taller. "I am neither a sergius to be commanded nor a corporal to be ordered about."

Marco surged in another step. "Nor a Lady to protect the Ancient's children!"

"Enough!" Kersei pushed between them, then faced him with a scowl. "It was not her fault. You and your men were yet clearing the tunnels when a Symmachian found me. He killed Theilig and drugged me."

He whipped around, brow dark and fierce. "It is good he is dead for failing me a second time!"

His acidic words seared her heart. "You should be ashamed of yourself! Sir Theilig was a good and honorable man." She sniffed and shook her head. "How ardently you throw around blame, Marco. If you seek someone to blame, to yell at, you have only to look in a mirror."

Face tightening beneath the beard that had grown scraggly in the weeks since his kyria's death, he speared her with those now-silver eyes. Nostrils flared, flinging attention to the sigil that once defined and directed his every action.

She braced for a torrent of his anger. Dreaded it. Hated that this man she had so dearly loved seemed a stranger to her now.

His lip curled, whiskers twitching. "We need to move."

Grieved, she wanted Marco Dusan of the Kynigos back. "What happened to you?"

"What happened?" he scoffed. Those brows hoisted upward, eyes widening. "*This!*" He snapped up his arm. "The brand destroyed everything I hoped for my future. Or don't you remember?"

Kersei recoiled at what she saw. Stumbled back a step. "*What* is that?" Not the brand—it was not even visible beneath the decay rotting his flesh. Ashen, crimson cracks pulsed at her. "Blood and boil, Marco. What happened?"

Face taut, he yanked down his sleeve. "Nothing." His gaze skittered around, from her to Jez. "I anak Ixion and my vanguard coming this way. Jez, are you able to reach Tigo, find out where they are? Where we can rendezvous?"

Grim-faced, Jez nodded and angled her gaze to the ground.

Even as she did, Kersei noticed Marco tense. He whipped to the right and stared, gaze piercing the . . . No, not his gaze. He was using his nose.

Suddenly, Marco caught her shoulder and nudged her toward a gnarly copse of scrub. "Get down."

"What's wrong?" she whispered, crouching there.

"A Symmachian—Eidolon."

"Just one?" Jez shifted into her Faa'Cris form, a sword now glistening in her hand. But as Kersei looked on, the shining armor flickered, then stabilized. It must be so painful . . .

He nodded. "A scout," they said in unison.

Kneeling at her side, Jez passed Aeliana to Kersei. "Tigo and your men are on the western side of the Plain of Adunatos."

Kersei's heart started. "That's a half-day's ride."

"Can you take them—" Without warning, Marco shot upward, arched over her, his boots kicking dust in Kersei's face.

Ducking to protect the babies, she heard a meaty thud. A crack.

Jez flew into motion, clearly ignoring her injuries, though her movements seemed sluggish.

Huddling the heirs close, Kersei prayed again for protection. Found herself staring down into green eyes, fixed on her. She shifted her gaze to Xylander, whose eyes flashed around, taking in the afternoon and chaos. But his cousin remained serene and focused. On Kersei. Who had the strangest sense this little one wanted to tell her something. Which was crazy.

Grunts and clangs rang as the two fought the Eidolon scout. Something struck Kersei's back, knocking her forward. She nearly lost her grip on Aeliana but caught her. Firmed her hold as the little one's hand flung out. Found Kersei's arm—the brand.

Fire erupted through her arm, then in rushed an icy, weightless feeling. Kersei blinked and it was gone.

"Take them to Deversoria, Jez," Marco said. "Hurry before—"

"I can't," Jez panted. "My wing—augh!"

"Can you take the babies?" Kersei asked, stepping forward.

"Perhaps—" Jez winced and touched her temple. "After some time in the sanitatem, I could come back for you."

"Very well." Kersei reached out to Jez, tried to pass her thoughts to her. Wished she had learned Lifespeech. *"Please hear me. I need you to hear this."*

Jez's eyes widened. *"Kersei?"*

Smiling, she expelled a breath. *"Take Aeliana to the Revered Mother or my mother. She's special. Mayhap not a Faa'Cris, but she is . . . not just human."*

"Okay," Jez said around a grunt, taking Aeliana. Then Xylander.

Marco was all business. "Kersei and I will travel north to the militia. But you can find us, aye?"

Jez nodded, jaw muscle working. She closed her eyes. Groaned—and was gone.

Feeling chilled, Kersei shuddered a breath, realizing this was the first time she'd been separated from her son. Even from Aeliana.

Marco started walking. "Stay close. We move quickly and quietly. Less for an enemy to track." Over the next ora, he stalked ahead, gaze constantly swinging back and forth, taking in the terrain, scents, and their course. Silent, brooding.

Amused at the thought, she must concede that, in that regard, he had not changed. She must also concede what he had been through since they met bordered on the inordinate. Though she shared half the brand and endured plenty of trauma as well, she could not fathom the anguish and physical pain from the torture of being trapped in the walls of a ship! Fighting off monsters. Returning to find his kyria alive . . . but then seeing her impaled.

Aches wove through her, burning her eyes. What she would not do to make his burden less.

"I do not need sympathy," Marco groused.

Heat shot down her spine at his words, yet she bristled that he would try to control her emotions as he did everything else. "You need *something*," she said. "Your treatment of the princess is abhorrent."

"Would you have me go to war with her in my arms?"

"Nay," Kersei challenged, "but mayhap in your heart."

With a growl, he turned and stepped into her space. "Do not claim to know what is and is not in my heart, Kersei. You do not know me."

"Mayhap, but—"

"You. Do. Not. Know. Me!"

Scalded by his vitriolic tone, Kersei felt that molten steel pour into her spine again. "Mayhap! But I do know what love looks like, and it is nowhere in those silver eyes when you look at your daughter." Boils, she did not want to argue with him. She must find a middle, calmer ground. "Know you that she is special, gifted? Every time she—"

"Did you forget I said not to talk?" He pivoted and continued, head ever sweeping to take in their surroundings.

"To think I admired you—"

He stopped short and wheeled around on her. "Quiet."

With a yelp, she drew up sharp, startled into silence by the ferocity in his eyes.

Another ora . . . then another. Blisters were forming on blisters in her boots. She could feel the letdown, the need to feed the babes. Where was Jez? Should she not have returned by now?

As daylight fell away, Kersei fretted more with each passing ora over Jez's absence, especially as she began to leak. Embarrassed and unwilling to bring attention to it, she adjusted the wrap to conceal the wet spots on her bliaut.

Marco glanced at her, his concern evident. "You are well?"

It should not humiliate her—nursing the heirs was natural and an honor, but to discuss it with him . . . "Aye," she managed wearily. "Tired."

Again he considered her. "There is more."

"I . . ." How could she divert him? "I am greatly concerned for Jez. She has yet to return."

"I had wondered of her absence myself." He darted her a glance. "It was not a deception, to send them off so you could remain to battle?"

Kersei started. "You think so poorly of me?"

He lowered his gaze, then let it drift across the small knoll on which they stood. "I know not what to think regarding many things these days." He nodded to their right. "We near water, a river mayhap?"

That would be a mercy. "The River Callista . . .?" She scanned the area, but even with the moonlight, she could not decipher where in Kalonica they were.

They climbed a small knoll that bent in the direction of Xanthus territory and afforded a view across the plains toward the wastelands to the southwest, and to the northeast, the River Callista. Oh, she ached for a bath. With privacy, of course. "I would so love to plunge myself into the water, clothes and all."

"The river lures me as well . . ." The normalcy of his words, lacking the vitriol more common these last oras, made her study him. With the shorter hair and beard, he was not wholly the revered hunter she had met on Cenon. But that sigil across his nose that pushed attention into his eyes radiated the intensity she had come to expect of him.

"But?"

Marco stilled. "Someone approaches. Over here." He caught her arm and jogged with her to a copse of trees. Nudged her against a large trunk and slid behind her. "Stay hidden."

Heart in her throat, Kersei tracked the rider as he came over the rise.

The rider trotted toward the trees. Moonlight slid over his form, revealing a longsword. Jerkin and trousers. Not Symmachian, as far as she could tell.

She shifted to look at Marco—who was not there! She startled. Jerked around. Where had he gone?

"Augh!"

Kersei whirled to the front. Saw the rider falling from his horse. Marco landing effortlessly—he'd swung from an overhead branch and struck the rider's chest with his boot.

"Oof!" The man impacted the ground hard, his breath audibly punching from his chest.

Marco whipped onto his feet and aimed at the man, a warble of red heat lighting the night. "Name yourself!"

"Whoa! Whoa!" The man held up his hands. "Haltersten, sire. Commander of your militia. I am the man the duchess Touched."

Those words pulled Kersei from safety, hurrying forward to see the man's face beneath the glow of that horrible weapon. "He speaks true," she said. "'Tis him."

Marco straightened and lowered his arm. "What do you out here alone at night?"

"We saw the ship go down and have been searching for you since, my lord.

I-if I may . . ." He slowly came to his feet. "The militia encamped for the night a klick northeast along the river." Deference poured off the man. "We would be honored to have you join us, sire. You and the duchess." He nodded to Kersei with a nervous smile. "There is food and cots."

For the entirety of the man's speech, Marco stared at him. Likely anak'ing him, taking in the scents and discerning if the man was honest. She did not doubt Haltersten's motives, not after the Touch. However, days had passed since that moment, and anything could have happened to the man or his adunatos in those oras.

Marco motioned Kersei to his side. "We would be glad for the provision. Have you water?"

"Indeed!" Haltersten went to his horse and reached for a waterskin.

"I would have the duchess ride—her feet are blistered. She has limped these last several oras."

"Of course, sire. Anything you require." Haltersten nodded as he handed the waterskin to Marco, who passed it to her, his stern gaze still on the man.

Feeling heat rise into her cheeks, Kersei marveled that Marco had noticed. She took a draught of the water. Had he also realized why she yet kept the wrap about her? The material had grown stiff and smelly from soured milk.

Aye, he must know.

Haltersten held the horse steady as she hoisted herself up into the saddle.

As they started toward the militia encampment, Marco positioned himself beside the horse. "How many men have you?"

"This is alpha troop here at the river," Haltersten explained. "There are three more detachments, each numbering at least five thousand."

Drinking the water, Marco choked. Coughed. Gaped at him. "In earnest? So many?"

With a deferential nod, Haltersten placed his hand on his chest—over the spot where Kersei had Touched him. "What started here spread. Impassioned me. Kalonicans are farmers, but they are not meek. After the duchess Touched my adunatos, my path seemed clear. I made it my mission to inspire the men—and even some women—to pick up swords and fight for our existence."

"Incredible," Marco said around a smile. "Well done, Haltersten. I am grateful."

"Thank the Lady," the man said, indicating to Kersei. "Without her, this never would have happened."

Kersei shifted on the horse. "The praise does not belong to me but to the Ancient."

Holding his heart again, Haltersten tucked his chin. "If you would not mind, Duchess, some in the militia want to know if you can do for them what you did for me. Mayhap after we sup?"

Heart in her throat, she did not know how to respond.

"I believe," Marco gruffed, "we would both appreciate food and rest first. It has been an arduous day."

They wound down into a shallow valley where an orchard hugged the river. Small tents and cots stretched as far as the eye could see. Shouts announcing the arrival of the medora brought bleary-eyed men to the front of the encampment.

"This way, sire," Haltersten said. "I would be honored for you to use my tent for you and the duchess. Captain Mient will be glad to help you with whatever you need."

Surprise snatched a breath from Kersei. "Sir Mient?" She eased forward on the horse. "Were you not friends with my father? Always did he speak so highly of you—and your very fine hunting grounds." She smiled at the memory.

The nobleman squinted up at her for a long moment before his eyes sprang wide. "You cannot be Mistress Kersei."

"Aye," she said, feeling every ounce of dirt and grime from the last few days. "I fear, however, the mistress side of me has long fled."

He moved closer to the horse and reached for her hand. Took it in his. "I am sorry for the loss of your family, my lady. They are dearly missed. Xylander was the best man I have ever known."

"I thank you. And I agree—they are terribly missed."

"Forgive us," Marco broke in, irritation scratching at his pale eyes. "But we would rest and sup."

Kersei dismounted, surprised that Marco was there to steady her when she stumbled. "My feet do ache," she managed awkwardly.

"This way, sire. Ma'am." Sir Mient stepped aside and motioned to a tent divided at the back into two halves. "It is not much but will afford some privacy. I will see what cook has for tonight, though I confess it's been gruel or broth and bread for what seems like forever."

"It is more than we have," Marco said. "Thank you."

DEVERSORIA

"Is she conscious yet?"

With a forlorn expression, Garai shook his head. "The damage to her wing was significant—cut straight through several tertials and fractured the coracoid." He sighed. "She also sustained blunt force trauma to her head. It is a wonder she folded successfully—a miracle she did it with two infants!"

"She has always been one of our finest." Alanathina moved from the sanitatem that held Rejeztia to the cradles where the Tyrannous heirs slept soundly after successfully nursing with Aliria, who had just returned to the city with her own newborn to wait out the war.

Stirring air delivered Nicea back to the medical bays. "How do they fare?"

"Well," Alanathina said with a nod. "Had Rejeztia not been in such condition, I would have refused them." Deversoria was not a crèche to watch over newborns. But these two babes were not mere newborns.

Though Nicea's surprise sparked, she held her peace.

"It will be interesting to see what gifts Xylander develops, having been born in a sanitatem."

The words irritated. It harkened back to the time when Faa'Cris coexisted with the Do'St, when both races sustained numbers because of the miracle waters and djell.

"You fear the Do'St will learn of this . . ."

"No fear. Rather—concern of once again becoming only a means to an end. We shook off that yoke long ago."

"And Aeliana?"

Warmth spread through Alanathina's core and pushed light and joy into her mood. "I already see so much of Deliontress in her." *And that, I do fear.*

"Yet I sense the peace and affability of Isaura, too. Not to mention the ferocity of her father." Nicea smiled. "There is also something . . . noble about her. Makes me think of Zarek?"

The words choked Alanathina. Stirred memories of that noble, gallant man whose love had persuaded her—of her own accord—to give him three sons before she felt the time had come to leave with Valiriana, and now, her

Daughter had given birth to her own son by Vorn. Aye, these stirred many memories. "Our grandchildren are incredible, are they not?"

Nicea smiled. "Very much."

Alanathina sighed, thinking of the Sister who had delivered them for safekeeping. "When Rejeztia is conscious, she will return to the battlefield." Her gaze lingered with her silent inference.

"But this is not our war," Nicea said. "When it is, we go. You know this."

"Aye." Alanathina peered down at the serene face of her granddaughter. Felt the pulse of peace and emotions from the child.

"Before she fell into unconsciousness, Rejeztia said Aeliana is special . . .?"

"Kersei's words," Alanathina corrected, lifting the child into her arms. Smiling when those riveting green eyes fixed on her as she came awake. "*Special* is too tame of a word for what this Daughter is. In fact, I sense in her something so deep and powerful, I am not sure this world is ready for her."

The meal was simple, the accommodations even more so. But Marco was glad for both. As he ate, he reviewed Haltersten's troop-mobilization plans. He had thought of everything—including a protection detail for Marco and Kersei. The man was surprisingly intelligent and strategic. Was that because of the Touch? Or had the Touch merely enhanced it?

"Have you military experience?" Marco asked as they sat outside the tent with a cheerful fire to chase off any chill and darkness.

Haltersten smiled. "I was once a machitis. Served in the Hardick Wars, remember? Left the service to try my hand at farming. Lost the crops, the farm, and my wife all in one season. Drove me mad."

Marco eyed him tentatively. *Such calamity would tempt any man to darkness.*

Before he could examine the thought too closely, he caught Kersei's nervous scent snaking out from the tent. Moving . . . down to the river. No doubt to take that plunge she'd mentioned earlier.

With all these men so near . . .?

"If you will excuse me." He rose and headed to bushes that lined the river. Putting his back to the water, he clasped his hands and kept his receptors attuned to the subtle splashing behind him. Crouched and plucked a blade of grass as he thought of all that had transpired in the last few days, the last week. His life had been overturned, his heart ripped from his chest.

Isa . . .

Men stalked toward him, unaware of his presence, but their effluxes said they were entirely aware of Kersei in the water. He swiveled up and squared his stance. "No further," he stated, holding their gazes. Quietly wondering if he should have allowed the protection detail nearer, but he hadn't wanted them spying on her either.

The men faltered. "We just wanted—"

"No. Further." Marco rotated his arm, feeling the heat riffle through the weapon.

"Yield to your medora!" A burly black-haired man rushed toward them, brandishing a sword. "Go on, Corim. Back to camp."

The shorter of the duo halted, gave a halfhearted acknowledgement of Marco's position, then started backing away. "Calm down, Raydin. We're going."

Thick-shouldered and broad-skulled Raydin dipped his head to Marco. "I beg your mercy for stepping in, sire. Corim is known for rebellion and debauchery. I would not have him here. Not with . . ."

Kersei. "Agreed. Now, if you will . . ." Marco nodded him away as well.

And none too soon. He caught Kersei's Signature, flush with embarrassment.

He appreciated her desire to bathe—he could even now smell his own rank self—but this was perhaps not the wisest. Eyeing the two stumbling back to camp, he heard Kersei draw near.

"I . . . I needed to wash . . ."

"You should have alerted me so I could stand guard."

Kersei hesitated, her scent rippling with irritation but also embarrassment. "I . . . see the wisdom of that." As she came around the brush, she nodded, her raven curls wet and springing free around her face over her shoulders. "But I . . . there were . . . reasons I could not wait . . ." She held wet clothes out, almost hiding that she now wore a man's tunic and trousers.

Though he wanted to feign ignorance, he had smelled her situation for the last half of the day. "I am sure Jez will return soon to deliver you to Deversoria and the children."

Kersei stiffened, clearly realizing he understood her dilemma. "I would hope so. Or at least for another Daughter to help me travel."

He cocked his head to the side. "That day, in Kardia . . . you had wings. Can you not"—what was it they called the moving from one place to another . . . ah, yes—"fold on your own?"

"If I had been raised as a Faa'Cris, trained, yes. And Ma'ma says I will find that side of myself one day, but . . . this is not that day. Though, I would do anything to relieve this ache—" She snapped her mouth shut.

Marco smirked. Looked down. Then back to her. "Brilliant, awkward conversation, eh?"

She sniffed a laugh. "Quite."

He nodded past her. "The guards are there. Stay with them. Though this is our militia, not all are trustworthy."

"Understood." She hesitated, glanced at the water, then seemed to catch his meaning that he would bathe and could not attend to her safety. "Be careful—there's a sharp shoal. I nearly sliced my leg on it."

After a nod, he waited for her to reach their tent, saw the guards acknowledge her presence, then he headed to the river. Bathed, and appreciated the solace. Mayhap lingered a little longer than he should have. When he re-entered the tent, he was surprised to find her sitting up, the dividing tent flap still tied open.

She drew in a breath and released it, shakily.

"You are well?"

"Aye." But her efflux said otherwise.

Marco hesitated, half wanting only to be abed and resting. "I am tired and anak your fear. Is there something . . . I should know?"

She sniffed. "Nay . . . I . . . upon your departure, I grew keenly aware that I was . . . alone. That I knew no one. The whole of it . . ." She swallowed, fear saturating the air. "It was as if reliving when the Eidolon set upon me and the babies. And Theilig . . ."

Doing his best not to drown in her sadness and fear—his own could fill an entire planet—he tensed. Nodded. "You are safe." He had no reserves for comforting her. "Get some rest. We set out at dawn."

"I—" She swung her legs over the cot. "How do you . . .?" She batted aside her unruly curls. "How do you do it, Marco?" The question was but a whisper.

He knew what she meant but did not want this conversation.

"The burden, the sadness and grief." She chewed her lower lip. "The loneliness. They pile up like an enormous silo of grain, overflowing as I stand looking at it, ready to bury me." Her eyes puddled with unshed tears. "All these things churn and burn through me, and I would crumble beneath them. I look at you and . . ." She shrugged, her curls bouncing in the light of a touchstone hanging from the center post. "I see the same exhaustion and pain. Yet you press on."

"Because I must." It took everything in him to voice those words. To shoulder away the oppressive weight on his chest.

"Aye," she said softly, lowering herself to the cot again. "We must. For the children." Hugging herself, she looked out to the encampment.

"Get some rest." He untied the canvas that separated their cots.

"Do you hate her?"

Marco froze. Knew she spoke of Aeliana. "What do you want from me, Kersei?"

Still her eyes were filled with tears. "To know you love Aeliana, that this fight, this darkness that you reek of, is not rotting you from within."

"It's not your concern." Marco let the curtain drop. Pushed himself to the cot and stretched out.

"I am your friend, Marco," she spoke through the fabric. "You can hide behind canvas as you do behind anger, but I see you are tormented."

Fisting his hand, he felt the weapon. Felt the anger. The will to be anywhere but here.

"It was not your fault that Isaura died."

The words punched him center mass. *You're wrong. I should have been there.*

"And I think she would be very hurt that you have not shown Aeliana your love."

"Kersei! Enough!" He yanked himself up. Stormed out of the tent and stalked away, sensing the guards trailing him. "Leave me." His growl snaked through the night to no avail. The men dropped back but did not leave even as he paced the river like a restless rhinnock.

Eventually, once Kersei's efflux quieted, indicating she had fallen asleep, he returned and dropped heavily onto the cot. Eventually, he drifted into a fitful sleep.

Minutes—hours?—later, he jolted awake, his receptors stinging with alarm. He leapt off the cot and landed on his knees, anak'ing an attack scent. Several of them. Shifting to the left, he shoved himself beneath the canvas that separated him from Kersei. He sidled to her cot. Touched her shoulder. "Kersei."

With a gasp, she flew awake in a panic and terror.

He clapped a hand over her mouth. "Hey. Hey. It's me. Marco."

She stilled, the whites of her eyes bulging in the dark.

"Raiders. Outside."

She took in a sharp breath.

"Down. Flat."

She obeyed without a word, sliding to the ground and pressing her belly to it.

Marco shifted to the side, slid his left hand beneath his right elbow and aimed—

"*Yah-yah-yah-yah!*" screamed a raider as he plunged through the tent with a dagger. With crazy speed and accuracy, he sent the blade spiraling, end over end, toward Kersei.

As she rolled for cover, Marco thrust up his arm, deflecting the blade against the rhinnock vambrace as he fired off a volley, shoving as much fury into it as he could.

The raider rained as ash.

The foul stench of another raider assaulted Marco's receptors. He angled, brought up his arm and aimed in that direction—through the canvas tent to where he anak'd the savage. He fired. Again. Again.

Shouts sailed through the camp, which came alive in response.

Lunging forward, Marco directed himself at the one to the left. Dived through the hole and nailed the next raider. They landed hard and flipped. Knowing the danger staying down presented, he whipped to his feet. Scanned the area, trusting his receptors more than his eyes in the dead of night.

Fitting words.

He saw no trace of Kersei, but probed with his receptors as his gaze swept the tent. As if in response, Kersei slid out with a javrod in hand—not the collapsible one but something standard issue. She was scared but safe.

A snarl came from his right.

Marco shifted, not before feeling a searing fire along his bicep—but then the knife hit the weaponized part. The blade sparked and bounced away. Using the trajectory of the dagger and the scent, Marco whirled around and fired a blast.

A scream erupted then died with its raider.

Marco shifted back and held his arm out, using the wake to guide his aim.

A hissed breath came with an acrid scent. Then another. And another. Three, maybe four. Reek! Beyond, the camp was in chaos as raiders and militia mixed in a violent melee. Where were they coming from?

He focused himself. Felt Kersei draw up next to him, heard the subtle *whoosh* of her javrod spinning as they faced the darkness. "I smell them but cannot see them." Baring his teeth, he aimed at the stench.

A dark shape blurred forward. Collided. Threw Marco backward and pounded him into the ground. The steady barrage of punches told him he wasn't fighting a raider. He struggled to get off the ground, back on his feet.

Discordant and fierce, a dark scent coursed past him. Toward Kersei.

No.

Unable to draw back his arm, he balled his fist. Imagined if they had killed her and his daughter. The blast erupted.

The Eidolon grunted, strained. Lifted.

A blade pierced Marco's shoulder, blinding him to the battle. "Augh!" Atop him dropped dead weight—the dead Eidolon. Shoving the Symmachian off him, he saw a shifting form.

Another Eidolon.

Marco rolled, hearing the thud of a heavy boot where his head had been. He came up onto a knee. Gritted his teeth at the blade still stuck in his shoulder. Struggling upward, he reached for it.

That boot connected with his head. Snapped it back. He flopped onto the grassy floor again. Groaned, feeling that blade dig deeper. He was going to die. Couldn't protect Aeliana. She would die—because of him. Like Isa . . .

These brigands were responsible for her death.

The thought forced him to vault another shot as he groaned. The Eidolon stumbled to his death.

Over him appeared a shadow—a raider!

Blazing Pyres! Was there no end? A tightness seized his gut. He wasn't going down this easy. Not with the entire Symmachian army waiting to devour his people. Scissoring his feet, he caught the raider's. Brought him down. The savage hit with a thud and seemed to simply bounce. Straight back up. He bobbed on his toes, the swirling, punishing marks of the Lady churning through his torso, arms, neck, and face. He sneered and snarled, sounding more like a criemwolf than a human.

A subtle *thwap* in the air drew Marco's gaze upward. Saw white hair sailing in the air. Directly over him. Met the eyes set with ferocity and intent. A glimmer of wire.

Wwhhhhrrrip!

Oh no. Anticipating blood spatter, Marco yanked his head to the side. Too late. Blood splotched his face and cheek as the sound of a neck snapping registered.

"On your medora!" Ixion's boots thumped ever so lightly on the ground next to Marco, the raider falling with a meaty thud. Then a smaller one for his head. The Stalker glanced at him and arced his eyebrow. "Quick nap before the real battle?"

Sniffing, Marco shook his head, thinking to wipe the blood away but couldn't care at this point. "Took you long enough." The raging fire in his shoulder forbade him from moving fast.

Around them in camp, the sounds of battle were dying down. Whatever this was, it had been poorly executed on the Symmachian side. Or perhaps in their arrogance they had grossly underestimated Haltersten's force.

"Stay," Ixion instructed and nodded to another.

Tigo trudged toward him with a grin. "We had to be sure you felt you'd given it your all. Would be unseemly for support troops to outshine the hero of the day." He shrugged out of his ruck and opened it. "Let me look at that."

"I am no hero," Marco gritted, trying to sit up.

"Whoa—hey, stay there! Let me make sure it's not near an artery."

With a huff, Marco sat and let the Eidolon tend him. "Your brothers-in-arms are taking every opportunity to wipe us out."

"Not all of them," Tigo said, instructing Kaveh to shine a light on the wound so he could probe it. "Jez and AO were part of my team, though I guess they both cheated."

"How's that?"

"Neither are truly Symmachian. AO is a Do'St and Jez, well . . ."

"Yeah. Speaking of—have you word from her? She took the babies to Deversoria and was supposed to return for Kersei, but that was half a day past." Across the road, he spotted Kersei having a cut stitched by Ixion.

Tigo faltered. "She's . . . not answering, and it's really ticking me off."

Marco grunted.

"So that arm blaster you have . . ."

"What about—*Augh!*" Every muscle and sinew convulsed in pain. He arched his spine. Clutched at his shoulder, groaning as the eruption subsided. "You could've warned me."

"They needed to see you were still human."

"There is little doubt of that."

Tigo removed his hand. "Hold this."

Taking the emergency aid pad, Marco pressed it to his shoulder. Felt the blood sliding along the edges and over his fingers.

"Actually, between your cold rejection of your heir and that blaster arm, there is great doubt."

Marco glowered at him.

Unrepentant, Tigo stuffed the wound with a clotting pad and began wrapping it. "And if we still had use of our gear, this would've taken two seconds and ten thousand nanites."

"Enough." Marco lumbered to his feet and moved to Ixion, Roman, and Hushak. "I am glad to see you."

Roman patted his arm. "I see you found the militia."

Marco turned his attention to the men grouping up, watching them. "Haltersten exceeded any expectation." He stretched his neck. "We were to head to the north side of the fire gorges at dawn. Symmachians are staging a few leagues out from there."

"I've been in touch with the general," Roman said. "They are nearly there."

Shoulder aching, Marco felt more than saw Kersei draw closer. He would have her in Deversoria, but it seemed the Faa'Cris had, once again, left them to their own devices. Though dawn had yet to lift her hem, he turned and sought out Haltersten. "Your men did well. They are testimony to your efficacy as a leader. Break camp and follow us to the gorges."

"Aye, sire."

Sir Mient came forward with two horses. "They are our best, sire. May they serve you and the duchess well."

Impressed, Marco smiled. "My thanks. A relief not to have to walk to battle." A ripple of laughter skated around them, and he took the man's forearm. "Well met, Sir Mient. See you on the battlefield." As he swung up into the saddle, and noted Kersei doing the same, a chorus of "Vanko Kalonica! Vanko Marco!" rang through the camp.

Marco lifted his arm. "Bring them war!"

Sunrise spread her light across the plain and welcomed the army to the northeastern side of the gorges. Roman and Ixion had ridden ahead to scout the gorge city of Ancra and secure lodging for Marco and his vanguard. The city leaders offered several structures built into the canyon walls for the medora's use.

Feeling useless and needing a way to avoid Marco, Kersei put herself to work, helping set up a kitchen and quarters for the officers. By midmorning, she stepped outside to find the entire mouth of the canyon full of tents and bedrolls, a temporary city in itself, which spilled onto the plains. At the far side of the gorge, using a steep, narrow path, Marco and a handful of his men picked their way up to a high outcropping.

"Duchess?"

Kersei turned and found Sir Mient coming toward her. "Ah, how—"

"Begging your mercy, Duchess, but the medora said you are to stay in quarters while he is gone."

Irritated, she should not be surprised that Marco would resort to such measures, not trust her, treat her as a prisoner . . . be too cowardly to talk to her himself . . . "I—"

"Apologies." The older man with gray at his temples shook his head. "He said you would argue, but I was not to allow it." Sir Mient seemed chagrined. "Please. Do not make this difficult for me. It would . . . I would be disappointed and it would hurt me to—"

"Calm yourself, Sir Mient." Defeated, Kersei lifted a hand. "I am well able to see myself back."

In her assigned quarters, Kersei hugged herself and paced, heart beating hard. Hating what was essentially captivity. Wished Darius were here—he would never stand for her being treated in this manner. Aches bloomed through her, the urge to nurse giving rise to missing her son—and Aeliana. Wished Jez had returned so she could be with the children. Wished she could do something.

"Ma'ma . . . Ma'ma, I need to be with the children."

No answer came.

"Ma'ma, please. *Help me come to them. Jez was supposed to return for me, but she has not."*

What if Jez was not injured but under orders not to return? The Ladies would not involve themselves in this war, so were they forbidding Jez from it as well?

I must do something.

But what?

Fold!

But . . . but she did not know how. Nobody had taught her.

"What is in us, our nature, Kersei, is not taught. It is imbued." Ma'ma's words from sabbatons past came back to her.

Thoughts colliding, Kersei stilled so she could think. Was it possible? Ma'ma had referenced the Touch, but could she fold as Jez had?

Calm and roll. Calm and roll, that was what Ma'ma had said.

Kersei closed her eyes. Recalled her ma'ma telling her to focus on the clypeus—her wings. With a shift of her neck and shoulder, she felt a gush of relief. Heard something crack against the floor. Startled, she looked to the side and saw a pitcher near her feet, water rushing over the hardpacked earth . . . toward her wings.

With a laugh of exhilaration, she drew herself around. Closed her eyes. Focused. *I can do this . . . I can reach my son.* "I . . ." She thought of Deversoria, where Xylander had been born. Where she had savored healing time with Darius.

Tugging came at her span. Something pulled her backward. "Ah!" she cried out, startled. Scared. Yanked herself forward. Stumbled. Her heart and mind spasmed, realizing it had nearly worked. If her fear had not stopped her.

Stretching her neck, she refocused. Felt that pulling again. It forced a strain against her spine. She gritted her teeth. Stilled herself. Thought of the Sisters . . . of Jez . . . of her ma'ma. Deversoria, so strange and vast . . . *"Home."*

A sensation not unlike falling—except not falling down, but up—pitched her forward. Kersei flung out a hand to catch herself, eyes snapping open. Halfway to the stone floor, she found her balance, her wings stiffening and righting. That's when it registered—the glorious coral marble floors. The echoes of sweet, soft voices.

Kersei froze. Sucked in a breath. Afraid if she moved, she would find herself back in the desert.

A noise came from behind.

She pivoted and spotted— "Ma'ma." She strangled a half laugh, half cry. "I . . . can't believe I did it!"

Smiling, Ma'ma came toward her. "I knew if I left you to it, you would sort it." She strode forward and embraced her. "You were always such a determined little thing."

Trembling, Kersei clung to her mother, the relief and freedom acute. "I missed my son. Where is he?"

Drawing her down the gaping corridor, Ma'ma smiled. "He has missed you. We had a nursing Daughter tend them, but he has been quite cantankerous."

"It was humiliating," she whispered, hearing her voice bouncing back to her in the cavernous halls, "not being able to nurse. And I feared . . .'"

"This will be faster." Ma'ma touched her shoulder, and in a blink, they were in a cozy room with gauzy curtains and warmth radiating from a touchstone firepit. A woman stood from a chair. "Thank you, Calliope. How fare the little heirs?"

Even as the two shared information, Kersei hurried to the sandy-haired head in the cradle. She peered down at Xylander, who lay on his back. When his gaze latched onto hers, he puckered his lip and belted out a wail, as if chastising her for being gone. She lifted him into her arms and felt that familiar tingle. "Oh, I have missed you." Situated on a settee, she fed him, relief sweet and her son beautiful.

Ma'ma joined her, now holding Aeliana, who yet seemed as peaceful and ambivalent as always. "It does me good to see you fight to come back to him."

"Ever did I have an acute frustration coursing through me, and I worried after Jez. How does she?"

"Rejeztia wakes for short periods, but the injury to her span and the internal damage was significant. But she is Faa'Cris and will recover."

"Tigo is quite worried."

Ma'ma gave a sniff. "I am certain it will be but a few more days, and she will, no doubt, return to him when she is able, or he will find his way here, as you have."

Kersei furrowed her brow and lifted Xylander to her shoulder, patting his back. "Whatever do you mean? How can he?"

Ma'ma explained about the Do'St. That Tigo was of that ancient line, and when he was ready to focus on it, he would step into a centuries-old role.

Kersei marveled. "Growing up, my most fanciful imaginings were of being able to spar with machitis, then being named one. Now to find there are so many supernatural things about our world . . ." She laid Xylander on the fur rug and gave him a toy to gum, then took Aeliana. "Do you think these ancient men will help in the war?"

"Tigo's father is doing his best, but there are not many of them, so do not count on a significant endowment of assistance."

With Aeliana in her arms, Kersei nursed her as well. Stared at the little beauty who seemed to have grown in the day since they had been separated. Crystal green eyes watched her as she drew in the sustenance. Kersei wiggled her finger into the tiny fist, and Aeliana gripped it tight. "I wish he would give you a chance . . . that you could know your ma'ma."

"Will you go back after you feed them? Now that you can fold?"

Kersei laughed, half startling Aeliana. "I succeeded once—and am not entirely sure how I did it." She snuggled in with the princess. "Besides . . . I . . . they need me."

"They will be fed and cared for if you are not here," Ma'ma said, "but I see in you a change, Kersei. There was a day you would have been champing at the bit to get back into the fight."

Stroking Aeliana's dark hair, Kersei tilted her head. Thought of her mother's words. Realizing she was right—something had shifted within her. Discovering she could fold . . . No, it was before that. When she realized she had wings? No . . . even farther back. "When I was here, when you told me of my identity as Faa'Cris . . . I think that"—she looked up at her ma'ma—"I think that is when I started accepting who I was. All my life, I was chastised for wanting to spar, yet I find it is in my blood. All those people who said I annoyed them, that I was not a proper lady . . ."

"I only wanted you to find acceptance in the world you knew."

"I hold no grief toward you for that, Ma'ma—well, then I did, but now I understand." She traced Aeliana's fingers. "Now, however, I know who I am." She kissed the little one. "And I know what fight is mine."

It felt poetic and right that this war came to a culmination in the continent's desert region known as the wastelands. Not far from here, he'd first come across Isa wielding those moon discs in a display that was impressive and beautiful. Like her. That's when he'd started falling in love with the shy, demure Moidian. Symmachians had stolen her from him, from his people. So, here in the place where she had grown up, he would deliver justice.

I vow it, Isa. Or I will deliver myself as a sacrifice for failing you.

Prone on an outcropping that overlooked the plain, careful to avoid too much pressure on his shoulder, Marco peered through his vambrace monocle. Took in the Symmachian army forming up a little over two leagues out, more than a league and a half from the edge of his own army's camp. A half dozen downed fast-attack crafts littered the western edge of the gorges, one even precariously wedged in a narrow crevasse.

"It's going to be a stiff, if not lopsided, engagement," Tigo muttered.

"Very lopsided—in their direction."

"Towers helped, though."

Marco grunted.

"I heard Kersei is missing."

Another grunt. "I anak her—she is safe. I assume in Deversoria by the scent coating her Signature."

"You think Jez helped her?"

"How else?" Marco shrugged. "We should go below and strategize."

"Right," Tigo muttered. "Need to make sure our deaths go according to plan."

After throwing him a glower, Marco headed back down into the canyon. Houses cut into the hardened clay made for much cooler living, but the monotonous browns and tans would grate quickly on his nerves.

A large house with a half dozen rooms had been offered by its owners to serve as a base of command. Already there were more than fifteen other structures being converted into a barracks, a storehouse, and a place of retreat for him and his men.

Marco entered the Command bunker and quickly realized that, despite its size, they would soon feel like rhinnocks stuffed into a cookpot, thanks to the heat and the many bodies. Seated in the center, he was surrounded by Roman, Ixion, Tigo, Bazyli, and his regia. "I consider you"—he met each of their gazes—"my commanders. I trust you and know your counsel to be filled with wisdom. We are not prepared—not one of us could argue otherwise, but we are here. Speak openly, and let us come together to defeat this enemy."

The general leaned forward, thick arms resting on his knees as he rubbed his knuckles. "Trachans were spotted coming from the east. Shau'li is sending all men of fighting age who remain. My brother Jencir leads our entoli this way—I saw Xanthus colors on the rise moments ago."

He paused, and Marco could not mistake the rush of emotion flooding him. He put a hand on Bazyli's shoulder. "How are Jherako and Hirakys doing after the bombardments?" His mind jumped to both leaders, men he had inadvertently befriended, Vorn and Crey.

"Though Crey took back his palace," Bazyli said, "Vysien has been besieged. I have it on good authority, however, that he is driving his rhinnocks north to rout the raider camp-city."

"What authority?" Marco asked.

Tigo angled into view. "Me. I was there when Jez charged him with the task."

"And you saw this—his herd coming north?"

At this, Tigo hesitated. "No, but I would assume—"

"We assume nothing," Marco snapped.

Roman shifted forward, arms resting on the table. "Forgelight fell a fortnight past—they were already heavily damaged when the kyria and I were there."

A reminder Marco did not need. He lifted his gaze to the master hunter. "Thumps from Rico regarding their fleet?"

Roman shook his head. "No word before the EMP. It is said their flight base collapsed beneath one of the bombardments, but that is not confirmed."

"So we know not how many of their men remain." It seemed a lost cause before they had yet begun. The only good thing to date . . . Marco eyed Haltersten. "We are grateful for all you have rallied in the militia."

"As said before, thanks should go to the Lady Kersei for . . . changing me."

"For that, send prayers to the Ancient, not the duchess." Marco moved on. "What of the smaller kingdoms?"

"Many rulers were killed in the attack that hit Forgelight while you were yet missing," Roman said. "The handful that remained belonged to countries or principalities. The harsh truth is we have a very small army, and Symmachia outnumbers us easily ten to one, possibly more."

"What of the other planets?" He looked around. "Vorn once said we had allies among other cultures."

"Some ships have come, it is true. But by and large, it is too hard to care when they are so far removed," Roman said calmly. "Little word from Kardia, save Jubbah arriving to help with the retrofit of the *Qirolicha* per your request; however, they have hit many roadblocks."

"What of the Faa'Cris?" Ixion asked from his post by the door. "Considering they have instigated this war, surely they will fight at our side."

Marco balled his fist. "I was unequivocally told this was not their war. As none are here, I would say they have made their intentions clear."

"So much for being the Blade of Vaqar to protect the innocent." Ixion eyed the onetime Eidolon commander. "What of that Lady of yours?"

Tigo snorted, but his efflux was rank with worry. "There has been no word from her since she left with the heirs. As for the Ladies"—his gaze struck Marco's—"when Jez and I left Deversoria, I am certain my interactions with them ended there. For such notable figures throughout history, they have lost their ability to inspire confidence or hope."

Frustration churned through Marco, the brand and weapon sending charges of heat through him. He scanned the crowd and found the younger Stalker. "Hushak. What word from the southern gorges and wastelands?"

The stoic man inclined his head. "My scouts returned two rises past, forced back by raiders and skycrawlers."

Marco roughed his hands over his face.

"If only there were a way for us to have a weapon like you have," Cetus said, indicating to Marco's arm.

"Nay," Roman broke in with a scowl. "It is a curse."

"I would take any curse that could stop those skycrawling scum from destroying our world," Cetus countered.

"It is easy to carelessly speak words when you have not lived beneath its demand," came Daq'Ti's trilling.

Marco started at the arrival of the Draegis. "Daq'Ti!" He caught the man's hand and patted his shoulder. "Good to see you again. How are the other pilots doing?" It must be hard, adapting to a planet with different oxygen levels and learning how to fight without a ship.

"They do their best," Daq'Ti said. "I would assist Duncan with work on the *Qirolicha*, but without power, I am of no use. If power is restored, I should return there, considering the complexity and their lack of Draegis systems knowledge."

"Agreed. If it comes back on, we'll find a way to get you there."

"Still cannot believe the skycrawlers have not tried to steal it," Ixion commented.

"It's dead as every other ship right now, but mayhap they yet plan to." It could be the Symmachians only waited for Daq'Ti and Duncan to finish their work. His mind worked hard, wondering if he could truly get it airborne. The timing would be delicate. "Think you it will fly again?" He gripped his friend's forearm—and stilled. Glanced down. "Your weapon . . ."

Daq'Ti trilled as he rotated his ashen arm.

Marco balked at the clear skin. "It's gone! What—? What happened?"

Pleasure and peace radiated from the Draegis, who lifted his chin with another quiet, long trill. "I let it go." He caught Marco's shoulder. "You should do the same."

Marco tensed. "Why would you— We needed that! We have no weapons against the Symmachians except these and a few pulse weapons taken off dead raiders—and with the EMP towers running, they're useless!"

Daq'Ti stepped uncomfortably close. "It is not worth it, Uchuvchi." He thumped Marco's chest. "The cost is too high."

"You crazy?" Cetus objected, coming to his feet. "I have a sword, which means close quarters. With an arm like that, he can target several at a distance. I'd kill for something like that."

Daq'Ti growled. "When I met him in Kuru, my arms were black, hard like stone. I was powerless to choose my path. They made me corrupt, took my will as their own."

"They were terrifying," Marco conceded. "Daq'Ti was nothing more than a machine obeying orders given by the same race of creature ultimately responsible for Symmachians being in the wastelands."

"Mayhap," Hushak grunted, "but those still work with the power down. Unlike this weapon." He hefted a pulse rifle, then jutted his jaw at Marco. "Sire, how did you get yours?"

The door flung open and Thorolf barged in. "Sire! Come quick—you should see this."

Out in the canyon floor, a mob of machitis surrounded something. Marco hurried over, with Ixion and Roman behind him. He stepped through and stopped at the sight of an Eidolon in light armor, standing with a wagon on which were stacked four large crates. "What is thi—"

Tigo barked a laugh. "Diggins!" He rushed toward the guy and pulled him into a hug. "What're you doing here?"

"The admiral sent some supplies."

Marco scowled. There were likely a couple hundred old-school assault rifles in those crates. "Where's the rest?"

"Yeah," Diggs said, rubbing his neck. "Sorry. Tough enough getting this many offship as it was. Couldn't do more without drawing attention and risking being intercepted."

Stunned by the too-brief flare of hope, Marco palmed the lip of the crate. It was like the Ancient was handing the Droserans breadcrumbs to sate a ravenous rhinnock.

"Better than nothing," Ixion muttered.

Later that night, they regrouped after a meal, and the general and his officers laid out their strategy.

Bazyli stood proud and confident. "We'll form up on the plains south of Shau'li." He touched the map on the table to his left. "Only machitis and aerios, other able-bodied men in these positions—here, here, and here—luring the enemy to funnel in. From the north, east, and south, we will drive them down into the fire gorges of the western plain. Those enemies who do not fall into the fiery pit, we cut down. What I will leave to you is the overall execution."

Ixion hovered over the map with Bazyli. "We have horses and they do not, so that will work to our advantage, especially in Shau'li lands."

"The hillier the better, because I can bet my life that they won't shed their light-armor suits," Tigo said, finally speaking up, "and that is weight you won't have to work around. Mech-suits without power demand abandonment because of the sheer weight. But that light armor will still protect them against most weapons. General, where do you train your men to target the opponent?"

"In this war, where our goal is to neutralize not incapacitate, the heart, throat, or head."

"Good," Tigo said, "but targeting the heart of a Symmachian will be ineffective."

"Because they don't have one?" Thorolf mocked.

Tigo made a face. "I assure you, they definitely have heart—as do I—but the light armor will deflect over ninety-five percent of weapons."

"Except the medora's weaponized arm," Cetus noted. "He put a hole straight through an Eidolon in the caves."

"A solid weapon," Tigo said, "but he is only one. For the rest of us . . . strikes to the joints, neck, or head are the best bet to take a Symmachian down." He stepped up to the table. "But do not expect them to go down easily."

"Are you trying to discourage us?" Cetus grumbled, rubbing the back of his neck.

"No," Tigo said, his young face one of experience and yet conviction, "but I also don't want you going out there under a blind assumption that because they don't have their tech, they're easy targets. Especially the ones in black and gold."

"Prepare the men," Marco said. "And remember—bring them war!"

"Vanko Marco! Vanko Kalonica! Vanko Drosero!"

An explosion of light seared his corneas, a pain that mirrored the icy-hot liquid charge through his PICC-line. Reef gritted through the fire and tried to listen for Eija—half expecting her to slam against a bulkhead. Head slowly clearing, he glanced around his couch . . . saw her floating toward the hatch.

Slag.

He scanned the array and controls . . . and the only thing he knew was that the ship was on autopilot. Had to be, since it was blurring along a pre-plotted course on the array. On the *Qirolicha*, Eija had said the trip would take days versus weeks . . . Which was interesting considering, in truth, time didn't exist in jumpspace. Nothing existed in jumpspace. Which still messed with his head. But hey, he wasn't complaining. Point being—he had a few seconds to secure Eija.

He released his harness and thrust himself up out of the cockpit. If he had a mech-suit, he could grav down, but as an Eidolon, he was skilled in navigating zero g. Using consoles and bulkheads, he swam toward Eija. Pressing two fingers to her carotid allayed fears she might be dead. But she wasn't in tip-top shape either. Secretly, he thanked Baru that her wings were . . . wherever they were. But he couldn't help but wonder if it was hurting her to have them hidden with that injury.

Hold up. Should he look for a medical bay or one of those healing pods the Draegis used? What would their pods do to a Faa'Cris?

Well, whatever it did, wouldn't it be better than dead? The pods hadn't hurt the Uchuvchi or Marco, right? Reef pushed from the cockpit and sailed down the grate gangway that held the hybrids. He scanned and searched through several hatches.

Opposite where Eija had initially delivered him, he found the medbay. He made quick work of getting topside and floating her down to the pod.

Maneuvering her body into the pod was a bit tricky in zero g but he managed it. As soon as the top closed, it hissed. A click indicated it sealed shut. The clear face shield ghosted gray, and a digital readout flashed with Draegis script—which his uni-com translated—displaying her biorhythms, oxygen levels, and myriad other readouts. The face shield cleared again, showing her in a tranquil sleep. No idea they were blasting back to the Quadrants. She'd be ticked when she woke up.

Voids, she was pretty. Sprinkling of freckles over her nose and beneath her eyes. He missed the braids she usually wore during HyPE training—they were . . . cute. She was cute.

Heart strained at the truth they'd agreed on, he shoved himself back to his couch and harnessed in. Skipped the PICC-line this time and went to work familiarizing himself with the ship. Two priorities: learn the weapons and targeting solutions, and figure out how to jettison those hybrid pods.

And just three not-days to do it in.

WASTELAND   GORGES,   KALONICA,   DROSERO

There was no way they would win.

I am one *man.*

One man with an injured shoulder and a weapon-arm he could barely control. Even now as he lay looking up at the stars where they met the mouth of the canyon, unable to sleep before setting out to battle at first light, he felt the ache of it, the stiffness spreading up into what had been a healthy shoulder. A rock pressed into his side and he shifted, aware of the snores around him. He was glad for the respite of a night in the open, away from the closed-in quarters in Ancra. Strategically, he had dispersed some commanders among the camp at the canyon's mouth in preparation for the morrow. Elsewhere on the plains, the gathered armies of Drosero likewise prepared. He glanced around him at the men laid out before battle . . .

As they will be when we dress them for burial. If any of us yet remain.

Morbid thoughts. True all the same.

The stone dug harder into his ribs. Marco reached to tug it out—and stilled at what his hand met. Jerking upright, he hauled up the bottom of his tunic. Stared at the spot where his belt met skin. Only . . . it wasn't skin.

"Holy Fires," he hissed. Yanked down his shirt. What the reek was happening to him? He moved to a spot where he was alone. Took a breath to steel his courage, then inspected the spot again beneath the moonslight. His gut cinched, and he was sure the jerky and bread he'd eaten was about to reappear, because a swath as wide as his arm stretched from armpit to just above his waistline. The entire right side had . . . hardened to what looked like ashes and embers in a firepit.

Like the Draegis.

Gut churning, he dropped back on his haunches and gripped his knees. This . . . this couldn't be happening. He wanted to look again, but now that he knew it was there, the feel of it stood out so distinctly.

And the fetor of it!

How could he stop it from spreading over his whole body?

Daq'Ti. He would know. Marco hopped up, skipped a step toward the resting men. Though he scoured them, he could not locate the one who'd come through the gate with him. The one who could help him understand what was happening and how to stop it.

He located and knelt at Ixion's bedroll. "Mavridis."

The man's eyes opened, and though he did not jolt upright, it seemed every nerve in his body was thrumming.

Or maybe that was Marco's pulse.

"A problem, sire?"

"Daq'Ti—do you know where he is? I must speak with him at once."

"Gone. Removed to the eastern edge of the camp and likely sleeping. As you should be, sire." Ixion was sitting now. "Is aught amiss?"

"Nothing." The lie did not sit well on his tongue. He patted Ixion's shoulder. "Rest. Sorry for the—" Marco whipped upright, spinning toward the attack scent way down the column, on the edge of camp nearest to the Symmachians. With horror he saw the shadows—not distinct individuals but an enormous mass—rushing across the plain. "Incoming!"

A piercing whistle came from his First.

"Rise, Drosero!! Rise!" Where were the sentries? How had the enemy effected such a charge? "*Bring war!*"

With a hop, Marco ran toward the fight, the swell of bodies around him thickening as men rose and raced to engage. From the enemy came a deafening roar that even made Marco falter. But not stop. He kept running, reminding himself of what they'd done. Who they'd killed.

Isaura . . . May I avenge you, my aetos.

Ahead, he saw the first clash of Symmachians and Droserans. Tents went up in flames, lighting the ferocious encounter. Where he had expected the skycrawlers to decimate his people, the lack of pulse weapons dictated a tough hand-to-hand battle. Raw, vicious fighting.

But then something registered. A feral, focused fury. Marco's gaze locked onto a stream of soldiers sprinting straight through the fray. Hiking over bodies. Deflecting blows but not staying to confront enemy targets. They were coming straight at him.

Straight for me.

Symmachians were targeting him. Had targeted him. This entire time. Snatched him and his Brethren. Attacked Stratios, killing hundreds, including Xylander and two of his daughters, to get at Marco's father and brother. Later, they wiped out his only remaining brother in Hirakys. They killed Isaura.

Rage exploded from his arm. He targeted the head of the lead Marine in black and gold.

Like a stag taken during a hunt, the Eidolon face-planted and slid forward, but the others jumped over him and continued. So did Marco. He fired. Missed the head, but an arm vanished. The Eidolon tripped, suddenly off-kilter, and went down.

On either side, Droserans engaged troops. But the river of Eidolons flooded toward Marco, unrelenting.

This . . . this was their tactic. Not stopping though a man died, the line still advancing toward the enemy, was—to them—a win.

Even as he reduced the next one to ash, he realized this weapon easily made him a target, whether or not he was the Progenitor. The newly delivered rifles a few Kalonicans wielded were filling his nostrils with a chemical detritus.

"Aetos!"

At his codename, Marco reeled toward Ixion—saw a raider flying at him. The dagger sliced along his face and neck.

Or would have. Had not a brilliant flash of light erupted in front of him. Whirling, Jez deflected the blade and relocated Marco to a spot farther back in the line.

He growled his frustration. "Nice of you to return."

"You're welcome." A frown gouged into her beauty. Her gaze slid to his side, then his arm, and her frown deepened. Wrapping them in her glory, she stepped into his personal space. "Let it go, Marco. Before it is too late."

"Release me, Jez."

Her brow rippled, considering him. "The thing distresses you, yet—"

"*Release me!*" he demanded. And not a second too soon—an Eidolon was fast approaching. Marco whipped up his arm and pulled a blast.

The Eidolon dove aside, avoiding the singed death. He rolled and came up. Reacquired Marco. Who followed the man down his arm's line of sight. When dark eyes met his, Marco squeezed off the volley.

No more Eidolon.

Fifty meters off, Ixion warred with two Eidolon and took a hammering. Even as Marco started that way, the Stalker hiked himself into the air, doing an aerial as he drew both swords, came down driving one into the neck of each Eidolon.

I really need lessons from him.

Myriad scents plagued Marco as he negotiated the battle, finding guilty pleasure in eliminating the enemy. He marveled that it did not drain him of energy. That he had an endless supply.

Even as the sun rose, climbed high into orbit, then laid herself to rest, the battle raged. Ever the ebb and flow went on, now one side advancing and then the other. Men rotated to the front in rhythmic waves, affording the survivors of each wave a brief respite in the rear guard. Fewer and fewer, it seemed. Marco raged, seeing so many Droserans as food for carrion while the stream of Symmachian infantry seemed as endless and relentless as ever.

Around the campfire that night, Marco kept to himself, afraid someone would notice. Afraid . . . *Am I going to look like the Draegis?* Become a mindless slave like them?

Panic darted through him, wondering—would he serve a Khatriza? Turn against his people?

He punched to his feet, the morose chatter around the fire suddenly dying—the men thinking his move a response to incoming trouble. "No, no. It's well. I just need . . . air."

A few chuckles pointed out the obvious—they had nothing but air out here. He stalked along the gorge, aware of his aching shoulder from the dagger wound but more aware of the stiffness in his body. He paced, trying to sort it. It would be fine. The war would end and he'd figure out how to get the weapon off his arm.

"Are you okay?"

Marco shook his head as the Faa'Cris haunted his steps. "If I needed your counsel, Jez, I would have asked. Why are you not with Tigo or—" He drew up straight. "Kersei—did you take her to Deversoria?"

Though not glorying, she stood in her Faa'Cris armor, looking as formidable and terrible—yet beautiful—as she had before. "She is there, but I did not take her. She folded herself."

Marco stared at her, trying to process those words, imagining the fiery daughter of Stratios now so wholly a Lady. He grunted. Focused on what mattered. "Are the heirs safe?"

"Last I checked." A confident efflux supported her words.

He squinted at her, the darkness playing tricks with his mind. "Your answers . . ."

Unwavering, she stood before him. "I am concerned about what is happening to your—"

"Be not." He silenced her with a slice of his hand.

"I am not commanded by men," Jez stated flatly.

So much for silencing her.

"Everything okay here?" Tigo strode toward them, his normally crisp clothes torn and stained.

"Brilliant," Marco groused as he shoved past.

"Sire."

He jerked up straight, stunned he hadn't detected Ixion coming. "Bleeding fires, can I get no peace?"

Ixion met his eyes, unfaltering. "Until this war is over, unlikely."

DEVERSORIA

Kersei knelt in the templum and clasped her hands. Prayed. Beseeched the Ancient to protect Drosero from the attack. Protect Marco in battle—and from himself. From that insidious weapon attached to his arm. "There is such darkness there. It seeks to corrupt what You have given—the brand." She feared for him. For them all, if Marco completely lost his way.

When her knees began to ache, she rose and started back to the home she shared with Ma'ma while here.

A flutter of wings delivered the Revered Mother to the steps of the templum. "Kersei."

She inclined her head. "Revered Mother."

It amazed and stunned to remember that this woman was mother to Darius and Marco. Wife to Medora Zarek. She had left so long ago, it had been easy to forget her visage. Sandy hair and blue eyes that favored Darius, but not Marco, framed a pretty, oval face. "May I walk with you back to the house?"

"Of course." Kersei smiled. "I am grateful for the refuge provided me and the heirs, especially at such a volatile time."

"I know my son is angry we will not join the war between Drosero and Symmachia."

It would be impossible to hide her thoughts from so skilled and ancient a Lady.

"Apparently," Alanathina went on, "he is not the only one."

"It is hard to fathom that you can be aware of the war, of what is happening—the slaughter—and yet . . . stay here."

"Trust that you are yet new to our ways and laws, and I am not."

Kersei paused and turned to her. "Why will you not help them? Your grandson and granddaughter live there. Their fathers—" She paused, realizing she had been about to say Darius lived there. "Marco rules there, like his father—your bound."

"Do you earnestly think I need a genealogical account of House Tyrannous?"

Kersei ducked and chewed the inside of her lower lip, feeling the brand stirring once more. Sensing an echo of the darkness roiling through Marco. It nauseated and worried her.

The Revered Mother stopped and glanced at her arm. "Your brand flares."

Feeling somehow guilty, Kersei nodded. "It had . . . settled after Iereania, but since his return . . ."

"Hm." Considering her for a moment, the Revered Mother bobbed her head down the street. "Would you come with me a bit farther? I have an idea."

"An idea?"

Alanathina nodded but said no more as they wound through the enormous city that defied limits and expectations, away from the more civic locations to the edge and a two-storied, narrow structure built into the wall that separated them from a very high drop to a river below. From her pocket, she drew out a ring of keys and used one to unlock the thick, carved door. The lettering over the door was one Kersei did not recognize, yet she knew its meaning.

"The palaestra." Her heart skipped a beat. "Library."

The Revered Mother stepped inside and held the door for her.

Though Kersei expected it to be dusty and dim, it was clean and well lit, but the musty smell of old paper could not be hidden as large, thick, leather-bound books dominated row upon row of shelving.

"Wait here."

Kersei did as instructed, and soon, the Lady returned and handed her a massive tome. "What is it?"

"Hopefully, answers. It is the Trópos anthology. Foretellings of a variety of brands of The Way. Yours and Marco's—the Fotiás—is in there. Mayhap this will help you understand why the brand has not yet quieted."

"Is that normal—for them to . . . quiet?"

Wise eyes held hers for a long moment. "I have never known one to continue to burn after it's been in the trough."

The trough . . . "Iereania." Kersei swallowed, glanced at the hefty book she held. "So . . . the brand is not yet fulfilled?"

The sun rose on the sixth straight day of combat. Weary, shoulder aching, Marco wanted nothing more than to dial back time and find himself in Kardia with Isa. Hear her voice. Feel the whisper of her words against his face as they lay abed talking.

He clenched his eyes and did what he had for the thousandth time—reached into the dreamspace. And once more felt the cold, empty void of her absence.

Angry, he pulled himself off the ground and geared up, strapping on his vambraces—of little technological use, but they did well in protecting his arms against blades. He slung his scabbard on, then sheathed the dagger in his boot and one at his thigh.

"Ready?" Ixion and a half dozen regia came toward him.

Marco gave his thoughts purchase on the battlefield. "I was thinking last night, we should post sentries on the towers."

"Tigo did that—"

"Marco!" A flutter of pale blue wings stirred the air with vanilla and patchouli as Kersei appeared near Ixion. "We must talk."

"We are leaving for battle."

"It is about the brands."

He stopped, his gaze instinctively landing on her arm, bare save a leathered epaulet that hung to her bicep. *What* was she wearing? With her standard omnirs and boots, she wore a gauzy tunic-like bliaut that hung to her thighs and atop that a stamped, leathered vest that gathered tightly around her small waist. Definitely not Kalonican attire.

She moved nearer, her mass of black curls in a ponytail. "Please, can we talk? It is important, or I would not have come."

The brands . . . His was hidden beneath the weapon. And her efflux warned she would again complain about it. "Later."

"Please—the brand—"

"Incoming!"

Marco dove to protect her, only to have her wings snap up and shield them both as they hit the ground beneath the detonation of a grenade.

Boom!

The concussion slammed over them, rocks and dirt raining down. Before the haze could clear, he coughed. Rolled free from her. "Get to safety, Kersei." Unable to see through the smoke, Marco threw himself in the direction of the Symmachians. Let his receptors lead. Detected his men behind him, grunts and blows filling the air. Kersei gone.

He plowed straight into the first Symmachian, barely stopping to run the man through. The strident scent of an Eidolon struck his receptors, and he ducked the incoming blow and whirled around, firing off a volley that turned the man's head to ash. He fell where he stood.

Marco battled, swung. Fired. Onward. Sweating. Volley. Took a slice to the side—but the blade merely *tsing'd* across the *chirish* that coated his flesh. The sound was not unlike a blade sharpening. *I seriously hope not.* That the *chirish* made him nearly impervious to injury fueled him.

As he made his way closer to the fallen ships and the Symmachians, Marco anak'd the others. Found Daq'Ti on the eastern side and a few times was sure he heard that trilling howl so unique to the Draegis. He feared for the alien without this weapon-arm, but he had survived this long.

Volley after volley helped Marco push on, and yet . . . though he had reached the first ship, the main camp was still at least a league off. The futility of it all struck him. Would they ever win? He had been told repeatedly and said himself that this war was impossible to win. Yet the despair of this moment showed him how much he had secretly hoped for an entirely different outcome.

What good am I if my purpose is only to help these people die? How was it any better to die with hope than to die without it? The end result was still the same—dead. The realization angered him. Pulled him around. A few meters away, a cluster of Eidolon were engaging the Droserans who had attacked, but . . . what was this? They backed up and glanced around for the next target rather than pursuing their enemies to the death.

What manner of combat was that?

A raider came from his left. Marco volleyed, still watching the Eidolon. Sure enough, they responded to attacks, moving and negotiating the battle, but then returned to their . . . position.

Roman jogged toward him, swinging hard at a raider and taking the man down with deft strikes. "Are you well?"

"Aye," Marco said absently as Roman pressed his back to the ship to protect his six. "Those Eidolon . . . they're guarding something."

Roman watched with him.

Receptors straining, Marco hauled in a breath and narrowed the scent cone, following it upwind to . . . "Or someone."

"Can't imagine a pilot or ship commander is that important."

"Agreed. We'll have to neutralize the guards."

"Ship's secured, so we need to find a way in."

"Or smoke them out," Marco suggested. "Not a fan of close-quarters combat. Without the Eidolon's static shields, my weapon is quite effective, but I cannot take a whole team out on my own."

"We need help against six Eidolon."

"Stalkers," Marco said, glancing about. Why hadn't he learned their whistles? He spotted Hushak. "Hang on." He wheeled around and sprinted to the Stalker. "Signal Ixion. I need as many Stalkers on me as possible."

Thumb and forefinger together, the Plisiázon set them in his mouth and let out a series of whistles.

A raider erupted in front of them. Marco fired and reduced the man to ash.

"There," Hushak said with a grunt as he went airborne and ripped his manriki, severing a raider's head. He landed and met Marco's gaze, no dizziness or disorientation. "They're coming."

"I really need to learn how to do that."

Hushak smirked. "I'd like to see that."

There was something sarcastic and almost sadistic in the man's efflux as they hurried back to the ship, where Roman was crouched, waiting. Within minutes, they had six Stalkers with them.

"There's a VIP in that ship," Marco said. "I want him."

The team made quick work of the Eidolon between the manrikis and the weapon-arm. Marco tic-tacked up the ship where the front flared out, and scrambled atop it, finding—just as he suspected—open hatches. With no electricity, most of the environmentals were down. A few fans could operate without electricity, but they needed solar and wind power.

Armed with two tunics soaked in ship's fuel, Marco used his dagger to pause the fan, set the accelerant inside the box, and sparked his dagger against his rhinnock vambrace. It took a few times but a flame caught. He blew on it to force the flame and smoke inward. Released the fan blade, and watched as the smoke plumed outward, then was sucked inside. Before he even turned away to slide down, he heard coughing.

He landed with a soft thump below the hatch. "Ready yourselves."

The lock disengaged.

Marco tensed, anxious and curious to find out who was inside. Even as the door lowered, he anak'd panic and alarm around the battleground. They'd been spotted routing the VIPs.

Smoke billowed out as the first man stumbled down the ramp, tripping and rolling.

Marco stuck out his boot and stopped the man. The second shuffled out, coughing and gagging. Letting his First deal with the other Symmachian, Marco flipped the first one over, aiming his weapon at the man's head. "Who—" The question died in his throat as the face registered. "This must be my lucky day. Hello, Rufio."

"Not even close," the man on the ground snarled. "You have no idea—"

Someone kicked him in the head, knocking him out.

Marco started, grabbing the tunic of the attacker. "Bazyli!"

Unrepentant, the general held his gaze. "I am disgusted to be related to him. He deserves death." He spat on the unmoving form.

"And Kersei deserves to be the one to deliver it."

"Sire," someone called from behind.

He turned around and stilled. Felt the rage of the weapon demanding to be sated. "Theon." Smirking, he shook his head. "My very lucky day. Rendezvous with the Hirakyn dogs gone wrong? No warning that your ship would suddenly stop working?"

"You can't keep them down forever."

"Oh, I don't need to. Just long enough to sever heads." He motioned to the headless Eidolon. "Care to join them?"

"I am a High Lord of the Ierean Temple," the man preened. "You would not dare set a hand against me."

Furious, recalling what this piece of meat had done to Kersei, Marco curled his lip. "I don't need to." He wanted Kersei to see both of these men who were responsible for her pain. He turned to Rufio, now on his knees and under the control of Hushak and Kaveh. "So." The nervous effluxes of the Stalkers had nothing on the refuse-of-a-man. "What shall we do with you?"

Ixion's expression darkened. "Tie him down in the canyon and shove a boulder from above, so that he might know what his brother and nieces felt."

Marco grunted. "And they say I am a monster."

"Desert justice," Ixion growled.

"He is right," Bazyli said. "My mother was his sister, Xylander my uncle, and nothing would give me greater pleasure than to see him pay for three hundred twenty-two who perished because of him."

"Not to mention what Kersei endured at the hands of the Symmachians and that machine." Marco grunted again, the words firming his resolve and belief that Kersei and all Stratians deserved justice. But was there anything painful enough for this man? He knew it would be painful for another. "Ready to answer to your niece, Rufio?"

TSC-C *CRONUS*, DROSERAN ORBIT

"Sir! Unrecognized light and energy source two light seconds distant!"

Domitas felt it in his gut as he flicked the arrays, scanning the reports from Lieutenant Loren. The readout showed a large pulse coming from . . . "Sicane." He thought of Slice and his report. Thought of what it meant.

He brought up an external image. Roughly six hundred thousand kilometers out, there was a fading burst of light . . . and—he leaned closer, squinting. Then magnified to maximum and studied the dark spots mottling the burst of light. And the dark ring haloing behind it.

"Another gate," the XO muttered as he stared at the same display, then glanced at Domitas. "You were right."

"Zarense, study what came through and work out weapons solutions."

"Yes, Admiral," she replied. "But are we sure they're . . . unfriendly?"

"That many ships coming through a gate that, according to TSC records, doesn't exist and"—eyes still on Pount, he spoke over his shoulder—"Loren, have they declared themselves or an intent?"

A brief pause came as fingers ticked over the system. "Negative, sir. No declaration or identity."

He cocked a nod to the captain. "Unfriendly. We should start toward them. Whatever their intent, we don't need them getting in the middle of our efforts on Drosero."

"Helm," Pount declared, his expression hardening. "Bring us around and put us on an intercept course for the flagship of that fleet. Use point three light speed."

"Aye, Captain."

Domitas tapped the console, opening a communications channel with all the ships, save the *Macedon*. He met Pount's and Dimar's gazes, being sure they noted the exception. "This is Admiral Deken. We have detected the arrival of an unknown fleet on a direct course for Drosero. Since there has been no declaration of intent or identity, we should assume unfriendly status and expect trouble. The *Cronus* is moving to intercept." He looked to weapons. "Get those weapons warmed and ready, Lieutenant."

Domitas gripped the edge of the console, watching as the dots grew larger at a painfully slow pace that was also, in the scheme of life, too fast. *"Renette, they're here."*

"We know. My span has never ached so violently."

"Heard from Meijatsia via Lifespeech. She's injured but en route, too." Though he wasn't sure where, only that she'd told him to help Commander Jadon. She'd winked out before he could clarify her instructions or position. *"I'll hold them off as long as I can and wipe out as many as I can."*

"Thirtieth time's the charm, right?" Reef muttered to himself as he keyed in the release sequence for the hybrids' pods. At least, he hoped that's what he was doing. The last twenty-nine attempts had failed. "It really shouldn't be so hard to vent a bay."

He moved his fingers over the control, sliding the bars up . . . up . . . Gaze skipping up and over the bulkhead as a thrum radiated through the ship, he felt a hitch of hope. "C'mon . . . c'mon . . ." Slow and steady, he drew the bars to the top of the schematic.

Screech!

A jolt lurched him forward and the bars dropped to the bottom again. "Augh!" He banged the console in front of him. "Slag. Slag. Slag." Head down, he resisted the urge to whimper. Or shout. Maybe scream like a little girl. Instead, he gritted his teeth and scanned the arrays. Glanced at the medbay pod. It'd taken him a full day to find the readout for her pod.

"*O'TISH UCHUN O'N DAQIA.*"

Reef stilled at the computer-simulated voice—which had a crazy amount of trill in it—announcing ten minutes to the gate. Heart racing, he straightened. "There has to be a way to get the bay to vent. What am I doing wrong?"

"There are . . . safeguards."

"Augh!" Reef jerked around—only to be yanked back by his harness. He strained to see over his shoulder. "You're . . . alive."

Eija grimaced as she dragged herself into the crash couch next to his, her face dotted with sweat.

He focused on the array. "So . . . what'd you say? Safeguards?"

"Release controls to me."

"You sure you should be doing this? You don't look so hot."

"That would be because I'm freezing."

"So the lectulo . . ."

"Helped," she said around a wince.

But not healed. Was that what she was saying? Was she freezing because of a fever?

Eija nodded. "The safeguard's down. Vent it."

Reef flew through the steps and slid the bars up. The ship thrummed . . . He held his breath, anticipating the rejection of his commands. Instead, the hull vibrated hard. The rectangle that symbolized the bay went red. "It worked?"

Eija nodded.

He wanted to release his harness and check, but they were too close to the gate. "How d'you know?"

"I can't . . . sense them anymore." Her head bobbed, the effort of holding it up seeming a strain. "The Khatriza are . . . there. Ready . . . flip and burn, then . . . kill the . . . gate." Her breathing sounded heavy. "Watch for the Uchuvchi . . . They need . . . to get . . . Drosero."

"You got them?"

"Flagship . . ." She huffed. "You clear . . .?"

Really did not like how much she was struggling. "Roger that. Go back to the medpod."

She ignored him, her fingers jittering on her console.

"*Dorvazoni beshdon . . . ta'rtto . . . a'tkozing . . .*"

The countdown made his muscles tense. "This is so slagged."

With a *twang-pop*, they rushed out of the jumpstream. Felt a weightless, empty void that felt more about his soul hanging in zero g than his body.

Despite her condition, Eija never missed a beat. She piloted the ship around and launched a salvo that perfectly targeted and destroyed the gate. Which released its own firing solution before it erupted in a ball of fire that died as soon as it started.

Reef hissed as they worked together to evade the— "Particle beams!" He gaped. "TSC doesn't have that tech!"

Neither did TSC have the tech to evade the beams, but this ship did and executed the maneuvers beautifully.

"Set course . . . Drosero."

"Right."

"Good," she said, her voice hoarse.

Reef eyed her, flinching at how pale she was. "Eij—go back to the pod. Please."

"Too . . . late . . ."

"Eija!"

"It's what . . . you wanted." Her eyes drifted closed.

"No! Not this." He tried to flick his harness loose to force her back into the pod, but the ship wouldn't release him because of its auto-maneuvering. She was dying and he couldn't do a scuzzing thing about it.

"Reef . . . you are not alone," she said, and Voids if his heart didn't try to jump into his throat.

"Eija! No! L-look—we're back." Panic drummed against his heart. "Can't you fold to your Sisters? Save yourself. Go!"

"The *Cronus*," she said, blinking. "Find it for safe . . . haven. Admiral . . . knowsssss." Her breath hissed to its end. An alarm sounded from her seat, indicating flat biorhythms. She was gone.

WASTELANDS, KALONICA, DROSERO

She had wings and could fold, but little else. No sword. Limited ability to fly or navigate the air. And once more it saddened Kersei not to be of use to her people while they fought for their lives. The days spent with the Ladies had trained her first to yield her will. In essence, to get out of the way and allow the Ancient to work.

"*Sometimes, the best thing we can do in a fight is kneel. It stills our bodies, slows our hearts, calms our pulse. Once you get out of your own way, you will hear, see, and know what it is you are to do or not do,*" Triarii Cybele told the hastati while Kersei sat in the amphitheater watching, learning as much as she could in the short time she was there.

Kersei stopped in her pacing, realizing even then that the Trópos book . . . it had basically said the same thing—that the wearer of the brand would know what its purpose was.

Yet, I do not.

An urgency had spread through her as she read and nursed the children—truly, one of the most beautiful things she had experienced, this bonding with them, protecting them by helping them grow, keeping them safe with the Daughters. As Marco had wanted. Desperately, she had wanted to speak to him, talk of the brand. Then again, she feared what he would say, how he would react. He was not himself.

"You. Do. Not. Know. Me!" His growled remonstration again choked her thoughts. Demanded she think of his silver-white eyes. The rage there. The . . . desperation.

She *did* know him. Better than she had ever known anyone in her life— including herself. It had been evident from the first time she'd encountered him on Cenon. The fierce and mighty hunter. Always had he been intense and brooding. Of late he had been more . . . feral. His eyes, once so pure and blue, now pulsed with a savage fury.

"You have nothing to fear of me." Had she not?

And the brand deepened that. Gave her an insight that, in part, felt unfair. Yet . . . did he not have that Kynigos ability to smell what she felt? She harrumphed. Mayhap things were fair now. Most insidious was . . . this . . . this thing on his arm . . . How it changed him! His actions were so merciless, cruel. His anger virulent and controlling.

"O Ancient, please . . ." She shoved the heels of her hands to her face and paced in the meeting room of the large structure that served as a Command center. Feared losing Marco to this war, to the weapon consuming his body and adunatos. "Please help him!"

"You. Do. Not. Know. Me!"

The words kept prowling her heart and mind. Hurt her. She had given up on his love, finally finding peace with Darius and accepting that Marco was bound to Isaura. And nay, she had not thought of Marco since Darius's death—not in that way. Things were too strained, too raw. He was too wounded after Isaura's death. Focused on helping Aeliana survive, she had been terrified the little one would die. Terrified of what his daughter's death would do to him. That it would send him over the edge.

But that happened anyway.

This man who raged and found no compunction in obliterating men . . . that was not Marco. Regardless of what he claimed, evidence lay in his action, the way he denigrated her in front of others, shouted, disregarded the feelings of friends . . . The Marco she knew had not returned from that other galaxy or universe or whatever they had named it.

Could she be surprised, though? Considering what he had been through . . . His anger was born of wounds. So very many wounds.

Please, Ancient . . . Ladies . . . help me.

Around her, something was different. Altered. She lifted her head, and even as her eyes focused on the room, her heart slammed into her ribs to find someone standing at the door. "Marco." Dashing away the tears, she wondered how he had entered without her hearing or knowing. "I am glad you are come. I would speak to you of our brands."

"Later." He thrust back the canvas covering the entry. "Come outside. You have a decision to make."

A decision? Blinking, she stepped out into the full rise of the day and shielded her eyes as she took in the dozen or so men off to the side. "What is—"

"Over there." Gruffly, Marco nudged her on. "Ixion thought to end this on the battlefield, but this judgment is not his to deliver."

Judgment? Kersei frowned as the band of aerios parted for her. "I do not understand. To what does this tend?"

Hushak and Ixion held captives at rifle point. Heads down and covered with burlap, two prisoners knelt on the hard ground, hands bound behind their backs. Their clothing hinted at offworlders. Who was this?

Even as her stomach squirmed at the display, she noted Marco nod.

In response, the hoods were removed. A tall, thin man squinted up at her, his nostrils flaring. Eyes consumed with loathing.

It took a moment to connect that hate-filled gaze with one she had seen before. "Theon," she whispered.

He sneered. "You will all die and then I'll have—"

Ixion slammed the hilt of his dagger against the man's temple, pitching him sideways into the second prisoner.

That second faltered and tried to break his fall, but with both hands bound, it proved impossible. He fell aside, and his face was on full display.

Kersei hauled in a breath, shock erupting as she staggered backward. Felt her own rage, unable to forget his betrayal carved into her adunatos. "Rufio." She flung out a hand, catching a sleeve to steady herself.

A touch on her shoulder brought her gaze to Marco. "Is this too much?"

Aye. Terribly so. She drew up her courage and spine as the two prisoners were righted, and her anger rose to the fore. "Nay." She glared at the one responsible for her father's death. Lexina's. Adara's! "*How?*" she raged. "How could you betray your own blood to the skycrawlers?"

"Advancement is too big a task for most people," he snarled. "I did what I had to do to help Drosero."

"*Help?*" Kersei fumed. "Does this look like help? My father—your own brother—is dead at your hand! The Symmachians are slaughtering the rest of us!"

"And, like the coward he is, Rufio sat in his ship with the high lord and did nothing." Marco fisted his hand. Looked at her. Waited.

Only then did she recall his words—*you have a decision to make.* What decision sat before her? *Judgment,* he'd said . . .

Taking in the machitis around her, their expressions hungry for vengeance, their postures tense, Kersei began to feel a little ill. "What is this . . .?" In Marco's eyes, the answer she feared found birth. She shook her head. "No . . . This—"

Holding her gaze, Marco raised his arm at the high lord and fired.

"No!" Kersei jerked back as heat blazed past her and incinerated the iereas. Crying out, she turned and stumbled a few paces, nearly falling. Hands stabilized her.

Roman's visage was flat, blank as he held her. "Steady," he murmured.

Clutching at his arms, she knew the image of the high lord vanishing into ash would never leave her mind. "How can you let him do this?"

"Kersei," Marco said, his voice hollow, void of emotion—save one: command. "Your call." He dipped the weaponized arm at her uncle.

Over her shoulder, she gaped. Straightened. "What are you doing, Marco? It is not—"

"What will it be? Life or death?"

Trembling, Kersei shook her head, then faltered, fearing his anger. His retaliation. "No." She shook her head more urgently. "This is not right."

"I agree!" he barked. "He knew you were in the reminding chamber and did nothing. Knew that blast would kill my father and brother, your father, sisters, and yet he did nothing save flee like the coward he is. Your uncle is responsible for the deaths of over three hundred Kalonicans, people whose protection I am charged with. A moment ago, I heard your anger and grief. So tell me, Daughter of Stratios, how can you not demand justice?"

"This is not justice!"

Marco's smile went feral. "You're right. Not yet." He aimed at Rufio.

"No!" Kersei lunged, reaching for her uncle. Instead, her hand caught the fiery wake of the volley. An angry red trail seared her fingers and thumb. As the pain registered, then flared, as her uncle turned to ash, she screamed her horror.

"Kersei!" Marco rushed to her, his brow forever furrowed in that angry scowl.

"No!" Hand held to her chest, she scrambled from him. "Stay away!"

"Pharmakeia!" Roman shouted, sliding in and holding her arm steady against his large frame.

Tears burned as she gaped at Marco. "You are right—I do not know you!"

Roman's arms were firm and comforting, like his voice. "Easy, Kersei."

Chilling waves and nausea rolled over her. "I . . . I am going to be sick." She saw Marco turn and hulk off. And truly, she could not ascertain if the clammy sickness was because of the scald or the monster prowling the wastelands with a crown and black heart.

What have I become? What is happening to me?

Storming away, Marco felt a piece of him die, recalling as he ended Rufio. Saw Kersei's shock. Her lunging. Hand extending. The fire burning her hand. And then her scream . . . that agonized, soul-piercing scream that had a razor's edge, carving through his chest.

He stretched his neck. Kept moving away from the campfire. Away from the aerios. Down the narrowing crevasse of the gorge. Holding his right hand, he kneaded the cramp in his palm. Much like the one in the center of his body. He touched it and staggered.

No . . .

Faltering, he debated looking. Gripped the collar. Tugged it out. Peered down. And his gut roiled to find the *chirish* had spread over his entire torso. Patting his stomach, he traced it from his belly button . . . his ribs . . . around . . .

Reek—

Something impacted his back. Sent him sprawling into the canyon wall. Scored his cheek. Ever the fighter, he hauled his instincts and receptors into line. Sensed a strike. He dropped and rolled, hopping up, even as a fist sent him reeling.

Shocked to find his master confronting him, Marco stumbled. Used it to his advantage—or tried to. After all day fighting and taking injuries, he wasn't fast enough. An uppercut caught his jaw.

He landed with a thud. "Enough!" he roared, feeling warmth sliding down his lip.

"Is it?" Roman demanded, crowding over him, ever ready. "I don't think so. What I saw back there will take months to beat out of you!"

Growling, Marco arched his spine and hopped to his feet. Pitched to the side. The *chirish* altered his weight and made him feel lopsided, but he made himself straighten, defiant. "Just try!"

Roman frowned, then slowly slung his head side to side. "Never have I seen you so far from your right course."

"My right course?" Marco hissed. "I don't have one. It was taken from me." He held his arms out to the side. "This? *This* is the Progenitor."

"No." Roman advanced. "*This* is bitterness. This is—"

"Sire!" An aerios raced up to them. "Sire, the Symmachians—they're dropping more troops."

Marco's gaze shot skyward, where a ship broke atmo, descended, got hit with a pulse, then slid in for a landing. Then another. And another. "Holy Fires," he whispered. "Why would they do that when they know the ships will only crash?"

"They don't care about the ships. They only care about winning, and that requires troop presence on the ground."

Marco watched another ship clear atmo as an idea forced its way into his thoughts. "Or because they expected it to make it to ground."

"What do y—" Roman's eyes widened.

"The towers."

Pop! Boom-boom-boom!

The earth rattled and trembled beneath his boots.

Marco swung around, scanning the direction the sound had come from—north. In the far distance, he saw a column of smoke. "The tower." He sprinted back to the camp. "Tigo!" He searched for the commander among those around the fire. "Where's Tigo?"

"Here!" The commander hustled toward him.

"Was that the tower they took out?"

"Wondering the same, so I asked Jez to find out." Tigo's cheek twitched with irritation. "It seems like the right location, and if they used explosives . . ." He looked south, as if he could see the tower that far away. "Jez should be—"

"They hit the tower," she breathed, appearing at his side. "Disabled it."

Tigo staggered to the side, uttering an oath, glowering at her.

Wings dusting the air, Jez seemed unfazed at how she'd startled him. "Slice lost two of his team, but he's already working on repairs. He's not sure he can get it working again, but he's trying. The other three towers are still working—for now."

Tigo pulled out a flex screen and swiped a hand over it. "Still dead. That's a good sign. We should be okay as long as the other three stay."

"Should?"

"It's never been used on planetary scale, so the logistics and data are experimental." Tigo roughed a hand over his face. "But I know Baric—if he sent one team to this tower, he sent teams to the others as well."

"We should send more troops to them," someone said.

"They'd never reach them in time," Tigo said. "But Jez and I could go."

Marco considered him. Remembered seeing Jez on the battlefield. "I'd hate to lose two swords here, but I think you're right." He eyed the Faa'Cris. "It'd be nice if the Daughters would actually help."

"Alanathina said—"

"I know: 'This is not our war.'" He grunted. "It wasn't my war either, until they put this brand on my arm." Marco felt unusually exposed in the middle of this group, as if they could discern the lavalike transformation happening beneath his tunic and armor. He prayed they couldn't.

"We cannot lose that EMP field," Ixion said.

"Agreed." Tigo squinted at them. "We knew that when they went up—it was a stop-gap measure, but Jez and I will make it last as long as we can."

With that, Jez stepped and they both vanished.

"That is . . . unsettling," Hushak said.

"Not as much as this." When would they stop sending ships? They'd lost two already . . . But either way, there were more troops here. More to fight. More to slay Droserans.

Marco knew he had failed as Progenitor. "We're going to be slaughtered."

HIRAKYS, DROSERO

Tigo blinked and he stood in a jungle.

The man working the tower dropped a tool and jumped back. "Slag!"

As the guy snatched the tool and went back to work, Tigo couldn't help his smile. Diggins had been his right hand on the 215. "Soil your pants, Diggs?"

"You can go to the Pyres," Diggs muttered.

"Can't believe they got you to come out of the Academy for this."

"Had a fundamental difference of opinion on the direction of HyPE. When I walked, your father talked. Waved me, asked if I was done sitting on my butt."

"Were you?" Tigo laughed, glancing around.

"I'm here, aren't I?"

The terrain around them was so vastly different from the one he'd been fighting on. The wastelands were dry, hot, and flat. This island wasn't entirely flat, and was more jungle, complete with the ninety percent humidity.

"Had any trouble?"

"Yeah. I'm talking to you." Diggs crouched and grabbed a different tool. "But if you mean with the tower—why d'you think I'm working on it?"

"I meant if you've been attacked. Where's the rest of your team?" Something thumped Tigo's chest, mud splatting his shirt. "What the—"

"You remember Neurotic." Diggs tightened a wire.

Tigo smiled, wiping the mud from his shirt. Jannsie Nurotsia from Metraxis 12 had been a quick riser in the Eidolon ranks. "Nice shot," he said to the thick vegetation, knowing she was likely staring at him through her scope. Rifle wouldn't work with the towers operational, but scopes didn't need tech, though it sure was nice with laser-guided ammo.

"So," Diggs said, replacing the panel. "What made you come down off your high horse?"

"Wanted to drag you off yours."

Diggs snickered. "Fair." He turned and nodded. "Sidra."

She gave the barest of nods. "The Kalonican tower was just taken out."

"Yeah." Diggs thumbed over his shoulder. "Had to do some modifications here to compensate." He gestured out into the jungle. "That's why the team is out there."

"Smart." Tigo extended his hand. "Proud to—"

Thwap. Thwap-thwap.

At the sound of weapons' fire, Tigo dove for cover, the others doing the same.

"I'll be back," Jez said as she folded.

"Great," he replied. *"Now I have no one to hide behind."*

"Psst."

Tigo angled toward Diggs, barely sighting a weapon sailing through the air. He snagged it, racked the slide of the old-world weapon, chambering a round. "Now we're talking. How many rounds?"

"High capacity."

"Symmachian or Rhiantan?"

"Nobody uses R-slugs anymore."

True, but nobody used old-world weapons either, and here they were. So. Thirty rounds. Should be able to make sure nobody destroyed the tower. With one down, they couldn't afford to lose another.

Hunkered to the side of the tower and outside the shielding, Tigo waited.

Click-thump.

Thud.

Pop-pop. Pop pop pop!

The last round was closer.

"Stand down!" It sounded like Neurotic. "I said stand dow—"

Thump. That would be the sound of her going down.

Slag. Tigo steadied himself, closing his eyes, listening. Wishing for a mech-suit to guide him. Rustling and a soft crunch pushed his gaze slightly right.

There, behind a trunk, two black-and-gold shapes.

Stealthily, he raised his weapon. Stared down the sights. Hated old-world sights. Unreliable. But he'd been trained on them, as all Eidolon had. For instances like this.

He drew in a breath, expelled it as his finger eased back the—

Jez was suddenly behind the shorter Eidolon. Her blade sang in the thick air, deadly, severing the head from the body.

The other Eidolon sprang forward, his weapon—an old-world long gun—aimed straight at the canopy.

Shock nearly choked Tigo. "Cleve!"

Skidding to a stop, eyes wild with determination and accusation, Arkin Cleve grinned at Tigo and unloaded his weapon on the tower.

Tigo did the same—but unloading on Cleve, aiming for that small head. Too small, if anyone asked him. A bullet struck. Another. Knocked Cleve sideways. He yanked back up, blood sliding down his eyes and cheek as he tried to aim again.

Lunging out, Tigo rapid-fired at his old nemesis. But the guy swung around, a spray of ammo peppering the thick, waxy leaves. Ducking, Tigo fired several bursts until Cleve crumpled to the ground like a dirty PT rag. Boot on the guy's chest, he stared down at him. "I've wanted to do that for a very long time."

Cleve smirked, blood pooling in his mouth. "Too late . . ."

Glad to see the light fade from the guy's eyes, Tigo wondered what he'd meant. And why the scuz did his head feel so heavy?

"Tigo!" Jez blurred into view, her expression contorted in panic. "No!"

"What?" Maybe that was him blurring. "I . . ." He frowned. "Why are you upside down?"

"Shut up. Keep still." Her beautiful lips said more he didn't hear. She shifted him, her voice warbling. It sounded a lot like she said he'd eaten a bullet. Her expression waxed soft but panicked. "I've got you."

The sky fell to the ground. Day became night and locked him in its icy brig.

44

DEVERSORIA

His adunatos was fading with each step she took. He would die before she reached the sanitatem. With Tigo in her arms, Jez folded back into Deversoria before the great stone bath. She used her boot to catch the lever.

"No, Rejeztia. No more foundlings. It is not our responsibility."

Ignoring the Revered Mother, she laid Tigo in the sanitatem.

"I told you—"

"If it is not ours, then whose?" Jez adjusted him in the basin so his head was in place for the oxygen snakes to reach his nostrils. "We are their guardians, yet we do not guard."

Irritation flashed through Alanathina. "There are things of which you are not aware—"

"Delay me further and he will die." Without a care for the disapproval, she hit the panel and watched the djell cocoon him. Touched his brown hair, avoiding the bullet hole that threatened to end his life.

Sadness wreathed the blue eyes and somber expression of the Revered Mother. "He is already dead, Rejeztia."

Shaking, she swallowed. "No."

"You sense it—his force gone. It's why you aren't arguing or attacking."

Anger spinning up, she struggled for a breath that did not hurt. "You stole the last man I loved. I will not be robbed of him as I was robbed of Jaigh's love." She shoved past the Revered Mother and palmed the lid. "Come back to me, Tigo." Tears rushed down her cheeks. "You are the best thing that has ever happened to me . . . and that's a lot of happenings." She touched his ear. His shoulder. "Please . . . don't make me beg."

Crying harder, she leaned into the sanitatem as the djell slid over his chest. "Come back. Tell me what I'm doing wrong. Because I am not supposed to love you." She squeezed her eyes against the tears and grief. "But I do. So very much. Do you hear me?" Breath shuddered through her as she entered the final sequence to seal the sanitatem.

As the lid closed, stone ground against stone, a sound that mirrored the ache of her adunatos.

"I love you. Come on!" she growled. "Tell me I don't know what love is. That I wouldn't see if it hit me on the lips!"

The djell climbed his throat . . . his chin . . .

She choked out a sob. "Tigo!"

It slid over his face, embraced him. "Come back to me, Tigo. Please!"

WASTELANDS, KALONICA, DROSERO

Had he not done this already? Come out to battle, incinerated raider after raider? Eidolon after Eidolon? Symmachian after Symmachian? Yet here he was, fighting, ever fighting, fatigued and angry. Around him rose and fell the Signatures of tired Droserans, drenched in exhaustion and grief, hopelessness. After the executions, after what he'd done to Kersei—the abhorrence in his men's eyes—Marco shared their despair.

The *chirish* was claiming him. And yet he was more accurate and relentless than ever. A good thing, was it not? Killing more Symmachians—definitely good. He veered to the side and aimed—a tightness in his spine and neck as he lobbed another shot. Another combatant down. His legs tangled and he struggled to stay upright.

Shouts carried across the wastelands. He looked to the sky as yet another ship crash-landed. As his gaze fell to the battle, to the . . . *Wait* . . . His heart fell as it dawned on him that the line of Droserans in some places was only one man deep. Beyond that, only Symmachians, Eidolon. Pushing harder toward him. Toward the camp. Miraculously, his men and the weapon had kept him safe.

Where . . . where were the rest of the Kalonican armies? He came around and spotted Ixion, shoulders stooped, head down and his white hair stained with blood, trudging toward him. "Have our men gone to camp?" It seemed to take so much energy just to talk.

"Nay," Ixion growled. "I know not the state of the other deployments, but we are overrun here." He spat blood to the side. "They are still dropping troops, and we have no replacements. We"—weariness darkened his gray eyes—"are lost."

Marco had known it. Felt it. Smelled the overwhelming stench of Symmachia drowning the lands, butchering Droserans. *I led them to their deaths.*

His First stalked toward him. "I have come to take you to safety. You must call a retreat to the gorge. There we can defend the funnel, hold out longer."

Marco started. "You would have me hide when my people are dying in droves? No!"

"Please, Marco."

That his First used his given name startled him. Once more, he looked out over what he could see of the plain. Two men . . . Eidolons took them down. "We can't . . . They will win."

"If we do not fall back, they have," Ixion growled. "I will not lose you as—"

Something warm and wet hit Marco's cheek. He cast about, searching for the source as he wiped his face. His fingertips came away red. "Wha . . .?" A heavy grunt from the side yanked him around.

The Stalker went to a knee, head bowed . . . tilting . . . forward. His entire body slumped. When he wobbled, grunting a breath, and could not stop himself from falling to the side, that's when Marco saw it—his arm. Gone!

Blood gushed from the wound.

"Ixion!" Marco dived to catch his First. Narrowly prevented him from colliding with rock and dirt. "Medic!" He yanked off his belt even as he searched the camp. Saw Hushak and Shobi already sprinting toward them, Roman behind them. Quickly, Marco used the belt to do his best to bind off the stump, hands slicking with his First's spilling lifeforce.

"Augh!" Ixion contorted as the leather constricted.

Though the blood slowed, with the severity and location of the wound, it was impossible to stop.

"Sir," Hushak said, face wrought as he went to a knee beside his elder. "I—" The man inexplicably vaulted backward. Landed with a thud . . . a gaping hole. He stared skyward, sightless. Dead.

Marco cursed. "Pull them back! Tell our army to fall back!" He shoved up under Ixion, and together with the others, rushed him back to camp. A handful of Stalkers and Kynigos protected their six as they moved.

Legs rubbery, Marco shuffle-ran, his gaze dropping. His body drooping. Ixion's head hung down, his neck bared to the darkening sky. His eyes closed. Face ghostly pale.

Don't do it, Marco warned him. *Don't you dare die.*

He could not lose another. Not today. He needed this man. Trusted him. Respected him. Like a brother, even if they were in each other's faces a lot.

"Here, my lord!" the pharmakeia shouted from a dwelling. "In here."

Inside, they lowered him to a table—and the other Kynigos shifted too fast. Ixion thudded against the wood. The jarring snapped him conscious. "Augh!" His howl raked Marco's adunatos.

The grim-faced pharmakeia scowled at the gaping wound.

"Do something!" Marco demanded.

"I . . . I can't. The wound—he is losing too much blood too fast."

"Stop it!"

"Fire!" Roman shouted. "Bring a torch."

"They're snuffed out," someone muttered. "No fire . . . no food . . . The people of Ancra have fled."

"Do something or so help me," Marco hissed. His hand caught, and he glanced down—surprised to find Ixion's bloody grip around his. He looked to his First. "Don't worry, we'll—"

"Your weapon," Ixion panted. Foam coated the corners of his mouth as he arched his back and howled, then settled, his eyes refocusing on Marco. "Use your weapon."

The weapon-arm . . .? What— *Oh.* The thought made him sick. "No—it's—"

"Do it," Ixion growled. "Or on your head be my death as well." He sagged, his breathing going labored.

"He's dying," the pharmakeia said.

"Do it, Marco," Roman snapped. "For once, use that thing to save someone, not incinerate them."

Pulling in a hard breath, he considered Ixion, the wound, then let the shaky breath tremor out. It would take a precise shot . . . He had not been forced to control it to any extent until now . . . Swallowing, nodded to the pharmakeia. "Ready salves and ointments—whatever you have for burns." He tore what was left of Ixion's sleeve and tunic away.

White-faced, the pharmakeia rushed out.

Roman grabbed the wood handle of a medical tool and glanced to Shobi. "Hold him down."

Bleeding plague of the apocalypse. Was he really going to do this?

Don't, and he dies.

Do, and he might die.

Bending over and looking into his First's eyes, he gave a grim nod. "Bite down."

The pharmakeia darted back in with supplies. Lifted a steel pike and nodded his readiness.

Marco cocked his head. Worked up the anger—enough existed watching his First go down. Blood spilling into the wastelands. He looked into gray eyes that were fading . . . Ixion was fading. Dying.

Balling his fist, he angled to the side. Pressed a hand on the leathered chest and begged Vaqar to make this work. Couldn't be a short burst. He had to be sure the skin melted. The heat warbled and surged. Rapidly, he contracted his fist and arm, firing off a shot.

It seared, flesh sizzling and burning. The acrid scent filling the air.

Ixion roared as the flame warbled and continued, the pharmakeia pressing the pike into the stream and forcing the skin to fold and meld.

The smell . . . *Holy Fires!* Trying to not inhale and have the taste of his First's burning flesh in his mouth, Marco focused. Ignored the howls. Tried to, at least. Didn't work.

Finally, the agony too much, Ixion collapsed. Silent. Unmoving.

Marco snapped his gaze to the pharmakeia, then Roman.

The master checked Ixion's pulse. "Faint, but still there."

"Done," the pharmakeia said, switching the pike for the other supplies.

The reek of Ixion's burnt flesh coated Marco's receptors. He stumbled out of the hut, hand over his mouth. Stomach heaving. He scrambled around the side and puked. Slumped back against the wall. Felt the friction of the *chirish* along his spine with the clay. Waiting for his gut to settle, he spat the rancid taste out. Braced against the wall, exhausted. Angry. Frustrated.

Somehow Kersei was with him, dropping to her knees, a waterskin in hand. She extended it.

He turned away. Couldn't face her. Didn't want to face any of them.

Sitting on her legs, she stayed there.

Marco pushed his gaze to the sky, where stars were beginning to appear. Symmachia was taking over the planet. They'd wipe out the existence people knew here on Drosero. Those they didn't kill, they'd oppress and subjugate. What was going to happen? How would he die?

And that creature, Xisya . . . Coming from Kuru. Where she'd turned men into beasts. *Just like me.* It was her tech, her machinations . . .

He growled, imagining her winning. Doing here as they had done to

Kuru. Anger churned and tossed his thoughts, his gut. Raged through him, the weapon pulsing, demanding he do something.

Her touch on his shoulder was light. "Truly, I am sorry."

Those words, coming from Kersei . . . So wrong. He grunted, shaking his head. "How . . . how is your hand?"

She angled the top to show him the inflamed part. "It will heal."

Detesting himself, he hung his head. Wiped his mouth again. "I—"

"Uchuvchi."

He snapped his gaze up and found Daq'Ti standing there. A sickening revulsion swept Marco. "You . . . It's your fault." He was on his feet, anger and shame roiling through his gut. "If you hadn't boarded our ship, taken me onto that dreadnought . . . If you hadn't led the coup to get off that ship, I wouldn't have this!" He brandished his weapon-arm. "People wouldn't hate me. I wouldn't be a cauterizing agent!"

"I told you to let it go." Daq'Ti's dark eyes radiated a sharp compassion that was thick with remonstration. He thumped Marco's chest. "It only makes dead what is living. It is bad. Makes you bad!"

"Say that again!" Weapon warbling, Marco raised it to Daq'Ti's face. "Say it again. Do it!"

"Marco!" Kersei gaped.

The Draegis shoved him backward.

Marco lunged. Aimed. Saw the heat and reveled in it.

"Marco, *no*!" Kersei threw herself between them, tripping and catching herself against his abdomen, gained traction to hold him back, shouting, crying. "Please, no. Stop! No!"

Light erupted, making the shadows bright as day. The flare punched Marco in the gut—right where Kersei had struck. He felt that lit hand reach up his stomach, sear past his lungs, and grip his heart. Choke his breath.

"Augh!" Gargling a howl, Marco staggered. He could not breathe. Could not move. Could not speak. In stark terror, as if he were held in the clutch of a powerful giant, he canted forward.

"M-Marco. Marco!" Kersei moved into him, and he fell against her shoulder.

His nose in her hair, he groaned. Could not think around the agony.

Her hand with that white-hot Touch rested on his stomach. The other found the back of his head. "Marco! I . . . I beg your mercy. I did not mean—"

"Help the medora!" came a shout.

The weapon . . . his arm went cold . . . icy cold. With a soft thump, something hit the ground. His eyes met Kersei's, her panic wild. His fury . . . bottomed out. "What have you done?" he wheezed, still paralyzed beneath that Touch.

Light exploded in the sky.

Though he could not move his limbs or speak or even breathe, Marco's gaze found the black. Only it wasn't black. A swirl of stars vomited a fleet into orbit.

No. No no no.

Eija had failed. The Khatriza had come.

And he now had failed. Had no way to fight them. No weapon. No will.

TSC-C *CRONUS*, DROSERAN ORBIT

Sweating out the hours as the distance erased between the *Cronus* and the alien fleet, Domitas had no trouble detecting the unusual stench of the Corrupt. The Faa'Cris had their idiosyncrasies, but these creatures . . .? Evil personified.

The display arrays spasmed to life with the alien fleet. There was a slight delay as the ship's systems processed and cataloged what it saw, throwing it onto the virtual screen and into something meaningful for the crew to work. Reasonable warship velocity would put the aliens in orbit in under twenty-three hours. However, this fleet—what should've taken them two days to traverse had taken a matter of hours.

"Time to intercept?" Domitas again looked at the external display, the ships noticeably bigger. The arrays were now more precise in identifying the component parts of this fleet. Surrounding the flagship, which looked to be carrier-class, sailed five battle cruisers, each easily the size of the *Macedon*. Behind them, seven somewhat bulky midsize ships brought up the rear.

"Twenty minutes, sir."

"Bring the ship to general quarters," Pount announced, "and full combat readiness. Bridge crew, survival suits." He glanced at Domitas with a nod.

"But who are they, sir? Who are we going after?" Lieutenant Loren gaped at him.

"More of Xisya's kind."

"How do you know that?"

Irritated with the questions, he knew they had to be answered. He'd handpicked this crew for a reason—their ability to think, exercise logic.

"The gate," Dimar answered. "They knew how to use it and where it'd lead them. Coming through with an entire armada kinda tells you they're not friendly."

Hackles raised at seeing those monsters come home to roost, Domitas flicked his fingers, activating the external display. There was no doubt why they were here—as a Do'St, he knew that. He thumbed the control and opened a channel to send out a broadcast message to the alien fleet. "Unknown armada that just came through our gate, this is Admiral Deken of the Tascan Command Fleet. Declare yourself and your intentions in our Quadrants."

He settled in his crash couch and thumbed his lower lip, waiting. Excitement drummed on his chest. It was here. All those years—decades— of biding his time . . . This was why he had endured the regime. The games. The impudence.

"Sir, messages from the *Argus* and *Apelles* wanting to know what we're doing."

Let them wonder. He had wondered about their idiocy for years. "Any response from the aliens?"

"No, sir," Loren said.

He thumbed the channel again. "Alien fleet, this is Admiral Deken of the *Cronus* and Tascan Fleet. You are ordered to brake velocity and power down. If you do not, we will be forced to fire upon you." He nodded to Pount. "Target the three lead ships for a simultaneous barrage."

Tension thrummed through the bridge, suppressing noise and chatter, dropping them into a strange silence.

Pount donned his suit and refocused. "Should we use disabling shots?"

"Captain, at our relative velocity," Domitas said, "no guarantee exists of any shot only being 'disabling.'" He huffed. "No, we're going to make sure we're not misunderstood. Lock solutions."

"You're sure about this response?"

Domitas eyed Pount. "Never been surer." He stroked his beard, feeling the calm that only came with radical commitment. "Recall, Captain, that these are the same creatures who developed the Engram, the same race torturing Kynigos—all things I have heard you voice dissent over. They've just jumped into the Quadrants, silent and unannounced. Not responding to waves." Though he addressed Pount, Domitas knew the rest of the crew needed to hear this. "Now, does that sound like they're just here to talk?"

Jaw muscle working, the captain straightened. "Firing solutions locked. On your mark, Admiral." He gave Domitas one more look. "You realize, the fleet—"

"I'm not worried about them. I know what I have to do."

"Sir," Zarense said, "the lead alien ship is one light second distant and not maneuvering."

"They're coming straight at us," Dimar muttered.

Domitas could feel it—the creature in charge of that ship. Knew she could sense him as much as he could sense her. Knew she wanted him dead as much as he wanted her dead. "Collision course."

"Yes, sir. They're—" Zarense hauled in a breath. "Main propulsion has lit off."

Accelerating. To ram the *Cronus*.

Domitas nodded to Pount.

"All batteries engage. You are weapons free."

"Sir, *Argus* and *Apelles* again request an explanation, and the *Titan* wants to know what's going on and if we need assistance."

Amazing how loyalties changed. The Xenocouncil had sought to exclude him and outmaneuver him, and now that they saw the threat the creature was, they were ready to listen.

"Update the *Titan* on what we know and tell them to join us."

"Ship One," Pount announced, "has slowed and weapons are coming online. The smaller ships are accelerating all out."

"Admiral!" Dimar nearly shouted. "The large craft—sir, dozens of small fast-attack crafts are vomiting from it."

"Keep firing! Give them everything we've got." He thumbed up the communications channel. "Ar—"

"Admiral"—Pount leaned toward him from his own chair—"there's an anomaly. Take a look." He flicked the frame to Domitas's array.

A midsize alien ship broke away from the others, arced in a wide curve, and unleashed its payload on its fellows. Jadon. Domitas finally understood what Meijatsia meant.

"It's attacking its own fleet," the XO balked. "Incoming fire!"

"We'll take all the help we can get," Pount said. "What damage are we causing?"

Domitas opened a communications channel to the nearest light cruiser. "*Damocles*, this is Admiral Deken."

"Sir, what the Voids—"

"Krissos, that is the Khatriza fleet, and they are not here to play nice. Bring your ship around and provide protection to that anomaly ship attacking its own. It is piloted by our own Eidolon, Commander Jadon." He then opened up a fleet-wide channel. "This is Admiral Deken. You are ordered to intercept the fleet that just came through. They are Khatriza and their endgame is our eradication. Deken out."

"Two minutes to impact!"

"Those little ships are like piranhas. Fast, maneuverable, and targeting our smaller ships, sir."

"What's happening with the hive ship?" Domitas asked.

"Nothing, sir. It's slowed and firing, but the barrage does not seem to be focused."

Domitas growled, eyeing the array. "Pay attention to the piranhas. They could become a problem." But then he had another thought and opened a channel. "*Apelles*, this is Admiral Deken. I want all your targeting solutions on that carrier. I have a feeling if we destroy it, those piranha ships might go dead in the water."

"*IMPACT IN TEN . . . NINE . . .*"

"Brace, brace, brace," Pount broadcast ship-wide.

The impact rattled through the hull and made Domitas's head throb. The barrage continued, one shot after another. The *Cronus* was a beast of a ship, its hull triple-reinforced with a strong but lightweight material. Multiple systems worked to deflect and fire countermeasures to draw ordnance off course, detonating far enough away to not cause irreparable damage. Yet still some got through.

"Damage reports," Pount demanded.

As the reports came in, Domitas watched the array. The small ships were barreling in now. And behind those, there was a second wave of midsize ships like the one Jadon was on.

"Sir, we have a message from one of the alien ships," Loren said, frowning as she listened, then her eyes brightened. "It's Jadon!"

"Give him to me." Domitas thumbed the channel. "This is Admiral Deken."

"Sir, Commander Jadon here, Eidolon Two-six-eight Beta, sir."

"Welcome back, Jadon."

"Thank you, sir. Not sure it's good to be back, but . . . Look, I don't know if you can see my ship, but the others like mine? You need to destroy every last one, sir. They're filled with what are basically assault troops—hybrid Draegis. They're the worst of the worst. My guess is they're headed for Drosero. Do yourself a favor and obliterate them."

Domitas bounced his gaze to the array. "The first line is distraction," he realized.

Pount nodded. "To keep us busy while the real trouble hits Drosero."

"Can you dodge the first line?"

"They're fast but they're . . . clunky. Impressive thrust-to-mass ratio." Pount shrugged. "It'll take expert handling."

Domitas waited. "Are you that expert?"

Pount almost grinned. "We'll find out."

"Captain has maneuvering," Domitas announced.

"All hands brace for heavy maneuvering!"

"He's gone—"

Jez whirled upward, her blade in hand, not sure how long she had sat against the bath of the sacred waters, praying, begging the Ancient for Tigo's life. "He's Do'St!"

Alanathina held up her hands. "Yes, Do'St. But not immortal."

Feeling the fury in her veins, she stared at the Revered Mother. "You are wrong. And cruel. To leave them to these butchers!"

"Symmachia and Drosero are both butchers in their own way. Would you not agree, after witnessing how Marco has fallen so far from the path laid out for him?"

"No, I will not. He has done the best he can with the limited tools available. As they all have. As Tigo did." She squared her stance and tucked her chin. *"Pro vita sua do mea—"*

For his life, I give mine, was no small commitment, but she meant it.

"Rejeztia, don't! *Think*!" Alanathina hurried forward. "Think what you are doing! Giving up your gifts for his life—it is an imbalance and impractical."

Jez lifted her blade, staying the Revered Mother's progress, glowering at her, daring her to tempt her blade. *"Ambulare cum eo in hoc primo plano."*

They had walked many earthly planes together, and she did not want that to end.

"By giving up centuries of experience, you put the focus on yourself and reject what the Ancient tasked us to do—protect the people."

"Which you are not doing! I did what you asked—I went with him, explored the options. Talked to the Do'St I could find," Jez roared. "And still you deem them unworthy. You sit in this Sacred City in arrogance and superiority, doing nothing." She held up her hand. "We have power to help them, and we do nothing! It. Must. Change!"

"I agree."

The voice came from behind, and Jez turned on her heels. "Magna Domine."

She took a knee and inclined her head. "I beg your mercy—"

"Why?" Eleftheria touched Jez's chin and brought her upright. "You have done what was ordained. You and Tigo helped reset the Faa'Cris on the path they were chosen for." She motioned behind Jez. "It is time."

What she saw stunned her. Stopped her. "What . . . what is this?"

Her Sisters, every Daughter who bore the rank of triarii or above stood there, spilling out of the hall and down the passage. Armored. Ready.

Had they come to arrest her? All of them?

She eyed the Revered Mother. "He dies and *now* you are prepared to do something?"

"Would you let his death be in vain?"

Jez tightened her jaw. "No."

Alanathina gave a nod. "Then let us war."

TSC-C *CRONUS*, DROSERAN ORBIT

Death rattle. *Cronus* shuddered beneath the bombardment, the weaker shields failing and shots penetrating. The same was true across the fleet.

Domitas bounced his gaze between the external displays. Saw a bright flash. "XO, what was that?"

"One of their transport ships is destroyed, sir!"

"Let's repeat that."

"Copy that, sir."

Again, he eyed the array that showed fleet placement. Saw the *Argus* stagger beneath a swarm of the piranha fast-attack crafts. His span ached with the presence of those things, and in him burned a vengeful fury to annihilate these creatures, a true diabolus.

Captain Pount gave a stream of orders that brought them around and slightly behind a transport and fired.

"Enemy ship showing multiple explosions—*Down!*"

Shouts went up across the bridge, the victory invigorating them.

"Sir," Loren called, "wave from the *Argus*. They have sustained heavy damage and are pulling out. The *Damocles* says—"

"Slag!" Dimar shouted. "*Damocles* is destroyed!" He stared open-mouthed at the array.

Domitas kept his gaze on the incoming Khatriza ships.

"Sir, the *Macedon* is moving away."

"No!" Domitas swung his chair around to the console and flicked his fingers, establishing firing solutions and locks on the battlecruiser. "*Macedon* does not leave."

Lieutenant Loren froze. "Sir?"

"The *Macedon* started this—that monster Xisya is responsible for all this. It's her infestation—she's a queen to these things. She does not get to walk." His clypeus thrummed with a need to respond to her presence here. "Lieutenant Zarense, if you see anything—a pod, a scout, anything eject from that ship, you fire and keep firing until there is nothing left. I've created a firing solution on Baric—if the *Macedon* tries to leave, we take it out."

Silence clanged through the bridge as the orders were processed.

"Sir," Captain Pount spoke up quietly, "since I am second-in-command here, I feel it's my responsibility to question that order, sir."

"Objection note—"

Boom. Boom!

The *Cronus* shuddered and slowed.

"Damage aft, Admiral. Main propulsion is down."

"Fire Control reports primary systems down. Secondary are online."

Even with the damage distraction, Domitas noticed the lieutenant had failed to confirm his orders. "Am I clear, Zarense?"

Her gaze skipped to the XO and captain even as another death rattle hit. "Aye, Admiral." The hull vibration and damages reported entered the thick tension.

"Sir?" Loren said in more of a squeak. "Message from the *Macedon*."

A sneer snaked through Domitas's mood. "Ignore it. My orders hold." There was a reason he'd handpicked the officers on this bridge for the new flagship—together, they'd been through engagements before, so he knew trust flowed both ways.

He saw a half dozen alien transports break away. Saw the anomaly ship enduring a heavy bombardment, no doubt a retaliation for attacking them. But then in swung more piranhas . . . a dozen, perhaps, firing on the transports and other piranhas strafing the anomaly ship. What in the Voids . . .?

Domitas wanted to help Jadon, but he had to address those four transports.

"Destroy those transports. Do not let them get past the fleet." He thumbed a communications channel. "*Crius* and *Titan*, brake velocity to maximum sustainable rate. Once those aliens sail past, target starboard and port— destroy them."

"Sir, the *Apelles* is hailing you."

Domitas nodded. "Admiral Waring."

"*Cronus*, we are heavily damaged. No shields. We have to abandon ship."

"Eject life pods," Domitas ordered. "But send everything you have before then."

"Yes . . . okay . . ." There was one thing Emesyn Waring wasn't— unconfident—yet that's all she now exuded. "Domitas, I . . . I can't understand it. We . . . we helped them. Built the gates."

Domitas grunted his agreement. "Like gullible idiots."

"I thought . . . we were allies. Why are they attacking us?"

"The only thing we are to them is expendable."

"They're . . . evil."

"Waring, get off that ship before it's too late. Send the order down the fleet." Grateful they finally saw the light, Domitas still needed them to send their full payloads before they were taken out or forced to abandon the fight. Because whatever landed on Drosero would make the Symmachian invasion look like a Baru Festival parade.

"Sir! Two enemy transports broke around us. They've made it into the atmosphere."

WASTELANDS, KALONICA, DROSERO

It felt as if his insides had been ripped out, rearranged, and put back in. And the physical pain was nothing to the thoughts haunting Marco as he lay curled on the cot, groaning. The weapon was gone. He had no means to fight the Khatriza. No chance . . .

"Water, sire?"

"No."

"Food?"

He groaned.

"I have blankets—"

"Out! Leave me!"

Finally alone in the darkness, Marco gripped his head. Shivered. Whatever Kersei had done . . .

He recalled when she had Touched the man in Lampros City. The light. The explosion. Just as Eija had with Daq'Ti.

Voids. Was that what Kersei had done to him—the *Ovqatlanish*. Taming.

Thoughts heavy, he lifted his shirt. Marveled at the mark in the center of his chest. Would it alter him the way Eija's had altered Daq'Ti? The thought repulsed him. He would not be slave to Kersei.

He was still Isaura's. But . . . it . . . There was a change. A shift. As if a veil had been pulled back on his heart, his life, his actions. Acute grief riddled him over his behavior. The lives he'd taken with the weapon. The darkness he'd let consume him. The cruelty with which he'd rejected so many. The callous words and temperament.

He paced, sorting through his feelings, the grief that overwhelmed him. *Isaura* . . . He slid down the wall and held his head again, unable to hold back the sobs. "Isaura!"

His beauty. His kyria.

Crying so hard his eyes felt they might burst, he struggled for air. He had not allowed himself to grieve. Blamed himself for that. Hated himself. And then— "Aeliana." Choking on the grief, he wagged his head. Banged it against the wall. What had he done? How could he have been so . . . merciless?

Galen.

Was it a just judgment? He knew not. "Forgive me," he whispered.

Rufio. Theon.

Undeniably they all deserved to be punished for their actions, but was it his place to mete it out? He knew not. Only that the rot which had eaten his adunatos put him in the wrong because he craved violence. Not justice.

But . . . Isaura . . . Aeliana . . . He slumped against the dirt and cried for them. *My aetos . . . little one . . . forgive me.*

Light stabbed his eyes. "Leave me!"

"Always were a grump when you first woke."

He groaned and stayed in the dirt for a while, then slowly dragged himself onto his knees. "Master." He pulled himself off the floor and dropped onto the cot, throbbing head in his hands.

Something pressed against his knuckles. "Drink. It's cordi."

"No," Marco said. "I . . . I'll be sick again."

Not one to be cowed by Marco's bad moods, Roman knelt at his cot. Held out something in the palm of his hand.

Shivering, Marco couldn't focus.

"It fell from your arm when . . . Kersei . . ."

The Touch. She'd healed him with the Touch. Marco peeled himself off the cot, holding his side. Feeling chilled. Changed. "It . . . that's what detached from the facility on Kuru and dug into my brand."

Rock in hand, Roman set the weapon on the table and smashed it. "Let's be sure it doesn't find your brand again." He considered him. "It fed off your light, Marco. The brand of light is purity, and this thing sapped it from you."

Gravely, Marco nodded, though his head felt like a thousand kilos. "But it gave me a weapon that helped me kill many Symmachians and save Ixion's life." He glanced at his boots, feeling exhausted and whole at the same time. "Without it, I am failed . . ."

"You know better than that."

"Do I?" Marco locked onto the master. "We had no hope, yet we survived these six days because of that weapon." Why did he keep arguing it when he could feel the difference in himself? Appreciated it?

"And the bravery of over a million Kalonicans and Droserans had nothing to do with that?" Roman shifted onto a stool nearby. "Marco, this technology did not make you the Progenitor." He caught his arm, turned it over, and shoved back the sleeve.

Marco jerked back. "Don—" He stopped short, staring at the brand. He had not seen it in months, not since . . . since the weapon. Even as he stared at it in the light of the touchstone, he saw the *chirish* fading. As water washed away clay. "I . . . I thought the weapon . . . that's why the Lady named me Progenitor. She knew I would go to Kuru, the thing would attach, that I'd bring this weapon back and—"

"No, you were chosen and named because of the blood in your veins." Roman pressed a hand to Marco's chest. "Because of this heart that beats for your people. Because of the man of honor and character you became, who hunted across galaxies, impacting lives, showing them honor and courage. You err in thinking that because you are named Progenitor the whole of the burden rests on your shoulders."

"But I cannot defeat Symmachia. No way to stop those creatures." He shook his head and looked to the master hunter. "The Khatriza came. We have no hope of winning."

Roman smiled sadly. "The war yet rages. Many have found their way here to the gorge to regroup. We yet survive. Who is to say what you will or will not do as we continue to war? Mayhap without that thing, you will fight better, stronger."

"I know not if it will be better or stronger, but I will fight." Even amid this sapping weakness. Pushing to his feet, Marco wavered. Found that the change that had been sparked by Kersei's hand left him unsteady. Served him right. "How is Ixion?"

"He came to not long ago, but he's weak. He's lost a lot of blood, but he's already barking orders. Clearly, he's going to survive."

"Sounds like him." Marco would never forget that moment.

Roman threaded his arm under him and caught his waist. "Ready?"

I feel his hand there . . . no chirish *. . .* With a grunt, he nodded. And with each step the unsteadiness fell away, but he didn't trust himself to walk alone. In more ways than one. "Thank you . . . Uncle."

Surprised, Roman met his gaze. A smile flickered through his face as he ducked and shoved the door covering outward to help him leave the damp, cool shelter.

Marco stepped out on his own, finding his legs stronger than he'd expected. Applause erupted, and he pulled straight, faltering but then finding himself steady. Slowly, his strength returned. His old self returned.

Bazyli stepped forward, offered his hand. "Good to see you on your feet, Your Majesty."

"I am glad to be up," Marco said, his voice scratchy. He turned and found Shobi there. "Well done, Plisiázon."

"You as well, sire."

Though Marco smiled, he did not feel the praise warranted, but he moved on, too tired to argue. Then he knew he must face one in particular. "Where is Daq'Ti?"

The subtle trill came from behind.

As Marco turned, the crowd parted, allowing the tall Draegis to lumber forward. He inclined his head. "Daq'Ti . . . I owe you a massive apology. I am grieved at my—"

"*Yuzma yuz,*" Daq'Ti said quietly, firmly.

Noting the uni-com hadn't translated that, Marco recalled the beast saying that to Eija. It meant "Hand to Face" or something like that. "I . . . don't know what that means."

"Loyalty," Daq'Ti said with a nod, holding out his hand. "Who I am is yours."

Accepting the handshake, Marco appreciated the vow. "I am grateful. And very sorry." He patted his friend—

He stilled, realizing he had never thought of Daq'Ti as a friend, but that's what the man was. Even as he opened his mouth to ask after the war effort, his thumper tapped him. His gaze darted to Roman, knowing only Kynigos had this channel. And this meant the towers were down. So, things had to be bad.

He swiped his thumper. "Go for Marco."

"Marco! You're not going to believe this."

"Rico, good to hear—"

"The Symmachians are pulling out of orbit."

Marco's gaze swung skyward, his heart thumping a little harder. "How? Why?" Unbelievable. He searched the cloudless sky, as if he could see the ships leaving.

"What is it?" Roman asked, gaining his side.

"Don't get too excited, though," Rico said. "Radar just lit up with new ships—and they don't seem friendly."

Not if Symmachia was leaving.

"Their emissions signature isn't registering, so we either have a lot of trouble or help at last," Rico said. "With the EMP towers down, we can probably get our ships back up in the air, too."

Roman gripped his shoulder, urging an answer.

"Symmachia is leaving orbit," Marco said.

A raucous round of cheers shot up around him, startling him and making it hard to hear Rico.

"But there are new ships arriving . . ." He covered his ear to better hear Rico. "What is Vorn's plan?"

"Lost a couple dozen ships between bombardments, but the cave-in sealed us out. He's gone to ground. He and his army are engaging the remaining ground troops. If Kalonica still has operable ships, you might want to get them airborne ASAP."

Marco ran a hand down the back of his neck. "Understood. Stay safe, Brother." He sighed, mentally gathering his thoughts and sorting options.

"Sire," General Bazyli said. "Scouts report Eidolon working their way to the gorges. Having their pulse weapons again is giving them an enormous advantage."

"What of the militia?"

"Returning from the north, but it won't be enough."

"Plisiázon have gone to rally the Ancrans and other gorge dwellers to help," Ixion said. "We'll need every able-bodied person to stave this off."

"You should be resting!" Marco said to his still pale-faced First.

"I can sleep when I am dead." Yet he rested on a barrel.

"We should consider moving you both to safe ground," Roman said.

"No," Marco said in tandem with his First, then smirked. "I need to address the troops." He looked around and found another barrel. He hopped up on it, surprised at how light—of heart and body—he felt without the weapon. "Listen up!" He raised his arm—grinned at the light of the brand winking back at him. "The arrival of unknown ships is forcing Symmachian ships to pull out."

Another round of shouts went up.

"We do not know what these other ships are or their intent, but this is our ora, our chance to defeat the troops yet on our lands. We need to push them back. Fight like never before. And I know—it's been an exhausting battle. The enemy had discouraged and depleted us, but they have not destroyed us! Let's do this. Arm up and head out. Do it for your families. Do it for our planet!"

Up went a round of "Vanko Kalonica! Vanko Marco!" Which then morphed into Marco's battle cry: "Bring them war!"

Marco hopped down and shouldered into Roman. Met his blue eyes. "Ready to hunt?"

It did Kersei good to watch from the back of the crowd as Marco rallied the people. There stood the man she had fallen in love with all that time ago. His step seemed lighter, his mood light— Nay. Marco had never been one to be light of mood. Intensity always coursed off those broad shoulders.

And what a miracle to then hear that Symmachia was leaving.

She had read in the Trópos book that the brands would burn as long as there was purpose. Returning to the plains, she had found that purpose. Unintentionally, but in healing Marco, she had a peace she never thought possible. One that erased her fiery determination to prove herself. She was proven. Her heart felt . . . fulfilled.

Kersei drew in a tranquil breath. Prayed the Ancient protected those going out, especially Marco. Not for her—for Aeliana.

As the men geared up and formed up to return to the battlefield, Kersei hugged herself. Marco was healed and rightly focused on his role—to vanquish the enemy from their lands. To war. Who would return? Who would not?

Knowing what they would face, she stood in place as they left.

Marco was with the first contingent, and even as he took the first step, his gaze swung back. Somehow found hers, then with the men, he returned to battle.

With great effort—though it was less than before—she folded back to Deversoria.

Sonorous and melodic, a great song climbed the stone walls, stilling Kersei before she moved toward the cradles. Though she could not be sure, it seemed all Faa'Cris were singing, their song radiating throughout the ancient city.

"Kersei."

She spun to find her ma'ma rising from her knees on the rug in her room. "Ma'ma, you startled me." She glanced about. "What is that singing?"

Ma'ma came toward her. "Stay here with the children. Do not return to celerus. Not until I return or it is over."

"What is over?" Her heart skipped a beat. "Ma'ma, you frighten me. What is this? Why are the Ladies singing? I thought it a celebration—"

"It is a commitment, our lives to the Ancient. Whatever may come."

Kersei shifted to face her straight on. "Ma'ma." She felt her throat tighten. "What—"

"They are here, Kersei. The Corrupt." Her brown eyes communicated so very many messages—strength, courage, fear, concern. "They have returned. The Corrupt can no longer fold, but they do know how to get into the city. The nearby passages are sealed, so you should be safe if you remain here."

"Should I join you in the fight? I am trained—"

"In the way of men," Ma'ma said with a smile. "Not with wings and flight." She pulled Kersei into a hug. "And I would not will this on anyone, especially not my daughter. I want you to live, to see your future happiness."

Kersei sniffed. "I fear there is little happiness to find, but I would be glad for my son and niece to have a realm to rule and peace in which to live."

Ma'ma framed her face with cool, firm fingers. "It is coming, Kersei. Sometimes the reward for our obedience, even in things we dread to face, is not what we want or fathom, but it will come." Tears pooled in her eyes. "I am so proud of you."

Throat raw, heart seized at the unexpected praise, Kersei choked back her own tears. "Ma'ma." She clung to her tightly. "Please come back. I cannot lose you, too." She felt the firm press of her mother's lips on her head and knew she would depart. "I love you. Thank you for pushing me to be better, stronger."

"You were always strong." Ma'ma stepped back and nodded, tears slipping from her eyes. "Remember. Remain here. Promise me—for the children, prom—"

"Fear not. I am here to protect them, and will not depart—" A question silenced her. "How will I know . . .?"

Rolling her shoulders, Ma'ma fanned out her wings. Light and glory smeared around her, eradicating every shadow and doubt. The air crackled as a sword manifested in her hand. "You'll know." She smiled—a rare thing from Ma'ma. That alone gave Kersei pause. "*Fac fortia et patere.*"

The charge to do brave things and endure seemed contradictory, especially since Ma'ma meant for her to stay in Deversoria. Babysitting. Kersei chastised herself for even thinking that. Yet all her life, she had fought—with a weapon. Sparred and trained with aerios. Earned herself a nickname she had once been proud of—Wild Daughter of Stratios.

Now . . . did staying to watch over the heirs, nurse them, mean she had become the *Mild* Daughter of Stratios?

Her brand flared, and she glanced at the arcs and lines in her forearm. Felt in her adunatos that Marco was in battle. She could sense his fury—no, his fierce focus. Her hand itched for the javrod or sword. To get out there and number among those who fought for their world. It was all she had wanted her entire life.

Xylander shot his legs out and bounced them, pulling her attention to his cradle. His gaze locked onto hers, and he unleashed a smile that would melt the coldest of hearts. Arms flinging out almost seemed to be reaching for her. And how could she resist? After checking on Aeliana once more to be sure the princess slept soundly, Kersei lifted her son from the cradle. Hugged him close, thinking how his father had already been lost in the preamble to this war.

The air around them was thick with tension, with the struggle unleashing on celerus. She wanted to help. Yet, somehow, combined with the peace that had struck her after the Touch healed Marco, truth dawned on Kersei: the bravest thing she could do right now was not to rush out into a fight she had little chance of surviving but to remain here. For truly, the child she held was not simply her son, nor just an heir to Kalonica.

No, what Kersei held and protected was the future.

WASTELANDS, KALONICA, DROSERO

"Augh!" Marco toed off the back of an Eidolon, the mech-suit providing traction, as he whipped into the air and spiraled at the PICC-neck to his left. Even as he drew back his sword, he saw the master sprint at the Symmachian and slide toward him, jamming a glo-rod up under the mechanized arm.

As sparks flew and the helmet muffled the scream of the Eidolon, Marco rotated and delivered a decapitating blow. His boots hit and skidded on the hardpacked desert.

Frankincense and cedarwood erupted from behind.

Without thinking, trusting the anaktesios, he whipped around, the sword an extension of his arm and his Kynigos training. Arcing his spine, he narrowly avoided a pulse blast and cut upward, grateful the attacker wasn't in a mech-suit. Even still, the Symmachian staggered against the slice across his torso, what could've been a death blow to a Kalonican. Roared and reacquired Marco, who had already thrust the man's weapon upward and driven his blade through the soft part of the light armor, which was more like connective tissue than bone. He whirled and extracted the blade as the Symmachian crumbled to the ground.

He thrust his back against his uncle's, ready for the next attack. No immediate threat, and he smirked at the amusement rolling off the master.

"That weapon-arm would've been faster," the master offered.

Marco grinned. "But not near as fun." Not the killing—each life invariably took a piece of his adunatos, as it should—but the being back in the hunt. In action.

To the right, the converted Haltersten made quick work of two mech-suits, using their limited mobility against them. Landing multiple strikes before he dispatched the last one, sparks flying as the electric network that supplied oxygen and power-assist died with its occupant.

Marco straightened and noted, "Ixion will be upset he missed this."

"I think not," Roman said, motioning across the plain to the edge of the gorge where white hair glared beneath the sun.

"Unbelievable." Marco gaped as Ixion flung his manriki. "The fool should be abed."

Roman chuckled. "Tell him that, but I assure you he will not last long. His body will eventually demand rest." He nodded to a cluster of light-armored Symmachians, and together they engaged the fight.

It went on for oras. A few cuts. Countless bruises. There were many limbs lost, even more lives. "It's endless," Marco huffed as the sun sank to hide behind the hills.

"Do they breed them in facilities?" Gripping his knees, Ramirus panted and caught his breath.

"The Khatriza do that with the Draegis. Let's thank the Ancient *they* aren't here." Even as he spoke those words, Marco would vow that creature had heard him. In the near distance, streaks of light flared against the darkening sky.

Wiping sweat from his face using the crook of his arm and peering at the anomaly, he caught an attack scent from behind. He pivoted, saw the Eidolon bearing down on him. Lifted his weapon, knowing it was too late. Cursed his exhaustion that left his limbs shaking and his reaction time too slow. He swung up.

The Eidolon punched him aside. Marco scrabbled for traction in the rocky dirt. Shoved himself forward with a growl, clamping the glo-rod and feeling the thrum of electricity. The mech-suit shot off a round. Marco ducked and swirled. Came up right into the warbling heat of the pulse weapon. *Reek!*

A dark shape blurred into him, shoved him aside with a roar. Marco stumbled, his legs weak, and swiveled around. Saw the burly Daq'Ti, face and arms bloodied from extended combat, using a javrod and a pulse weapon to kill the Symmachian.

Shaking off the shock, Marco rushed in to ensure the Eidolon was down for good.

Face marred with blood, sweat, and dirt, Daq'Ti inclined his head.

"Thank you," Marco huffed as thunder pulled his attention to the far plains. "What is it?"

The skulking skies lit up with fast-entry pods that burned a path straight to the ground. They impacted a few leagues off, the combined resonance like thunder rumbling in the distance.

"Symmachia!"

Screams sparked as the pods collided with horses and people alike, disregarding the life on this planet and the existence Droserans fought for. The pods were landing on the most southwestern plain, very close to Shadowsedge.

"Near the fire gorges," someone commented.

"Voids," another muttered.

At the skycrawler term, Marco glanced to the left and found the dark-skinned officer who'd worked with Tigo. "Diggins." Beside him were more Eidolon, their light armor altered, apparently so Droserans would recognize them as friends. "I thought your people were pulling out—why are more troops dropping?"

Diggins cocked his head. "Those aren't Symmachian." He paused, squinting to see better in the fading light. "Scuz." His eyes met Marco's "Didn't you say something about more ships arriving?"

Reek! Marco's gut clenched even as he anak'd a spate of new scents—Draegis. Khatriza. Here.

How in the 'verse were they going to survive?

A trilling howl went up from his left—Daq'Ti. Head tilted back, he cupped a hand over his face and shouted. *"Xatrimaza bizni qul qish uchun qeytib keldi. Biz ulerge ruxset baremizi?"*

"What's he saying? And to whom?" Roman asked, looking at Marco.

"His pilots," Marco grunted. "He's warning them the Khatriza have come to retake them as slaves, if they will let them."

"Biz ozodmiz. Biz ozodmiz! Biz ozodmiz. Biz ozodmiz!" came the reply.

"They say they will not."

Taking in the Kuru infestation, Marco fought the swell of panic. "I've seen what these things can do." He shook his head. "There is no hope against such beasts. They are vicious, ruthless. Nothing means anything to them, except the Khatriza's commands."

"And they want this planet wiped out."

Marco nodded, then shook his head again. "I had a modicum of hope two minutes ago." In disbelief, he watched as the Draegis formed up and started running. Toward the fight. Toward him.

A scream from the right yanked them around. As if bolstered by the arrival of the aliens—did they think the Draegis allies?—Symmachians were making use of the air assault distraction to advance their line. A dozen or more Eidolon had lined up and were pushing forward, crushing horse and human alike.

Anger pitched Marco back into the fray. With the master, Ramirus, and others, they fought the battle at hand. But his mind and receptors were racing with the arrival of those beasts. Oras they spent, fighting. Somehow they ended up on the south side, nearly in Hirakyn lands.

A light-armored Symmachian barreled at Marco, who saw the attack too late. The man took him to ground, drove a punch. Turning just in time, Marco protected his nose but took the brunt full in the ear. Heard something crunch, even as he extracted his dagger and thrust it up into the skycrawler's neck. Though he felt and detected the man shout in agony, he heard little. Realized something had happened to his hearing.

All good. He was a Kynigos after all. Relying on sight and sound too often got him in trouble. Like this. He pitched the dead Symmachian off him and hopped to his feet, wobbling, realizing his bleeding ear made him unsteady, too. Imbalanced.

The ground shook and rattled as a pervasive keening strafed the air. With a growl, he hunkered, as if he could get away from the sound, half expecting his left ear to start bleeding, too. "What is . . ." Wait.

"—arco!"

He came up—and the entire right half of his peripheral vision got swallowed by an enormous beast.

Heart in his throat, he threw himself aside, landing on his rear. He tried to scramble away, but the enormous rhinnock slammed its snout against his chest.

The impact popped his hearing. "Augh!" Air gusted from his lungs as a massive muzzle the size of a fermented cordi barrel thumped him against the ground. Hot, rancid breath huffed at him, rifling that reek over his receptors.

"Ugh!" Marco stilled, peering up the scaled-hide head and horns, up the spine to the silhouetted figure who sat atop it. Laughing. "Crey!"

"Yer looking a little piqued, Dusan."

"Get him off me." Irritation and embarrassment raced through his veins. "Now."

"Do yeh think I order this amazing beast around?"

"Aye," Marco growled, trying a third time to get up, all too aware of the chuckles and amusement dusting the warriors. "Now back off!"

"But Barly has taken a liking to yeh. Who am I to argue?"

Shouts around them told Marco this was wasting time and putting lives at stake. "Crey, there's a battle—"

The rhinnock lumbered around—much faster than would seem possible with that bulk—and thrust its head. A mech-suit went flying.

"Aye. Are yeh planning to join us in battle? Or would yeh like another break, maybe for yer cordi?"

The rhinnock again focused on the Symmachians, allowing Marco a chance to hop to his feet. He glowered up at Crey. "It's about time you joined the war. What took you so long? Did you need to breed and nurse the rhinnocks yourself?"

Sword in hand, Crey scowled at him. Then burst out laughing. "I knew yeh had some snark in there somewhere." He nodded. "Well, I cannot stand around looking pretty like yeh. I have a war to win."

"He thinks too much of himself."

Marco started at the figure that strode toward him, a phalanx of bare-chest warriors around him. "Vorn!" He clasped the king's forearm and pulled him into a shoulder hug. "Thank the Ancient. Good to see you."

Hair braided back, Vorn nodded. "Seems we are a little outdone here." He scanned the battlefield. "Seems blackened beast is on the menu for our celebration feast to pledge Teague with your daughter."

Was that what the Jherakan king had named his son?

Marco smirked. "How are they? Safe?"

Vorn's expression darkened as his men and the vanguard formed up around them. "The Queen is mad as an aetos whose aetlet is threatened, but she yielded to my request to take him and return to Deversoria until this is ended. At least that way, I ensure my heir is yet there to take the throne should I fall." He had a smile that never made it past his eyes. "She tells me the Kalonican heirs are there as well. Safe."

Relief swirled through Marco at hearing that directly stated. "My thanks. Now," he said, searching the plains, "a tip—the blackened beasts? Cut off their right arms. Without it, they have little save their daggers. They rely overmuch on those blasters." His thumper pulsed behind his ear, and Marco thumbed it. "Rico?"

"Aye, I'm here with Duncan at the *Qirolicha*. Since the power was restored, he's been working nonstop. Recruited some locals, too. He thinks if we can get Daq'Ti back here, he could get the *Q* airborne. An Interceptor is en route for him."

The *Qirolicha* . . . It was one ship, but it could do some damage to the fleet. Perhaps stop the flood of invasion. "Find Daq'Ti!" he shouted to those around him as he scanned the skirmishes nearby. Finally spotted his tall form finishing off a Symmachian. "Understood. Land on the northeastern edge of the Ancran gorge. He'll be there."

"Copy that."

Infused with an unexpected flicker of what was dangerously close to hope, he decided it couldn't hurt to have contingencies in place.

Vorn gripped his arm, his expression somber as he considered the ongoing battle. "This does not look good."

Why was there not some prophecy to promise things would be well? "Aye, but neither is it yet over." There he went again, toeing that thread of hope. He started toward Daq'Ti, who was now jogging in his direction.

"Head to the gorge," Marco said. "Duncan needs your help with the *Qirolicha*." He pointed to the Interceptor already coming in for a landing.

Daq'Ti trilled but hurried to meet the craft.

A blast of heat and rage erupted from behind.

Once more he hated that these beasts had no scent. But the warriors around them did, and the area exploded with panic.

Apparently reading the same alarm, Vorn dove into Marco.

A thud that popped them from the ground for a split second was followed by a scraping noise. Dust and rocks erupted as a rhinnock ground to a stop in front of them.

Marco leapt to his feet, only then registering Vorn's strident scent. He glanced down and saw the massive welt across his back. "On your king!" he shouted to the Furymark, the Jherakan king's elite guards. He then used the dead rhinnock's horn to tic-tack atop the beast. Saw the dead rider. Not Crey.

Though he intended to use the vantage to scout his next target, what Marco saw froze him. "Reek," he whispered, unable to move. Think.

"Sire!" Haltersten shouted from the ground. "We are lost. All is lost."

Gut clenched, Marco swallowed, taking a knee on the yet-warm scaly hide. *Vaqar . . .* He ran a hand down the back of his neck. *What are we supposed to do?*

So great a foe, the Va'Una Issi Desert had grown mottled with the Draegis, hybrids, and Khatriza. They were a tsunami against an ill-prepared country. Heart sick, he watched the slaughter.

I am a gnat. He fisted a hand, grieved. Felt the air swell with the same emotion as the outlook grew grimmer with the darkening day, as if the planet, too, knew the dark hour had come.

Slag. Slag. Slag. He was dead.

D. E. A. D.

On a collision course with one of the alien battlecruisers, Reef decelerated sharply. Saw the umpteen fast-attack crafts whizzing toward him. The hard deceleration flipped his couch and pressed him hard into its hold. Fluids zapped into his PICC-line to keep him awake and intact. As the transport finished its hard deceleration, he flipped the ship and went for a hard burn, which rattled his skull. Spiked him with adrenaline as he shot away from the alien fleet and aimed for the planet. And he prayed the Symmachian barrage would miss his ship.

Earlier, he'd comm'd with Admiral Deken, but now the ships weren't responding to his waves. Or maybe they weren't getting them. Either way, he was scuzzed.

He pushed the ship to point three light speed, which, if the hyperactive rattling was any indication, was beyond safe parameters. But it didn't really matter since he was already dead.

Then he had a blinding flash of the obvious. Comms implant! Had no idea if it still worked. "Symmachian fleet, this is Commander Reef Jadon of . . . the . . . the only alien ship getting attacked by other alien ships. Please do not fire on me." He manipulated the controls and got back on vector for the fleet. Direct course for the biggest ship—that one had to be the *Cronus*. Slag, how long had he been gone? He hadn't realized it'd left dock.

Accelerating, he felt a strange warning at the back of his neck. His gaze shifted to the virtual display.

It was afire with incoming bombardment warnings! From . . . everyone.

He swung his transport around and down. Felt the crushing effect of maneuvering so hard. "*Cronus*," he said into his comms, "appreciate it if you don't fire missiles or pulse cannons at me. Maybe target all the other ships that look exactly like mine?"

It was futile. He was de—

Boom. Crack!

The vacuum that devoured breathable air popped Reef's ears.

No no no. He didn't have time for this. His thumbs raced over the controls. Straining, fighting to stay alert, he keyed up the weapons controls. With the torn hull, the transport vibrated until he felt like he was in a blender.

His muscles wouldn't work right. He struggled to stay alert. Groaning, temples straining against the deprivation of oxygen, he tried to lock in a firing solution, but this transport ship wasn't loaded with an arsenal of high-tech weapons like a battlecruiser.

A green light blipped—weapons away!

He monitored the array. Saw red dots. What was that? Trouble?

His heart convulsed—those dots weren't on the screen. They were in the void around him. Crimson droplets. Blood.

I'm bleeding . . .? He glanced down. Saw the hole in his side, metal punching through it. Struggling for a breath, he realized his survival suit was failing. His body was failing.

With that terrible truth, he slid into another painful awakening: *"Eija . . . I was wrong . . ."* Brittle cold consumed him. Sucked the air from his lungs. Squeezed his chest in a vise until he heard nothing . . . saw nothing . . . felt nothing. Except grief. "Eija . . ."

SHADOWSEDGE PLAINS, DROSERO

The spawn would feast on Droseran blood.

And Marco would not let them. Limbs aching, feet blistered, bearing a dozen or more cuts, he threw himself at the Draegis powering up its arm. He hiked into the air and brought down his sword with all his might. Severed sinew and bone.

Howl reverberating in his ears, he landed. Twisted around and—

The beast slammed his fist into Marco's chest. Punched the air from his lungs. Marco staggered backward. Saw the warbling heat of another weapon-arm powering near his face. Dropped to a knee as he forced air into his lungs.

Twisted and drove his blade into the pulsing red lines of the beast's chest.

Even as the thing stumbled, Marco felt air swirl behind him. Another! He toed the one in front of him, ticked then tacked in a backflip, extracting his blade from one and ramming it down into the soft neck of another. He wished Eija were here. Or Kers—

No. No, he did not will her here. And he thanked the Ancient that Isaura was not here to endure this or see him fail so miserably.

"Sire, look!" The defeat coursing through Haltersten, who indicated the skies, mirrored the many warriors—aerios, machitis, regia, militia, Daq'Ti's Uchuvchi—on this battlefield. Hope was swiftly losing.

Narrowly avoiding another barrage of superheated air, Marco swiveled aside. Glanced up. And his heart plummeted. "More . . ."

More alien pods dropping.

Merciful Vaqar. What are we to do?

He stumbled but caught his balance.

A hand clamped on his shoulder.

Marco reeled around, snapping his dagger up—and found gray eyes there. "Ixion. You should be resting!"

Face clammy, eyes rimmed in exhaustion and pain, he panted. "Fall back, my lord."

"Where are we to fall back to?" Marco barked a laugh. "They are everywhe—"

He felt her. Felt the searing reek of her essence.

Might not be able to detect her drones, but the Khatriza . . . He pivoted, sword up, not one to linger in fear, to panic. Yet the size of her . . . the ferocity of her razorlike appendages . . . dropped him into a dark pit, thick with memories of being tortured. Of being strapped into that machine, dosed with a paralytic. Then the bubble burst.

Righteous fury snapped through him. "No!"

Behind her roared a legion of beasts and hybrids, howling and trilling as they slaughtered.

"*No!*" he repeated, feeling that hum of power. As if the weapon were still in his brand. As if he could eviscerate them. But it was just him . . .

Overhead whirred a strange noise. The odd, high-pitched *whir-whir-whir* drew his gaze skyward. Barely in time to see the glittering crescent ship rush into the atmosphere. He swiped the thumper. "Rico, was that the *Qirolicha?*"

"Yes, got word from the admiral that the Khatriza ship was about to break orbit. We had no time to retrieve you, so Daq'Ti took it to confront them."

Oh no. *Daq'Ti* . . .

Even when Marco had considered flying it to the Khatriza fleet there had been little thought of it being anything but a suicide mission. He searched the skies, the *Q* now out of sight. "Do we have Interceptors to assist him?"

"Negative. Fuel stores are too low right now."

Reek! "Keep me posted." Heart heavy, he returned his attention to the ground battle.

The Khatriza queen screeched and catapulted toward him. Appendages crackling and snapping.

No . . . No, it wasn't the appendages crackling.

Marco backed up, suddenly and acutely aware of the brightening of the day. Twinkling and rippling, the field came alive in the glory of the Faa'Cris. Something sparked in his chest.

His mother stood before him. Time seemingly frozen as she turned to him, terrifyingly beautiful in all her armor and skill. "*This*"—she nodded to the Corrupt—"is our war."

The band that held time still snapped loose.

With a shriek, the creature Xiomara leapt straight into the light-fired sword of Alanathina, who whipped up into the air, spiraling her blade through the black darkness of that Khatriza.

Hope exploded with the creature, raucous shouts and near-glee flooding the battlefield.

Unable to see beyond the fifty or so around him, Marco could well imagine Faa'Cris had greatly evened the battle.

With a smirk, he tucked his chin. Embraced that dangerous hope. "Thank you, Ancient."

TSC-C *CRONUS*, DROSERAN ORBIT

It would all be over soon. Domitas huffed and refocused on the close engagement with the enemy ships. Felt the pull of Renette on Drosero, urging him to assist them.

"Admiral," Lieutenant Zarense called from his right, "the *Macedon* has lit thrusters. They're pulling away."

Domitas all but sneered at the array, silently thanking Baric for giving him a reason to end him. He tapped in a direct channel. "Captain Baric, you are ordered to power down and wait for escort. Any ships or pods that leave the *Macedon* will be destroyed."

"Sorry, Admiral," Baric drolled. "I no longer follow your—"

"Tactical," Domitas barked. "Disable their engines and weapons arrays. Notify me of any escape pods."

"Aye, sir."

Though Domitas would not hesitate to destroy Baric, there were thousands of innocent Symmachians on that battlecruiser who did not deserve death because their captain was a traitor.

"Dom, it's time," came the quiet, strident words of his beloved.

"I—"

The *Cronus* shuddered. Again. And again.

Domitas snapped his gaze to the display, seeing a barrage of weapons' fire assailing the ship. Slag.

"Admiral," Zarense announced. "The Khatriza flagship and the remaining two midsize ships are throwing everything at us. Shield buffers are down to five percent, sir."

Repeatedly shuddering, the *Cronus* groaned at the attack, warning of its own demise.

"Target—"

Boom. Boom-boom!

Domitas felt that last one rattle his chest.

Groaaan.

"Shield buffers are down."

Anger curled along his clypeus and heated the back of his neck. He opened a channel to all ships—save the *Macedon*. "Tascan Fleet, this is Admiral Deken. Target all weapons immediately on that flagship."

Even though weapons opened up, rather than a fiery waterfall, it looked like a piddle.

"Domitas, they're on the planet. You're missing the fun."

He gritted his teeth. *"I may not make it. Slay a few for me."* Eyes on the external array, he saw the enemy fleet, largely limping along save that massive flagship. Which would likely end them. "Captain, begin ship-wide evacuations. All personnel to pods."

"What the scuz?" Dimar shouted. "Sir—a ship just erupted from Drosero."

"They've been—" Wait. *From* Drosero? His gaze lit on the external array. Saw what seemed a glorious gold . . . "The sphere-craft!"

"It's on intercept for the flagship," Loren announced excitedly. "It's . . . alight . . . with weaponry. I've never seen anything like it."

"Moving fast," Dimar said, then snapped his gaze to Domitas. "On a collision course!"

Disbelief silencing him, Domitas watched the external array as the sphere-craft whirled like a bolt of spinning lightning toward the Khatriza flagship, whose weapons were suddenly redirected to the craft, hitting it . . . without effect.

He chuckled but then stilled. Wondered who was flying it. Who was sacrificing their life . . .

"Sir, the weapons on that ship . . . they're too hot . . ." Loren trailed off, her gaze flicking from her display to the external array.

"We're too close," Pount whispered. He looked to Zarense. "Divert all power to forward shields, now! Radiation incoming!"

From the *Cronus*, the collision—detonation—was enormous.

Brilliant. Silent. Deadly.

Even as the particles of radiation from the blast rippled across the *Cronus*, Domitas knew it had succeeded. Inwardly, he thanked the hero who had piloted it, given their life to stop that Khatriza infestation. Prayed it hadn't been Marco.

A general sense of awe and relief washed over the bridge officers as Dimar announced the flagship destroyed.

"Life signs?" Domitas asked, doubting the possibility of any survivors.

"No organics, sir," Pount stated flatly. "They're gone."

Dimar heavily exhaled a breath he seemed to have been holding.

Patting the XO's shoulder, Domitas nodded. "Good job, *Cronus*. Now, let's support our fleet and Drosero. Finish off the rest of the Khatriza ships."

Damage reports came in but were insignificant.

"My job here is done." He stepped back. "Captain, you're in charge and have the ship."

"Sir?" Pount asked, frowning.

"It has been a pleasure, *Cronus*. Warrior on." Domitas rolled his shoulders and stretched his neck as the wings unfurled on the deck, drawing gasps and shouts of surprise. He smirked. "There's a beauty below who needs my help."

A hybrid leapt at her, his mouth a series of razor-edged teeth.

Jez angled and used her wing as a shield. Heard a crack even as she bent her knees and shot upward, thrusting the hybrid off. It landed atop one of its own, their bodies mangled and broken. Aloft, she scanned the field. They had done much to give the Droserans hope, but . . . there were so many. So very many.

From her high vantage, she spotted a Khatriza attacking the Jherakan king. She hiked up and dived for the creature. As she closed the distance, she could not help but wish Tigo were here. Or the Licitus who had trained to fight with them. The Resplendent had chosen to depart without the men, believing them too new in their training to be effective.

She saw the maneuver for what it was—the Ladies afraid of losing men who had become important to them.

Just as I lost Tigo.

The momentary distraction, the strangle of grief, was a costly mistake. She hadn't seen the Khatriza come around. Shoot upward. Though not able to fly, the distance she erased in her leap had caught Jez off-guard. Their bodies collided.

The Khatriza shrieked in her ear. Sharp fingers dug into her shoulder.

Jez gritted against the pain. Shot into the sky, folding her wings around them as she spiraled rapid-fire up into the darkening blue, spinning . . . spinning even as the creature stabbed her. Trying to reach the clypeus. The higher she went, the weaker the creature got. Rejeztia went faster and faster, never losing her focus or orientation. As clouds drenched her hair and face, she gritted her teeth against the pain and the slick warmth sliding down her spine. When her hearing popped, she jolted to a stop. Thrust out her arms and wings.

Weakened from the centrifuge-like motion, the Khatriza shrieked as the sudden, unexpected stop flung her away.

Rejeztia gulped a breath, the exertion of that maneuver sapping every bit of strength she had left in spite of the injury. Her head swam as she watched the Corrupt plummet back to the earth. Vision graying, she struggled to keep aloft.

"Rejeztia!"

The clear-as-a-bell voice of Alanathina snapped Rejeztia into the awareness that she was falling. Jez slid out her hands, angled her span—felt the piercing pain of the gashes where the Khatriza's fingers had cut her—and alighted. Her legs crumpled beneath her. She dropped onto all fours but pushed up, knowing down would mean death.

Bodies hit her. Shoving her back to the dirt. Pluming dust in her face and eyes. Fists pummeling. Growling.

Hybrids had her pinned. One pounded its thick paw against Jez's injured shoulder. She cried out but fought to regain her feet. Drew up her sword and sliced and stabbed with swift, efficient, familiar strikes.

The four were dead, their bodies littered around her feet. More were coming.

Two Draegis sent fiery blasts at her.

No. Not at *her*. At the bodies. They erupted into flames like a pyre.

With no choice, despite her injured wing, Jez shoved into the air. Agony lanced through her. She wavered. Dropped—but she adjusted and landed away from the fire. She staggered. Nearly fell. Found a knee. Dug her sword into the ground and pushed up even as the hybrids were already barreling down on her.

Streeeeeee-crack! Thud. Thud. Boom!

She dared not search out the strange sound, but a roar grew. Absorbed the air. The ground and heavens were drenched in the roar that seemed to alter the very air it stirred.

The beasts faltered, their course erratic for a moment, then refocused on her.

As she tried to push up, Jez saw the space between her and the beasts fill . . . with wings.

Black and gray. Do'St! He stood with his back to her, his span enormous and dark. "No!" With that thunderous shout, he shot into the hybrids. Crashed into them. They were dust and ash in seconds, before he even landed.

Jez gave an incredulous laugh. Grateful, she struggled to her feet. Lifted her sword.

Driving a long, black lightblade into another hybrid with the effort most men took to walk, he straightened and turned.

Her heart leapt into her throat and strangled her shout. "Tigo!"

Waggling his eyebrows, he angled his wings from one side to the other, modeling his new armor. "What do you think? Sexy, huh?"

She flew at him, tears blurring her vision as she careened into him. "How?" She held him tight. "How is this possible? I saw—you were dead!"

"That's not how you say Do'St." He touched his throat, the way AO had. "At the back of the throat."

With a laugh, she rejected the idea of slapping him and lunged into him again. Noticing how very soft his wings were. Which was the biggest dichotomy, since nothing about him was soft.

"You know I'm all about this hugging thing," Tigo said, "but I think we have a few hundred diabolus to slay." He sidestepped, snapped a wing at one enemy. Brandished his black lightblade into not one but two Draegis. Then grinned at her, nodded to the field. "See? Licitus rule the day."

It was only then, at his mention of the men of Deversoria, that Jez saw the ones he had trained, the ones who had sparred with and learned to fight with the Faa'Cris, yet battled on this field with her Sisters.

Dispatching another Draegis, he seemed in his element. Deed done, he alighted next to her. "C'mon. Say it." He cupped her mouth as if making her speak and said, "'Oh, Tigo. You were right all along. I should have trusted you.'" He stepped back. Held out his arms in his cocky, self-assured way. "Aw, Jez. So nice of you to say. I'm glad we could get past bygones to kill some overcooked Draegis. But you know—" He two-handed his sword, shuffled sideways and swung upward, delivering a Draegis of his pulse arm, then of his head. Swaggering back, he smirked at her. Slid his arm around her waist and winched her to himself. "I'm kinda sad it took my dying for you to realize that."

She rolled her eyes, never happier. Even in the midst of a bloody battle. "I suppose you want a kiss."

He looked offended. "I *died* for you."

"No, you died because you were too dense to duck."

"Ouch." His expression went serious, his eyes hooded. "Definitely want that kiss."

"Okay."

His eyebrows lifted. "Really?"

"After we win this war . . . I might even take a life-oath with you."

Tigo froze. His expression blanked. Then his eyes sparked. "Done."

They warred together, moving in tandem, terrifically effective and deadly.

Night paused for no one. Neither did the many varied warriors who fought on the plain. A heavy price had been paid; the evidence lay with the bodies. Soaked in blood, Marco felt the grit and ash of the dead in his eyes and nostrils. Grieved the losses. Relished the victories. To the south, nearer Hirakys, where Crey and the remaining rhinnocks thundered over raiders and Symmachians, skirmishes still raged. The fighting was dying, the rage and exhaustion beating against his receptors. Smoke rose, a ghostly phantom in the dark skies.

Looking up, Marco sought Daq'Ti's unique Signature, but it was not there. He swiped his thumper. "Rico . . . any word?"

"He's gone." Rico's pronouncement was leaden with grief. "He flew straight into the flagship—destroyed it and himself."

Heaviness shrouded Marco, watching the skies. Knowing the Draegis protector had made the ultimate sacrifice. Come all this way . . . fought for a people not his own . . . and died ending the incoming Khatriza.

And yet, he felt something . . . undone. Unfinished. Anak'd that rancor that had smothered his senses on . . . He drew his head up and glanced around. "Xisya!" He fisted his grasp on the pulse weapon he'd taken from an Eidolon.

With a whirl and gust of minty air, the Revered Mother appeared, her visage urgent. Her weapon glorious against the black of night. "She's come." Surprisingly, her efflux hung with panic. "I cannot find her, but she's here."

Marco stepped back, anak'ing. Tucked his chin, rolled his shoulders. Hauled in scents. One rose to the fore: Vanilla and patchouli spiked with panic.

"Kersei."

His mother caught his arm. "The heirs!"

In a flash they were in a room that assaulted his senses with mint and fear. In a ready stance, he scanned the rug, the bed, the tapestry, the . . . cradles. "What is this? Where are we?"

"Deversoria. The nursery—Kersei was here when we left for battle." She motioned to the door that hung crookedly from its last hinge. "Xisya shouldn't have been able to fold into here, but if she remembered the canyon route—"

"I sense her."

"Kersei?"

"My daughter. She brought me home across galaxies. Think you she could not draw me through this place?" He tensed at the scent that struck his receptors. "Troub—"

His mother transported away.

With a growl, he closed his eyes and sprinted from the room. Let the anaktesios guide him through halls and out into the open. He felt an absence and opened his eyes. Saw the Draegis, facing away from him.

Marco toed a balustrade to stairs that led to a cobbled road and vaulted into the air. Drove his weapon down into the joint of the shoulder, separating that weapon-arm from the beast. He landed on the stone, boots sliding. Putting too much distance between them. With a growl, he dug his sword into the stone, stopping himself. Even as he reacquired with the pulse weapon, he faltered.

Saw his mother in her Faa'Cris glory whipping like a tornado at the beast, shredding it.

Marco shielded his face. Clearly, she had that well in hand. He angled his head again and locked onto Aeliana's minty-floral scent.

"Do not stop," his mother said around huffed breaths as she gained his side. "I will deal with the vile beasts." She stilled. "She's close. I can—"

He bolted away, trailing that scent like a bloodhound. An offensive analogy since Kynigos had better, more refined receptors than dogs. He skidded around a corner and saw movement ahead in the dim light of the touchstones that lined this alley. But there was no doubt now. He stalked forward, his gift sorting what lay ahead. The wail of a baby drew him on. It was not Aeliana. How he knew that when he had so abhorrently avoided her, he knew not. But he now could find Kersei's Signature as well.

Ahead, the dark shape of the Khatriza shifted and unfolded—struck the touchstone, dousing them in shadow. Touchstones nearer him seemed to grope for the creature. "Xisya!" It was hard to discern shadow from form.

Until she turned.

Revulsion and fury spat through him. "Come home to die?"

"No," Alanathina said, shoving past him. "This is my battle."

"I think not. Do you know what she did to me and to so many of the Brethren? To Kersei in the Engram? Her leeches murdered Isaura—and now she hunts my daughter!"

"I know. I am sorry." His mother touched his arm again. "But I was part of the caste who banished her. It is my responsibility to—"

"*Heeee-yah!*"

Marco snapped to the far end. Saw a ruffle of wings.

A glint of a sword, a radiant form scattered the shadows along the walls of the alley. Black curls.

"Kersei! No!" He darted forward, firing with the pulse rifle at the pale, translucent torso of Xisya. Before he'd cleared ten paces, he slid to a stop as the Revered Mother appeared between him and Xisya.

Her glory was blinding. Her wings cracking like whips at the creature who shrieked and shrilled. The chaos of their battle was horrific.

"Kersei!" he shouted past them, searching through the fray to the dark end of the passage. "Kersei?"

"I am here," came her strained voice.

"Get somewhere safe." And with that he drove himself into the fight. Managed to pull off a pulse shot and nail one of Xisya's legs. The creature wobbled to one side but never stopped her fight with his mother, who was a frightening sight, her face flecked with the near-purple blood of the Corrupt. She struck and thrust the blade home. Slashed. Moved in. Cornered Xisya in an alcove. And suddenly there were more Resplendent, including Jez.

Marco staggered, his legs weak from countless hours and relentless days of warring. Watched the Faa'Cris deliver the Corrupt from this life. The dichotomy of darkness and light could not have been more obvious. It was done. Xisya would never continue her work here. Never harm another person he loved.

He shifted to the side—and collided with someone. Dark curls. The unusual attire he now understood as that of the Ladies. He caught the shoulders. Looked into brown eyes. "Kersei."

Blood splatters across her face told of the moment she had attacked the creature. "Here." She shifted a bundle into his arms as if the weight of holding it was too much.

He looked down. Surprised at the babe in his arms. Saw the bloody mess of Kersei's side and abdomen. "You're wounded!"

Sweat mottled her lip and brow. "She . . . she was about to attack you." Kersei grimaced. "And she's . . . *fast.*"

She had saved him? Attacked Xisya to save him! Aeliana cradled in one arm, he guided Kersei, who held Xylander close, out of the alley.

"Alanathina said Xisya . . . could not get in the city. But . . . she found us." She motioned to a stone bench near a fountain and collapsed onto it, nearly dropping her son.

The air swirled with mint again, and Jez knelt at her side. "We need to get her into the sanitatem." She passed the boy to Marco and hooked her arms beneath Kersei.

"Here, I—"

They were gone. Marco stood there, a babe in each arm. There was a time he would have complained about this. But as he peered down at the heirs, he realized with the war done, with Xisya dispatched, these two were his focus. These two were the future.

"Rico and I negotiated the return of nearly a hundred Brethren from various Symmachian ships, and they are recovering at the Citadel."

"I am glad to hear it, Master," Marco replied via his thumper. "We must make every effort to ensure Symmachia destroys those insidious things. The Engrams are as evil as the creature responsible for them."

"Agreed. The Citadel would be grateful for a visit."

Marco grunted. "Someday mayhap. For now, I am needed here."

"For honor, Marco."

Now that he had reevaluated himself, his roles, Marco could say honestly, "For honor." He swiped the thumper and headed back into the house, where he found what remained of his vanguard gathered in the dining hall.

"It will take months and a detailed census to know how many Kalonicans died," Bazyli said from the large table where the vanguard sat, "but we know the numbers are close to twenty thousand. Shau'li was devastated, and my own entoli suffered greatly." The man's efflux was drowning in grief.

"Friend," Marco said, "what grieves you?"

Tightlipped, Bazyli stared at the marble floors. "My bound . . ." He looked around, as if seeking escape. "I am told she was among the dead. With our younger children. Ares and Yalena yet live, I believe."

"You must go back, help them—"

"Aye." He swallowed. "I would appreciate time . . ."

"Of course. At once." Marco shifted. "You have served me and Kalonica well. I begrudge you nothing in returning to tend to your children, family, and the Xanthus." His gaze slid to Kaveh, who nursed a wounded leg but stayed near him all the same, ever vigilant. "We have an opening—Commander of the Armies. Interested?"

Kaveh started. "I would be honored, sire, but we are short on regia at the moment."

"Especially ones as gifted as you. We will backfill the positions. All will be well." Marco lowered himself to a chair and leaned forward, elbows on his knees as he rubbed his knuckles. "As long as there are no more prophecies about me." He laughed with them, but his heart was yet heavy.

The grief assailing the air from north to south was overpowering.

"'Tis quiet without the Kynigos about," Kaveh noted.

Marco nodded, feeling that loss as well.

A messenger arrived, one of the dozens they'd sent out to gather reports from the various clans. As he hurried to Bazyli to relay the news, Marco rose. He would let them handle the news, compile a report to discuss on the morrow. For now, he had something else to take care of. "If you will excuse me." He made his way upstairs to one of the six bedrooms and knocked on a door.

"Enter!"

Marco sniffed a laugh and opened it. "Any meaner and you would scare the plaster off the walls."

"Good," Ixion growled, shifting on the bed, his missing limb a gaping reminder of what they'd been through. "It is driving me crazy. One more day of forced bedrest and I will lose my mind."

"You should have gone to bed immediately after the wound was . . . sealed." Shame still bit at Marco over that weapon-arm. "Continuing to war caused infection. The pharmakeia said—"

"I know what he said."

Amused with his First's irritability, Marco parked himself in front of the window and saw the great Stratios Hall in the distance. Then shifted his gaze to the city on the hill, a haze lingering from the fires. Amid it, the crumbling ruins of Kardia. Arches still remained, part of the upper levels, but gaping holes made it structurally unsound.

"You going to rebuild?"

Turning the Tyrannous sigil ring on his little finger, Marco nodded. "Have an architect coming from Avrolis next week." He shifted and tucked his hands under his armpits. "What of you?"

"Prokopios took damage—not good, but not as bad as the other provinces. Not like Hirakys or even the northern edges of Jherako and Forgelight." He reached for a glass of water and hissed, bracing his hand over the bandaging, then reached slower this time. "I am stepping down formally as elder and the elder-in-place will take over permanently."

"Then you will remain in the north?"

Ixion shrugged and winced. "I am no good as a Stalker now. What else would I do?"

Marco snorted. "I will not take offense that your role as First is not challenging you."

"Never did I speak such words."

"Didn't have to, and it is my greatest hope that life in the north *will* be quiet from here on." The last days of the battle dug into his thoughts again.

"Thank you," Ixion said quietly.

"For what?"

"Not pandering to me."

"I would not do that to an invalid."

Ixion glowered.

"A jest."

"A bad one," Ixion gruffed, then eyed him. "Kita tells me a solicitor came earlier . . ."

Marco nodded. "Aye, representing the Mient estate. Apparently, Sir Mient was wounded in battle and succumbed to his injuries, but not before amending his will." He scratched his beard. "The entirety of his estate, including Aetos Rest, has been left to House Tyrannous."

"You will need a home for you and the princess until Kardia is rebuilt."

"So it would seem." Nodding, Marco took in the room. Thought of this grand estate, this home but a small taste of what would be again. "Kersei and Xylander are the last of the Dragoumis line."

"Especially after you removed her uncle's head."

"I am not sure she will forgive me for that, but the thought of him living . . . knowing what he had done . . ." Marco lowered his head. "Not my best moment."

"Oh, I think it was your best," Ixion said. "Though it shocked, nothing gave me greater pleasure than seeing that man die after all he orchestrated. The coward!"

A soft rap on the door drew Marco's gaze to where Kita stood with a nurse.

"I need no food, nor do I need my dressing changed," Ixion barked as she stepped in.

"That may be true," Marco muttered, "but you need that attitude changed for speaking to your future bound like that."

"Get out."

"You forget whom you speak to," Marco teased as he moved to the door.

"Get out—*my lord*!"

Marco looked at ever-patient Kita and pointed to the invalid. "Wash his mouth out while you're at it."

A wad of dressing flew across the room.

Laughing, Marco ducked out. He passed the nursery and peeked in. Danae was laying Xylander in a crib, and Aeliana slept soundly . . . and his heart sagged. He would not wake her.

Even as he backed out, he heard her cry.

Danae straightened and spotted him, curtseyed. "Your Majesty."

"Will she go back to sleep?"

"Nay," Danae whispered, "she is likely hungry."

Yeah, he did not need to be here for that. "I'll return."

"Would you like to hold her?"

Marco hesitated on the threshold. Felt out of his depth. Wanted to leave. Yet felt keenly the rebukes of Kersei and Roman—even Tigo!—over ignoring her.

Danae cocked her head to the side. "'Tis very simple. Have a seat."

He entered, feeling more unsure than he had as a First Year at the Citadel. He sat and she brought Aeliana to him. The transition was awkward, but thank Vaqar he did not drop her.

When she laid a cloth over his shoulder, he felt ridiculous. Like a nursemaid. Would she ask him to wear corsets and petticoats now?

"Lift her to your shoulder and pat her back."

"I'm not an idiot." *Indeed you are.* Marco huffed, doing his best to hide how awkward he felt. But then his attention was ensnared by the tiny human he held. *My daughter . . .* Her face was filling out and had his olive complexion and dark hair. But those eyes . . .

Aeliana yawned, scrunching up her tiny face and chin. Her arms shot in the air and she grunted, arching her back in a power stretch, then settled back in his arms. Those little eyes focused on him. Chin tucked, she grinned.

His heart stirred that she'd smiled at him.

"'Tis probably gas," Danae said from the side. "Be sure to burp her." She left them alone.

"We both know you were smiling at me," he whispered to Aeliana. "It can be our secret." Entranced by the tiny green eyes, he let out a breath. "Hello, little aetos." The nickname felt right, a derivation of what he had called Isaura. "You are . . . a marvel." Cupping the back of her neck and her bottom, he lifted her and kissed her cheek. "She was right . . . how could I avoid you?"

Another smile, this one scrunching her nose, her mouth opening and closing.

"Ha! See." He smiled at his daughter. "I knew it." The most amazing part . . . anak'ing her emotions. Sensing her happiness that grew as he held her. Bent forward, sitting her on his knees, he framed her back with his forearms, noting his brand glittering along her side.

"You are so much more your mother. Thank Vaqar," he said softly, visually tracing her face and head. "She would have loved you . . ." Marco stretched his jaw and blinked to fend off the tears. "Your mother was good at everything, and she would have taken such good care of you, loved you so deeply. I will do my best to make up for her absence. It's my fault, you not having her. I pray one day you forgive me."

How could a building be so full of people yet feel so lonely?

Trudging up the stairs, Kersei used the back of her hand to push aside her rogue curls. Blasted hair wouldn't stay tied when she helped feed those who had taken refuge here at Stratios. Strange how life almost seemed to have fallen into a normal routine, yet a sabbaton past they were fighting for their very existence.

Oh, she was ready for a warm bath and a nap.

As she rounded the corner to the bedchambers, she spied Danae standing a few feet from the nursery, staring into its dim sanctum. Concerned, Kersei hurried forward. "What is—"

Danae wheeled around with her finger to her lips. "Shh. He's with her again." "Who?"

"The medora!"

Kersei froze.

"It is so sweet," Danae cooed. "He is so fierce and handsome, but to see him with—"

"Remember that he is your medora," Kersei said, resenting the woman's giddy exclamations riddled with her attraction to Marco. "He will not be pleased to find us gawking."

Properly chastened, Danae hesitated, then nodded and headed downstairs.

She should not spy on him, yet she could not resist either. Kersei peered into the nursery. Head down, Marco was bent forward with Aeliana lying along his forearms, her head cradled in his large, capable hands. She was smiling. He was smiling, whispering to her. He knuckled away a tear.

Never had she seen anything more beautiful, save when Darius had first held Xylander. Kersei tucked herself back at the threshold, watching Marco talk to Aeliana. This bigger-than-life man wrapped up in such a tender moment. It was precious, though he would balk at the term. On the table by the chair, she noticed the bottle, which they had prepared so Marco could have some bonding time with his daughter. Why had she yet to be fed? The two were so ensconced with each other. A moment later, Aeliana's lower lip stuck out. Her chin puckered.

Uh-oh. Time to sup . . .

She let out the slightest of complaints.

"You will have to do better than that," Marco teased, and then the princess widened her eyes, looking at him.

Aeliana seemed to love the sound of his voice.

"If you want something," he said, "demand it."

Kersei nearly laughed at his instruction.

"You may be the prettiest thing I have seen, but I will not let you wrap me around your tiny fingers."

Another cry. This one louder.

"Better," Marco said, but now he sounded a little less confident.

Then a staccato series of cries.

"Let's not overdo it. Nobody likes a showoff."

Sensing the frustration on both of their parts, Kersei slipped into the nursery.

Marco exhaled heavily. "I wondered if you would stand out there all day."

With a small laugh, she crossed the room and lifted the bottle. "She is hungry."

His gaze met hers miserably. "I know."

"Then feed her."

He stood. "I must go." Tried to pass the infant to her, but she resisted. "There are matters—"

"Marco," she laughed, guiding him back to the chair. "Feeding her is not scary."

"I make war, not milk."

The words had an unintended impact—reminding her of all that had been lost. Of the moment he had nearly killed Daq'Ti. When she intervened. Healed him. The look in his eyes.

"I am sorry." His words were quiet, repentant.

She looked back, sight still blurry. Drawing up her courage, she set the cloth beneath Aeliana's chin, then handed Marco the bottle. Uncertain, he fed her.

The little one nuzzled into it, her shoulders hunched, hands clutched beneath the bottle. She pulled in long draughts, the gulping clearly audible. A moment later, she paused, her breathing half moaning.

"Oh my!" Kersei laughed. "Never have I seen her drink so fast and so much." She looked at Marco. "It's because of you."

And it was . . . All of it. Everything. Because of him.

Too many demands. Too many people. Too many scents.

Marco strode out of the meeting room and down the hall. Saw an aerios coming that way and diverted to the stairs. Just needed time alone. Where could he find that, though? At the far end of the upper level, he eyed the window and hesitated. Rotated his arm, testing his range of motion. Stiff but not pained. He raised the window and climbed out onto the sill. Holding the framing, he pivoted and caught a beam sticking out. He hiked up and caught a lower window ledge. Toeing the brick, he made quick work of scaling his way up to the roof.

Perched atop the framing of a third-floor window, he gauged the widow's peak above—the window set in it was open. He shoved and caught the edge. Dangling there, he glanced down and grinned at the heights. The people below unaware their medora was scaling walls like a spider.

He eyed the upper frame of the window. Drew up his legs and dug his toes in. Hiked, then shoved upward. Caught the top of it.

A face was there. Screamed.

Scared the diabolus out of him. His fingers slipped. As he dropped, he sucked in a breath.

"Marco!" Hands clapped hold of his, stopping him. Eyes wide with fright, Kersei pulled.

Gave him the second he needed to gain traction. Haul himself up onto the ledge. Heart racing, invigorated by the endeavor, he grinned at her. "Thanks." He perched on the edge, one leg in the widow's peak, one on the sill, hugging his knee.

Shuddering a breath, she placed a hand to her chest, a breeze throwing her curls into her face. "I have a mind to shove you out."

The words punched him back to that moment in the camp when he . . .

"No doubt," he said quietly. "I . . . I did not mean to intrude on your"—he skated a look around the dusty attic—"privacy."

"You realize there are perfectly good stairs to reach this attic."

"I needed the workout."

"After what you went through in the war, I expected you would lie abed for a month!"

"I let Ixion do that for me."

She laughed, then sobered. "How fares he?"

"He is up and about now, so not quite as miserable." He adjusted on the ledge and dangled both legs out the window, relaxing.

"Marco—come back in. 'Tis not safe."

Despite the nerves in her efflux, he rejected her plea. "I am perfectly stable and safe."

"Stable," she sniffed. "You climbed a wall!"

With a chuckle, he stared down at the people, the women cooking and hanging clothes out. Men chopping wood, others preparing materials to be hauled to the city for use in rebuilding homes and shops. Across the plain and the river that glittered beneath the midrise sun, he saw the broken ruins of his ancestral home. Crumbling arches, missing walls said to be impenetrable. It lay in ruins.

Like me.

The ledge eased down a bit more beneath her weight as she joined him. Fully, he had expected her to leave. He glanced at his arm and started to rotate it. But again felt the shame of what he'd done.

Pushed his gaze to Lampros City, yet his mind wandered back to the wastelands. "I am sorry," he managed, the words thick and coarse on his tongue. When she did not respond and her efflux wavered with anger and grief, he peered aside. "You were right to be angry with me for killing Rufio. I should not—"

"My anger—" Her words caught in her throat, which she cleared. "My anger was not that my uncle was killed." She swallowed and bit her lip, her chin trembling. "What upset me . . . I will never forget the rage in your face, your eyes ablaze, hungry for retribution. It was—*you* were horrifying."

Marco looked down.

"And after the Touch—I would ask that you not hate me. I—"

"Hate you?" He barked a laugh. "You *healed* me, Kersei."

Her brown eyes widened. "You were so furious with me when I Touched Haltersten."

He groaned, sloughing his hands over his face. "I was furious with the world, with myself. Anything and everything. Rage was consuming me—I realize now it was because of the weapon. It stirred a thirst for violence. And after Isaura died, I was so . . . lost. So angry. I wanted those who had hurt her to hurt, to feel the full fury of my vengeance."

A strange scent peppered the skies, but he saw nothing.

"As well, you took neither reason nor counsel in deliberating guilt, the judgment to deliver. You were judge and executioner." She shook her head, those long spirals dancing over her shoulders. "It would be easy to place the blame on that weapon, say it made you do those things. But Marco . . ." A pause lingered and drew his gaze back to hers. "You were wrong. Terribly wrong. And I could not let you kill another and risk your adunatos."

Head hung, he knew no matter the words he spoke, he could not alter his actions, nor his motive. "You are right." He nodded. "And I . . . I thank you for that wisdom. For . . ." He looked at her hand. "The Touch." The *chirish* remained only in a gray pallor around his brand. He recalled that the Touch could not take effect without a willing participant.

She folded her arms, putting her hands out of sight. "You looked at me like I was the diabolus when I helped Haltersten, and not far from it when I Touched you on the battlefield, yet here you offer thanks?"

He sniffed. "I was wrong." He glanced up at the skies and sighed. "I would ask your forgiveness for what I put you through, both for judging you over the gift and for what I forced you to witness and do at camp." He shook his head. "It was abhorrent."

"You have it."

He peered up at her standing there. "So easily?"

"Nay, not easily," she said with an airy laugh. "This past week, I have struggled to sleep, but I made peace with the Ancient, and now you." Yet there was something heavy in her efflux that wedged between them. "I just do not think I can ever forget your face in that moment when you killed him."

"Understood."

"What of you? Can you forgive?" She nodded toward his stomach.

"Forgive?" Marco scowled, catching sight of two men who appeared suddenly on the lawn, wings folding away. He shoved himself out, whirled, and caught the ledge amid Kersei's panicked shout.

Tigo strode with his dad across the lawn to the structure that looked like something out of a history doc-vid.

Marco jogged toward him with a grin. "I am glad to see you. Last I heard, you had died."

"Yeah, Jez wanted to kill me when I made her make good on that promise to marry me." Tigo faked surprise. "Oh, you meant when my fellow Symmachian shot me in the head."

With a laugh, Marco shrugged. "I do not know. Those Faa'Cris . . ." He extended his hand to the onetime fleet commander. "Admiral."

"No more," Tigo corrected. "He resigned. Right?"

"Command felt it a conflict of interest." His dad grunted and scratched his beard, squinting in the afternoon sunlight. "I kind of agree." He waved the air. "Besides, I was bored and annoyed with politics. When you've lived as long as I have—"

"Yeah, yeah, got it." Tigo rolled his eyes and shook his head. "We really do have a point for being here."

His dad smacked the back of his head.

"Ow, hey!" What, did he have a "Smack Here" sign taped to the back of his head? "Annnywaaay, we were asked to bring this." He handed Marco a device. "The Tertian Space Coalition invites you and any Droseran delegates to come to Symmachia—"

"Not while I'm breathing."

"—for a . . ." Tigo nodded. "Knew you'd say that."

Dad shouldered in, gesturing to the device. "The TSC asks you to use that disc to list grievances and losses, so they can offer reparations."

Marco eyed it. Knew there was no way he'd do that.

"I wouldn't take it seriously," Tigo said. "It's just their way of trying to get a foothold here. They know the elefthanite ore is valuable—even if it's not all that Xisya creature promised—and they don't want to lose the chance to make an alliance and start digging."

Marco cracked the device in two and dropped it in the dirt. "The only thing they can dig is their graves."

Dad snickered. "Knew I liked you. By the way, the gates have been destroyed. Nobody's going to be coming through."

"What about the technology Baric developed with Xisya's help?"

Tigo grimaced. "Yeah, they want you to be unsuspecting and gullible and think that since she's gone, so is that tech. It's not. Which will only create a repeat of this."

"Are you telling me the TSC will always be our enemy?"

"Not an enemy, but neither would I turn your back on them."

"My lady, you are sure of this?"

Kersei hefted the javrod in her hand as she considered the target downrange. "Why do you aerios keep asking me that?" With a grunt, she sent the weapon spiraling across the stable yard to the end, where it thudded heavily into the target. Center mass. "Hoyzah!" She fisted her hands in the air and turned a circle, laughing.

Applause rippled across the north lawn of Aetos Rest, and she gave a mocking bow to the visitors—members of the Five Houses and the Council.

"Brava, Cousin." Bazyli strode toward her and handed her a ribbon. "For your victory."

Inclining her head, she smiled. "I am *rewarded*, Cousin."

"Come. Walk with me." He angled his elbow out for her.

"Gladly." She threaded her arm through his and breathed in deep of the mountain air. "It has been six months, yet I still find I much prefer to be out in the open than cooped up and surrounded by walls."

"For me, it will be a lifetime too soon if I see the wastelands again."

"Heartily can I agree with that." Too much had happened there for her to ever want to return. She shuddered at the thought. "I am glad you have come today. How is Xanthus?"

"Recovering, though I fear it a long road."

"Mm. For many of us." She took in the thick wooded area that surrounded the new seat for House Tyrannous. "I never expected to be invited to such a grand affair."

"Why would you speak such an offense? You are Stratios House!"

"Because," she said, toying with the ribbon, "I have lost the medora's favor."

"Nay, I do not believe it."

"What happened, what I did to him—the Touch . . . you saw how he reacted regarding Haltersten. To have it happen to him, I deserve his censure. Though, I never meant it to happen."

"Of course not."

"He did ask my forgiveness for his actions, which I readily gave. He conceded that the Touch healed him, but when I asked for the same forgiveness, he scowled and left. He has not spoken to me these many months."

"Much has consumed his time, Kersei. The entirety of Kalonica must be rebuilt."

Yet the ache was there all the same. She had hoped for reconciliation, friendship. She paused, taking in the gap in the tall trees where one could stand and look out over the whole of Lampros City and all the way down across the country. "How incredible. How is it Zarek I chose the cliffs of Kardia rather than this place to build his castle?"

"It is said he believed it easier to come and go unnoticed, but I think it was the ocean that lured him."

"I think this a brilliant place to find peace and quiet."

The onetime Mient estate, situated perfectly in the Mountains of Kardia and surrounded by tall trees and lush gardens, towered behind them. Though only three levels, the house sprawled along the mountain. Four cottages, tucked among the trees, now housed several of Marco's most trusted— Ypiretis, Ixion, and Kaveh had taken up residence in the smaller buildings, but the main grand house was left to the medora. To Marco.

"How is Stratios Hall coming along?"

"Wonderfully. All that is left is the west hall, so I returned last week. I've secured staff and sergii, and at last have felt the faintest semblance of normalcy."

"And Xylander?"

"Ever his father's son. Passionate, obstinate—"

"Do you describe his father or his mother?"

Kersei laughed. "Fair. In all honesty, he is a very good baby. There is a tenderness about him that I believe will make him an amazing friend and ally. The ferocity of his temper will work well for a machitis." She plucked a long reed with a coral bloom as they walked in the quiet of the afternoon.

"Any suitors offering to set petition?"

"For Xylander?" she teased, then shook her head. "Too soon, Cousin. Besides, I fear that being mother to a prince, I am seen as too much a liability for most houses."

"Most men would be glad to align themselves with House Tyrannous in any respect to bring that notoriety and fortune to their own houses." He grunted. "Nay, I would think more are fearful of your name, the Wild Daughter of Stratios."

Kersei stroked the reed between her fingers. "I confess, I am not offended." She lifted her jaw, then settled into a comfortable silence as they walked. Yet her mind niggled that there was more to these questions. "Bazyli, to what do these queries tend?"

He feigned surprise. "Can I not inquire of my cousin?"

"Aye, but already these things are known to you, as you are part of the medora's Council."

"It is not the same as hearing it from you," he said, continuing along the path, directing them up the slight incline. "But I concede. You have guessed true—I wanted to inquire what plans, if any, you have to reestablish the Stratios machitis training. As I am sure you are aware, Kalonican law requires each entoli to have its own machitis ready to fight in the name of the medora and realm."

So . . . there it was. Kersei had wondered how long it would take before someone forced the issue of a man being in charge of Stratios. "Think you because I am a woman and widow that I—"

"Nay, nay," he said, lifting a hand. "You should know me better."

She beat down the rising defensiveness. "I . . . I know that while I did spar and train with aerios and regia, I am no training master." Frustrated, still hurting over the loss of her father and their machitis, she looked aside. Knew not what would come of her father's legacy.

"Might I make a suggestion?"

With a halfhearted laugh, she shrugged, certain that things about her and Stratios had already been decided in secret deliberation. "Why do you pretend at what the Council has already determined?" She lifted her chin. "Tell me. Please . . . do me the decency—"

"I would prefer you not accuse your medora, family, and friends so easily."

Kersei deflated. "You . . . are right. I simply do not want to surrender my father's land and name to another just because his only heir is a woman."

"Which is why I wanted to recommend . . . myself."

Stunned, she stopped and look at him. "What say you?" She searched his eyes and that trim blond beard threaded through with silver.

"Jencir served as elder-in-place while I commanded the armies. Our entoli trusts him, they forged a connection that I cannot take away. Nor do I want to. I . . ." His gray eyes seemed sad. "In truth, I no longer feel I belong there. Not with Deianara and the littles gone."

"Oh, Cousin." Kersei touched his arm. "I beg your mercy."

"We both have our losses, do we not?" He gave her a tight smile. "I thought since your father was my uncle and we share the same blood . . . if you . . ." He squared his shoulders. "I know I ask much, but if I could train the machitis of Stratios, live in the cottage with Yalena—Ares has a commission to join the aerios at Kardia—then I would yet be close enough to Kardia when the medora would have need of me, and—"

"Aye!" Kersei hugged him. "Of course. It is a perfect solution to both of our dilemmas. I would be glad of your company and aid."

Cheers and applause seemed to celebrate the decision, pulling their attention toward the house. A crowd had gathered.

"Ah, it is time," Kersei said. "The grand announcement. I wonder what it could be."

When they emerged onto the lawns, Ypiretis stood on the steps of the back terrazza speaking to the gathered. "And now, His Majesty, Marco, First of His Name, Son of Zarek and the Lady Alanathina. Medora. Kynigos. Progenitor. Victor!"

Shouts went up and the doors to the house opened.

Head up, shoulders back, Marco stepped from the double doors of the mansion. He cut an impressive figure in his black doublet, pants, and boots. Ever did he look the fierce hunter, save this time no cloak or quarry. How well he presented. Tall, athletic, he had grown his hair—some but not much. The sides and back were trimmed short, but at least it was no longer shaved. That trend had fallen away, it seemed, with the weapon that had nearly stolen him from them. The hair on the top looked as if he'd shoved it back from his face before emerging.

She nearly laughed, imagining him frustrated over the "frivolity" of such fancy clothing. It summoned images of when first she had seen him in that royal jacket. On Iereania. The brooding hunter who had her willpower on its knees—right along with her heart. Which now thrashed in her chest.

Oh, Marco . . .

She silently pleaded with him to release bygones. Grant her mercy for the Touch, one she did not regret—he was, after all, returned to them. Whole. Healthy. Yet when she asked for forgiveness, he leapt from the ledge as if forgiving her were the last thing on earth he would do.

Drifting nearer, she eyed the guests. All entolis were represented in some manner, along with the regia who had served him and the kyria—Kaveh and Cetus, who now bore a terrible scar across his neck, half his ear missing. No hunters, since the masters had gathered them all back to Kynig. Then there was Tigo with Jez and his father, a contingent of Faa'Cris. No surprise that Alanathina would be here, or Jez. Vorn had arrived with his queen, and a handful of others she did not recognize.

"Thank you," Marco spoke to the gathered. "I will make this short, as I know you are ready for the food and dancing—and I am ready to be done with speeches." He let the laughter filter out, then nodded. "We have all been through much, and there are yet loved ones who whisper in our dreams, ever alive in our hearts. Sadness and grief defined us for a time, but in the time of hostility, mistakes, and death . . . came hope. It is time for war to be set aside, for us to find peace and community. To that end, I am creating an alliance of people and planets that will include representatives of the Faa'Cris and the Do'St"—he indicated the Dekens and Faa'Cris—"and of Jherako and Hirakys." Ah, the surly Crey of Greyedge stood beside the striking king, Vorn. "Of other planets. More will be shared in the days and months ahead."

Marco nodded, clearly pleased with himself and the news. "Now, before we part, I have some titles to bestow. First, since they sacrificed everything and fought for us, defending our skies and lives with their ships, and since they have been deemed traitors on Symmachia, I have offered Domitas and Tigo Deken this estate to call home—well, once I vacate it upon Kardia's completion." Laughter tittered around the crowd as he waved the two men to the dais. "In welcoming them to our lands, I feel it imperative to be able to call on their counsel and years of experience. We do not expect Symmachia or the Tertian Space Coalition to leave us alone. Therefore, I am bringing both men onto my Council and hereby grant them the titles Viscount and Baron of House Drusus. The five entolis are now six."

A rumble of applause went up as Tigo and his father were bestowed with the vestments of their new titles.

"As well," Marco continued, pausing for a moment, his gaze contemplative above that sigil, "for gallantry and incredible efforts in raising a militia that made the difference between utter defeat and victory, I recognize Harkon Haltersten and confer upon him the Order of Vaqar. I also knight him and name him baron and elevate him from militia commander to lieutenant commander of the Kalonican armies."

Cupping her hand over her mouth and fighting tears, Kersei watched the dark-haired man whom she'd Touched jerk with shock.

Face crimson, Haltersten climbed the stone steps.

After shaking hands with him, Marco affixed his new Order of Vaqar collar around the man's shoulders. He stepped back as the Council members congratulated and welcomed the commoner into their ranks. "And our final installation of nobility is that of Kaveh Naderi, who served and protected at Kardia and is thereby elevated as well to the title of baron."

The investiture of the regia went smoothly, and Marco shifted aside once more as the new barons congratulated one another and received well-wishes from those around them.

Kersei spotted a flash of white next to Marco, who stood facing the new barons, but his attention was divided by someone at his side.

When she angled around the crowd to see the source of his distraction, a pang darted through her chest.

In a stunning white gown with green embroidery stood Lady Danae. Blonde, sweet, and demure . . . As she talked to him, he leaned a shoulder closer, tugging at the cuff of his doublet. Smiling, he straightened and said something to her. To which the lady laughed. Touched his arm.

A burn started in Kersei's lungs and spread up her throat. It surprised that he would so soon consider another kyria . . . Swallowing the hurt came with the realization that Danae so perfectly fit the type of woman who interested Marco.

And I do not. At least, no longer. She was deemed too wild, too unruly.

Mayhap she had been. She chewed her lower lip, rubbing her brand and working to once more accept that it had served its purpose.

Was Danae why he had not spoken to her since Stratios?

Kersei could watch no more. She fingered the embroidered overlay of her omnirs and made her way inside to the banquet hall. Just past the stairs, she spied lines of tables and enormous floral arrangements, candelabras, and sergii adding finishing touches. With a plate in hand, she filled it with sweets and confections, going a little heavy on them, especially the chocolate and cream petit fours. She tucked one in her mouth and turned toward the punch fountain for a glass of chilled cordi—oh, Marco would be so annoyed.

"I would speak with you."

Sucking in a sharp breath that he appeared so stealthily at her side, Kersei also sucked in the cake. It went down the wrong way. She coughed, but tried to stifle it. Choked. Coughed. Blood and boil, she was going to humiliate herself.

Marco touched her elbow, brow furrowed. "Are you well?"

Cheeks puffed around another cough, she held up her finger dusted with powdered sugar. Then grabbed a glass of punch and took a gulp. Thankfully, it washed down. She cleared her throat and managed a smile. "Confections always get me in trouble."

"I remember another gathering where you had a plate of pastries."

Kersei slowed, amazed he remembered . . . and even more, that he would mention it. That had been a very different time. One where they . . .

She cleared her throat again, willing away those thoughts. "You would speak with me?" Mercy, he was powerfully handsome in his Kalonican greens.

His expression tightened as he motioned her down a hall.

Afraid of another choking incident, Kersei abandoned the confections and fell in step with him. "The house is lovely."

"Hm." It was more grunt than word and seemed to match a suddenly serious mood.

"How fares Aeliana?"

"Well," he said with a nod, lines crinkling at the corner of his eyes. "Crawling all over the place. I have considered building a corral for her, but she would climb it."

Kersei laughed. "Xylander was the same. It is hard to believe he nears his first birthday." She shook her head. "Time is an unrelenting foe."

"Mm." Marco walked with her, but it seemed his thoughts were elsewhere. Those eyes looking at nothing in particular, yet darting all over the property and guests.

"All is well?"

Marco shrugged and bobbed his head. "As well as can be, I think."

"I have not seen Elder Mavridis."

His chest heaved a breath. "He is convinced he's useless. I fear it will take a command from his medora to get him back to work. I would throttle him for the way he does not fulfill his petition for the Lady Kita. Could not even get him to come out of his cottage for the alliance and elevating heroes of the war. He fears she would pity him."

"He is here? Even now?"

"A hundred paces beyond the hedgerow."

Kersei bristled. "He harms Kita and her future delaying to such an extent.

If he breaks the petition, she is unlikely to have anyone set again for her."

"He will do it, if I have to order him. Mayhap for the celebration next year."

"Celebration?"

Marco continued, chin tucked and gaze taking in their path. "I had thought to host some sort of event to mark the victory over the Symmachians. I realize a year is a length, but with planting season upon us, and many still building homes, I felt it insensitive to do it sooner. But I would help the people remember what we accomplished and honor those who gave their lives. Our minds and hearts are too fickle, desperate for the next great thing. Hard times too easily forgot."

"Victory Day," Kersei said with a smile. "That would be wonderful." She thought through ideas. Discarded one as too costly. Another as too difficult to master on a big scale. "Oh, for all of Kardia? Or just the Council, like this party?"

"All of our people."

Our people. Inwardly, she smiled at how that had changed. "It should be grand . . . a sign that we revel in life." She held up her hands, palming them across the air as she spoke. "A week-long festival that culminates in a grand ball. Streets filled with foods from all entolis, games, auctions to raise money for the rebuilding of Kardia—"

"Then you will do it?"

She stopped and looked at him. "I beg your—what?"

"I had come to ask if you would organize the festivities."

"Me?" Her heart jolted. "Why me? I am naught but a mother and—"

"During the war, you kept your head. Your peace. You cared for the people. Challenged even me." He shrugged. "This seemed a good fit."

"A good fit."

"Yes, a good fit." He drew her aside, then released her arm and toyed with that cuff link again. "Will you do it?"

Kersei stared at him—wondering at the fact he had never forgiven her. Yet here he was, asking her to organize the medora's celebration. "I would be honored."

He huffed a sigh. "Thank Vaqar."

They walked on, talking of the house, the dark paneling he did not like and the portraits of people he did not know. "I would have one done for Isa." His gaze flicked to hers. "And Darius should have one."

Gnawing her lower lip to stop from tearing up, she smiled. "That would be lovely."

He stared at the canvas of a lady for a long moment. "I have never met this woman, but I am curious about her. Where did she get the jewels? Whose eyes does she have? Those questions keep her alive." Marco stepped back with a sigh. "That is what I want people doing hundreds of years from now for Isaura—remembering, asking those questions."

His love for her was deep. He would never let go. Never move on. "I think it would be good, too, for Aeliana to have a way to look upon her mother."

"Yes!" Marco brightened. "Exactly. Xylander, too."

She smiled, heart warmed.

He touched her elbow and directed her down another hall. "Tell me, what do you think of Kaveh? He's been elevated to baron in light of the changes."

Kersei blinked, glancing back to where the onetime regia conversed and laughed with nobles. "I . . . am glad for him, and you."

Marco glanced at her with a frown. "For me? Why?"

"You are surrounded by heroes. Good, strong men."

Another of those grunts. "But what of Kaveh?"

What was this? "I . . . am glad he has been rewarded for his courage on the battlefield . . ." It came out like a question, but she did not understand what he was getting at.

He smirked. "I meant, what do you think of him as a person?"

"Oh, is that what you meant?"

"You mock me."

She laughed. "I fear I do, mayhap a little." She peered up at him. "It is good to see you smile again."

His gaze held hers. "And you, Kersei."

Blood and boil, what he did to her heart when he spoke her name and looked into her eyes. *Do not go there—recall he . . .* "I . . . um, Kaveh has always been kind and formidable as a regia. I believe Darius thought very well of him." She should not mention Isaura's death. "I know he was beside himself for not being in the castle when . . . Isaura—"

Expression tight, Marco grunted. "It was an impossible situation. Grace should be extended, especially in light of the war."

Kersei did her best not to look at him, not to bring up the fact he had not forgiven her.

"He is older than you, yet he said he had sought you out a few times."

Surprise made her look up at him. "Did he? I . . . I had not known."

"I fear Darius's interest in you silenced many a man." When she gaped at him, he wiped a finger over his nose. "But his character—would you speak to it?"

Kersei stopped and frowned. "I beg your mercy, but I do not understand—"

"I am considering a petition . . ."

Her heart faltered. "Petition?" It was the duty of the medora to review all petitions, and with his questions regarding Kaveh . . . She nearly choked on the word. *Please, Ladies, do not let it be for me.* "I-I am surprised you would ask my opinion on this matter at all."

Marco swung around. "Why? I value your thoughts. You see what others do not."

"Do I?" The thought of being bound to yet another man she did not love nauseated her. She pulled her gaze. Mayhap she should leave and return to the gardens.

He frowned. "Have I offended you, Kersei?"

She blinked. "No, but . . . I had thought . . ." There was nothing for it. "In truth, I was surprised to have received an invitation at all for today's investitures."

A deeper frown. "Why would you not?"

"You . . ." She wanted to growl. "You resent me. Withheld your mercy regarding the Touch."

"I *what*?" He cocked his head at her. "Why would you think that?"

"When we were in the widow's peak, I asked if you would grant mercy, and you scowled"—she indicated to his face—"as you are even now doing, and left. Out the window. It has been months since, and you have not spoken to me." Did she sound desperate? "So, it seemed clear the injury I had done, taking away the weapon, was found as unforgivable to you as the Touch of Haltersten."

"What I find unforgiveable is that you have lived these months believing that." He huffed a laugh. "Kersei, there is nothing to forgive, no mercy to grant." He smoothed a hand over his beard. "What you did needed to be done." He twisted that ring again. "I was told once that the *Ovqatlanish* can only be effected upon a willing participant."

Kersei considered him speculatively.

"In other words, as much as I had lost myself to the weapon, there was a part of me that wanted freedom. To be freed from it. Then you . . ." He looked into her eyes for a long moment, touched her elbow. "You *healed* me, Kersei—I told you that in the cottage. And as I have thought of that moment since, it became clear to me why you bear the other half of our brand."

Though she tried not to draw in a breath that he referred to it as "our" brand, she failed.

"Had you not . . ." Marco shook his head, lifting his gaze to the cornices. Walked a few more paces with that smirk that was both endearing and condescending. "I remember when I had tucked your hair under my vambrace and it nearly killed you—"

She drew back. "You did what?"

He seemed chagrined. "I may have conveniently forgotten to tell you that story."

"My hair?"

He nodded. "On Cenon, when you passed out in the stone courtyard"—he looked at her, waiting for her to nod that she remembered—"I carried you to the iereas. Your hair snagged on the buckles of my vambrace. I realized it sated the fire of the brand, so I kept it there. Kyros later told me I nearly killed you."

She touched her hair, mute.

"I am sorry for that, by the way."

With a shrug, she pursed her lips. "I recall how terrible the fury of the brand was before the Temple. What I recall more was the power that erupted when we touched the halves together." And the moment in his solar after the brand's fulfillment when she had jumped into his arms and kissed him passionately. The way he held her so tight, she was not sure she could breathe. Did not care if she did.

Nervous jellies swarmed her belly, and she braved a look into those eyes. So pale and intense. So beautiful. He was beautiful. "We have changed much since then."

Marco's lightness, his near smile, evaporated.

Cursing herself, Kersei knew she had pushed too far. Too soon. He was yet grieving Isaura, and she thought only of herself.

"My lord?" a sweet, feminine voice reached down the hall.

A practiced smile swept beneath his beard as he looked in that direction. "Lady Danae. Thank you for coming." He nodded to Kersei. "Duchess." And he left.

Just like that.

Leaving Kersei with only one possible answer to the abruptness with which he abandoned her. The petition he had mentioned—it was not for Kaveh. But for Marco and . . . Danae.

Hand on the portfolio, Kersei peered out the window of the royal carriage as it conveyed her, Kita, and Xylander to Kardia. One month until the big celebration, and Marco had insisted she remain at Athina House so she would not be strained and slowed in making final preparation and decisions.

It had been almost a year since she walked Aetos Rest with him, and since then, they had met once a month to discuss plans, work through issues that had come up with the vendors, and mete out minute details. It had become harder and harder to be around him, her heart surrendering more and more of itself to him. Though he knew it not. She had learned how to master her feelings and not throw them in his face, respect that he intended to bind with another. Yet she was grateful they were at least friends. She would have that over nothing.

"Open the gate for the Duchess of Stratios!"

Gaze yanked back to the present, Kersei peered out at the door, smiling when she saw the gilt aetos once more on the iron gate that swung open to allow the royal carriage entrance. They lumbered along, pulling up to Athina House on the right, facing the south side of Kardia.

"Look!" Kita gaped. "So much has been done!"

Three-fourths of the first level had already been restored, the windows replaced, plaster washed and painted, flowers replanted, pavers reset. To the far right, just shy of where the cliffs of Kardia accepted the rage of the Kalonican Sea, scaffolding lined the entire east side of the castle. The north side of the castle was yet visible with stalwart arches that once bore beautiful stained-glass windows standing defiant against the winds' bombardments.

They rounded the circle, bypassing the pretty house, and aimed for the castle. "Oh no," Kersei said. "He is taking us to the wrong place."

Kita rapped on the roof. "We are to go to Athina House," she shouted.

Yet the carriage pulled to a stop at the front terrazza, where she had once stood to welcome Isaura to her new home. Oh . . . mercies. It was good to remember the gracious kyria who yet occupied her hunter's heart.

"I will tell the driver," Kita said, reaching for the door.

"Xylander." Kersei clapped her hands at her son, who sat on the floor playing with wood toys Bazyli had carved for him. "Come. We will be there—"

"Oh!" Kita stepped out and shifted aside. "Your Majesty."

Kersei started, her gaze flicking out. Caught a black jerkin and trousers. Mercies, what was *he* doing receiving the carriage?

"Good rise, Lady Kita."

His voice, so deep and resonant, stole her breath. Every time.

Xylander strained to the edge and grabbed the frame of the door.

"Give care," Kersei said as she stepped out, reaching for the handle to steady her descent, but instead, Marco caught her hand. "Oh! My lord." She curtsied. "We apologize for intruding on your time. I am afraid we were delivered to the wrong house."

"Not at all," Marco said, grinning. "You are here at my instruction." He indicated to the house. "Come, I would show you what has been accomplished."

When Kita gave her a wide-eyed look that asked what was going on, Kersei had no reply. "Our things . . ."

"They will take them to the cottage." He angled and pointed to a side door. "This way."

Kita, Mnason, and Xylander went on ahead with the servants.

"I hope you do not mind," Marco said, waiting for Kersei, his hand worrying that ring again. "I thought it might be of use to see the hall as you plan for the final preparations."

"It would indeed." Kersei hugged the portfolio to her chest. "However, there is no need to distract you from your duties."

The door opened and Marco gave the waiting sergii a curt nod. "Is that your way of trying to get rid of me?"

"No!"

He laughed and waited for her to enter.

Kersei moved into the house and paused. "Oh my!"

Marble had been replaced, the walls papered, and electric lights glared brightly along the hall that bore pictures and decorative alcoves with various aetos sculptures. There was a particularly poignant one of a royal woman—kyria? princess?—with a baby. She paused to admire it.

Marco stopped with her. "I am surprised you noticed . . ."

"It is beautiful."

"Come." He motioned down the hall and led her to a door he opened. "The real reason I would have you here—"

He would?

"—was for this." He grinned. "Close your eyes."

What was this? What manner of man had he transformed into? "You seem to be enjoying this far too much."

"And I would have you enjoy it." He nodded. "Eyes closed."

Sighing, Kersei complied, suddenly and acutely aware of her hammering heart. Never had she seen him so alight, so . . . giddy. It seemed wrong to call this fierce hunter-medora by such a term.

Holding her arms, he guided her forward. "No peeking."

"Then hurry. I fear you lead me to a cliff."

"I told you once"—his breath skated along her ear, sending chills down her spine—"you have nothing to fear of me."

"Marco—"

"Okay, open them."

Afraid to, afraid she might somehow disappoint him with her reaction, she slowly opened her eyes. And gasped as she took in the large room and at the far end, a blue stained-glass depiction of a raging ocean and an aetos soaring high above. Walls on either side bore life-size portraits of the medoras and kyrias who had gone before.

"Behind you," Marco gruffed.

Kersei twitched at his nearness and turned as he swept aside, out of her way. With a yelp, she slapped her hand over her mouth. Tears burned.

There on the wall were two new enormous portraits . . . Darius in his royal uniform, looking austere and somehow . . . "He looks arrogant."

"Not arrogant," Marco said as he stood beside her, gazing upon his brother, "confident. Assured. I never saw him any other way."

Her heart squeezed. "It is an incredible likeness."

"I had two painted, so that Xylander can always look upon his father when he has need."

Kersei slowly pushed her gaze to Isaura's likeness. The Heart of Kalonica crown with its arches and emerald droplets sat atop golden hair done up with twists. The amulet she had always worn, carved with the *Trópos tis Fotiás*, on a gold chain. And her gorgeous gown of green and gold. "Isaura the Gracious."

"What?" Marco frowned at her.

"I told her that should be her title as she was ever gracious, always so gentle. So beautiful." *Everything I was not nor could hope to be.*

Marco chuckled. "Is that where it arose? I heard it spoken by sergii and wondered."

"She was a perfect kyria." No surprise she yet had Marco's heart. *Next to you, I never had a prayer . . .*

Marco fell silent. "You look longer upon Isa's portrait than Darius's."

"I—" Kersei faltered. "The details, the way her crown seems real—"

"She makes you sad."

"I—" She sighed. "No, she makes me realize all the places I have failed and still fail. I am neither gracious nor gentle." She eyed the wastelander beauty again and thought of Danae, wondered if she had yet arrived for the gala. "Nor blonde."

Marco laughed, but it sounded as raw as her heart.

She started for the door. "We should—"

"Kersei."

Gah! He had that way of saying her name that made her heart leap from her chest.

"I would not have you be those things." He nodded to the kyria's portrait. "Isaura was what I needed after the terrible grief, facing an impossible war. She was an anchor in the storm of my life. A gift I did not deserve. She was also what this realm required in my absence."

A terrible grief . . . "Aye," she agreed.

"For us both much has changed"—he glanced at the paintings again—"and is better because of them."

Could he hear her thundering heart as he peered at her with— "Your eyes!"

"What?"

"They're blue again!" Leaning in, she checked both. How had she not noticed in all their meetings and discussions?

"It has been a gradual alteration since you healed me." He shuffled closer, his gaze on hers. "No one has noticed but you."

Her breath caught at that. Realized she touched him. Yet he had not removed her hand. Rebuked her. "How could they not? It is remarkable." *Like you.*

A glimmer of a smile ghosted through his features as he eased away. "Come. Let us review the plans to make this victory celebration the grandest Kardia has ever seen."

Would the celebration tonight go as planned? Or would it come crashing down, unable to give substance to what roiled through his veins?

Perched atop Athina House, named for his mother and built for VIP guests, Marco tried not to think of Kersei readying herself beneath this roof. She had come a month past, and they had spent much time together. Not wanting her to suffer loneliness, he'd invited her up for dinner. Happened upon her along walks . . . walks he had deliberately interrupted, testing the waters. Her reaction.

Kardia had been swarmed by her scent, her attraction.

And yet . . . Isa.

He scanned the city, relieved at the progress made. Lives resuming, laughter stirring the air and his receptors. Much better than eighteen months ago on that plain. Crouched, he swiveled and stared over the courtyard and cobbled drive.

Scaffolding hugged the beleaguered palace on all sides as workers spent months removing stones, strengthening support columns, and stabilizing the entire first level of the castle. The cliff face had been reinforced, the wall repaired with the aerios quarters inset, the courtyard and statue of Eleftheria restored. Kersei had arranged with Duncan, their official city engineer, for the terrazza to be aglow with electric lights. Even now, as carriages began filtering in to drop off guests for the grand celebration, machitis were sparring in the yard. Normalcy was returning to Kardia.

He anak'd the irritated scent a tick before a whistle carried through the air—Ixion calling him to his side. Finally, Marco had learned the various pitches, lengths, and beats—to call Stalkers to group up. With a smirk firmly in place, he slanted his legs and slid down the roof. Sailed out, twisting, and caught the ledge. He dropped down to the window, then toed the stone fireplace. Scaled it, landing silently.

"You want to be a spider, go be a spider. I'm not chasing you anymore,"

Ixion groused. "Not that I could."

"Will you be this foul all night?"

"Since you made me wear this get-up—*aye*!" Ixion followed him up the side path into the house, scratching at the stiff collar.

"It is your wedding, not to mention a celebration of my rule and the Victory Ball, as the duchess has named it. If I have to wear a doublet and crown, the least you can do is wear a doublet. You are, after all, the groom and my First."

"You should have named someone else your First. I am of no use—just a villager now."

"I pity Kita when your first child is born."

"Mm." But he scowled again, giving him a sidelong glance. "Why?"

"Then she will have two infants to deal with." In his solar, Marco strode straight for the bath, where sergii had prepared hot water and spiced soap. He growled at the scent. People may like perfumes and spices, but it only grated on his receptors when he had to wear them. He would need to instruct the new staff better.

"See?" Ixion gruffed. "I should not bind with her. She deserves better."

"I might agree," Marco called as he scrubbed down, then toweled off. "Unfortunately, it is of no avail—Lady Kita has accepted your petition, despite your many arguments." Even sliding into his jerkin, he heard the Stalker's grunt. He stepped into his trousers with the gold ribbon down the outer seam. "And I will run you through if I hear you speaking such words to her. She will be your wife. Honor her. Stop your wretched complaining."

In the dressing chamber, Marco threaded his arms through his doublet as sergii used a tool to secure the gold buttons and another helped him into his boots and began lacing them.

"Remember the last time you wore that?" Ixion's voice came from behind.

Jaw tight, Marco tried to push that memory away. He did not need the complication of it, especially knowing she would be here. Of the things he had spent the early rise considering as he watched the waters rush into the cliffs.

"Will it be hard . . . having Kyros here for my binding?"

"Nay." It would not be hard because it already was hard. Thinking of the high lord spurred his thoughts to the day on Iereania, when he'd expected it to end one way, only to have it destroy every hope. Throw them apart. And he was reaching with his receptors before he knew what he was doing. As if they had a mind of their own, his receptors flung out and caught her Signature. He retracted them. Closed them. Did not need that plaguing his thoughts. Yet his brand thrummed, confirming she was near. Another reminder he did not need.

Hm, should he go to her? What if she needed something? A last-minute detail that warranted his attention.

He should not want to see her so much. Recalled at the Rest how her scent had flooded his receptors with attraction. It nauseated. Hurt. Made it hard to focus.

"Did you come to a decision?" Ixion's voice was weighted with the topic neither of them would name.

"Nay." Marco hung his head. "It has been nearly two years, yet I could continue with her in my heart for the next ten and be content."

Ixion stood much closer. "It is not wrong to love again."

"It *is* wrong! Must be wrong." Growling, he roughed his hands over his face and beard. "I do not want to betray Isaura or her memory. She was the best of us, leagues better . . ."

"Aye."

He huffed. "No pity from you, eh?"

"You get what you give." He clamped a hand on his shoulder. "But I repeat—it is not wrong to love again. Isa would not want you alone."

"I am not. Aeliana—"

"You know what I mean." Ixion bumped his shoulder intentionally. When a knock came at the door, Ixion went to answer.

Leaving Marco to the internal longing and debate. Isa . . . *My aetos* . . . He drew the amulet from his pocket. Its gold chain so odd a combination with the wood-carved circle. Nearly two years . . . The ache had lessened a fraction, yet the emptiness still gaped. She had truly left an enormous void.

Returned, Ixion motioned into the solar. "Your rooftop antics have made you late to my wedding. They ask for you."

"I'll tell Kita you were stalling."

"She will not believe that."

"*You* do not lie well, my friend," Marco teased, returning his words. "Come. It will be a long night." He winked as weight settled on his head from the heavy crown, a winged aetos attacking, its eye a large emerald. Green eye.

Like Isaura. As if she watched over him. How apropos.

They stepped from the solar, and there waited the detachment of regia in their white and golds. Impressive!

"Vanko Marco! Vanko Kalonica!" reverberated across the marble floor and ceiling as he strode to the front of the line, Ixion on his right, Bazyli on his left, and behind them, Kaveh Naderi.

He turned to the new baron with a smirk. "You ready?"

Stiff-backed Kaveh produced the cylinder. "Nervously so."

Marco took it and handed it to a sergius, who hurried it into the great hall. "It is a good match."

"Tell that to the general."

Horns in the great hall blared, and silence fell over the guests. Scents of expectation and excitement mirrored his own. His people had earned this night, this celebration, and he would revel in it with them.

Attendants pulled wide the doors and Marco strode forward.

A thunderous applause beat against his chest as he made his way to the dais at the far end of the hall. There, he waited for the adulation to die down, both hating it and appreciating that they were so ardently his supporters. "Thank you! Tonight we have many festivities planned, lots of food, and dancing!"

The crowd again erupted in applause, and from the right he felt a spearlike jolt of attraction wrapped in vanilla and patchouli. He stretched his neck, praying it was true and ripe. However, knowing the schedule was tight, he quieted them. "Tonight will see the joining of two houses. It is my great privilege to witness the binding of a man I consider my friend, confidant, challenger, father-in-law, and warrior. I know few men so gallant." He motioned to the door. "Tonight, Ixion Mavridis binds with Lady Kita Lasdos."

The doors opened and in glided Kita, resplendent in a pale peach gown that made her glow. At her side walked her son, Mnason, in the green machitis uniform, a gift from Marco for the boy who had begun his swordsmanship with his new father.

But behind Kita walked . . . a vision. Kersei. A navy velvet gown unfairly hugged curves his fingers yet remembered.

Marco cleared his throat. Resisted the urge to step back.

A small tiara nestled among raven curls that were piled atop her head and cascaded around her face and bare neck. At the hollow of her throat rested a sapphire necklace with dangling diamonds that seemed like falling stars.

A hand thumped his back—Kyros urging him aside so he could conduct the binding—and he only then realized he'd not breathed since she entered. He moved to stand next to Ixion, his traitorous gaze again flicking to Kersei, who swung to face the lady she stood with. At her back, the thin straps of her gown clasped a sheer navy train trimmed in crystals that draped down to the floor. She looked as if she herself sailed among stars at night.

His thoughts bounced back to the Stardeck on the *Kleopatra*. Their kisses . . .

Reek. He yanked his attention back to Ixion and Kita. Again, cleared his throat and thoughts. Eyed the high lord. Had no idea what the man was saying.

Was her gown intentional? To remind him of what they once had? Of his powerful passion that had forced him to break the Kynigos Codes?

Kersei had never done anything *un*intentionally. It was one of the things he lo—*admired* about her.

A shout went up, and Marco flinched. Realized he had yet again lost track of the present. Ixion and Kita were bound. It was done.

"Medora Marco?"

Clapping with the crowds, he blinked at the iereas. What had he missed this time?

Kyros frowned and edged closer. "Was it tonight? You were—" He nodded behind Marco. To Kaveh.

Ah! "Yes." Marco wanted to beat himself over the head with his crown. He climbed the dais to address the people.

Saw her bare neck in his mind's eye. Remembered kissing her nape, her intake of breath . . .

He stretched his jaw. "Since tonight is a celebration, I have been asked by yet another for a moment of your time." He took the cylinder from High Lord Kyros and held it aloft. "I have here a petition." He tapped the petition against his hand and decided to do things a little differently tonight. "Who sets this petition?"

Kaveh lifted his hand. "I do, Medora Marco."

Marco grinned at the cheers from aerios and regia. "Baron Naderi, name your intended."

"I set petition for Lady Danae Sebastiano."

An exultant shriek echoed through the hall. Danae shoved through the crowd. When she reached the baron, Bazyli moved to stand beside her.

"Kaveh," she whispered, shaking her head, wiping tears.

Enjoying this immensely, Marco asked, "General Sebastiano, a petition has been set for your sister. Since you are the eldest of your family, do you accept this binding?"

"I do, my medora."

Marco nodded. "Lady Danae, Baron Naderi has set petition. Do you agree to this?"

Murmurs rippled through the room, confusion emanating about the questions he posed. No lady had ever had a say in her binding.

Exquisite in her green gown and updo, she beamed. "Absolutely!"

Laughter met Marco's own chuckles. "Then it is done." He motioned to Kyros, who performed the betrothal ceremony.

Afterward, Marco regained the dais and spoke to those gathered. "You may have noticed the questions I posed for this petition are different from what you are used to. After what our country and this planet have been through, after all we have done to fight for our freedom and our lives, I thought it only fitting that we secure freedom for all of us. I have seen and know intimately the great pain a lack of voice in binding can have on people."

He smoothed a hand over his beard, struggling not to focus on Kersei's scent that gushed with adoration and that blessed—*accursed*—scent of attraction, but he must see in her eyes that she understood this was for her. Because of what happened to them. Never again would it happen to another couple. His heart cinched to see grateful tears in those brown eyes.

"This morning, I signed a decree that no woman will be bound without her own consent." He indicated to Kaveh and Danae. "As you can see, Danae has agreed to this binding—which will take place when they set a date."

"Very soon," Danae said, earning more laughter.

Happiness was the course for the night, and Kersei was pleased for the magnificence with which this celebration had occurred. Despite a few hiccups with a certain confection that had collapsed, all had turned out well. Standing with Kita as she said her vows—though the woman would have preferred her wastelander friend, Isaura—was an honor.

Seeing Marco accept the petition, then tell the crowd he was freeing women from bindings they objected to, Kersei's heart nearly burst. From there, the guests broke into dancing and merriment. Which swirled around her like a dizzying torment, since none asked her to dance.

Marco . . . Marco had laughed and talked with his regia. Seemed as at home here as he had anywhere before. There were more smiles, more handshakes . . . If one counted all the times Marco Dusan, the Kynigos hunter, had smiled in his life, she was sure this night outpaced that number by a hundred.

Relieved, exhausted . . . and so very lonely, she started for the side door, feeling every ounce of grief from the last year as she watched others celebrating, making merry. Yet here she stood . . . alone. No family. No dance partner. No friend. She had sent her son home with the governess two rises ago, knowing she herself would yet return after this.

"Excuse me," an elderly noblewoman asked. "Could you fetch me a glass of punch?"

Stunned—did the woman think her a sergius?—Kersei relented and delivered the refreshment. And she yet again stood with the elderly and women whose condition did not allow dancing.

Stark loneliness pushed her out of the hall into the fresh air, salted by the sea. Lured toward it, she made her way down to the courtyard where the statue of Eleftheria ruled again. From there, Kersei saw up the hill and through the windows of the hall to the revelers and spotted Marco talking with Bazyli.

Forlorn, she shifted her attention to the statue. Thought of all that this revered woman had helped orchestrate to effect a violent end to a dark, wicked race who had ravaged millions of lives. Most of all . . .

"Thank you," Kersei whispered to Eleftheria, "for bringing him back. Even if I cannot have him, at least he is here. Kardia is better for it. I . . . wish he did not have to know grief. That Isaura was still here with him and Aeliana. They deserve that . . . He deserved her love and to have happiness."

She thought of the winsome beauty, full of grace and mercy. Grievously killed. "She was a better person than I am. So very much better." So much that she won Marco, had his love, his child . . . Tears coursed down her cheeks. "I wish—"

"Isaura was a saint." Marco's voice stabbed into her solace.

Kersei whipped around, her thick hair batting her face and making it hard to see him in the night. "Marco."

Crown and vestments gone, he worked his way toward her slowly, deliberately. "When I first met Isa, I thought her a child—a girl. Silly, flighty." He motioned, a softness to his expression rarely seen. "She was so lighthearted but wise. Iron for blood, and fierce against injustice. Yet there was a . . . frailty to her. Insecure, unsure of herself." His eyes glossed, but he nodded, pursing his lips. "You spoke true—Isa was one of the best."

"I believe most who encountered her would agree."

He smoothed a hand over his mouth and beard, looking past her to the sea, shifting his stance. "I loved her in a way I never fathomed being able to." He tucked his hands under his armpits, standing close enough to touch. "Loving her—I could not believe it. It was so unexpected. *She* was unexpected."

His words were an affirmation of what she had known—his love for the kyria was still entrenched. He need not rub it in. "I . . . I am glad you . . . had her." But it hurt too much. If he had come to reminisce over Isaura, she would not be the ears for those words.

No, that was not true. She would. Because he had done so much for so many. He had endured much. And she would be whatever he needed from her—even if it was her absence.

She wandered down to the new stone balustrade that had been erected to trim the edge of the cliff. Large, flat stones pressed into the earth formed a small terrazza with a few benches curling along the edge.

Moving into view next to her, Marco leaned down and palmed the balustrade, staring out across the waters, which were serenely behaved this eve. He hiked onto the balustrade in a single jump, then sat down, his legs dangling over the sea. Remained there, silent, thoughtful. So striking a visage, his hair cut short around his ears and neck. The wind taunted the longer strands atop his head, dropping them along his brow. His jaw, so tightly set, bounced the muscle beneath the beard.

The salty, damp air and cool night sprayed a shiver across Kersei's spine. But she would not depart. Did not know if she should. Or if he wanted her there.

But he had not sent her away. In fact, he followed her to the small terrazza. She eased onto the balustrade, debated facing the same direction—it would be inappropriate to hike her legs up—but then, she never had been proper.

She shifted around, swinging her legs over—her shoe caught her hem, and she lost her balance. Fell against Marco. With a yelp, she panicked, thinking she would fall to the cliffs below.

Marco caught her. "Kersei!"

She laughed, her heart pounding at the near disaster. Steady, she put her feet back on solid ground and hugged herself with a nervous laugh. "That was not my brightest idea."

Marco again hopped up onto the balustrade and stood.

She yelped, scared he would fall, but he flipped backward and landed beside her. She laughed and shook her head. "What—"

"I miss doing that." He grinned down at her, then reached toward her.

Her breath slowed, watching . . . waiting . . . Was he . . .? Would he . . .?

He tugged free a lock entangled across her forehead. Even still, the barest trace of his touch lit fire across her skin. Slowing, hand yet near her cheek, he met her gaze. "You know that I can anak what you feel . . ."

She should look away. A proper lady would. Kersei looked up at him, glad that he could detect it. Tired of hiding it.

His thumb traced the line of her jaw. "It is not fair." He worked the coil that dangled near her ear down to her bare shoulder.

"What?"

"This dress."

Her heaviness lifted. Surprised and happy he had figured it out, she smiled. "I did not think you noticed." She had not been too subtle with the details, and those efforts paid off. And it felt glorious.

"How could I not?"

Was that a statement about her looks or the dress? Or its meaning? "You understood what—"

"The Stardeck."

Now that he named it openly, she felt a little brazen having a dress made to deliberately invoke that memory. Ashamed, she caught her lower lip. "I . . . I ordered it made because it seemed my last . . ." She sniffed, fearing if she bared her adunatos to him now, it would be too soon. He would reject her. Leave.

"Your last?" he prompted, words husky.

"After the Rest, I thought you sought Danae's affections." And she dared not break this moment, the spell it cast over her racing heart. "When you neither wrote nor came, I thought . . . 'Danae is so much like Isaura,' and you seemed so well a fit . . ."

Boots grinding dirt and rock beneath them, Marco shifted nearer. Not moving. Not touching. Just . . . standing there. A heady something imbued her brand, but then he dropped his gaze. Turned away.

"Stay," she said around a shiver. "You block the wind."

He chuckled. And then something went . . . strange in his expression.

Warmth pressed against her back—his hand. She drew in a breath, gazing into his pale blue eyes. Breathed out, battling her own emotions, knowing how they vaulted into his receptors. Teeth chattering, she cared not because of the fire in her breast that this man stirred.

He removed his doublet and slid it around her shoulders, tugging the collar closed. He slowed, his hand tracing her chin again. Her jaw.

Oh, she ached to be in his arms, to know his passion again.

Forehead to hers, he ground out, "Kersei . . ."

Her name was an agonized breath, rustling her curls and making her pulse thrash wildly in her chest.

Nose pressed to her cheek, his mouth swung toward hers. "We should not . . ."

Desire flashed through her, and she tilted her head, wanting his kiss. If that was what he would give.

With a groan, he angled in, his breath dancing over her mouth. Lips teasing hers.

He veered off with another moan, but did not move.

Kersei gripped his tunic to steady herself, to stop him from pulling way.

Then his mouth caught hers. He enfolded her into his arms, his kiss hungrily claiming her. She curled into him, tears dashing down her face to finally have this. To know his love once more.

But like a bucket of ice water, he broke off. "No." He stepped back, swallowed, looking miserable. "No."

Shocked, she stood there, her nerves still vibrating. Stunned. Heartbroken. What was he saying? Was he really—

"Sorry." He looked down. "I—"

"Augh!" Kersei hiked up her skirts and fled back up the hillside, refusing to let him hurl some excuse of honor or grief at her. Fool! "Stupid, stupid girl!" *Thinking he would love you!*

Running toward the house, she ignored his shouts that chased her. She reached over her shoulder and grabbed hold of the crystal veil that hung down her back. Ripped it off. No more stars. No glittering hope of love. No more. No more would she be the one they would mock.

Sprinting for the courtyard, she spied a destrier being led to a carriage.

She skidded toward it and leapt astride. "Hiyah!" They bolted out of

Kardia. Sobbing, she rode down the mountain . . . across the plains . . . back to Stratios. As far from that place and Marco as she could get.

These two years, she had set her hope on him. On them finding love. On a vision of them married with their own sons. A vision he had told Isaura when asking her to bind with him.

Yet he will not ask me.

At Stratios oras later and ignoring calls as to her welfare, she raced up the stairs and to her room. Threw herself into the bedchamber and slammed the door, feeling every bit the impetuous Wild Daughter of Stratios. Well, no more. Tonight, that girl died. She buried her face in the pillow and cried herself to sleep.

54

KARDIA, LAMPROS CITY, KALONICA, DROSERO

"What happened?"

Limping, Marco stormed down the hall to his apartments, mood foul, heart wrenched. "She misunderstood."

"What is there to misunderstand when you set petition?"

Irritated, he gritted his teeth and yanked off the jerkin and adornments. "I did not get that far."

Ixion frowned. "Let me guess—you kissed her."

Marco stabbed a finger at his First. "*Do not* start with me." He tossed the clothes aside and donned his blacks. "Aye, I kissed her, but I stopped." Pausing, he sliced a hand through the air. "I wanted to do it right. Not have someone happen upon us and demand honor's price. I wanted—needed— her to believe it was of my own free will. When I tried to explain that—she tore off like a Rapier."

"She is a woman in slippers. How did you not catch up and stop her?"

With a growl, he flung up a hand. "I tried, but"—humiliation galore— "she kicked off her shoes. I narrowly missed tripping on them, only to end up entangled in her blasted veil! Twisted my ankle. By the time I hobbled to the courtyard, she was gone. Stablemaster said she stole a destrier. Bolted out of here."

Ixion's chuckle started low and grew.

"Go away! You are bound and should be entertaining your wife." He threaded his arms through a tunic.

"Oh, this *will* entertain her."

Marco strapped on his leather Kynigos vest. Vambraces.

"What are you doing?"

"Going after her."

"Tonight?"

"Aye, and I'm taking every available aerios. I want her to understand one thing: I come for her and her alone. She will not mistake me this time."

"Sire, it will be the middle of the night by the time you reach Stratios," Ixion said as Kaveh slipped into the room. "Wait until morning."

"Nay. I will not let another minute pass with her believing I do not love her." He looked to the baron.

"They are ready."

"Send them. Surround the house. Do not let her leave." As Kaveh hurried out, Marco grabbed a ruck and stuffed it with his Kalonican doublet, crown, and vestments.

"What are you doing with those?"

"Like I said, she will not mistake me." Marco strode down the hall to the royal treasury and opened the vault. He scanned the pieces and pulled one out. Tucked it in his pocket. He strode out of the house to the stable yard and pulled up short.

Kaveh, Ixion, and Bazyli sat mounted, the former holding the reins of a fourth mount. Four regia waited with them. Marco flung himself onto the destrier, and they set out. The long ride gave him time to figure out what to say. How to apologize for being so inept at communicating his love to her.

Isaura . . . you took a piece of my adunatos with you. Mayhap that is how I am so sure you grant me this release. Never will you be forgotten.

STRATIOS HALL, KALONICA, DROSERO

"My lady."

Kersei moaned against the void that clung to her, holding her to the bed.

"My lady! Aerios surround the house, my lady!"

Bolting upright, Kersei blinked away the dregs of sleep and grief. "What say you?" She flew across the room and pulled back the curtain. Shock rooted her feet to the floor as she stared down to the north lawn where at least twenty regia arched around the property, touchstones in hand.

"It was just a destrier . . ." she murmured, her breath blooming across the leaded glass.

"Lady Kersei," a gravelly voice called. "You are ordered to present yourself forthwith."

"What did you do?" Elerine whined as she hurried toward her with a long cloak to put over her nightgown.

"Nothing." Kersei wondered if this was about the destrier. "I took a horse—borrowed. But it would be returned on the morrow."

"Lady Kersei!" the voice demanded again. "You have two minutes to present yourself, or we will come in after you."

"Check Xylander. Keep him." She stuffed her feet into boots and hurried down the stairs. "Get the mead and cordi."

"This be not a party, miss," a bent sergius said. "They are the medora's men. What you done? We got no other jobs."

"'Tis a misunderstanding, I am sure." She motioned him back toward the kitchen. "Ready something for the regia. They have had a hard ride."

Smoothing a hand down her long cloak, she stepped into the night. "What manner of rudeness is this?" she demanded, going out to them. "What crime could I have possibly committed that you come before even first rise?"

When no answer came, Kersei moved out farther, thrumming with nerves and hugging herself as thunder rolled in the distance. "Have you nothing to say for yourself?" Mercy—that was not thunder but more riders! "Tell me what you want of me, or I will return to the house."

Silence met her demand once more. She frowned, confused. Frustrated. Tired. Heartbroken. "Very we—" Even as she turned, the middle of the column broke apart.

Three riders jutted through and veered to the sides. Kaveh. Ixion. Bazyli.

"Cousin," she called. "Pray tell, what is this madness?"

Yet one more destrier trotted into the center, bearing—

"Marco," she whispered. What was he doing here? He had said no, refused her. What could he possibly want?

Holding his Black steady, he was formidable in the ebony winter cloak trimmed in fur, the crown she knew he hated wearing pressing against his brooding brow. He folded his arms over the pommel of his saddle. Stared at her. "Mistress Kersei."

Her heart did that jangly thing at the term he had used for her on the *Kleopatra*. "What is this, my medora? We soundly slept when your men—"

"A misunderstanding," Marco announced, then hiked his leg over his Black and slid down effortlessly. As he stalked toward her—was he limping?—he removed his gloves. The ferocity in his gaze pushed her back. "You absconded with a destrier—"

"Do you jest?" *That* was what this was about? "It is there, in the barn. I only . . . borrowed it. To hasten my way home."

"Hm." Marco advanced, favoring a leg. "As I was saying, you absconded with a destrier, and in my attempt to thwart your hasty exit from Kardia, I wrenched my ankle, tripping over this." He pulled something from a pocket and held it aloft.

"My veil," she murmured. He had hurt his ankle . . . *chasing* her? "I . . . did not know."

He raised a hand to stay her from speaking. "Had I not been injured"— he stalked closer, shortening the gap between them—"I would have intercepted you. Prevented this"—he motioned around the yard—"whole misunderstanding."

What was he doing? She did not understand. "I beg your mercy." She could not bring herself to look in his eyes.

"And," he said, stepping even nearer, "if you had not rushed off in such a panicked, desperate state, I could have finished my thought."

"Thought?" Finally, she met his gaze. "'No' is pretty definitive, my lord. I did not mistake that."

"I said 'no,' Mistress, because I would not do this the wrong way."

"Wrong what?" She blinked. "I mean—way wrong?" She growled and touched her forehead to hide her embarrassment. "My medora, it is late and—"

He erased the last proper distance and caught her hand, shoving her breath into the back of her throat. "Do you recall," he spoke for her ears only, "when Isaura lay dying, she said, 'love her'?"

Mortified that he spoke of the kyria's death, Kersei nodded. "Of course. And you have loved Aeliana, honoring that wish—"

"No." Marco smirked and it did crazy things to her stomach. "That is what I thought as well—that she meant Aeliana, yet it nagged at me. A buzzing at the back of my thick skull." He sighed. "After you came to the Rest, thoughts of you tormented my risings and slumberings."

Lips parted, Kersei searched his face to be sure he did not taunt her. "I—"

He pressed a finger to her lips. "Whose hand did Isaura put on mine that terrible day?"

Oh. Kersei started, recalling that terrible moment. "Mine." The word was no more than a breath.

Marco smirked again. Nodded. "She meant you, Kersei. Even then, Isa was giving me permission to love again." Somehow, though there was no space between them, he pressed closer. "To love *you*. Again."

Chin trembling, she resisted the urge to ease away. "Do not do this—mock me—not in front of all these regia, Marco. I cannot endure it—"

"Mistress Kersei," Marco shouted, making her flinch, as his piercing eyes held her still, "I would have your permission to set petition for you." He went to a knee, brandishing an emerald ring. "Will you grant it?"

Cupping her hands over her mouth, she burst into tears. Stumbled backward, so exhausted, weary. Stunned. Elated. Crying.

Marco rose and pulled her into his arms. "I know . . . I know . . ." He kissed her temple. "I love you, Kersei."

She clung to him, sobbing into his shoulder.

"Kersei."

Trying to compose herself, she shuddered through a few more choked tears.

"Can you grant mercy and give an answer before Ixion runs me through for kissing you on the cliffs or ruins this moment with a demand?"

She laughed and cried at the same time. "Aye, yes. Always."

Chuckles skittered around the yard, and Marco put the ring on her finger. He claimed her mouth and heart in a kiss that sealed their lives together.

EPILOGUE
EIGHT YEARS LATER
CLIFFS OF KARDIA, KALONICA, DROSERO

Wind tugging at the collar of his hide jacket, Marco climbed the stone steps. Little hands nearly strangled him, and he braced his son perched atop his shoulders. "Easy, Darius," he said with a laugh, releasing the hand that had clung to his as they made the journey.

"I am scared, Papa," the five-year-old said. "It is too high."

"Nonsense, this is where our home will be." He shifted around and reached to aid Kersei, who negotiated the path with their three-year-old on her hip and her swollen womb challenging her.

Pausing, she huffed and blew a curl from her face.

"Here," he said, taking Roman from her.

On the top level, barriers were erected to protect workers from falling. Past the scaffolding that marred the eastern wing where they were building a new addition—a larger balcony, and above their solar, a landing pad for his scout—Marco breathed in deeply and set down the boys. He offered a hand to Kersei.

"I am a warrior's daughter—"

"And a medora's very pregnant wife."

"Careful . . ." With a glower, she gained the top. "I would have words with said medora about the state he has yet again put me in."

Moving behind her, he slid an arm around her, cradling the unborn heir within her womb, and kissed the crown of her head. "Can I help it if you are powerless against my charm? I believe you called me handsome on the *Kleopatra*."

She rolled her eyes. "Air sickness."

He laughed. "More like lovesick."

Leaning back against him, she lifted her hand to caress his face. He caught it and their brands kissed, a flare of light and energy in a permanent reminder of their journey.

"Papa?" Raven-haired Aeliana joined them, reaching across Kersei's arm to touch his.

Thunder roared. Lightning splintered the dark sky and momentarily seared his vision. No, not lightning—the brand. It erupted in a rage of blinding light, charged by the Touch of his daughter.

Marco sucked in a breath, staring at Aeliana.

Who smiled at him with suddenly violet eyes. "Ma'ma loved it here on the balcony."

How could she possibly know that?

Tendrils of lightning snaked through the sky, illuminating the surrounding lands, the sea, and Lampros City.

Nerves rifled from Kersei, giving him a look regarding Aeliana. "We should go," she said, lifting Roman back into her arms. "I do not want to be drenched before the ball."

Still startled, he drew Aeliana to his side. Hugged her. Peered into her eyes—green again. *What the reek?* Even then, looking around at Kersei, wind whipped about by the incoming storm, and the boys laughing and doing their best to tic-tack . . . a tingling awareness flickered through Marco. Made him pause. Hold his breath.

This . . . this is . . . familiar.

Something fumbled at his hand. He glanced down. Kersei's delicate fingers wrapped his. Swathed in glittering green, gold, white, the arm led to a face bursting with brilliance as the sun parted the clouds. The gold circlet she favored, the one with the emerald that dangled at the center of her forehead, encircled hair barely visible beneath the glare.

Marco shielded his eyes and squinted. His heart jarred. "Kersei!"

She smiled at him. "Our sons"—she nodded to the right—"have at last understood."

He looked to where she indicated—and froze. Just as in that vision ten years ago on the cliffs, he saw their children, Xylander, Zarek, Darius, Roman, and Aeliana at their side—all with hands to chests, speaking the aerios oath . . . one they would take in the future to swear protection of the realm.

"They have understood their duty as the heirs of Kalonica."

Exhilaration raced through him as he jerked back to her. "Kersei! This is it!" He caught her shoulders. "This is it—my vision! The one I had after Iereania." He laughed and threw his head back, arms held out. "Thank you,

Ancient! Thank you! Thank you for these gifts, my wife, my children, this realm."

Something tugged at his tunic. He pivoted to the left.

Mop of curly black hair tussling in the wind, little Darius squinted up at him. "Papa, will the baby be a girl this time?"

ACKNOWLEDGEMENTS

Special thanks to Reagen Reed for your incomparable editorial skills. This series would not have been what it is without you! Thank you for pushing me to write the story of my heart, despite being exhausted mentally and physically. So grateful for you!

Thank you, Lindsay Franklin, for UN-retiring so you could do line edits on WAR. I am very grateful to have your careful eye on this last installment. THANK YOU!

Thank you to Katie Williams for your proofreading—great catches. I appreciate your careful eye. Thank you also to Jamie Foley for the wonderful formatting and maps. You are so gifted!

One-hundred-thousand thank yous to Rel Mollet for always being there for me, for reading and letting me brainstorm ideas.

Kim Gradeless, thank you for reading and helping hunt down typos and mistakes. For laughing with me, and for [fruitlessly] begging me to resurrect dead characters.

Thank you, Katie Donovan, for reading through these stories and tracking down typos as well. You are a blessing!

ABOUT THE AUTHOR

Ronie Kendig is a bestselling, award-winning author of over thirty books. She grew up an Army brat, and now she and her Army-veteran husband have returned to their beloved Texas after a ten-year stint in the Northeast. They survive on Sonic & Starbucks runs, barbecue, and peach cobbler that they share—sometimes—with Benning the Stealth Golden. Ronie's degree in psychology has helped her pen novels of intense, raw characters.

Ronie can be found at: www.roniekendig.com

Facebook: www.facebook.com/RapidFireFiction
Twitter: @RonieKendig
Goodreads: www.goodreads.com/RonieK
Instagram: @KendigRonie

THE DROSERAN SAGA

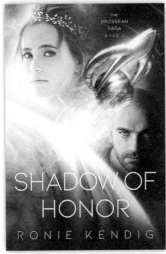

THE ABIASSA'S FIRE TRILOGY

Available Now!

Embers

Accelerant

Fierian

IF YOU ENJOY

THE DROSERAN SAGA

YOU MIGHT LIKE THESE NOVELS: